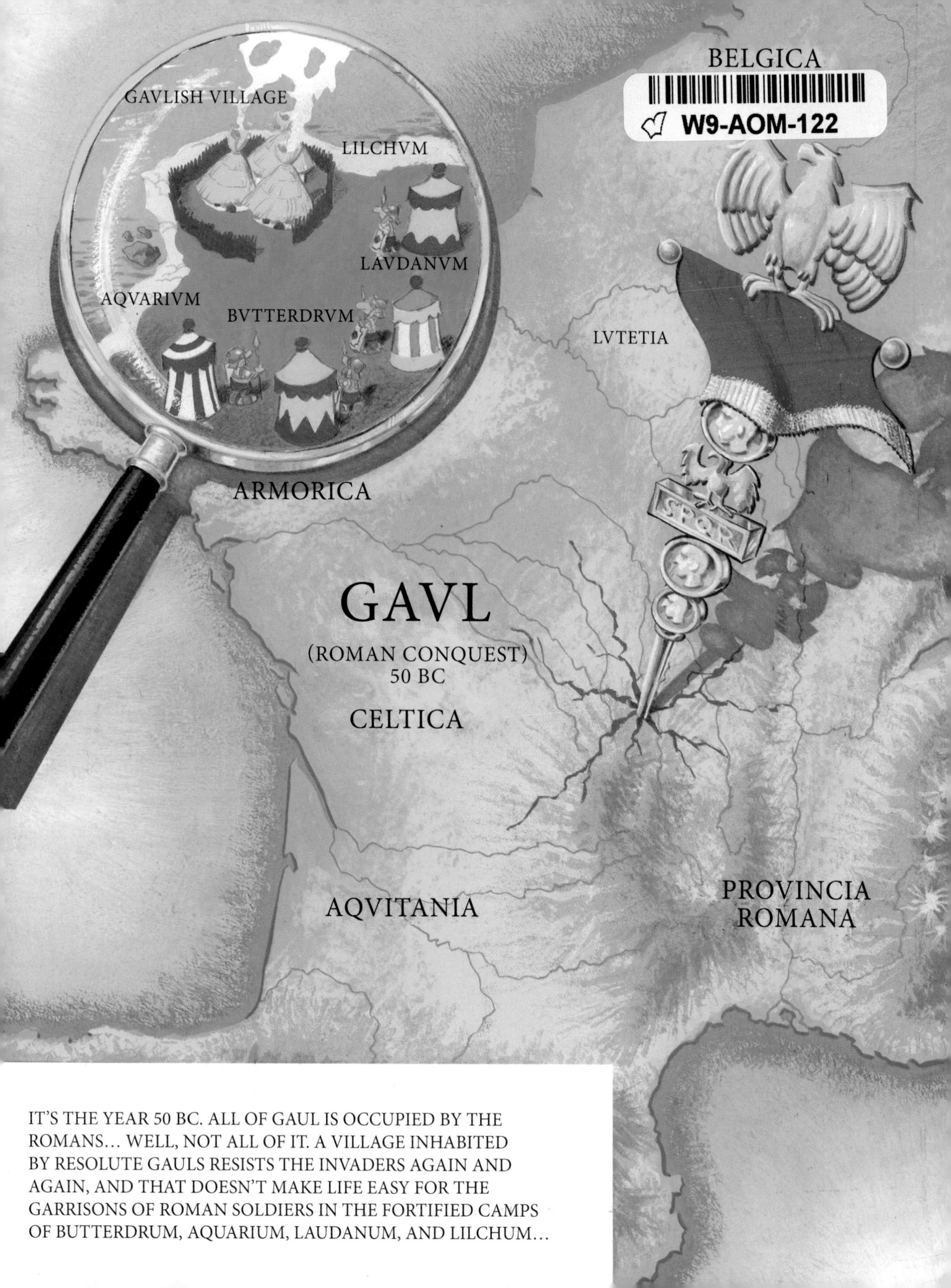
BELGICA
GAVLISH VILLAGE
LILCHVM
LAVDANVM
AQVARIVM
BVTTERDRVM
LVTETIA
ARMORICA
SPQR
GAVL
(ROMAN CONQUEST)
50 BC
CELTICA
AQVITANIA
PROVINCIA
ROMANA

IT'S THE YEAR 50 BC. ALL OF GAUL IS OCCUPIED BY THE ROMANS… WELL, NOT ALL OF IT. A VILLAGE INHABITED BY RESOLUTE GAULS RESISTS THE INVADERS AGAIN AND AGAIN, AND THAT DOESN'T MAKE LIFE EASY FOR THE GARRISONS OF ROMAN SOLDIERS IN THE FORTIFIED CAMPS OF BUTTERDRUM, AQUARIUM, LAUDANUM, AND LILCHUM…

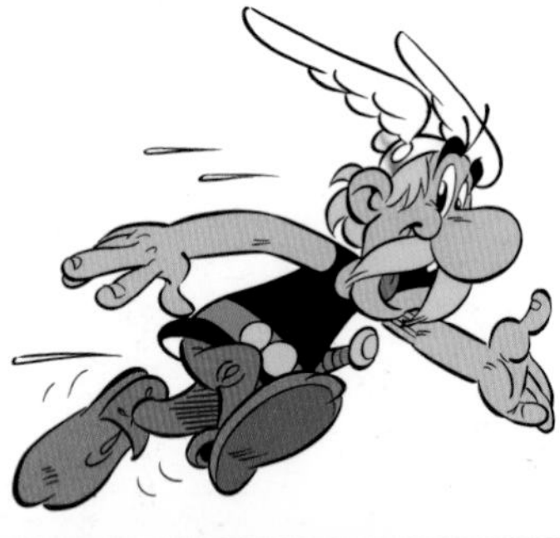

ASTERIX, THE HERO OF THESE ADVENTURES. A SHREWD, LITTLE WARRIOR WITH A KEEN INTELLIGENCE. ALL DANGEROUS MISSIONS ARE ENTRUSTED TO HIM WITHOUT HESITATION. ASTERIX GETS HIS SUPERHUMAN STRENGTH FROM THE DRUID PANORAMIX'S MAGIC POTION...

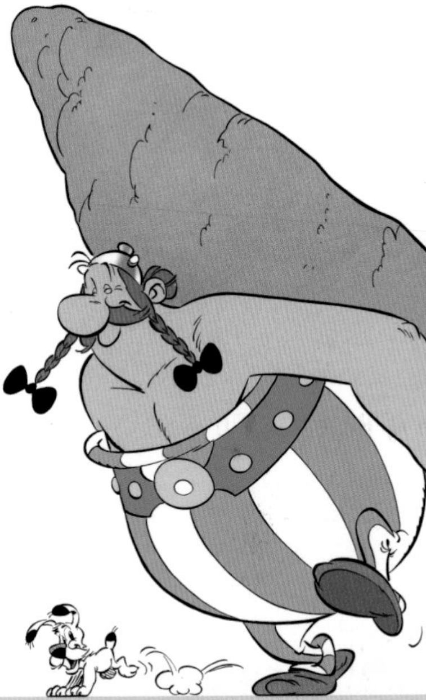

OBELIX IS ASTERIX'S CLOSE FRIEND. A MENHIR (TALL, UPRIGHT, STONE MONUMENTS) DELIVERY MAN, HE LOVES EATING WILD BOAR AND GETTING INTO BRAWLS. OBELIX IS ALWAYS READY TO DROP EVERYTHING TO GO OFF ON A NEW ADVENTURE WITH ASTERIX. HE'S ACCOMPANIED BY **DOGMATIX**, THE ONLY KNOWN ECO-DOG, WHO HOWLS IN DESPAIR WHENEVER SOMEONE CUTS DOWN A TREE.

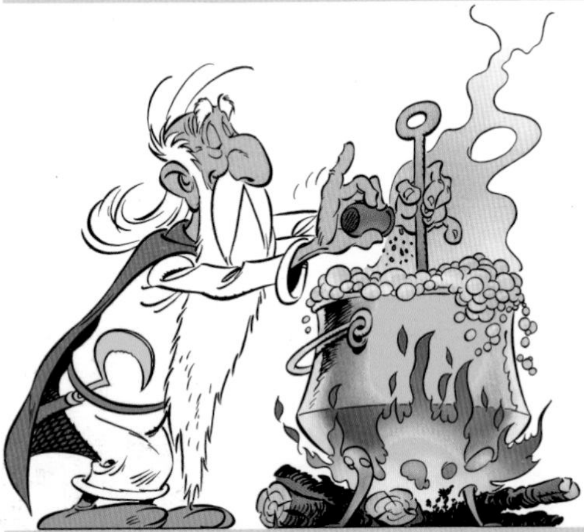

PANORAMIX, THE VILLAGE'S VENERABLE DRUID. GATHERS THE MISTLETOE AND PREPARES MAGIC POTIONS. HIS GREATEST SUCCESS IS THE POTION THAT GIVES SUPER-STRENGTH TO THE USER, BUT PANORAMIX HAS OTHER RECIPES UP HIS SLEEVE...

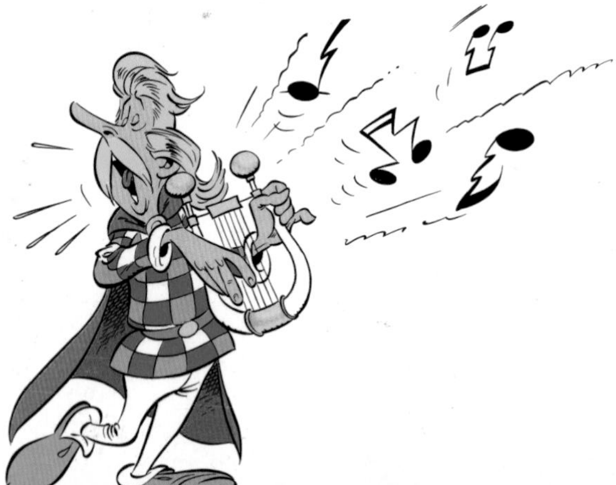

CACOFONIX IS THE BARD. OPINIONS ABOUT HIS TALENTS ARE DIVIDED: HE THINKS HE'S AWESOME, EVERYBODY ELSE THINKS HE'S AWFUL, BUT WHEN HE DOESN'T SING ANYTHING, HE'S A CHEERFUL COMPANION AND WELL-LIKED...

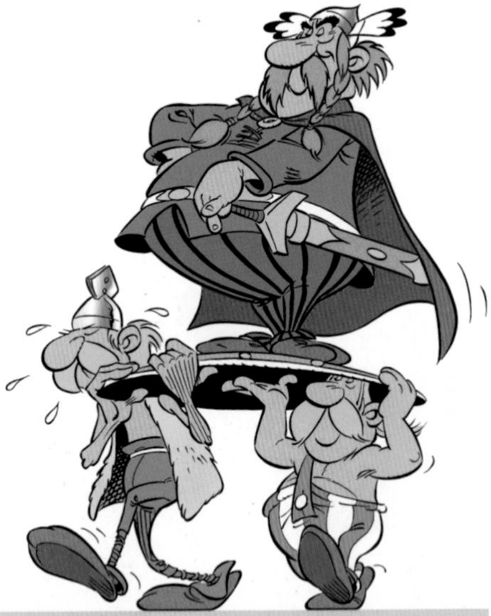

VITALSTATISTIX, FINALLY, IS THE TRIBE'S CHIEF. MAJESTIC, COURAGEOUS, IRRITABLE, THE OLD WARRIOR IS RESPECTED BY HIS MEN AND FEARED BY HIS ENEMIES. VITALSTATISTIX HAS ONLY ONE FEAR: THAT THE SKY WILL FALL ON HIS HEAD BUT, AS HE SAYS TO HIMSELF: "THAT'LL BE THE DAY!"

Asterix®

VOLUME THREE

PAPERCUTZ™

GRAPHIC NOVELS

Paperbacks

Coming Soon

Vol. 1

Vol. 2

Vol. 3

Vol. 4

Hardcovers

Coming Soon

Vol. 1

Vol. 2

Vol. 3

Vol. 4

Vol. 38

ASTERIX graphic novels are available in paperback for $14.99 each and in hardcover for $22.99 each; ASTERIX Vol. 38 is available in hardcover only for $9.99 each at booksellers everywhere. Order online at papercutz.com. Or call 1-800-886-1223, Monday through Friday, 9 – 5 EST. MC, Visa, and AmEx accepted. To order by mail, please add $5.00 for postage and handling for first book ordered, $1.00 for each additional book and make check payable to NBM Publishing. Send to: Papercutz, 160 Broadway, Suite 700, East Wing, New York, NY 10038.
ASTERIX graphic novels are also available digitally wherever e-books are sold.
PAPERCUTZ.COM

VOLUME THREE

Collecting
ASTERIX AND THE BIG FIGHT
ASTERIX IN BRITAIN
ASTERIX AND THE NORMANS

Written by RENÉ GOSCINNY
Illustrated by ALBERT UDERZO

NEW YORK

VOLUME THREE

Collecting…
Asterix and the Big Fight
Asterix in Britain
Asterix and the Normans

ASTERIX® - OBELIX ® - IDEFIX ® -DOGMATIX ®

Original titles: *Le Combat des chefs, Astérix chez les Bretons, et Astérix et les Normands*
© 1966 GOSCINNY/UDERZO
© 1966 GOSCINNY/UDERZO
© 1967 GOSCINNY/UDERZO
© 1999 HACHETTE LIVRE
© 2020 HACHETTE LIVRE for this omnibus and its American translation

Published by: Papercutz
First Papercutz edition: October 2020

Printed by Ultimate Print, Malaysia

Paperback ISBN: 978-1-5458-0571-8
Hardcover ISBN: 978-1-5458-0570-1

JOE JOHNSON – Translation
JAYJAY JACKSON – Design
BRYAN SENKA – Lettering
JULIE TILLET, LAURA STAUFFER – Special Thanks
ERIC STORMS – Editorial Intern
JEFF WHITMAN – Managing Editor
JIM SALICRUP
Editor-in-Chief

Papercutz books may be purchased for business or promotional use. For information on bulk purchases please contact Macmillan Corporate and Premium Sales Department at (800) 221-7945 x5442.

Distributed by Macmillan

www.asterix.com 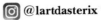 Asterix and Obelix 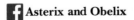 @lartdasterix

R. GOSCINNY ASTERIX A. UDERZO

Asterix and the Big Fight

Written by René GOSCINNY

Illustrated by Albert UDERZO

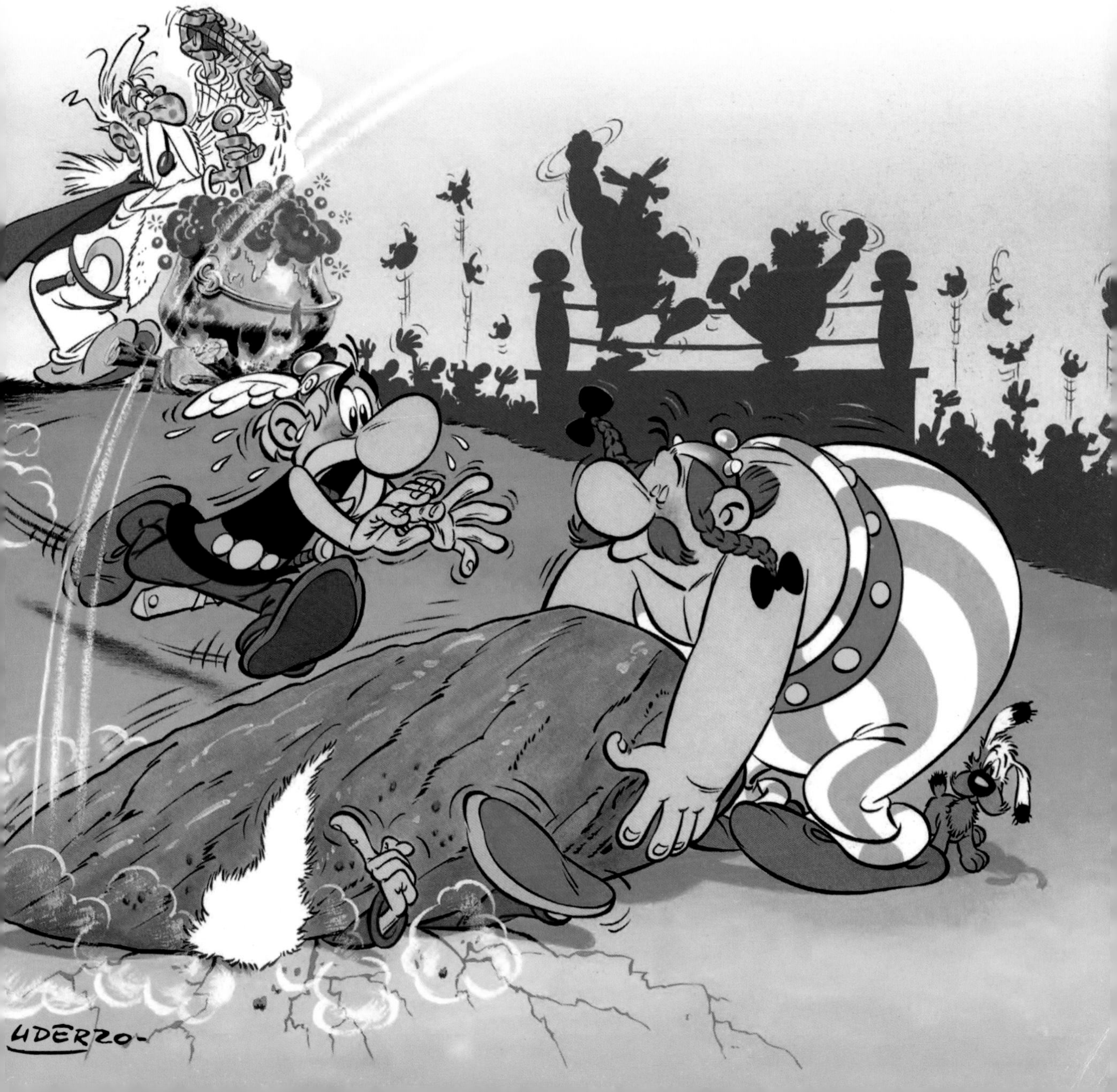
UDERZO

ASTERIX AND THE BIG FIGHT

Written by RENÉ GOSCINNY *and illustrated by* ALBERT UDERZO

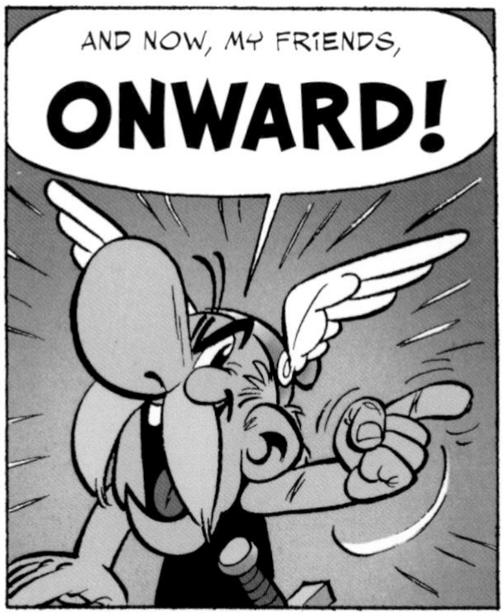
AND NOW, MY FRIENDS,
ONWARD!

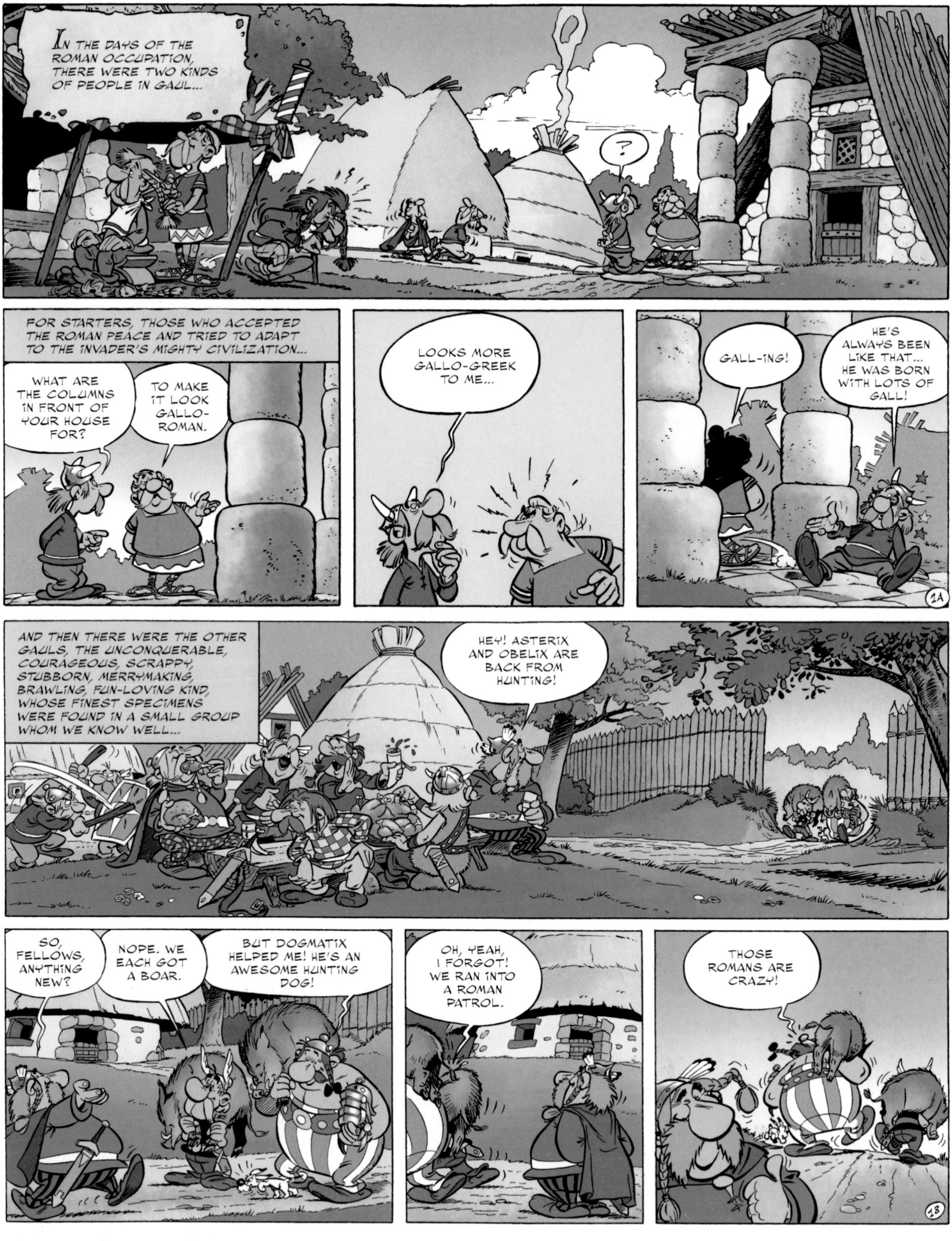
IN THE DAYS OF THE ROMAN OCCUPATION, THERE WERE TWO KINDS OF PEOPLE IN GAUL...
?
FOR STARTERS, THOSE WHO ACCEPTED THE ROMAN PEACE AND TRIED TO ADAPT TO THE INVADER'S MIGHTY CIVILIZATION...
WHAT ARE THE COLUMNS IN FRONT OF YOUR HOUSE FOR?
TO MAKE IT LOOK GALLO-ROMAN.
LOOKS MORE GALLO-GREEK TO ME...
GALL-ING!
HE'S ALWAYS BEEN LIKE THAT... HE WAS BORN WITH LOTS OF GALL!
AND THEN THERE WERE THE OTHER GAULS, THE UNCONQUERABLE, COURAGEOUS, SCRAPPY, STUBBORN, MERRYMAKING, BRAWLING, FUN-LOVING KIND, WHOSE FINEST SPECIMENS WERE FOUND IN A SMALL GROUP WHOM WE KNOW WELL...
HEY! ASTERIX AND OBELIX ARE BACK FROM HUNTING!
SO, FELLOWS, ANYTHING NEW?
NOPE. WE EACH GOT A BOAR.
BUT DOGMATIX HELPED ME! HE'S AN AWESOME HUNTING DOG!
OH, YEAH, I FORGOT! WE RAN INTO A ROMAN PATROL.
THOSE ROMANS ARE CRAZY!

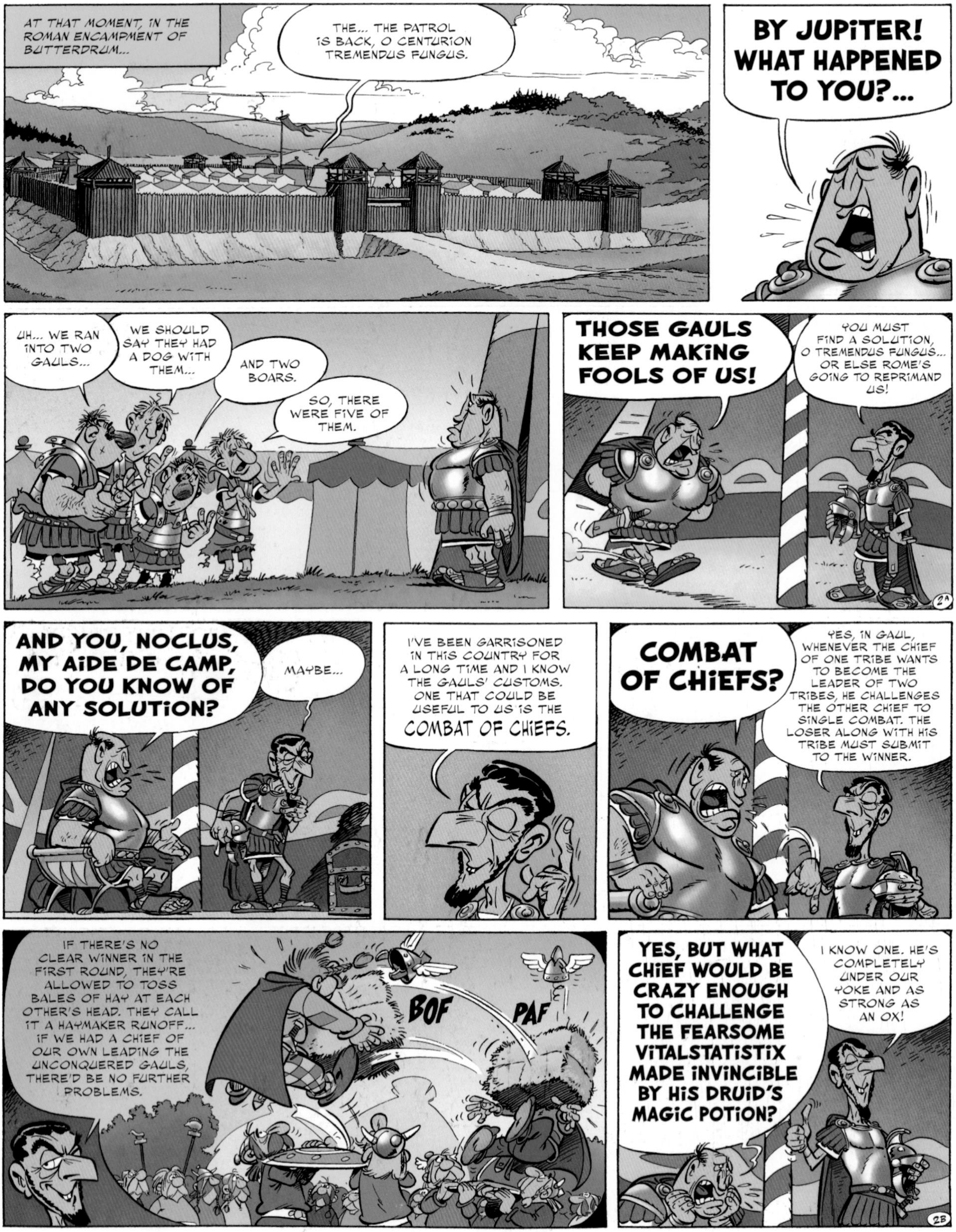
AT THAT MOMENT, IN THE ROMAN ENCAMPMENT OF BUTTERDRUM...
THE... THE PATROL IS BACK, O CENTURION TREMENDUS FUNGUS.
BY JUPITER! WHAT HAPPENED TO YOU?...
UH... WE RAN INTO TWO GAULS...
WE SHOULD SAY THEY HAD A DOG WITH THEM...
AND TWO BOARS.
SO, THERE WERE FIVE OF THEM.
THOSE GAULS KEEP MAKING FOOLS OF US!
YOU MUST FIND A SOLUTION, O TREMENDUS FUNGUS... OR ELSE ROME'S GOING TO REPRIMAND US!
2A
AND YOU, NOCLUS, MY AIDE DE CAMP, DO YOU KNOW OF ANY SOLUTION?
MAYBE...
I'VE BEEN GARRISONED IN THIS COUNTRY FOR A LONG TIME AND I KNOW THE GAULS' CUSTOMS. ONE THAT COULD BE USEFUL TO US IS THE COMBAT OF CHIEFS.
COMBAT OF CHIEFS?
YES, IN GAUL, WHENEVER THE CHIEF OF ONE TRIBE WANTS TO BECOME THE LEADER OF TWO TRIBES, HE CHALLENGES THE OTHER CHIEF TO SINGLE COMBAT. THE LOSER ALONG WITH HIS TRIBE MUST SUBMIT TO THE WINNER.
IF THERE'S NO CLEAR WINNER IN THE FIRST ROUND, THEY'RE ALLOWED TO TOSS BALES OF HAY AT EACH OTHER'S HEAD. THEY CALL IT A HAYMAKER RUNOFF... IF WE HAD A CHIEF OF OUR OWN LEADING THE UNCONQUERED GAULS, THERE'D BE NO FURTHER PROBLEMS.
BOF
PAF
YES, BUT WHAT CHIEF WOULD BE CRAZY ENOUGH TO CHALLENGE THE FEARSOME VITALSTATISTIX MADE INVINCIBLE BY HIS DRUID'S MAGIC POTION?
I KNOW ONE. HE'S COMPLETELY UNDER OUR YOKE AND AS STRONG AS AN OX!
2B

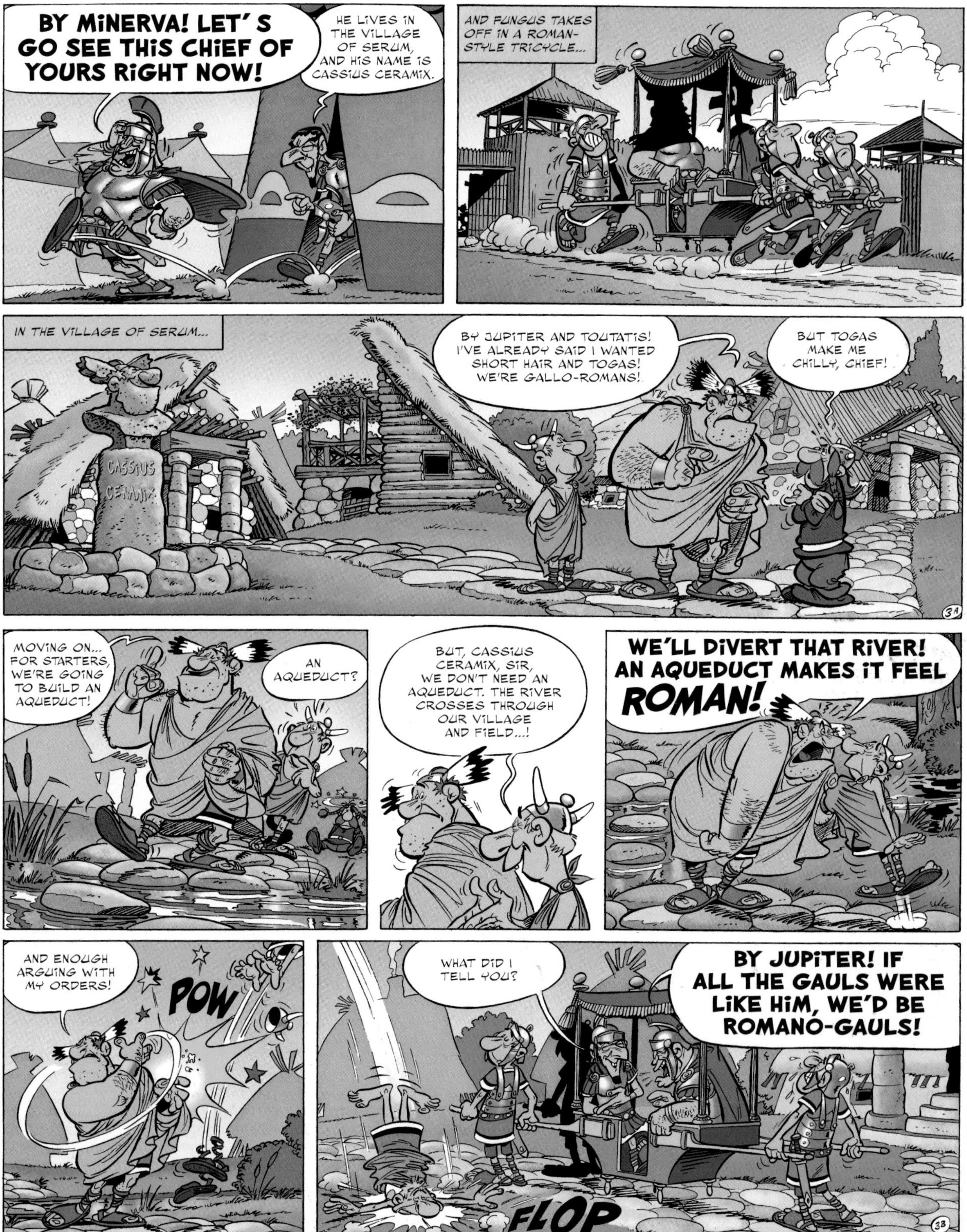
BY MINERVA! LET'S GO SEE THIS CHIEF OF YOURS RIGHT NOW!
HE LIVES IN THE VILLAGE OF SERUM, AND HIS NAME IS CASSIUS CERAMIX.
AND FUNGUS TAKES OFF IN A ROMAN-STYLE TRICYCLE...
IN THE VILLAGE OF SERUM...
CASSIUS CERAMIX
BY JUPITER AND TOUTATIS! I'VE ALREADY SAID I WANTED SHORT HAIR AND TOGAS! WE'RE GALLO-ROMANS!
BUT TOGAS MAKE ME CHILLY, CHIEF!
MOVING ON... FOR STARTERS, WE'RE GOING TO BUILD AN AQUEDUCT!
AN AQUEDUCT?
BUT, CASSIUS CERAMIX, SIR, WE DON'T NEED AN AQUEDUCT. THE RIVER CROSSES THROUGH OUR VILLAGE AND FIELD...!
WE'LL DIVERT THAT RIVER! AN AQUEDUCT MAKES IT FEEL ROMAN!
AND ENOUGH ARGUING WITH MY ORDERS!
POW
WHAT DID I TELL YOU?
BY JUPITER! IF ALL THE GAULS WERE LIKE HIM, WE'D BE ROMANO-GAULS!
FLOP

O, CASSIUS CERAMIX!

?

HAIL, CAESAR! WELCOME TO OUR BELOVED INVADERS!...

SORRY FOR INVADING YOUR SPACE, BUT THE CENTURION TREMENDUS FUNGUS AND I WOULD LIKE TO HAVE A LITTLE CHAT WITH YOU.

COME IN THEN! MY HOUSE... MY DOMUS, RATHER... WILL BE HONORED BY YOUR PRESENCE.

CERTAINLY.

4A

YOU KNOW ABOUT THE CUSTOM OF COMBAT OF CHIEFS... WE'D LIKE FOR YOU TO FIGHT A CHIEF AND TAKE COMMAND OF HIS TRIBE, AFTER YOU WIN.

ROME SWEET ROME

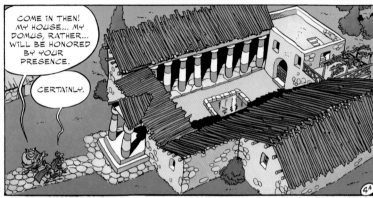

NOTHING EASIER... WHO'S THE UNFORTUNATE CHIEF? IT'LL BE A MASSACRE.

VITALSTATISTIX!

VITAL... VITALSTATISTIX!? BUT THAT WOULD BE A MASSACRE!

NOBODY DREAMS OF CHALLENGING VITALSTATISTIX! THE DRUID PANORAMIX'S MAGIC POTION GIVES HIM SUPERHUMAN STRENGTH!

UH, YES... LET'S NOT DWELL ON THAT!

ON THE CONTRARY, LET'S DO!

SINCE THE PROBLEM IS THE DRUID'S POTION, LET'S GET RID OF THE DRUID. NO MORE DRUID, NO MORE POTION. NO MORE POTION, NO MORE PROBLEM.

4B

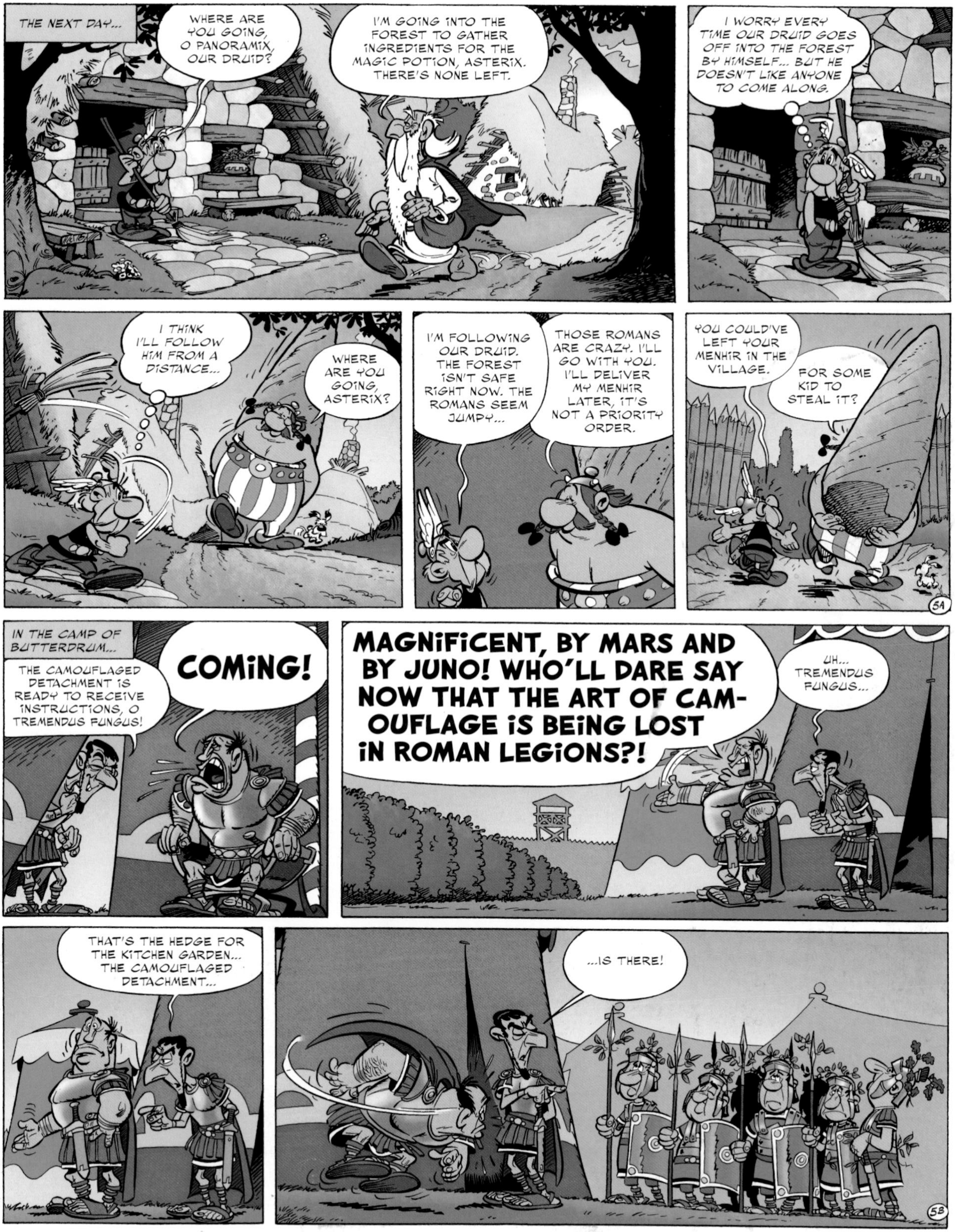
THE NEXT DAY...
WHERE ARE YOU GOING, O PANORAMIX, OUR DRUID?
I'M GOING INTO THE FOREST TO GATHER INGREDIENTS FOR THE MAGIC POTION, ASTERIX. THERE'S NONE LEFT.
I WORRY EVERY TIME OUR DRUID GOES OFF INTO THE FOREST BY HIMSELF... BUT HE DOESN'T LIKE ANYONE TO COME ALONG.
I THINK I'LL FOLLOW HIM FROM A DISTANCE...
WHERE ARE YOU GOING, ASTERIX?
I'M FOLLOWING OUR DRUID. THE FOREST ISN'T SAFE RIGHT NOW. THE ROMANS SEEM JUMPY...
THOSE ROMANS ARE CRAZY. I'LL GO WITH YOU. I'LL DELIVER MY MENHIR LATER, IT'S NOT A PRIORITY ORDER.
YOU COULD'VE LEFT YOUR MENHIR IN THE VILLAGE.
FOR SOME KID TO STEAL IT?
5A
IN THE CAMP OF BUTTERDRUM...
THE CAMOUFLAGED DETACHMENT IS READY TO RECEIVE INSTRUCTIONS, O TREMENDUS FUNGUS!
COMING!
MAGNIFICENT, BY MARS AND BY JUNO! WHO'LL DARE SAY NOW THAT THE ART OF CAMOUFLAGE IS BEING LOST IN ROMAN LEGIONS?!
UH... TREMENDUS FUNGUS...
THAT'S THE HEDGE FOR THE KITCHEN GARDEN... THE CAMOUFLAGED DETACHMENT...
...IS THERE!
5B

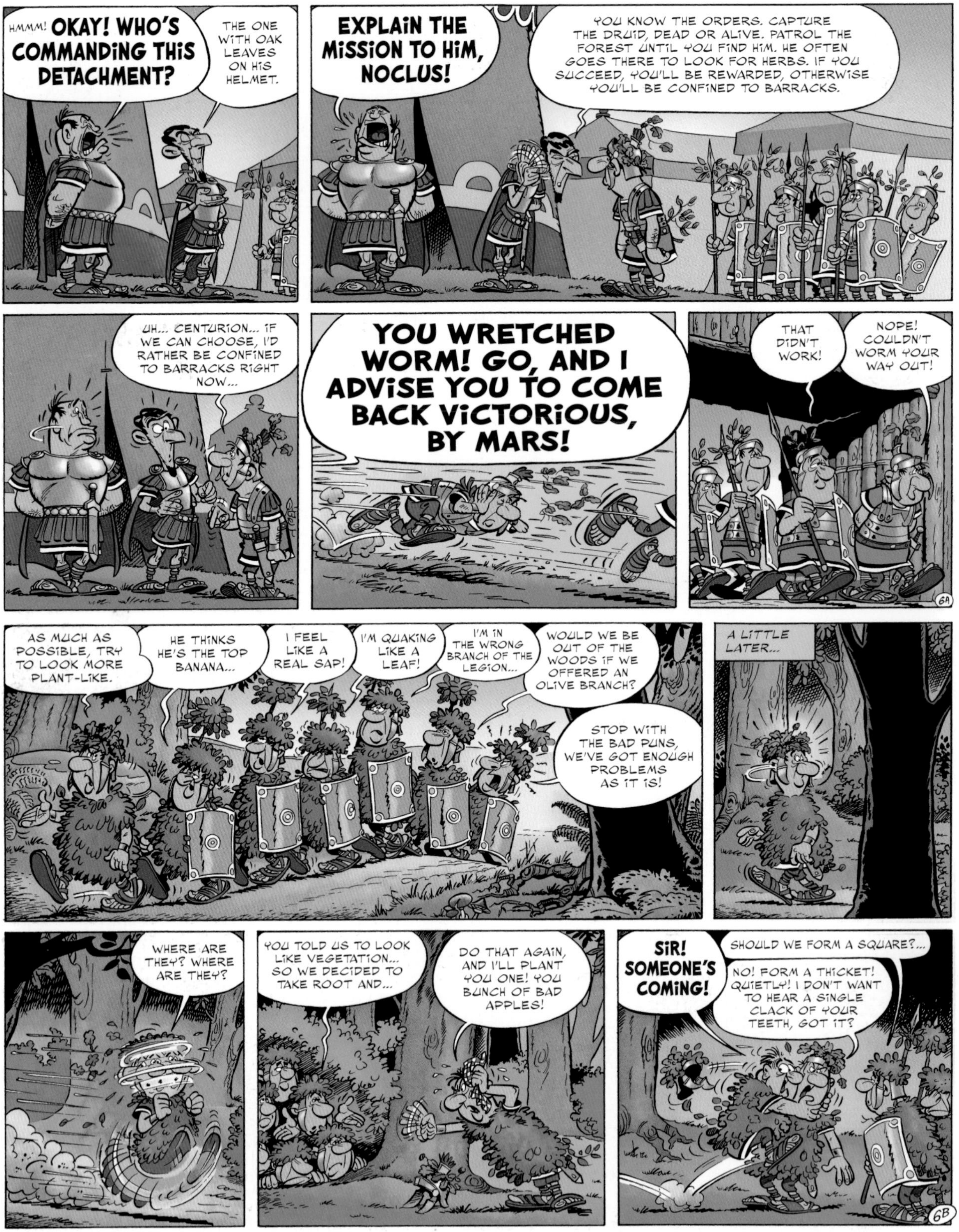
HMMM! OKAY! WHO'S COMMANDING THIS DETACHMENT?
THE ONE WITH OAK LEAVES ON HIS HELMET.
EXPLAIN THE MISSION TO HIM, NOCLUS!
YOU KNOW THE ORDERS. CAPTURE THE DRUID, DEAD OR ALIVE. PATROL THE FOREST UNTIL YOU FIND HIM. HE OFTEN GOES THERE TO LOOK FOR HERBS. IF YOU SUCCEED, YOU'LL BE REWARDED, OTHERWISE YOU'LL BE CONFINED TO BARRACKS.
UH... CENTURION... IF WE CAN CHOOSE, I'D RATHER BE CONFINED TO BARRACKS RIGHT NOW...
YOU WRETCHED WORM! GO, AND I ADVISE YOU TO COME BACK VICTORIOUS, BY MARS!
THAT DIDN'T WORK!
NOPE! COULDN'T WORM YOUR WAY OUT!
6A
AS MUCH AS POSSIBLE, TRY TO LOOK MORE PLANT-LIKE.
HE THINKS HE'S THE TOP BANANA...
I FEEL LIKE A REAL SAP!
I'M QUAKING LIKE A LEAF!
I'M IN THE WRONG BRANCH OF THE LEGION...
WOULD WE BE OUT OF THE WOODS IF WE OFFERED AN OLIVE BRANCH?
STOP WITH THE BAD PUNS, WE'VE GOT ENOUGH PROBLEMS AS IT IS!
A LITTLE LATER...
WHERE ARE THEY? WHERE ARE THEY?
YOU TOLD US TO LOOK LIKE VEGETATION... SO WE DECIDED TO TAKE ROOT AND...
DO THAT AGAIN, AND I'LL PLANT YOU ONE! YOU BUNCH OF BAD APPLES!
SIR! SOMEONE'S COMING!
SHOULD WE FORM A SQUARE?...
NO! FORM A THICKET! QUIETLY! I DON'T WANT TO HEAR A SINGLE CLACK OF YOUR TEETH, GOT IT?
6B

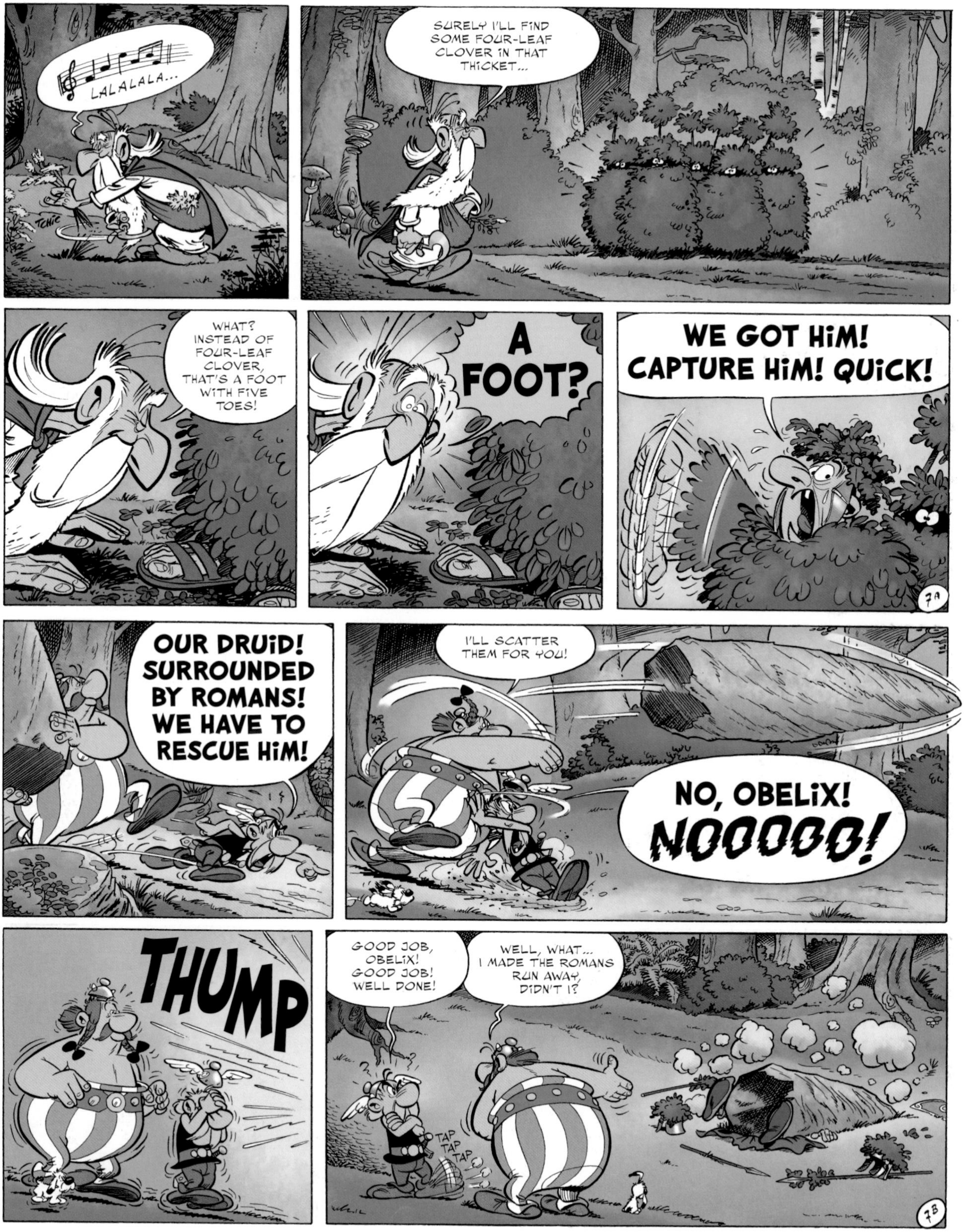
LALALALA...
TCHIC
SURELY I'LL FIND SOME FOUR-LEAF CLOVER IN THAT THICKET...
WHAT? INSTEAD OF FOUR-LEAF CLOVER, THAT'S A FOOT WITH FIVE TOES!
A FOOT?
WE GOT HIM! CAPTURE HIM! QUICK!
7A
OUR DRUID! SURROUNDED BY ROMANS! WE HAVE TO RESCUE HIM!
I'LL SCATTER THEM FOR YOU!
NO, OBELIX! NOOOOO!
THUMP
GOOD JOB, OBELIX! GOOD JOB! WELL DONE!
WELL, WHAT... I MADE THE ROMANS RUN AWAY, DIDN'T I?
TAP TAP TAP
7B

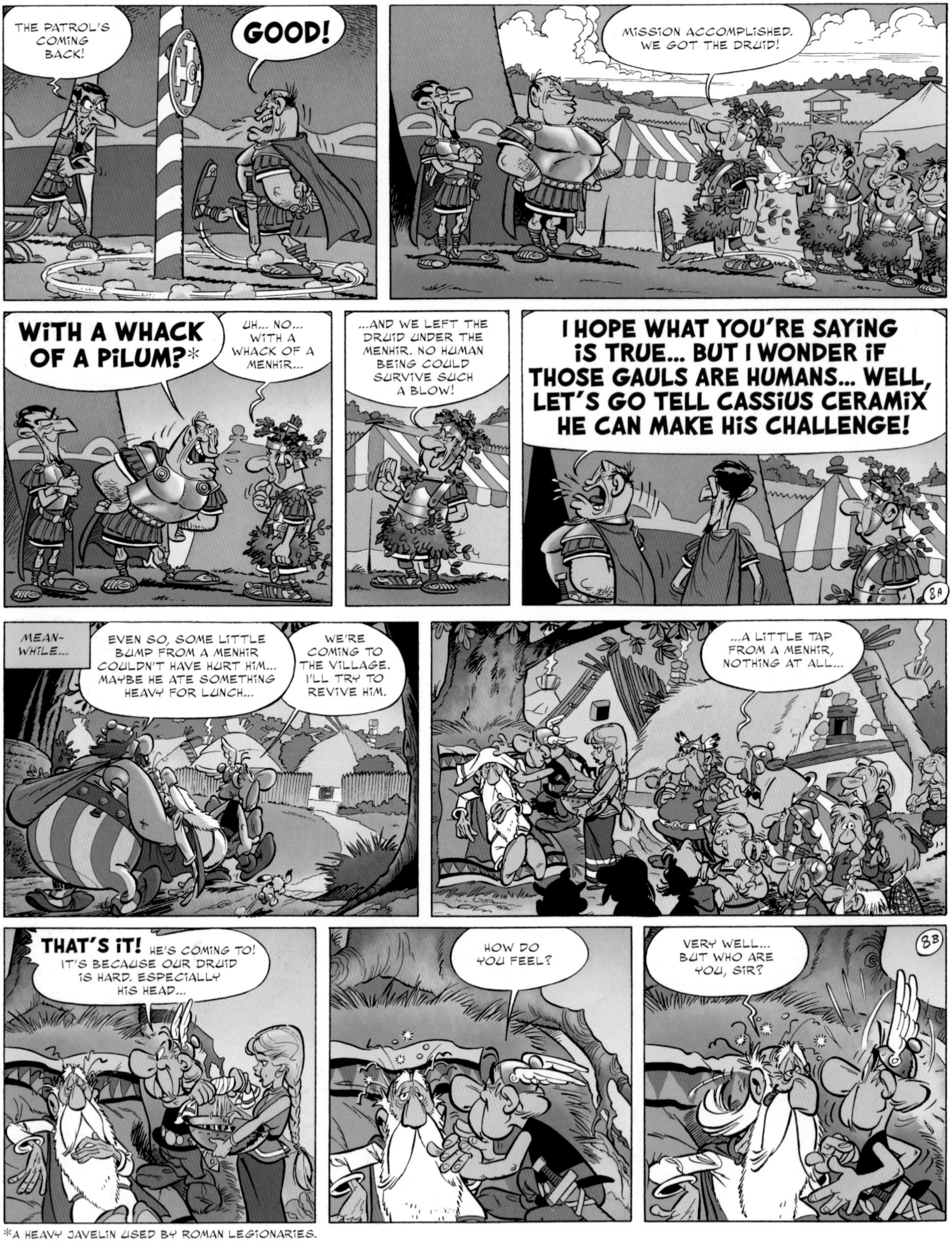
THE PATROL'S COMING BACK!
GOOD!
MISSION ACCOMPLISHED. WE GOT THE DRUID!
WITH A WHACK OF A PILUM?*
UH... NO... WITH A WHACK OF A MENHIR...
...AND WE LEFT THE DRUID UNDER THE MENHIR. NO HUMAN BEING COULD SURVIVE SUCH A BLOW!
I HOPE WHAT YOU'RE SAYING IS TRUE... BUT I WONDER IF THOSE GAULS ARE HUMANS... WELL, LET'S GO TELL CASSIUS CERAMIX HE CAN MAKE HIS CHALLENGE!
8A
MEAN-WHILE...
EVEN SO, SOME LITTLE BUMP FROM A MENHIR COULDN'T HAVE HURT HIM... MAYBE HE ATE SOMETHING HEAVY FOR LUNCH...
WE'RE COMING TO THE VILLAGE. I'LL TRY TO REVIVE HIM.
...A LITTLE TAP FROM A MENHIR, NOTHING AT ALL...
THAT'S IT! HE'S COMING TO! IT'S BECAUSE OUR DRUID IS HARD. ESPECIALLY HIS HEAD...
HOW DO YOU FEEL?
8B
VERY WELL... BUT WHO ARE YOU, SIR?

*A HEAVY JAVELIN USED BY ROMAN LEGIONARIES.

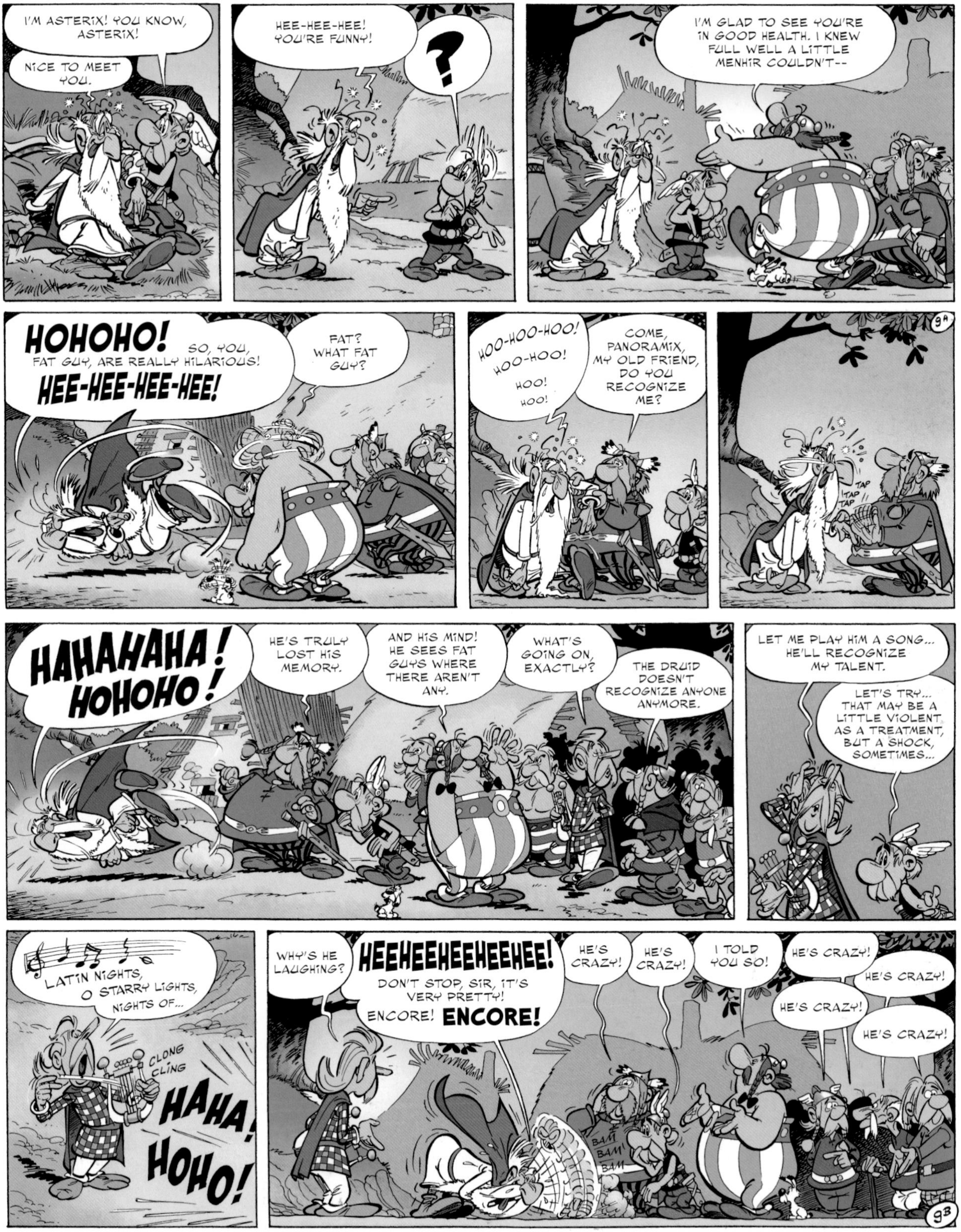
I'M ASTERIX! YOU KNOW, ASTERIX!
NICE TO MEET YOU.
HEE-HEE-HEE! YOU'RE FUNNY!
?
I'M GLAD TO SEE YOU'RE IN GOOD HEALTH. I KNEW FULL WELL A LITTLE MENHIR COULDN'T--
HOHOHO! SO, YOU, FAT GUY, ARE REALLY HILARIOUS! HEE-HEE-HEE-HEE!
FAT? WHAT FAT GUY?
HOO-HOO-HOO! HOO-HOO! HOO! HOO!
COME, PANORAMIX, MY OLD FRIEND, DO YOU RECOGNIZE ME?
TAP TAP TAP
HAHAHAHA! HOHOHO!
HE'S TRULY LOST HIS MEMORY.
AND HIS MIND! HE SEES FAT GUYS WHERE THERE AREN'T ANY.
WHAT'S GOING ON, EXACTLY?
THE DRUID DOESN'T RECOGNIZE ANYONE ANYMORE.
LET ME PLAY HIM A SONG... HE'LL RECOGNIZE MY TALENT.
LET'S TRY... THAT MAY BE A LITTLE VIOLENT AS A TREATMENT, BUT A SHOCK, SOMETIMES...
LATIN NIGHTS, O STARRY LIGHTS, NIGHTS OF...
CLONG CLING
HAHA! HOHO!
WHY'S HE LAUGHING?
HEEHEEHEEHEEHEE! DON'T STOP, SIR, IT'S VERY PRETTY! ENCORE! ENCORE!
HE'S CRAZY!
HE'S CRAZY!
I TOLD YOU SO!
HE'S CRAZY!
HE'S CRAZY!
HE'S CRAZY!
HE'S CRAZY!
BAM BAM BAM

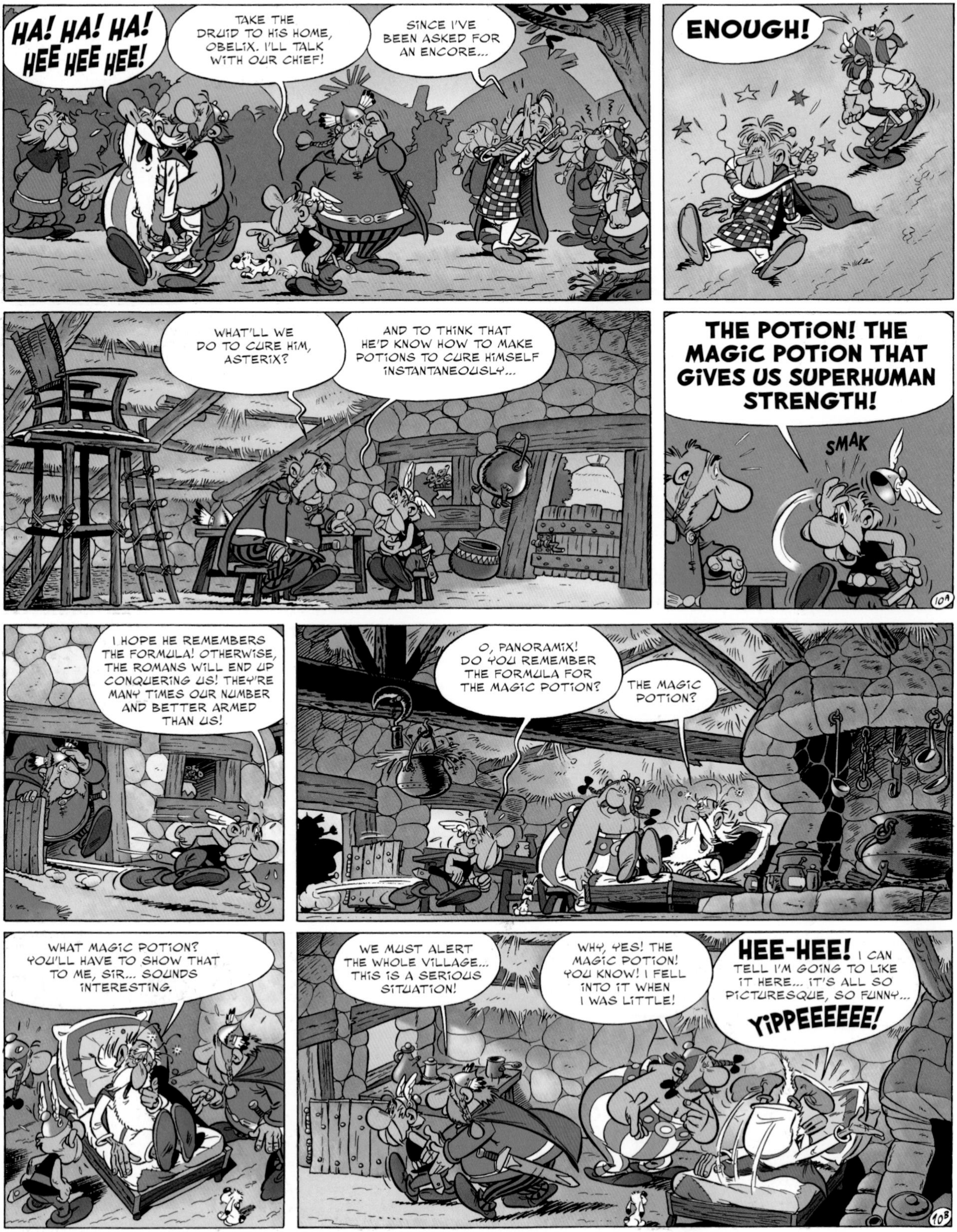
HA! HA! HA! HEE HEE HEE!
TAKE THE DRUID TO HIS HOME, OBELIX. I'LL TALK WITH OUR CHIEF!
SINCE I'VE BEEN ASKED FOR AN ENCORE...
ENOUGH!
WHAT'LL WE DO TO CURE HIM, ASTERIX?
AND TO THINK THAT HE'D KNOW HOW TO MAKE POTIONS TO CURE HIMSELF INSTANTANEOUSLY...
THE POTION! THE MAGIC POTION THAT GIVES US SUPERHUMAN STRENGTH!
SMAK
10A
I HOPE HE REMEMBERS THE FORMULA! OTHERWISE, THE ROMANS WILL END UP CONQUERING US! THEY'RE MANY TIMES OUR NUMBER AND BETTER ARMED THAN US!
O, PANORAMIX! DO YOU REMEMBER THE FORMULA FOR THE MAGIC POTION?
THE MAGIC POTION?
WHAT MAGIC POTION? YOU'LL HAVE TO SHOW THAT TO ME, SIR... SOUNDS INTERESTING.
WE MUST ALERT THE WHOLE VILLAGE... THIS IS A SERIOUS SITUATION!
WHY, YES! THE MAGIC POTION! YOU KNOW! I FELL INTO IT WHEN I WAS LITTLE!
HEE-HEE! I CAN TELL I'M GOING TO LIKE IT HERE... IT'S ALL SO PICTURESQUE, SO FUNNY... YIPPEEEEEE!
10B

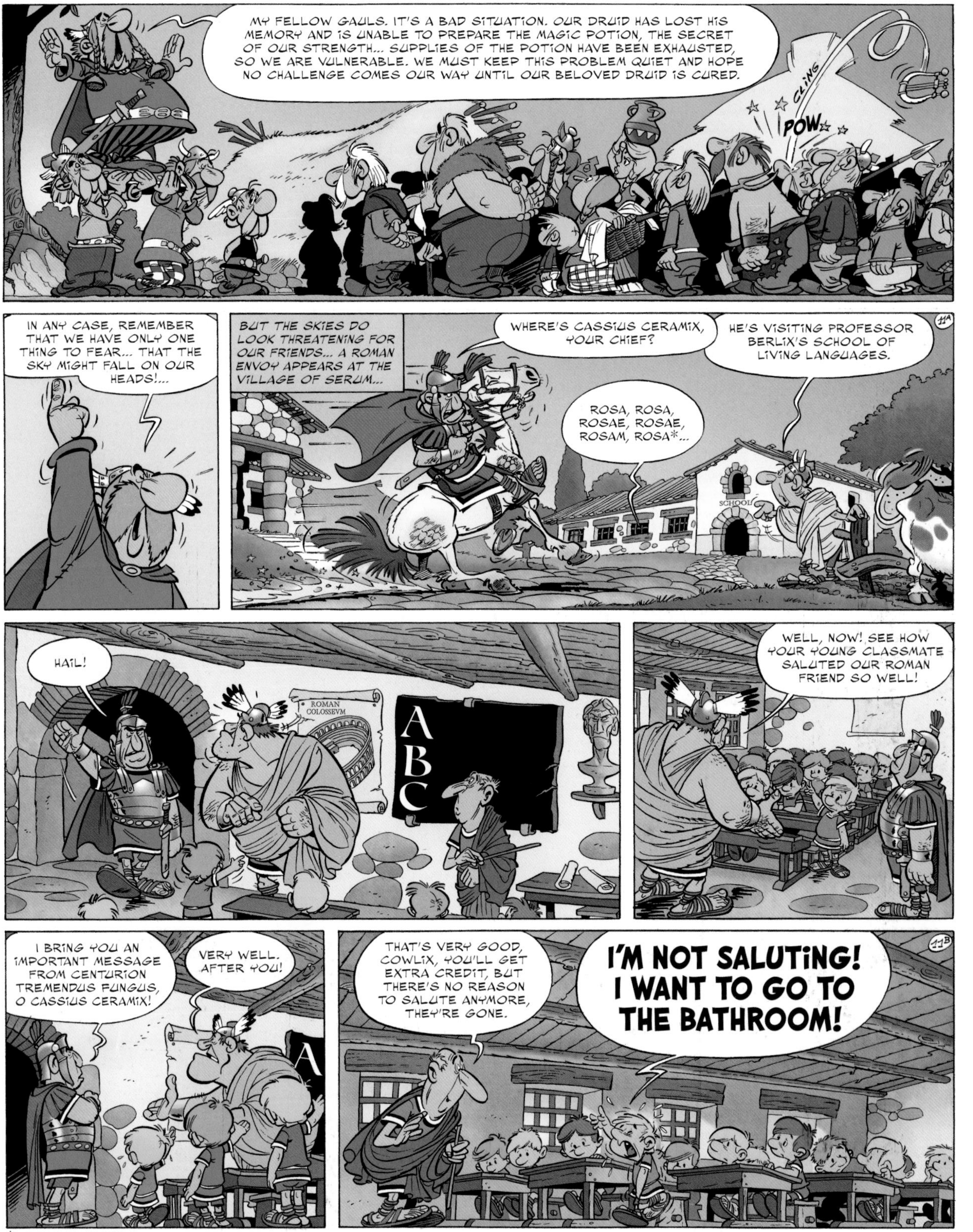
MY FELLOW GAULS. IT'S A BAD SITUATION. OUR DRUID HAS LOST HIS MEMORY AND IS UNABLE TO PREPARE THE MAGIC POTION, THE SECRET OF OUR STRENGTH... SUPPLIES OF THE POTION HAVE BEEN EXHAUSTED, SO WE ARE VULNERABLE. WE MUST KEEP THIS PROBLEM QUIET AND HOPE NO CHALLENGE COMES OUR WAY UNTIL OUR BELOVED DRUID IS CURED.
CLING
POW
IN ANY CASE, REMEMBER THAT WE HAVE ONLY ONE THING TO FEAR... THAT THE SKY MIGHT FALL ON OUR HEADS!...
BUT THE SKIES DO LOOK THREATENING FOR OUR FRIENDS... A ROMAN ENVOY APPEARS AT THE VILLAGE OF SERUM...
WHERE'S CASSIUS CERAMIX, YOUR CHIEF?
HE'S VISITING PROFESSOR BERLIX'S SCHOOL OF LIVING LANGUAGES.
ROSA, ROSA, ROSAE, ROSAE, ROSAM, ROSA*...
SCHOOL
HAIL!
ROMAN COLOSSEVM
A B C
WELL, NOW! SEE HOW YOUR YOUNG CLASSMATE SALUTED OUR ROMAN FRIEND SO WELL!
I BRING YOU AN IMPORTANT MESSAGE FROM CENTURION TREMENDUS FUNGUS, O CASSIUS CERAMIX!
VERY WELL. AFTER YOU!
THAT'S VERY GOOD, COWLIX, YOU'LL GET EXTRA CREDIT, BUT THERE'S NO REASON TO SALUTE ANYMORE, THEY'RE GONE.
I'M NOT SALUTING! I WANT TO GO TO THE BATHROOM!

*LATIN FOR "ROSE."

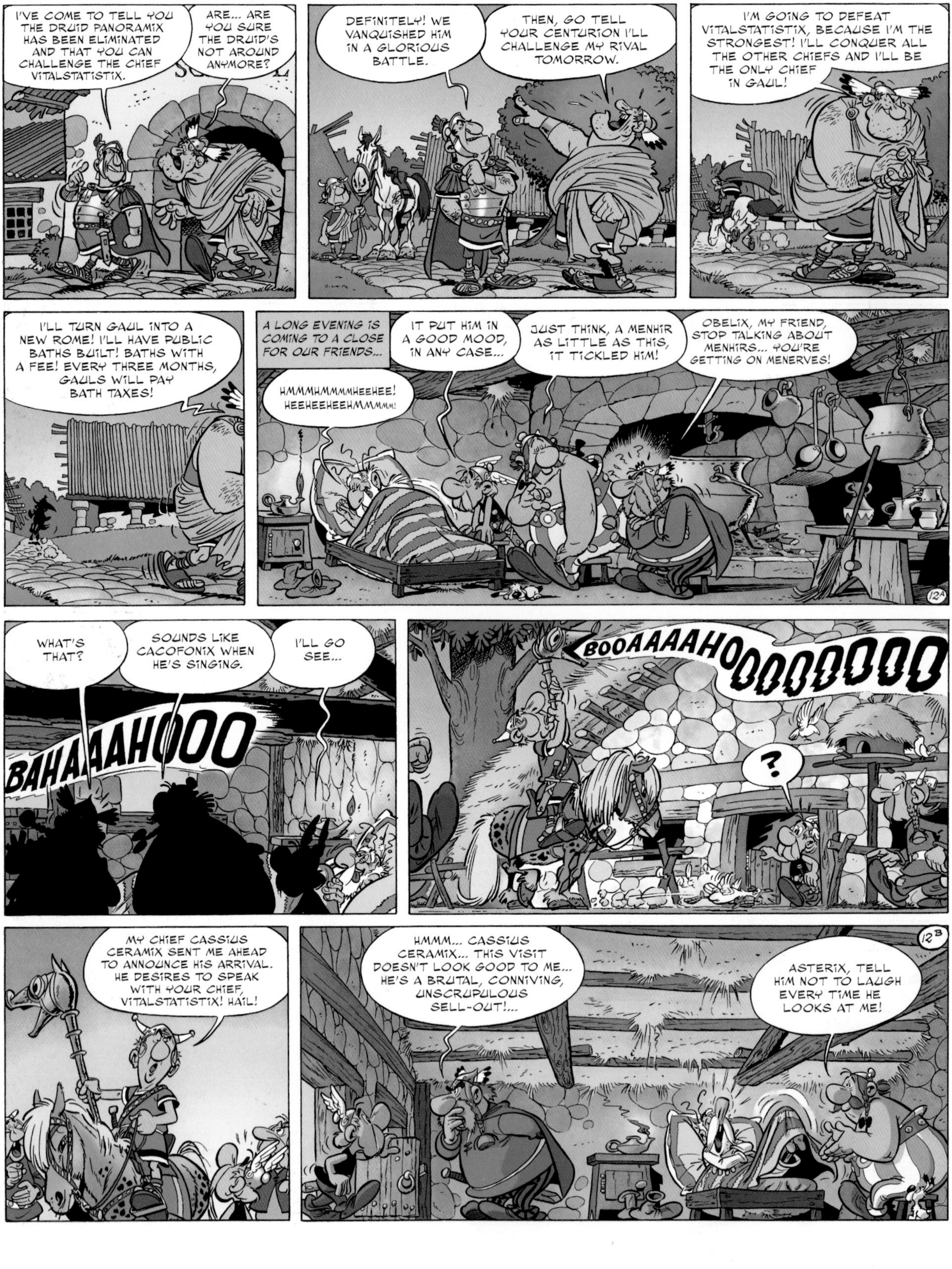
I'VE COME TO TELL YOU THE DRUID PANORAMIX HAS BEEN ELIMINATED AND THAT YOU CAN CHALLENGE THE CHIEF VITALSTATISTIX.
ARE... ARE YOU SURE THE DRUID'S NOT AROUND ANYMORE?
DEFINITELY! WE VANQUISHED HIM IN A GLORIOUS BATTLE.
THEN, GO TELL YOUR CENTURION I'LL CHALLENGE MY RIVAL TOMORROW.
I'M GOING TO DEFEAT VITALSTATISTIX, BECAUSE I'M THE STRONGEST! I'LL CONQUER ALL THE OTHER CHIEFS AND I'LL BE THE ONLY CHIEF IN GAUL!
I'LL TURN GAUL INTO A NEW ROME! I'LL HAVE PUBLIC BATHS BUILT! BATHS WITH A FEE! EVERY THREE MONTHS, GAULS WILL PAY BATH TAXES!
A LONG EVENING IS COMING TO A CLOSE FOR OUR FRIENDS...
IT PUT HIM IN A GOOD MOOD, IN ANY CASE...
JUST THINK, A MENHIR AS LITTLE AS THIS, IT TICKLED HIM!
OBELIX, MY FRIEND, STOP TALKING ABOUT MENHIRS... YOU'RE GETTING ON MENERVES!
HMMMHMMMMHEEHEE! HEEHEEHEEHMMMMM!
12A
WHAT'S THAT?
SOUNDS LIKE CACOFONIX WHEN HE'S SINGING.
I'LL GO SEE...
BAHAAAHOOO
BOOAAAAAHOOOOOOOOO
?
MY CHIEF CASSIUS CERAMIX SENT ME AHEAD TO ANNOUNCE HIS ARRIVAL. HE DESIRES TO SPEAK WITH YOUR CHIEF, VITALSTATISTIX! HAIL!
12B
HMMM... CASSIUS CERAMIX... THIS VISIT DOESN'T LOOK GOOD TO ME... HE'S A BRUTAL, CONNIVING, UNSCRUPULOUS SELL-OUT!...
ASTERIX, TELL HIM NOT TO LAUGH EVERY TIME HE LOOKS AT ME!

CASSIUS CERAMIX IS HERE, CHIEF!

HURRY IT UP NOW! THIS IS ON ME!

IF YOU'D STOP FIDGETING ALL THE TIME!...

DOWN! THEY'RE HERE!

THAT'S IT! THAT'S IT!

BAAAAHOOOOOOUUUUUU

BAAAAAOOOOUUUULLLUUUHHH

WHAT A RACKET!

IT HAS A NICE MELODY!

13ᴬ

HAIL!

HELLO!

THIS IS A HIGH-LEVEL MEETING!

TELL US ABOUT IT!

I'VE COME TO CHALLENGE YOU! A CHALLENGE TO A COMBAT OF CHIEFS!

?!!

A CHALLENGE!

A CHALLENGE!

YES, BUT--

THE WINNER, ACCORDING TO OUR LAWS, WILL BECOME THE CHIEF OF THE DEFEATED ONE'S TRIBE! THE COMBAT WILL TAKE PLACE AT THE NEXT CALENDS!*

13ᴮ

*THE CALENDS IS THE FIRST DAY OF A ROMAN MONTH.

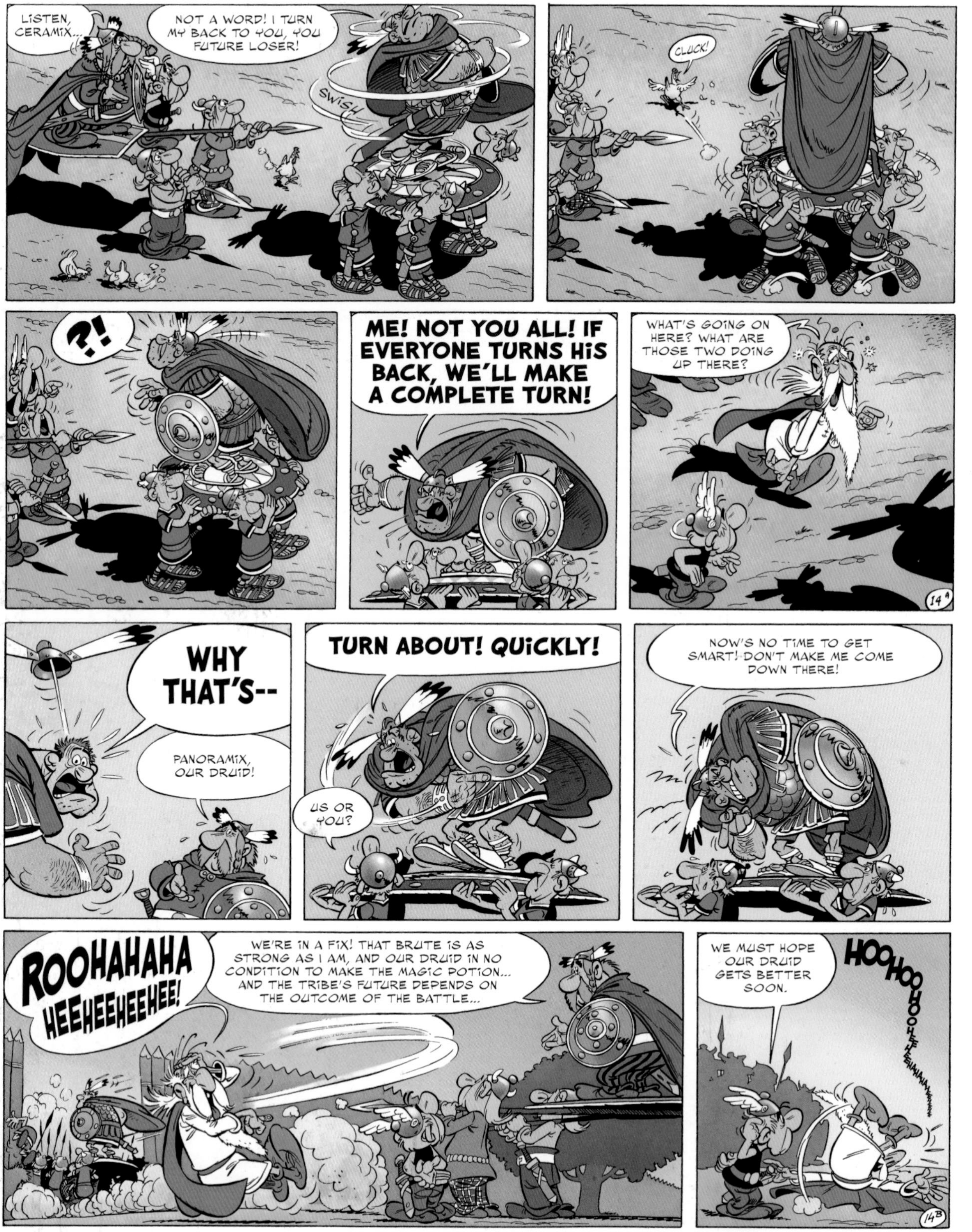
LISTEN, CERAMIX...
NOT A WORD! I TURN MY BACK TO YOU, YOU FUTURE LOSER!
SWISH
CLUCK!
?!
ME! NOT YOU ALL! IF EVERYONE TURNS HIS BACK, WE'LL MAKE A COMPLETE TURN!
WHAT'S GOING ON HERE? WHAT ARE THOSE TWO DOING UP THERE?
14A
WHY THAT'S--
PANORAMIX, OUR DRUID!
TURN ABOUT! QUICKLY!
US OR YOU?
NOW'S NO TIME TO GET SMART! DON'T MAKE ME COME DOWN THERE!
ROOHAHAHA HEEHEEHEEHEE!
WE'RE IN A FIX! THAT BRUTE IS AS STRONG AS I AM, AND OUR DRUID IN NO CONDITION TO MAKE THE MAGIC POTION... AND THE TRIBE'S FUTURE DEPENDS ON THE OUTCOME OF THE BATTLE...
WE MUST HOPE OUR DRUID GETS BETTER SOON.
HOOHOO
14B

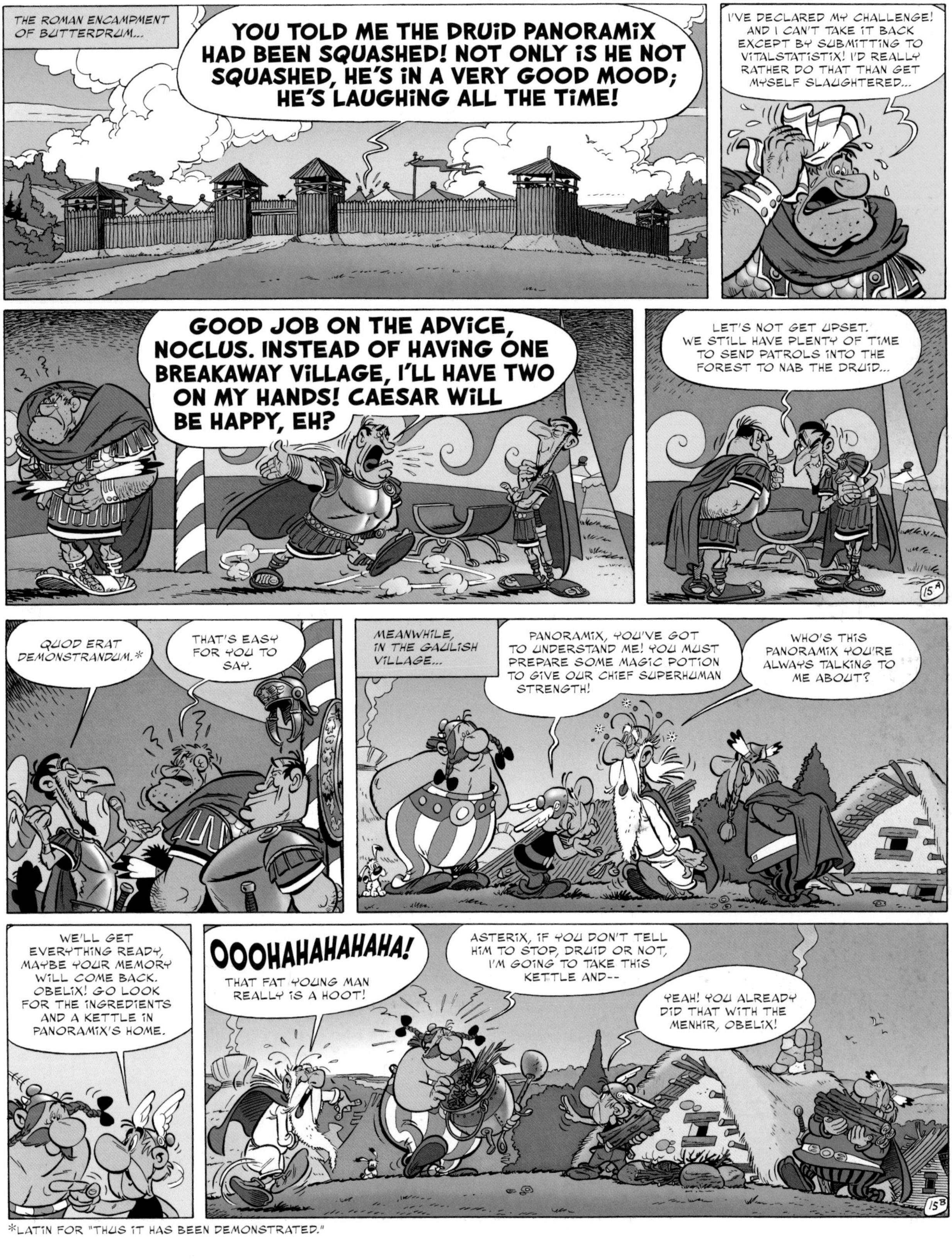

THE ROMAN ENCAMPMENT OF BUTTERDRUM...
YOU TOLD ME THE DRUID PANORAMIX HAD BEEN SQUASHED! NOT ONLY IS HE NOT SQUASHED, HE'S IN A VERY GOOD MOOD; HE'S LAUGHING ALL THE TIME!
I'VE DECLARED MY CHALLENGE! AND I CAN'T TAKE IT BACK EXCEPT BY SUBMITTING TO VITALSTATISTIX! I'D REALLY RATHER DO THAT THAN GET MYSELF SLAUGHTERED...
GOOD JOB ON THE ADVICE, NOCLUS. INSTEAD OF HAVING ONE BREAKAWAY VILLAGE, I'LL HAVE TWO ON MY HANDS! CAESAR WILL BE HAPPY, EH?
LET'S NOT GET UPSET. WE STILL HAVE PLENTY OF TIME TO SEND PATROLS INTO THE FOREST TO NAB THE DRUID...
15A
QUOD ERAT DEMONSTRANDUM.*
THAT'S EASY FOR YOU TO SAY.
MEANWHILE, IN THE GAULISH VILLAGE...
PANORAMIX, YOU'VE GOT TO UNDERSTAND ME! YOU MUST PREPARE SOME MAGIC POTION TO GIVE OUR CHIEF SUPERHUMAN STRENGTH!
WHO'S THIS PANORAMIX YOU'RE ALWAYS TALKING TO ME ABOUT?
WE'LL GET EVERYTHING READY, MAYBE YOUR MEMORY WILL COME BACK. OBELIX! GO LOOK FOR THE INGREDIENTS AND A KETTLE IN PANORAMIX'S HOME.
OOOHAHAHAHAHA!
THAT FAT YOUNG MAN REALLY IS A HOOT!
ASTERIX, IF YOU DON'T TELL HIM TO STOP, DRUID OR NOT, I'M GOING TO TAKE THIS KETTLE AND--
YEAH! YOU ALREADY DID THAT WITH THE MENHIR, OBELIX!
15B

*LATIN FOR "THUS IT HAS BEEN DEMONSTRATED."

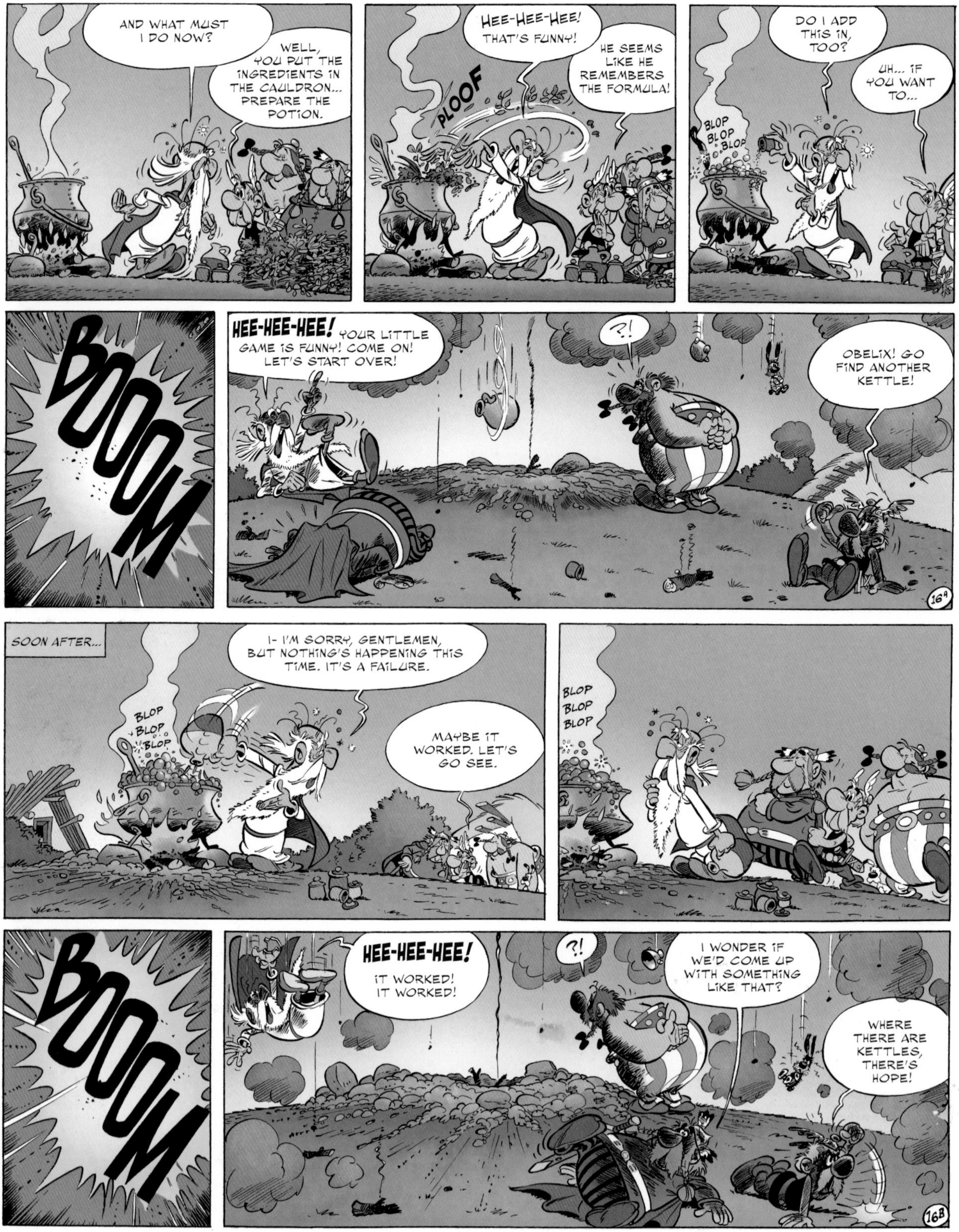

AND WHAT MUST I DO NOW?
WELL, YOU PUT THE INGREDIENTS IN THE CAULDRON... PREPARE THE POTION.
HEE-HEE-HEE! THAT'S FUNNY!
PLOOF
HE SEEMS LIKE HE REMEMBERS THE FORMULA!
DO I ADD THIS IN, TOO?
UH... IF YOU WANT TO...
BLOP BLOP BLOP
BOOOM
HEE-HEE-HEE! YOUR LITTLE GAME IS FUNNY! COME ON! LET'S START OVER!
?!
OBELIX! GO FIND ANOTHER KETTLE!
16A
SOON AFTER...
I- I'M SORRY, GENTLEMEN, BUT NOTHING'S HAPPENING THIS TIME. IT'S A FAILURE.
BLOP BLOP BLOP
MAYBE IT WORKED. LET'S GO SEE.
BLOP BLOP BLOP
BOOOM
HEE-HEE-HEE! IT WORKED! IT WORKED!
?!
I WONDER IF WE'D COME UP WITH SOMETHING LIKE THAT?
WHERE THERE ARE KETTLES, THERE'S HOPE!
16B

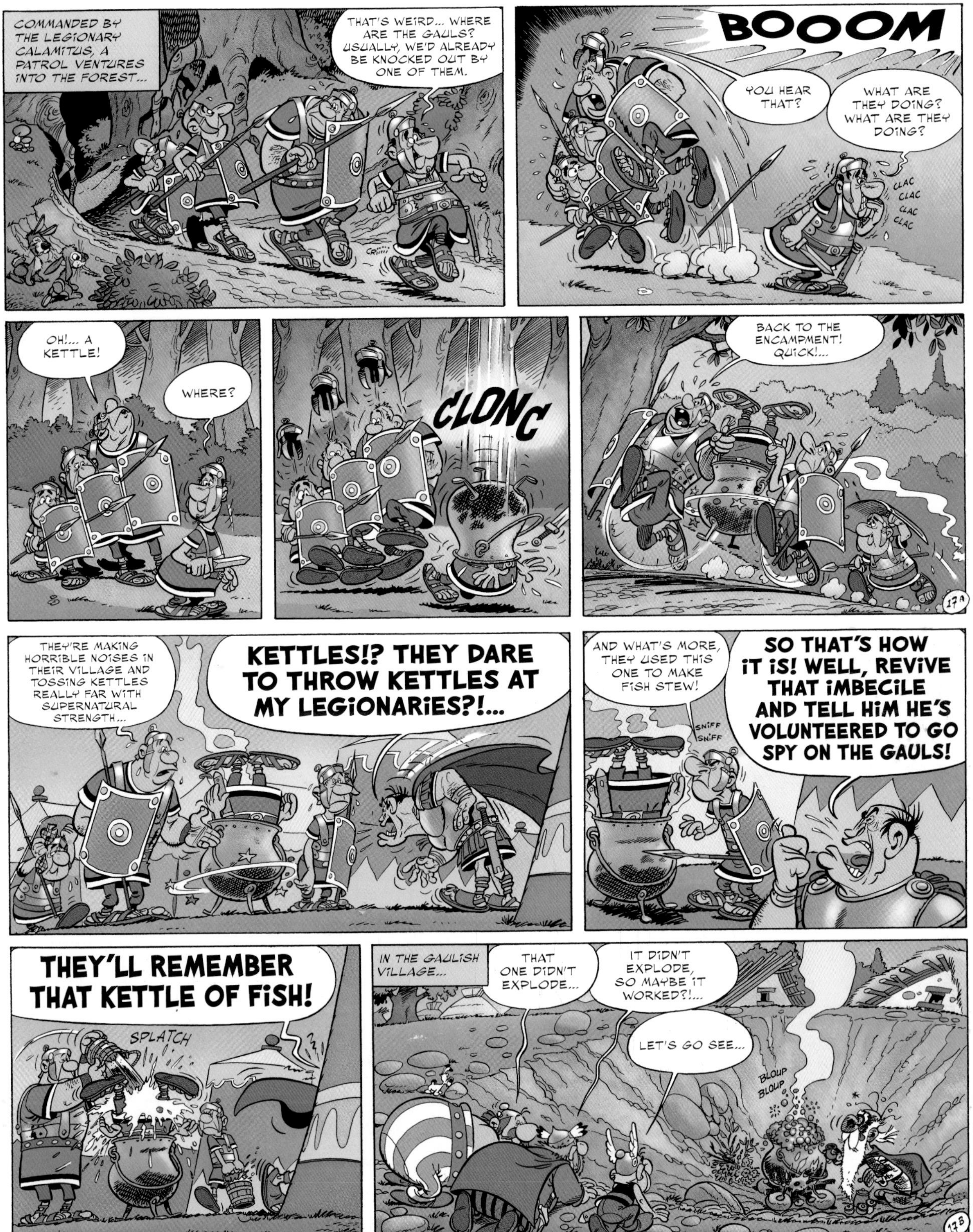
COMMANDED BY THE LEGIONARY CALAMITUS, A PATROL VENTURES INTO THE FOREST...
THAT'S WEIRD... WHERE ARE THE GAULS? USUALLY, WE'D ALREADY BE KNOCKED OUT BY ONE OF THEM.
CRiiiii
BOOOM
YOU HEAR THAT?
WHAT ARE THEY DOING? WHAT ARE THEY DOING?
CLAC CLAC CLAC CLAC
OH!... A KETTLE!
WHERE?
CLONC
BACK TO THE ENCAMPMENT! QUICK!...
THEY'RE MAKING HORRIBLE NOISES IN THEIR VILLAGE AND TOSSING KETTLES REALLY FAR WITH SUPERNATURAL STRENGTH...
KETTLES!? THEY DARE TO THROW KETTLES AT MY LEGIONARIES?!...
AND WHAT'S MORE, THEY USED THIS ONE TO MAKE FISH STEW!
SNIFF SNIFF
SO THAT'S HOW IT IS! WELL, REVIVE THAT IMBECILE AND TELL HIM HE'S VOLUNTEERED TO GO SPY ON THE GAULS!
THEY'LL REMEMBER THAT KETTLE OF FISH!
SPLATCH
IN THE GAULISH VILLAGE...
THAT ONE DIDN'T EXPLODE...
IT DIDN'T EXPLODE, SO MAYBE IT WORKED?!...
LET'S GO SEE...
BLOUP BLOUP

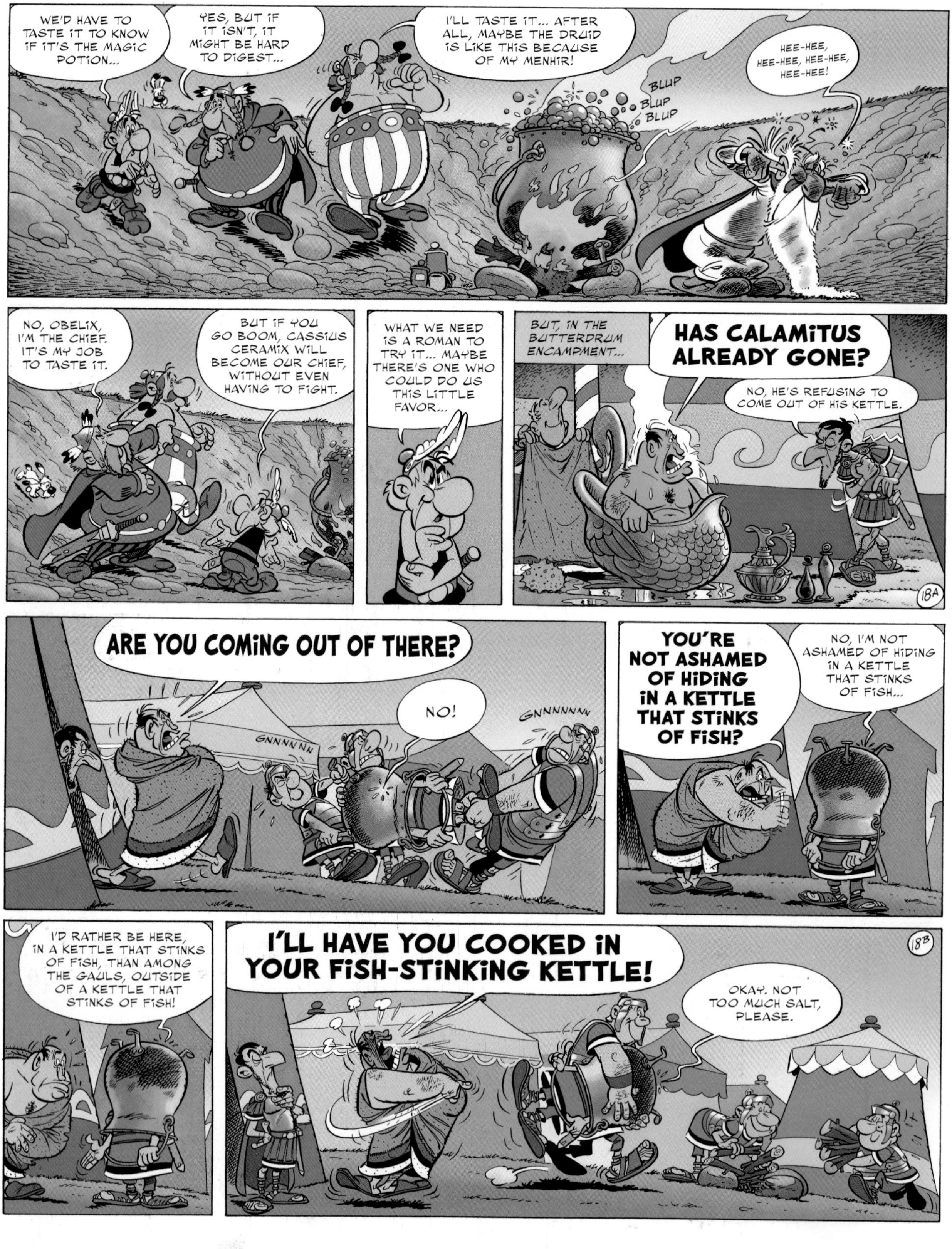

WE'D HAVE TO TASTE IT TO KNOW IF IT'S THE MAGIC POTION...
YES, BUT IF IT ISN'T, IT MIGHT BE HARD TO DIGEST...
I'LL TASTE IT... AFTER ALL, MAYBE THE DRUID IS LIKE THIS BECAUSE OF MY MENHIR!
BLUP BLUP BLUP
HEE-HEE, HEE-HEE, HEE-HEE, HEE-HEE!
NO, OBELIX, I'M THE CHIEF. IT'S MY JOB TO TASTE IT.
BUT IF YOU GO BOOM, CASSIUS CERAMIX WILL BECOME OUR CHIEF, WITHOUT EVEN HAVING TO FIGHT.
WHAT WE NEED IS A ROMAN TO TRY IT... MAYBE THERE'S ONE WHO COULD DO US THIS LITTLE FAVOR...
BUT, IN THE BUTTERDRUM ENCAMPMENT...
HAS CALAMITUS ALREADY GONE?
NO, HE'S REFUSING TO COME OUT OF HIS KETTLE.
18A
ARE YOU COMING OUT OF THERE?
GNNNNNN
NO!
GNNNNNNN
YOU'RE NOT ASHAMED OF HIDING IN A KETTLE THAT STINKS OF FISH?
NO, I'M NOT ASHAMED OF HIDING IN A KETTLE THAT STINKS OF FISH...
I'D RATHER BE HERE, IN A KETTLE THAT STINKS OF FISH, THAN AMONG THE GAULS, OUTSIDE OF A KETTLE THAT STINKS OF FISH!
I'LL HAVE YOU COOKED IN YOUR FISH-STINKING KETTLE!
18B
OKAY. NOT TOO MUCH SALT, PLEASE.

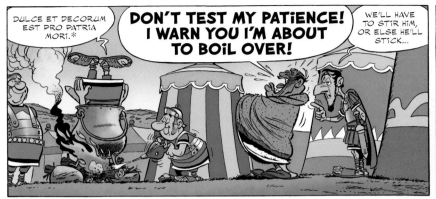

DULCE ET DECORUM EST PRO PATRIA MORI.*

DON'T TEST MY PATIENCE! I WARN YOU I'M ABOUT TO BOIL OVER!

WE'LL HAVE TO STIR HIM, OR ELSE HE'LL STICK...

SO, COMING OUT OR NOT?

I-- I'M NOT READY YET...

OH, ALL RIGHT ALREADY... I'M COMING OUT... WHAT IN BLAZES? ...BUT I PROTEST!

I CONGRATULATE YOU FOR YOUR UNPREMEDITATED HEROISM! YOU'RE GOING TO GO SPY ON THE GAULS... IF YOU'RE WELL CAMOUFLAGED, YOU RISK NOTHING!

SOON AFTER...

LOOK! CALAMITUS!

HE DOESN'T LOOK TOO HAPPY!

AND HE STINKS OF FISH!

THAT'S ONE FISHY TREE!

HEE-HEE-HEE-HO! HAHAHA!

IMBECILES.

THE VALIANT LEGIONARY ENTERS THE FOREST...

I'M PRETTY CLOSE TO THE GAULISH VILLAGE... I'LL PLANT MYSELF HERE.

HOOHOO!

?

GO AWAY, FILTHY BEAST! YOU'LL GET ME NOTICED! SHOO!

HOO?!

SHOO! SHOO!

HOO! HOO!... A TREE GIFTED WITH SPEECH AND SMELLING OF THE TIDE, WHAT A MIRACLE! I'LL NEVER PART COMPANY WITH IT!

*LATIN FOR "IT IS SWEET AND FITTING TO DIE FOR ONE'S COUNTRY."

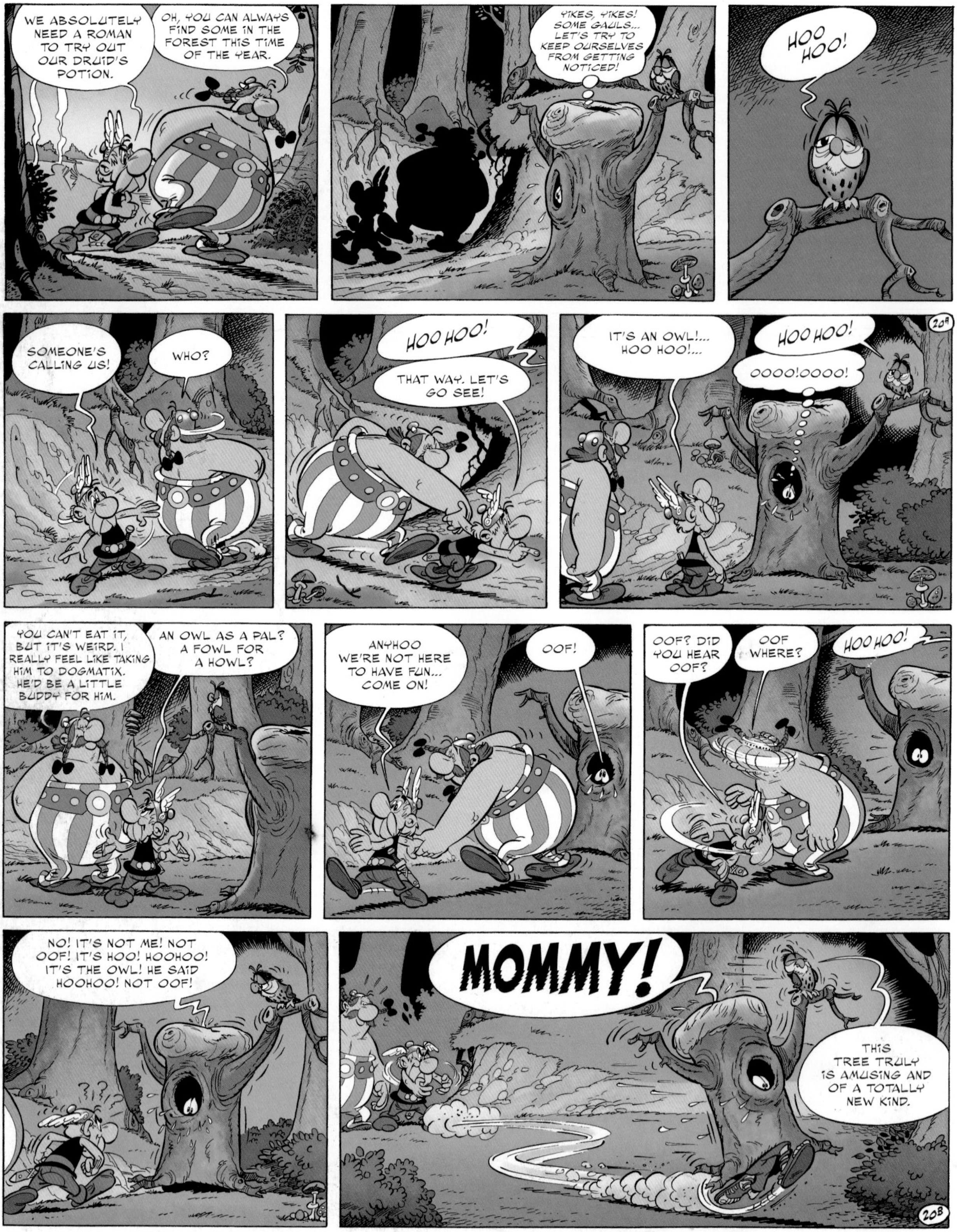
WE ABSOLUTELY NEED A ROMAN TO TRY OUT OUR DRUID'S POTION.
OH, YOU CAN ALWAYS FIND SOME IN THE FOREST THIS TIME OF THE YEAR.
YIKES, YIKES! SOME GAULS... LET'S TRY TO KEEP OURSELVES FROM GETTING NOTICED!
HOO HOO!
SOMEONE'S CALLING US!
WHO?
HOO HOO!
THAT WAY. LET'S GO SEE!
IT'S AN OWL!... HOO HOO!...
HOO HOO!
OOOO!OOOO!
YOU CAN'T EAT IT, BUT IT'S WEIRD. I REALLY FEEL LIKE TAKING HIM TO DOGMATIX. HE'D BE A LITTLE BUDDY FOR HIM.
AN OWL AS A PAL? A FOWL FOR A HOWL?
ANYHOO WE'RE NOT HERE TO HAVE FUN... COME ON!
OOF!
OOF? DID YOU HEAR OOF?
OOF WHERE?
HOO HOO!
NO! IT'S NOT ME! NOT OOF! IT'S HOO! HOOHOO! IT'S THE OWL! HE SAID HOOHOO! NOT OOF!
MOMMY!
THIS TREE TRULY IS AMUSING AND OF A TOTALLY NEW KIND.

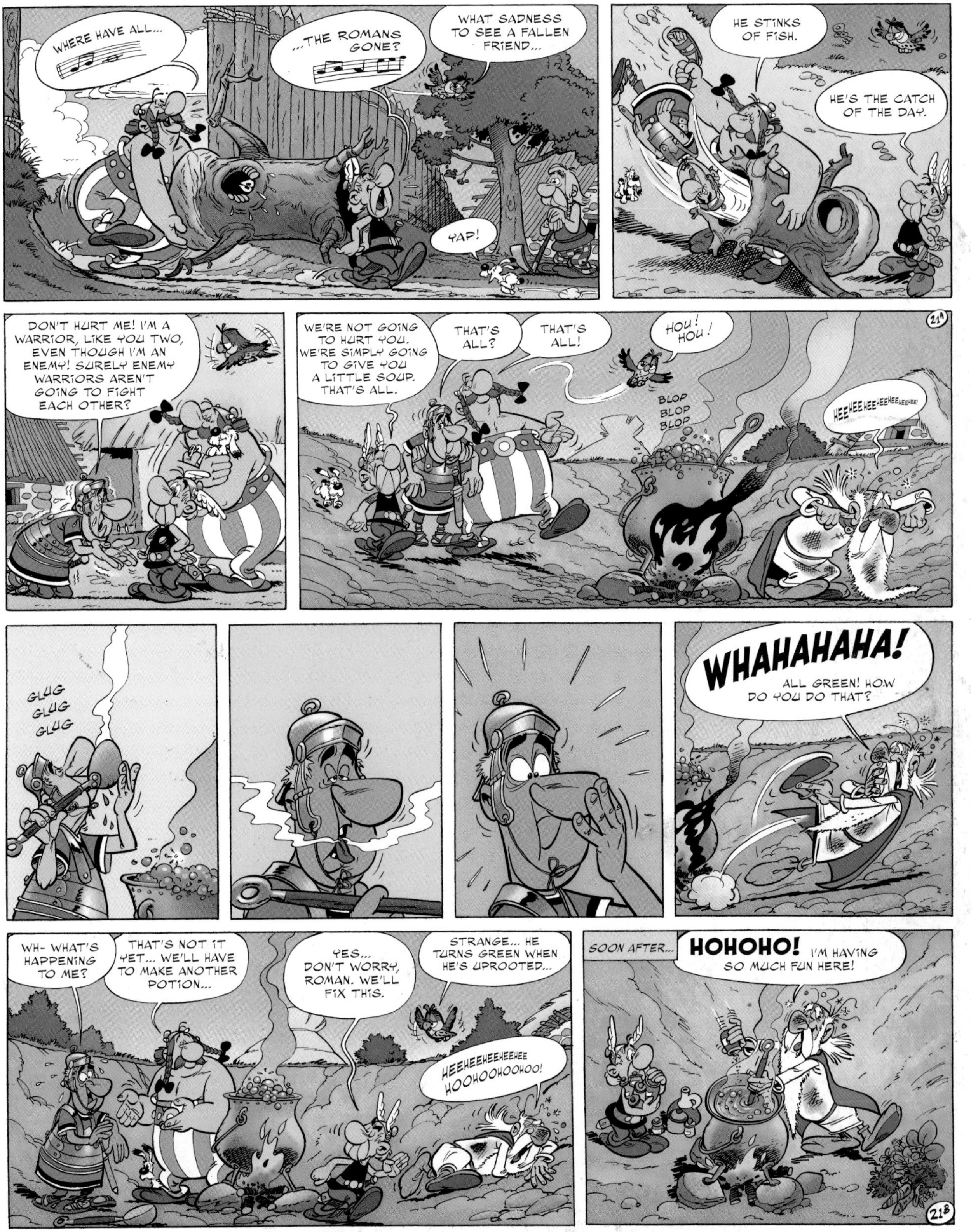
WHERE HAVE ALL...
...THE ROMANS GONE?
WHAT SADNESS TO SEE A FALLEN FRIEND...
YAP!
HE STINKS OF FISH.
HE'S THE CATCH OF THE DAY.
DON'T HURT ME! I'M A WARRIOR, LIKE YOU TWO, EVEN THOUGH I'M AN ENEMY! SURELY ENEMY WARRIORS AREN'T GOING TO FIGHT EACH OTHER?
WE'RE NOT GOING TO HURT YOU. WE'RE SIMPLY GOING TO GIVE YOU A LITTLE SOUP. THAT'S ALL.
THAT'S ALL?
THAT'S ALL!
HOU! HOU!
BLOP BLOP BLOP
HEEHEEHEEHEEHEEHEEHEE!
GLUG GLUG GLUG
WHAHAHAHA!
ALL GREEN! HOW DO YOU DO THAT?
WH- WHAT'S HAPPENING TO ME?
THAT'S NOT IT YET... WE'LL HAVE TO MAKE ANOTHER POTION...
YES... DON'T WORRY, ROMAN. WE'LL FIX THIS.
STRANGE... HE TURNS GREEN WHEN HE'S UPROOTED...
HEEHEEHEEHEEHEE HOOHOOHOOHOO!
SOON AFTER...
HOHOHO! I'M HAVING SO MUCH FUN HERE!

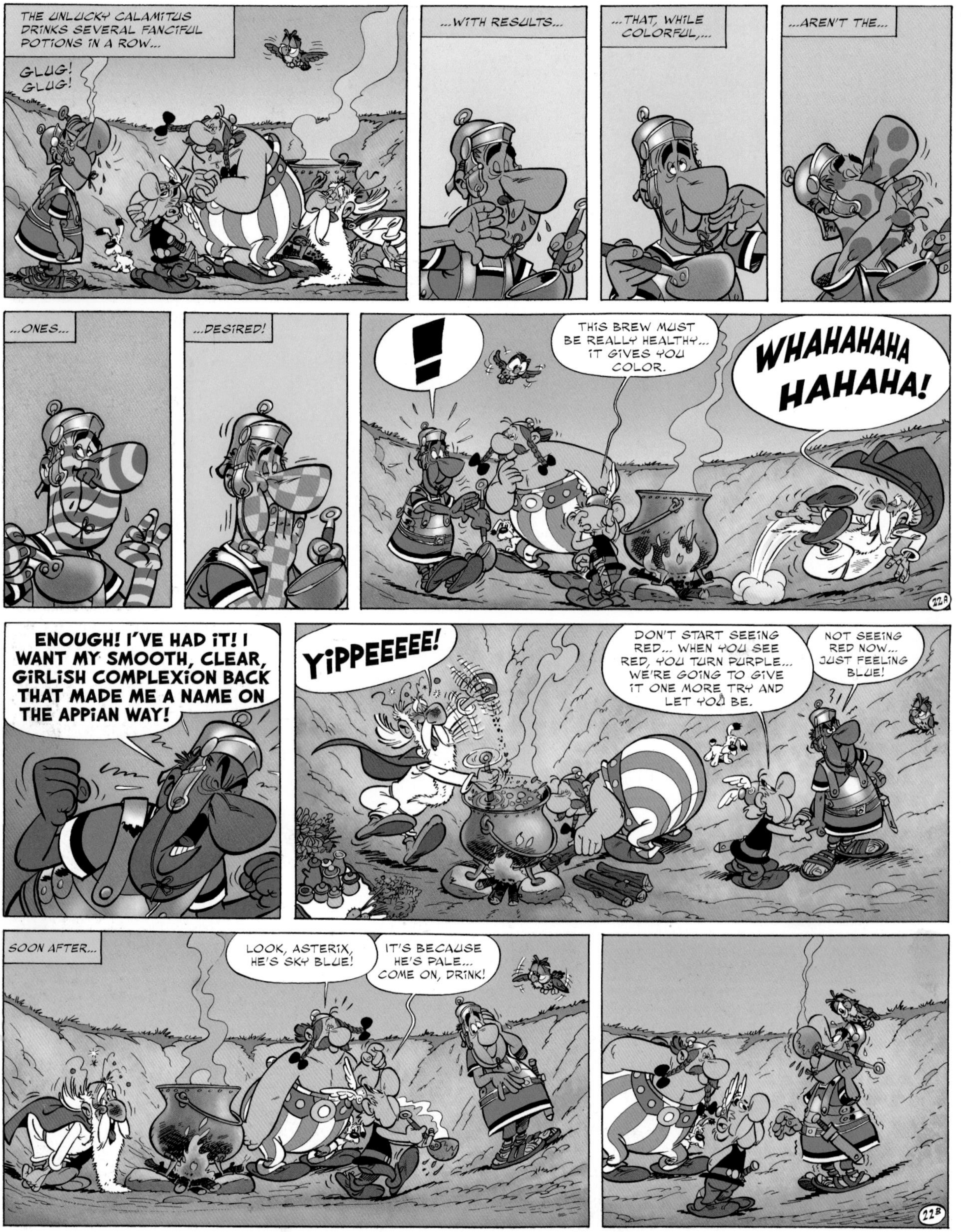

THE UNLUCKY CALAMITUS DRINKS SEVERAL FANCIFUL POTIONS IN A ROW...
GLUG! GLUG!
...WITH RESULTS...
...THAT, WHILE COLORFUL,...
...AREN'T THE...
...ONES...
...DESIRED!
!
THIS BREW MUST BE REALLY HEALTHY... IT GIVES YOU COLOR.
WHAHAHAHA HAHAHA!
22A
ENOUGH! I'VE HAD IT! I WANT MY SMOOTH, CLEAR, GIRLISH COMPLEXION BACK THAT MADE ME A NAME ON THE APPIAN WAY!
YIPPEEEEE!
DON'T START SEEING RED... WHEN YOU SEE RED, YOU TURN PURPLE... WE'RE GOING TO GIVE IT ONE MORE TRY AND LET YOU BE.
NOT SEEING RED NOW... JUST FEELING BLUE!
SOON AFTER...
LOOK, ASTERIX, HE'S SKY BLUE!
IT'S BECAUSE HE'S PALE... COME ON, DRINK!
22B

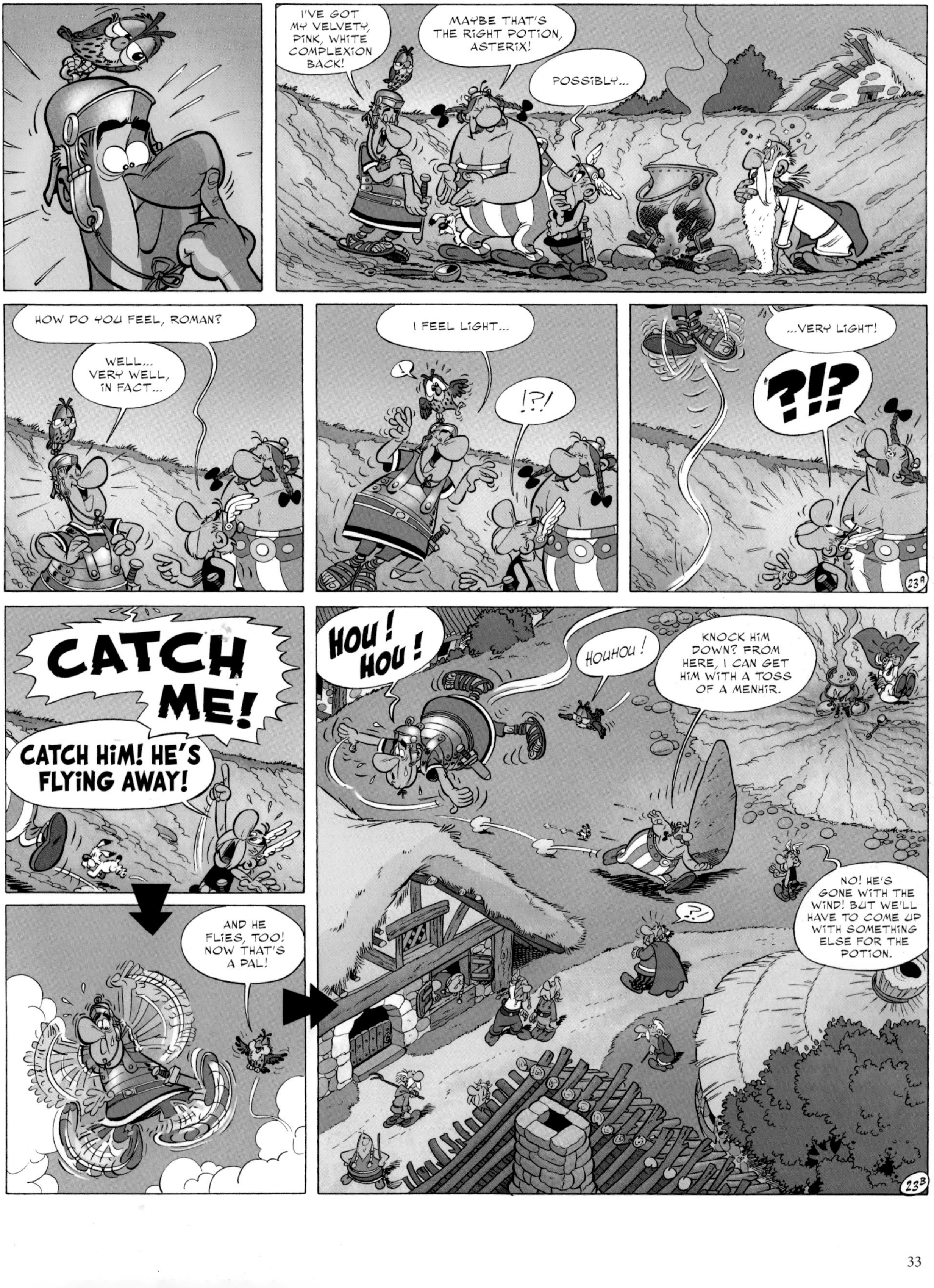
I'VE GOT MY VELVETY, PINK, WHITE COMPLEXION BACK!
MAYBE THAT'S THE RIGHT POTION, ASTERIX!
POSSIBLY...
HOW DO YOU FEEL, ROMAN?
WELL... VERY WELL, IN FACT...
I FEEL LIGHT...
!?!
...VERY LIGHT!
?!?
CATCH ME!
CATCH HIM! HE'S FLYING AWAY!
AND HE FLIES, TOO! NOW THAT'S A PAL!
HOU! HOU!
HOUHOU!
KNOCK HIM DOWN? FROM HERE, I CAN GET HIM WITH A TOSS OF A MENHIR.
NO! HE'S GONE WITH THE WIND! BUT WE'LL HAVE TO COME UP WITH SOMETHING ELSE FOR THE POTION.

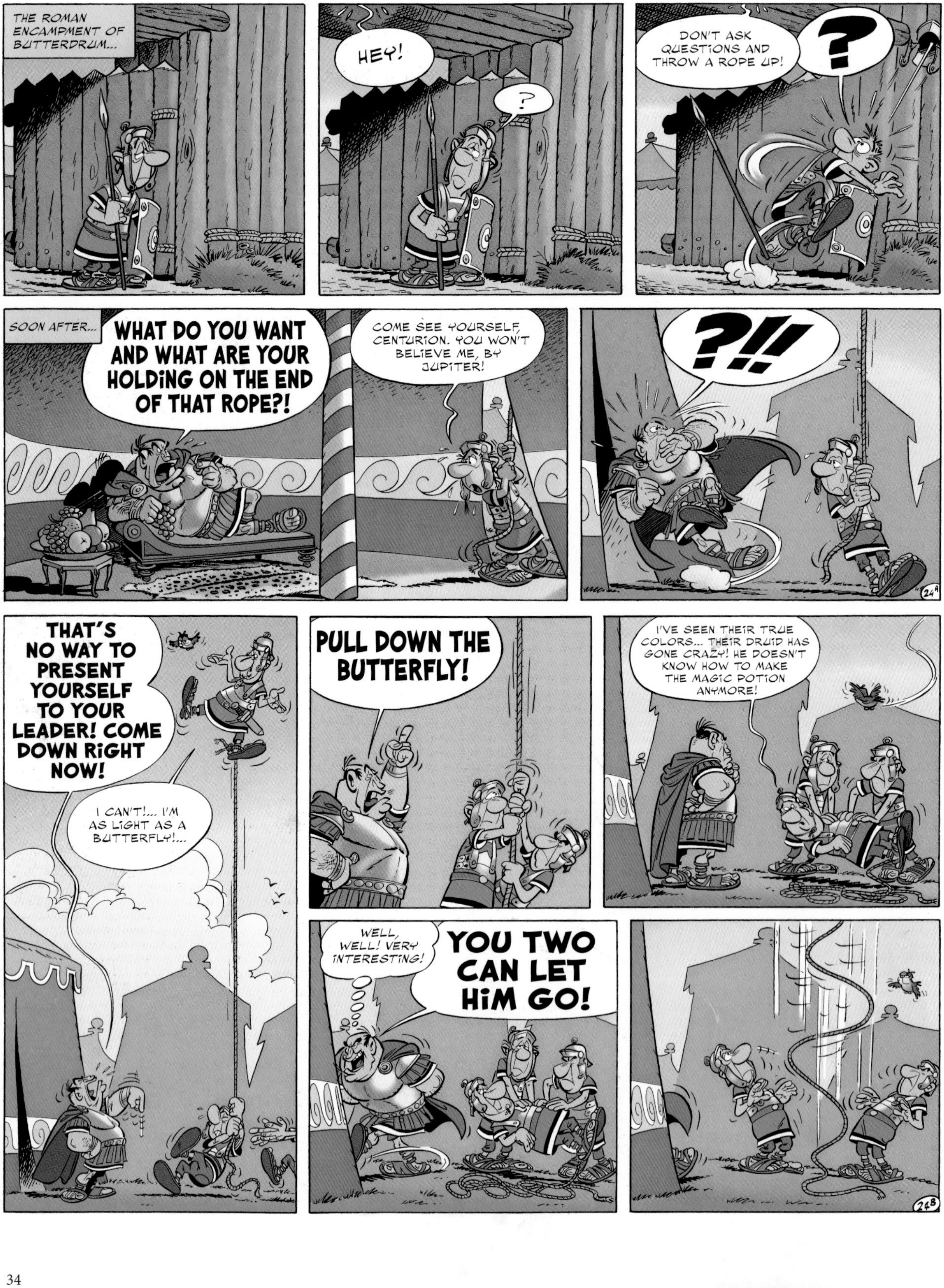
THE ROMAN ENCAMPMENT OF BUTTERDRUM...
HEY!
?
DON'T ASK QUESTIONS AND THROW A ROPE UP!
?
SOON AFTER...
WHAT DO YOU WANT AND WHAT ARE YOUR HOLDING ON THE END OF THAT ROPE?!
COME SEE YOURSELF, CENTURION. YOU WON'T BELIEVE ME, BY JUPITER!
?!!
24A
THAT'S NO WAY TO PRESENT YOURSELF TO YOUR LEADER! COME DOWN RIGHT NOW!
I CAN'T!... I'M AS LIGHT AS A BUTTERFLY!...
PULL DOWN THE BUTTERFLY!
I'VE SEEN THEIR TRUE COLORS... THEIR DRUID HAS GONE CRAZY! HE DOESN'T KNOW HOW TO MAKE THE MAGIC POTION ANYMORE!
WELL, WELL! VERY INTERESTING!
YOU TWO CAN LET HIM GO!
24B

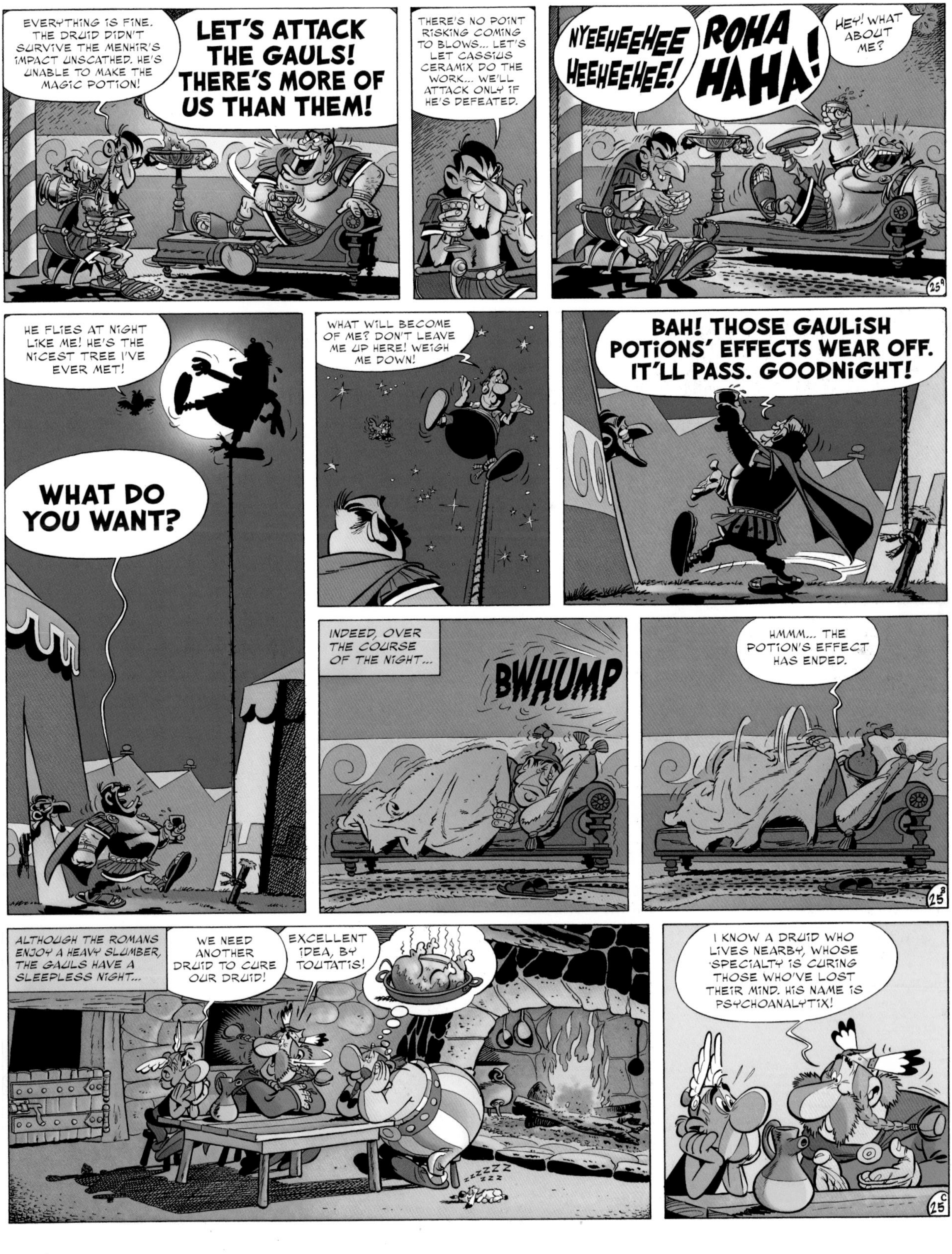
EVERYTHING IS FINE. THE DRUID DIDN'T SURVIVE THE MENHIR'S IMPACT UNSCATHED. HE'S UNABLE TO MAKE THE MAGIC POTION!
LET'S ATTACK THE GAULS! THERE'S MORE OF US THAN THEM!
THERE'S NO POINT RISKING COMING TO BLOWS... LET'S LET CASSIUS CERAMIX DO THE WORK... WE'LL ATTACK ONLY IF HE'S DEFEATED.
NYEEHEEHEE HEEHEEHEE!
ROHA HAHA!
HEY! WHAT ABOUT ME?
25A
HE FLIES AT NIGHT LIKE ME! HE'S THE NICEST TREE I'VE EVER MET!
WHAT DO YOU WANT?
WHAT WILL BECOME OF ME? DON'T LEAVE ME UP HERE! WEIGH ME DOWN!
BAH! THOSE GAULISH POTIONS' EFFECTS WEAR OFF. IT'LL PASS. GOODNIGHT!
INDEED, OVER THE COURSE OF THE NIGHT...
BWHUMP
HMMM... THE POTION'S EFFECT HAS ENDED.
25B
ALTHOUGH THE ROMANS ENJOY A HEAVY SLUMBER, THE GAULS HAVE A SLEEPLESS NIGHT...
WE NEED ANOTHER DRUID TO CURE OUR DRUID!
EXCELLENT IDEA, BY TOUTATIS!
ZZZZZ
I KNOW A DRUID WHO LIVES NEARBY, WHOSE SPECIALTY IS CURING THOSE WHO'VE LOST THEIR MIND. HIS NAME IS PSYCHOANALYTIX!
25C

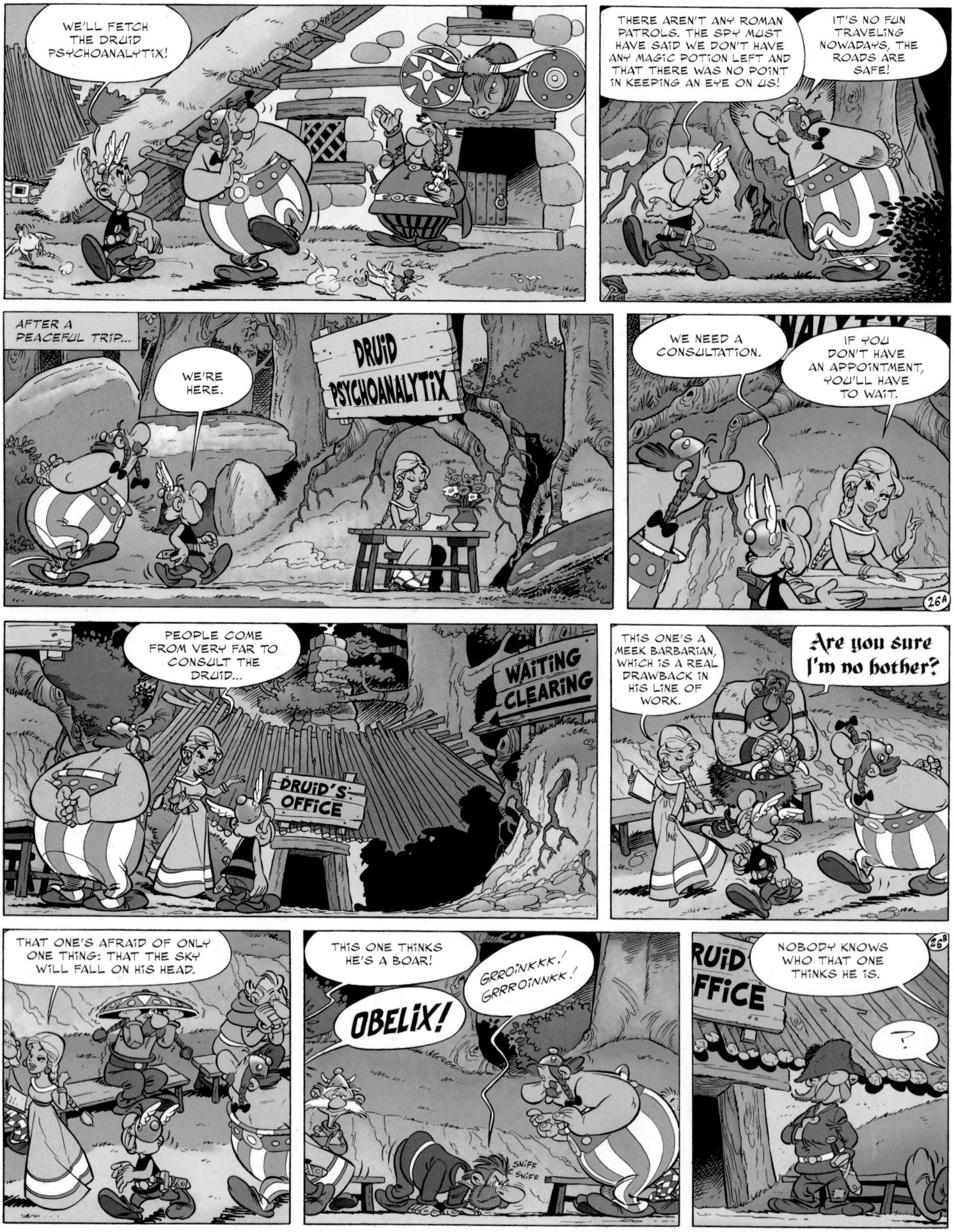
WE'LL FETCH THE DRUID PSYCHOANALYTIX!
CLUCK!
THERE AREN'T ANY ROMAN PATROLS. THE SPY MUST HAVE SAID WE DON'T HAVE ANY MAGIC POTION LEFT AND THAT THERE WAS NO POINT IN KEEPING AN EYE ON US!
IT'S NO FUN TRAVELING NOWADAYS, THE ROADS ARE SAFE!
AFTER A PEACEFUL TRIP...
DRUID PSYCHOANALYTIX
WE'RE HERE.
WE NEED A CONSULTATION.
IF YOU DON'T HAVE AN APPOINTMENT, YOU'LL HAVE TO WAIT.
26A
PEOPLE COME FROM VERY FAR TO CONSULT THE DRUID...
WAITING CLEARING
DRUID'S OFFICE
THIS ONE'S A MEEK BARBARIAN, WHICH IS A REAL DRAWBACK IN HIS LINE OF WORK.
Are you sure I'm no bother?
THAT ONE'S AFRAID OF ONLY ONE THING: THAT THE SKY WILL FALL ON HIS HEAD.
THIS ONE THINKS HE'S A BOAR!
GRROINKKK! GRRROINNKK!
OBELIX!
SNIFF SNIFF
26B
DRUID OFFICE
NOBODY KNOWS WHO THAT ONE THINKS HE IS.
?

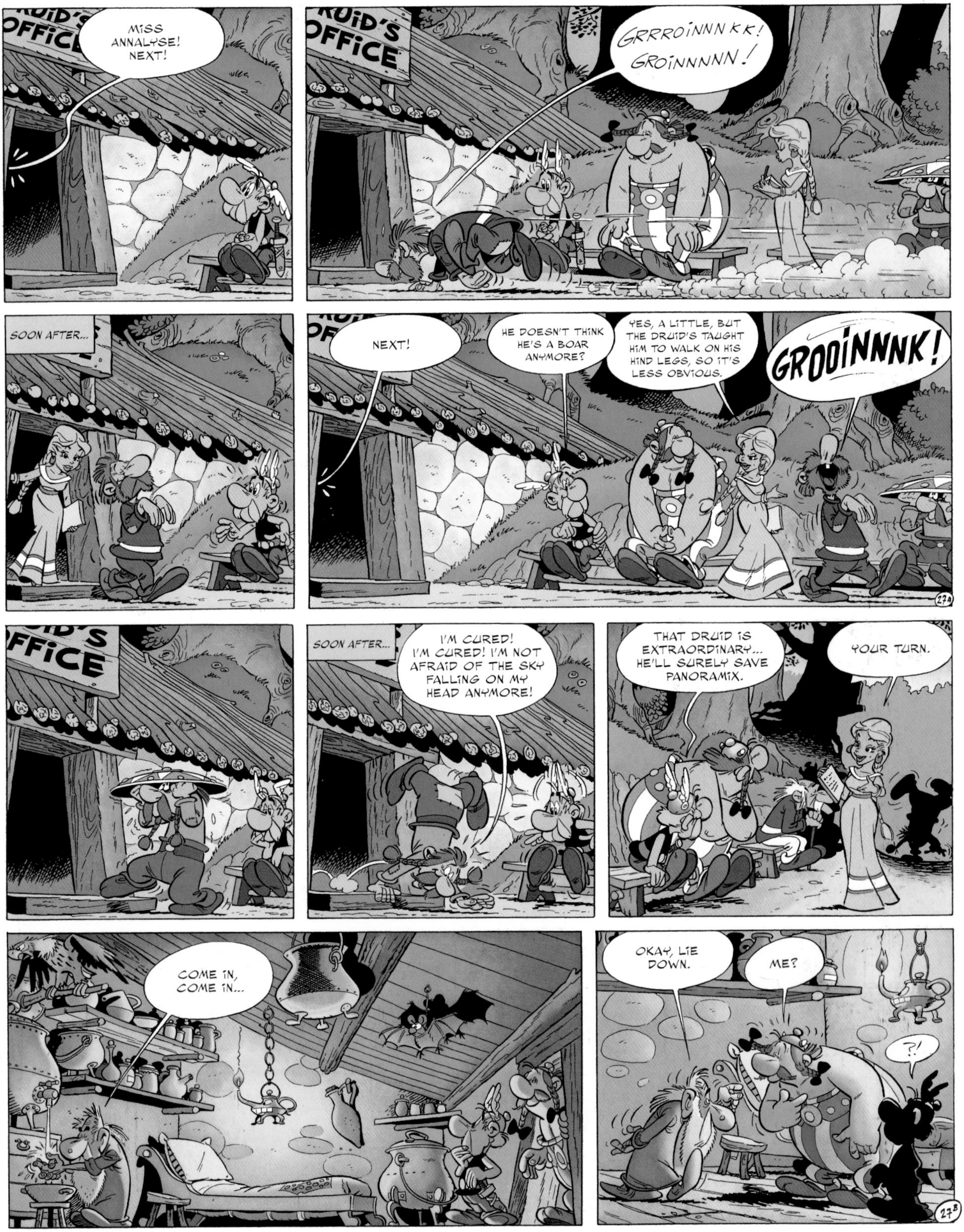
DRUID'S OFFICE
MISS ANNALYSE! NEXT!
DRUID'S OFFICE
GRRROINNNKK! GROINNNNN!
SOON AFTER...
NEXT!
HE DOESN'T THINK HE'S A BOAR ANYMORE?
YES, A LITTLE, BUT THE DRUID'S TAUGHT HIM TO WALK ON HIS HIND LEGS, SO IT'S LESS OBVIOUS.
GROOINNNK!
DRUID'S OFFICE
SOON AFTER...
I'M CURED! I'M CURED! I'M NOT AFRAID OF THE SKY FALLING ON MY HEAD ANYMORE!
THAT DRUID IS EXTRAORDINARY... HE'LL SURELY SAVE PANORAMIX.
YOUR TURN.
COME IN, COME IN...
OKAY, LIE DOWN.
ME?
?!

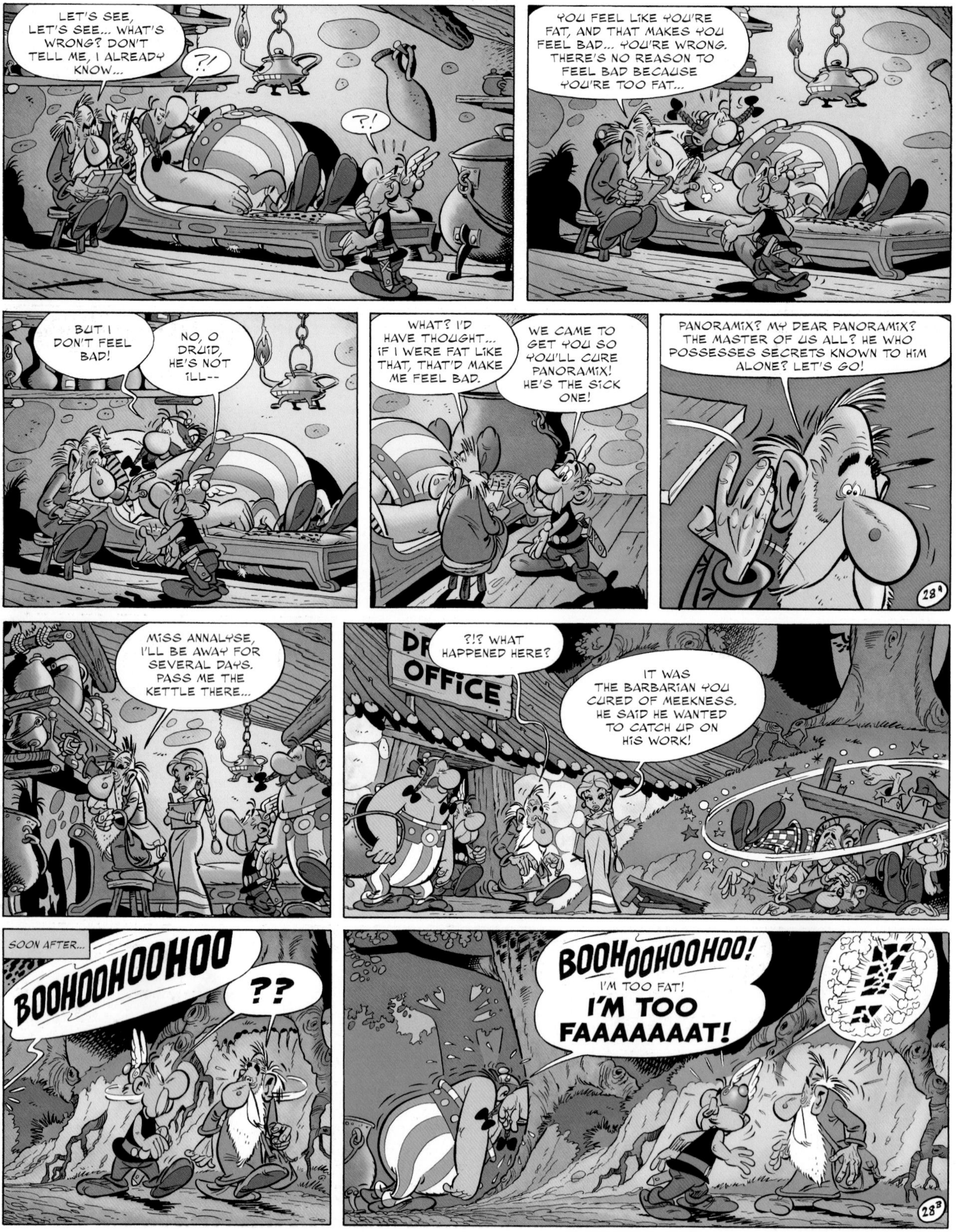
LET'S SEE, LET'S SEE... WHAT'S WRONG? DON'T TELL ME, I ALREADY KNOW...
?!
?!
YOU FEEL LIKE YOU'RE FAT, AND THAT MAKES YOU FEEL BAD... YOU'RE WRONG. THERE'S NO REASON TO FEEL BAD BECAUSE YOU'RE TOO FAT...
BUT I DON'T FEEL BAD!
NO, O DRUID, HE'S NOT ILL--
WHAT? I'D HAVE THOUGHT... IF I WERE FAT LIKE THAT, THAT'D MAKE ME FEEL BAD.
WE CAME TO GET YOU SO YOU'LL CURE PANORAMIX! HE'S THE SICK ONE!
PANORAMIX? MY DEAR PANORAMIX? THE MASTER OF US ALL? HE WHO POSSESSES SECRETS KNOWN TO HIM ALONE? LET'S GO!
28a
MISS ANNALYSE, I'LL BE AWAY FOR SEVERAL DAYS. PASS ME THE KETTLE THERE...
OFFICE
?!? WHAT HAPPENED HERE?
IT WAS THE BARBARIAN YOU CURED OF MEEKNESS. HE SAID HE WANTED TO CATCH UP ON HIS WORK!
SOON AFTER...
BOOHOOHOOHOO
??
BOOHOOHOOHOO!
I'M TOO FAT!
I'M TOO FAAAAAAT!
28B

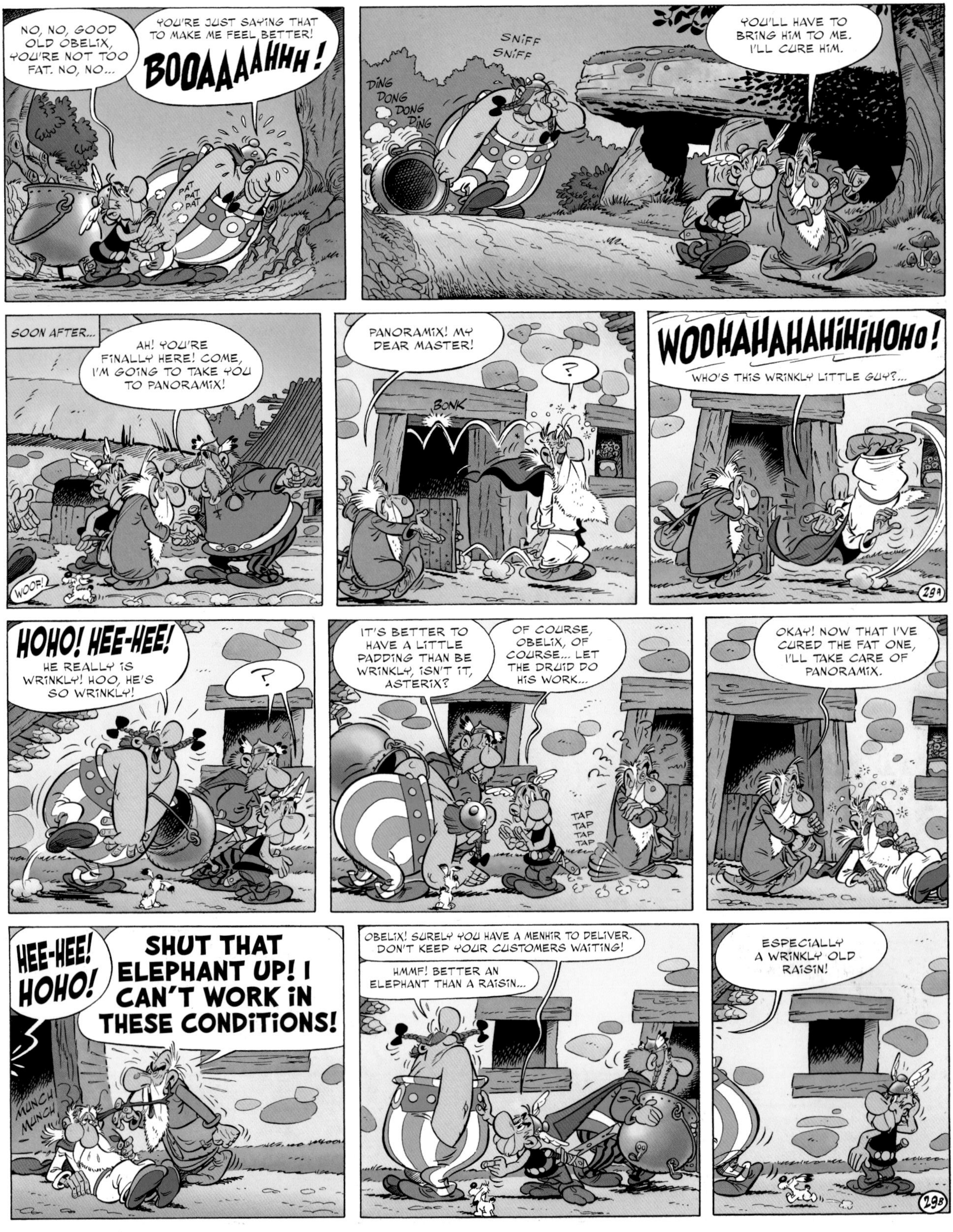

NO, NO, GOOD OLD OBELIX, YOU'RE NOT TOO FAT. NO, NO...
YOU'RE JUST SAYING THAT TO MAKE ME FEEL BETTER!
BOOAAAAHHH!
PAT PAT PAT
SNIFF SNIFF
DING DONG DONG DING
YOU'LL HAVE TO BRING HIM TO ME. I'LL CURE HIM.
SOON AFTER...
AH! YOU'RE FINALLY HERE! COME, I'M GOING TO TAKE YOU TO PANORAMIX!
WOOF!
PANORAMIX! MY DEAR MASTER!
BONK
?
WODHAHAHAHIHIHOHO!
WHO'S THIS WRINKLY LITTLE GUY?...
29A
HOHO! HEE-HEE!
HE REALLY IS WRINKLY! HOO, HE'S SO WRINKLY!
?
IT'S BETTER TO HAVE A LITTLE PADDING THAN BE WRINKLY, ISN'T IT, ASTERIX?
OF COURSE, OBELIX, OF COURSE... LET THE DRUID DO HIS WORK...
TAP TAP TAP TAP
OKAY! NOW THAT I'VE CURED THE FAT ONE, I'LL TAKE CARE OF PANORAMIX.
HEE-HEE! HOHO!
SHUT THAT ELEPHANT UP! I CAN'T WORK IN THESE CONDITIONS!
MUNCH MUNCH
OBELIX! SURELY YOU HAVE A MENHIR TO DELIVER. DON'T KEEP YOUR CUSTOMERS WAITING!
HMMF! BETTER AN ELEPHANT THAN A RAISIN...
ESPECIALLY A WRINKLY OLD RAISIN!
29B

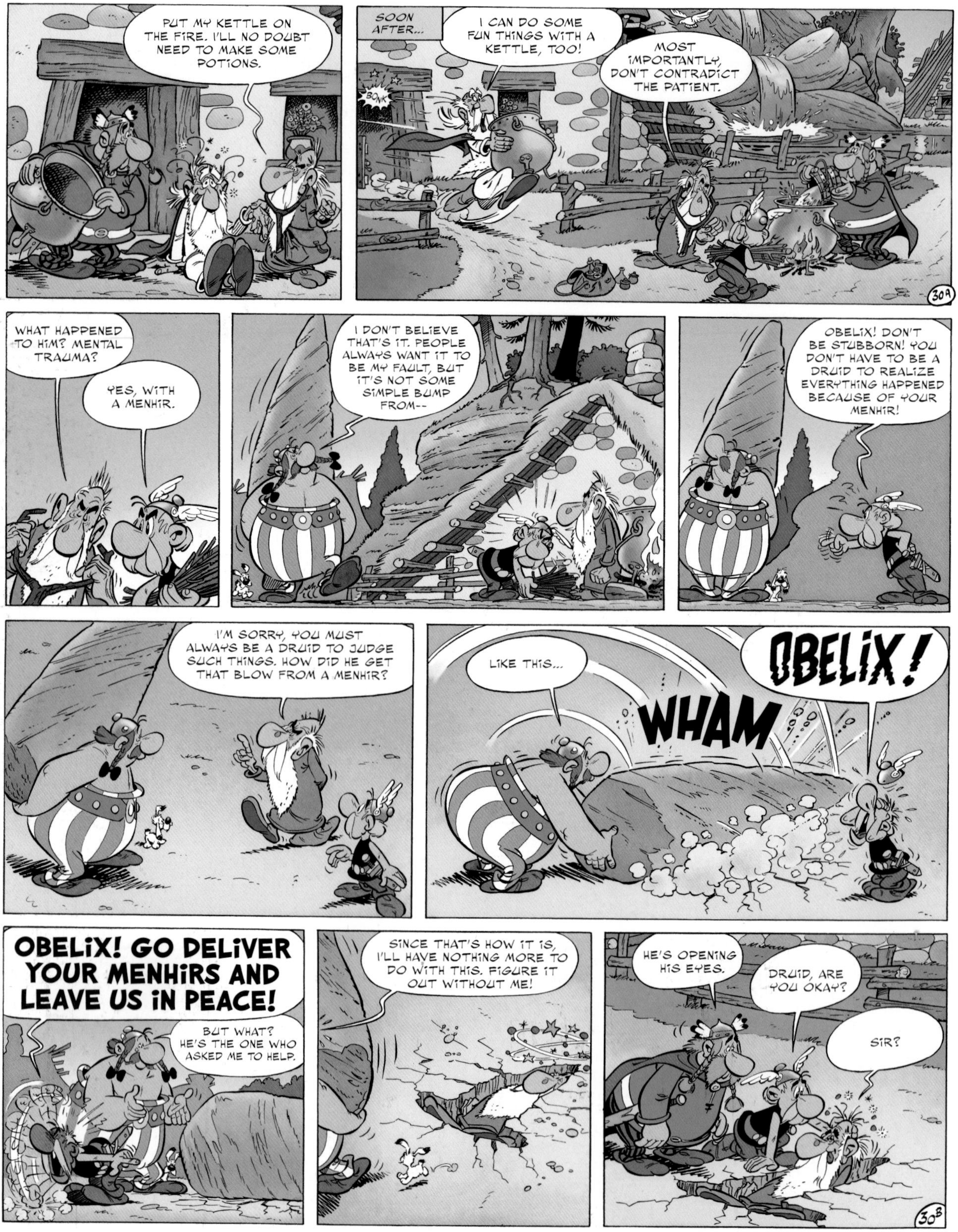
PUT MY KETTLE ON THE FIRE. I'LL NO DOUBT NEED TO MAKE SOME POTIONS.
SOON AFTER...
I CAN DO SOME FUN THINGS WITH A KETTLE, TOO!
BONK
MOST IMPORTANTLY, DON'T CONTRADICT THE PATIENT.
30A
WHAT HAPPENED TO HIM? MENTAL TRAUMA?
YES, WITH A MENHIR.
I DON'T BELIEVE THAT'S IT. PEOPLE ALWAYS WANT IT TO BE MY FAULT, BUT IT'S NOT SOME SIMPLE BUMP FROM--
OBELIX! DON'T BE STUBBORN! YOU DON'T HAVE TO BE A DRUID TO REALIZE EVERYTHING HAPPENED BECAUSE OF YOUR MENHIR!
I'M SORRY, YOU MUST ALWAYS BE A DRUID TO JUDGE SUCH THINGS. HOW DID HE GET THAT BLOW FROM A MENHIR?
LIKE THIS...
WHAM
OBELIX!
OBELIX! GO DELIVER YOUR MENHIRS AND LEAVE US IN PEACE!
BUT WHAT? HE'S THE ONE WHO ASKED ME TO HELP.
SINCE THAT'S HOW IT IS, I'LL HAVE NOTHING MORE TO DO WITH THIS. FIGURE IT OUT WITHOUT ME!
HE'S OPENING HIS EYES.
DRUID, ARE YOU OKAY?
SIR?
30B

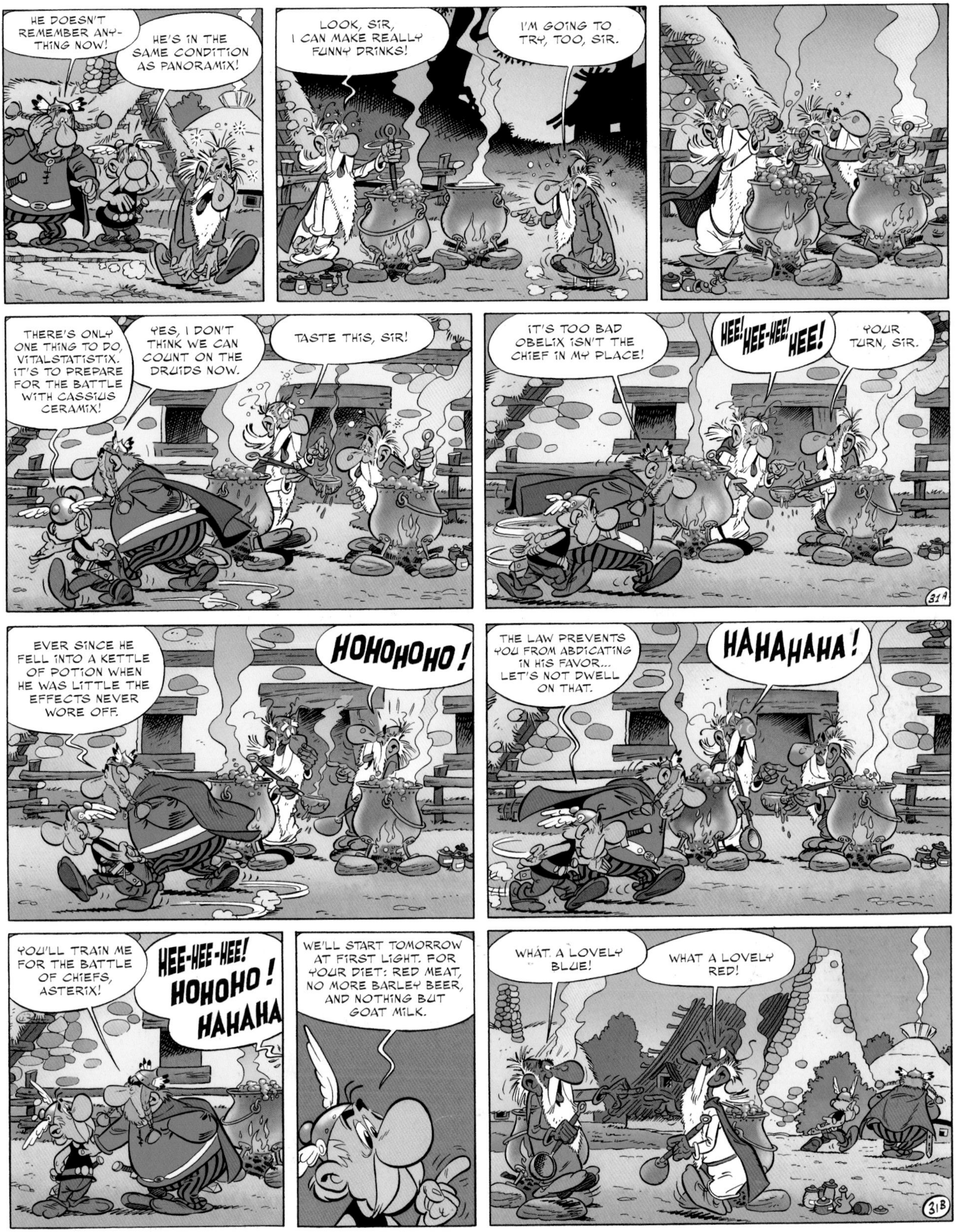
HE DOESN'T REMEMBER ANYTHING NOW!
HE'S IN THE SAME CONDITION AS PANORAMIX!
LOOK, SIR, I CAN MAKE REALLY FUNNY DRINKS!
I'M GOING TO TRY, TOO, SIR.
THERE'S ONLY ONE THING TO DO, VITALSTATISTIX. IT'S TO PREPARE FOR THE BATTLE WITH CASSIUS CERAMIX!
YES, I DON'T THINK WE CAN COUNT ON THE DRUIDS NOW.
TASTE THIS, SIR!
IT'S TOO BAD OBELIX ISN'T THE CHIEF IN MY PLACE!
HEE! HEE-HEE! HEE!
YOUR TURN, SIR.
31A
EVER SINCE HE FELL INTO A KETTLE OF POTION WHEN HE WAS LITTLE THE EFFECTS NEVER WORE OFF.
HOHOHOHO!
THE LAW PREVENTS YOU FROM ABDICATING IN HIS FAVOR... LET'S NOT DWELL ON THAT.
HAHAHAHA!
YOU'LL TRAIN ME FOR THE BATTLE OF CHIEFS, ASTERIX!
HEE-HEE-HEE! HOHOHO! HAHAHA
WE'LL START TOMORROW AT FIRST LIGHT. FOR YOUR DIET: RED MEAT, NO MORE BARLEY BEER, AND NOTHING BUT GOAT MILK.
WHAT. A LOVELY BLUE!
WHAT A LOVELY RED!
31B

DAWN HASN'T RISEN YET...

ZZZ! ZZZ!

?

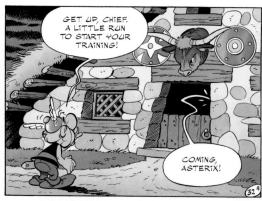

GET UP, CHIEF. A LITTLE RUN TO START YOUR TRAINING!

COMING, ASTERIX!

COCKADOODLEDOO!

ONE, TWO, ONE, TWO, ONE, TWO! LET'S GO! PUT SOME OOMPH INTO IT, BY TOUTATIS!

?

NO, NO, NO!.. THAT'S NOT HOW IT'S DONE, VITALSTATISTIX! I'LL SHOW YOU!

IT'S BETTER LIKE THAT!

MUCH BETTER!

A LOT BETTER!

HMMM! IT LACKS OOMPH!

NOW I'M GOING TO TRAIN YOU TO FIGHT. YOU NEED AN OPPONENT...

HUFF! PUFF! HUFF!

I CAN DO THAT...

I DON'T KNOW IF--

HE'S RIGHT. OBELIX IS IDEAL FOR THIS ROLE. I WON'T BE AFRAID OF HURTING HIM.

OKAY, WELL, LET'S STA--

KA-POW

BRAVO! BRAVO, OBELIX! WITH YOU, WE DON'T NEED ROMANS IN GAUL ANYMORE!

I WAS IN SUCH A HURRY TO DO A GOOD JOB...

O, VITALSTATISTIX, MY CHIEF, YOU HAVEN'T LOST YOUR MEMORY, AT LEAST?

NOT ONLY HAVE I NOT LOST MY MEMORY, I WON'T FORGET THAT PUNCH ANY TIME SOON!

WHILE VITALSTATISTIX IS TRAINING, , HIS FORMIDABLE FOE, THE CHIEF CASSIUS CERAMIX, IS TRAINING TOO, IN THE VILLAGE OF SERUM.

NEXT!

KA-POW

NEXT!

I'D LIKE FOR THIS FIGHT TO BE OVER ALREADY!

YES, THIS TRAINING IS A KILLER!

IT'S ALWAYS ON-THE-JOB BRAINING!

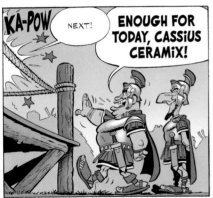

KA-POW

NEXT!

ENOUGH FOR TODAY, CASSIUS CERAMIX!

YOU CAN'T LOSE. DEPRIVED OF THE MAGIC POTION, YOUR OPPONENT WON'T BE ABLE TO BEAT YOU!

NO MORE THAN THE OTHER GAULISH CHIEFS. I'M GOING TO CHALLENGE THEM ONE BY ONE AND I'LL BECOME THE ONLY CHIEF OF ALL OF GAUL!

THUMP

(MURMURS) HMMM... THAT GAUL IS A LITTLE TOO AMBITIOUS. HE MIGHT BECOME DANGEROUS.

(MURMURS) I THOUGHT ABOUT THAT. AFTER HIS VICTORY, WE'LL SEND HIM TO TAKE A LITTLE TOUR OF ROME... COVERED IN CHAINS, HE'LL FIND OTHER OPPONENTS, IN THE ARENA OF THE CIRCUS MAXIMUS.

YOU CAN BE SO SMART, NOCLUS!

WAP

A LITTLE TOO SMART! AFTER CASSIUS CERAMIX'S VICTORY, YOU'LL ACCOMPANY HIM TO ROME, TO SERVE AS HIS OPPONENT IN THE CIRCUS MAXIMUS!

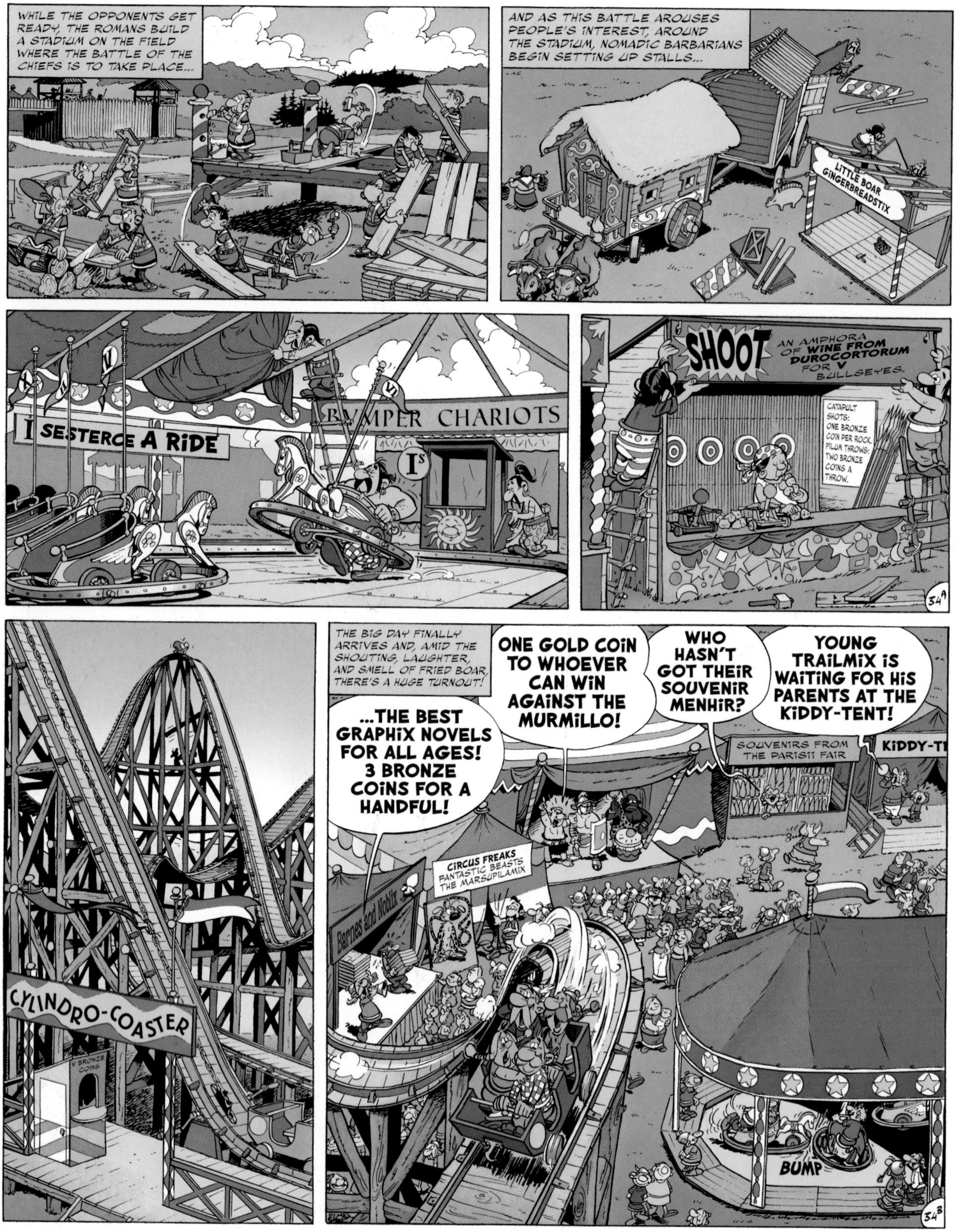
WHILE THE OPPONENTS GET READY, THE ROMANS BUILD A STADIUM ON THE FIELD WHERE THE BATTLE OF THE CHIEFS IS TO TAKE PLACE...
AND AS THIS BATTLE AROUSES PEOPLE'S INTEREST, AROUND THE STADIUM, NOMADIC BARBARIANS BEGIN SETTING UP STALLS...
LITTLE BOAR GINGERBREADSTIX
I SESTERCE A RIDE
BUMPER CHARIOTS
I S
SHOOT
AN AMPHORA OF WINE FROM DUROCORTORUM FOR V BULLSEYES.
CATAPULT SHOTS: ONE BRONZE COIN PER ROCK. PILUM THROWS: TWO BRONZE COINS A THROW.
34A
CYLINDRO-COASTER
V BRONZE COINS
THE BIG DAY FINALLY ARRIVES AND, AMID THE SHOUTING, LAUGHTER, AND SMELL OF FRIED BOAR, THERE'S A HUGE TURNOUT!
...THE BEST GRAPHIX NOVELS FOR ALL AGES! 3 BRONZE COINS FOR A HANDFUL!
ONE GOLD COIN TO WHOEVER CAN WIN AGAINST THE MURMILLO!
WHO HASN'T GOT THEIR SOUVENIR MENHIR?
YOUNG TRAILMIX IS WAITING FOR HIS PARENTS AT THE KIDDY-TENT!
SOUVENIRS FROM THE PARISII FAIR
KIDDY-T
CIRCUS FREAKS
FANTASTIC BEASTS
THE MARSUPILAMIX
Barnes and Noblix
BUMP
34B

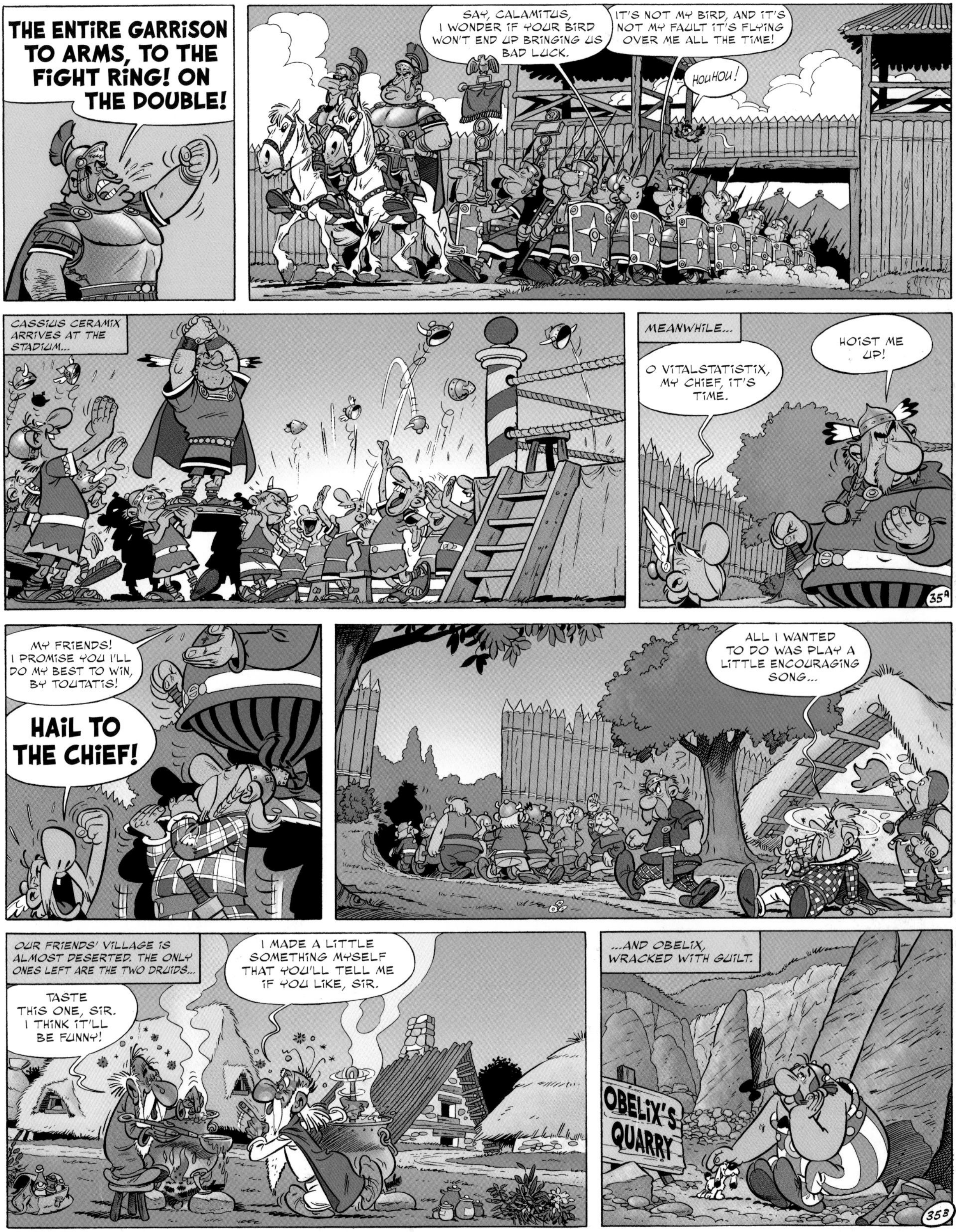
THE ENTIRE GARRISON TO ARMS, TO THE FIGHT RING! ON THE DOUBLE!
SAY, CALAMITUS, I WONDER IF YOUR BIRD WON'T END UP BRINGING US BAD LUCK.
IT'S NOT MY BIRD, AND IT'S NOT MY FAULT IT'S FLYING OVER ME ALL THE TIME!
HOUHOU!
CASSIUS CERAMIX ARRIVES AT THE STADIUM...
MEANWHILE...
O VITALSTATISTIX, MY CHIEF, IT'S TIME.
HOIST ME UP!
35A
MY FRIENDS! I PROMISE YOU I'LL DO MY BEST TO WIN, BY TOUTATIS!
HAIL TO THE CHIEF!
ALL I WANTED TO DO WAS PLAY A LITTLE ENCOURAGING SONG...
OUR FRIENDS' VILLAGE IS ALMOST DESERTED. THE ONLY ONES LEFT ARE THE TWO DRUIDS...
TASTE THIS ONE, SIR. I THINK IT'LL BE FUNNY!
I MADE A LITTLE SOMETHING MYSELF THAT YOU'LL TELL ME IF YOU LIKE, SIR.
...AND OBELIX, WRACKED WITH GUILT.
OBELIX'S QUARRY
35B

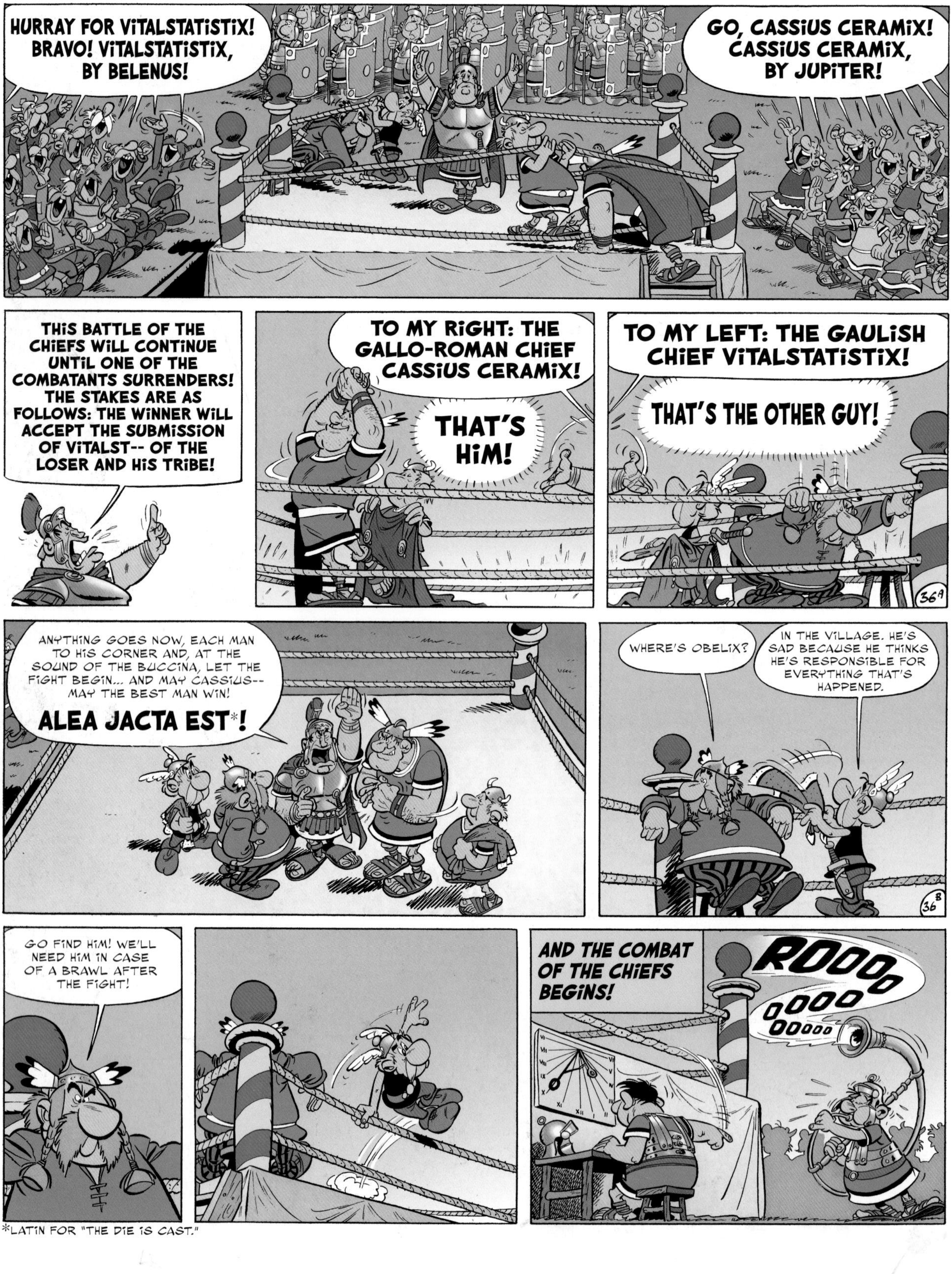
HURRAY FOR VITALSTATISTIX! BRAVO! VITALSTATISTIX, BY BELENUS!
GO, CASSIUS CERAMIX! CASSIUS CERAMIX, BY JUPITER!
THIS BATTLE OF THE CHIEFS WILL CONTINUE UNTIL ONE OF THE COMBATANTS SURRENDERS! THE STAKES ARE AS FOLLOWS: THE WINNER WILL ACCEPT THE SUBMISSION OF VITALST-- OF THE LOSER AND HIS TRIBE!
TO MY RIGHT: THE GALLO-ROMAN CHIEF CASSIUS CERAMIX!
THAT'S HIM!
TO MY LEFT: THE GAULISH CHIEF VITALSTATISTIX!
THAT'S THE OTHER GUY!
ANYTHING GOES NOW, EACH MAN TO HIS CORNER AND, AT THE SOUND OF THE BUCCINA, LET THE FIGHT BEGIN... AND MAY CASSIUS-- MAY THE BEST MAN WIN!
ALEA JACTA EST*!
WHERE'S OBELIX?
IN THE VILLAGE. HE'S SAD BECAUSE HE THINKS HE'S RESPONSIBLE FOR EVERYTHING THAT'S HAPPENED.
GO FIND HIM! WE'LL NEED HIM IN CASE OF A BRAWL AFTER THE FIGHT!
AND THE COMBAT OF THE CHIEFS BEGINS!
ROOOO OOOO OOOOO

*LATIN FOR "THE DIE IS CAST."

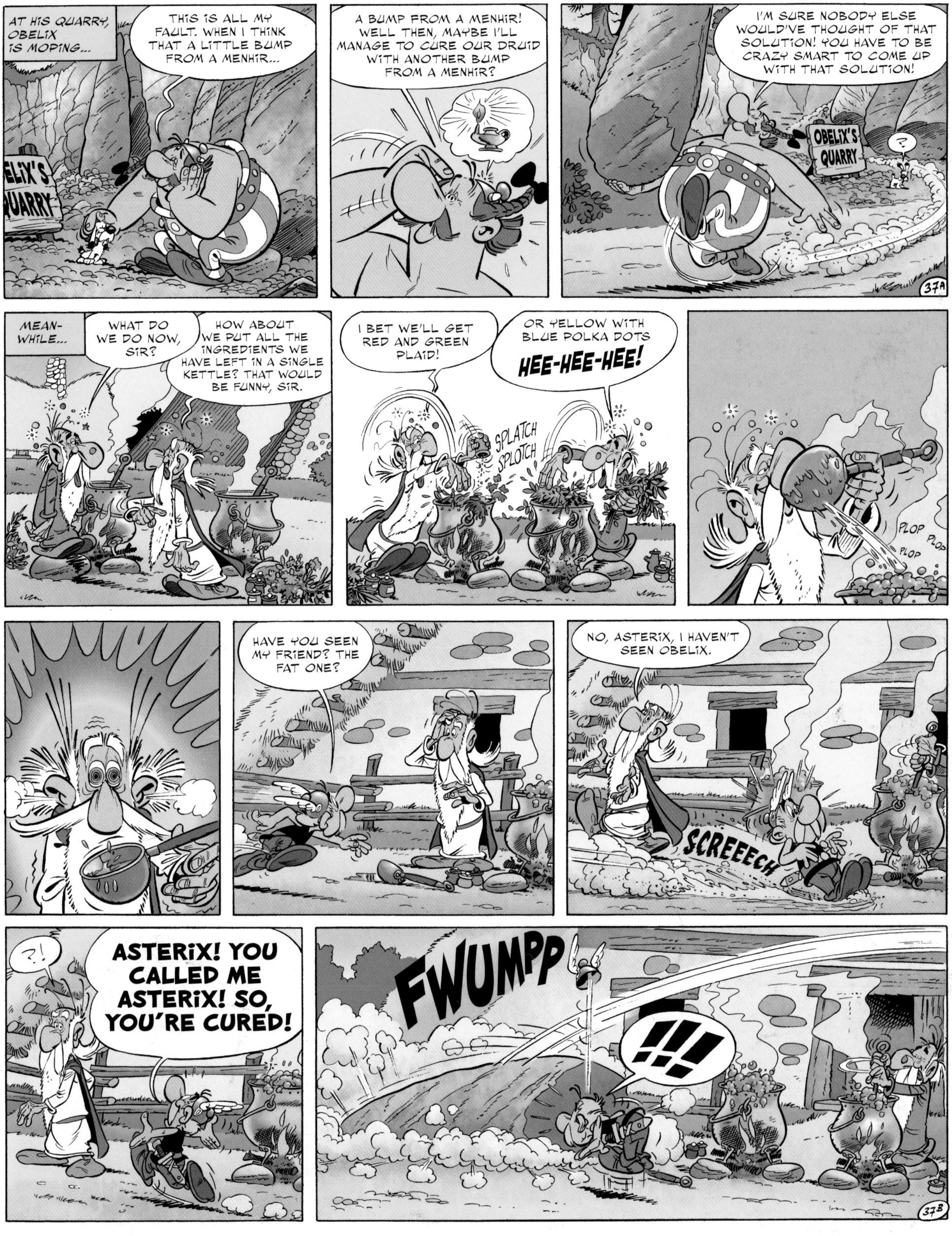
AT HIS QUARRY, OBELIX IS MOPING...
THIS IS ALL MY FAULT. WHEN I THINK THAT A LITTLE BUMP FROM A MENHIR...
ELIX'S QUARRY
A BUMP FROM A MENHIR! WELL THEN, MAYBE I'LL MANAGE TO CURE OUR DRUID WITH ANOTHER BUMP FROM A MENHIR?
I'M SURE NOBODY ELSE WOULD'VE THOUGHT OF THAT SOLUTION! YOU HAVE TO BE CRAZY SMART TO COME UP WITH THAT SOLUTION!
OBELIX'S QUARRY
?
37A
MEAN-WHILE...
WHAT DO WE DO NOW, SIR?
HOW ABOUT WE PUT ALL THE INGREDIENTS WE HAVE LEFT IN A SINGLE KETTLE? THAT WOULD BE FUNNY, SIR.
I BET WE'LL GET RED AND GREEN PLAID!
OR YELLOW WITH BLUE POLKA DOTS
HEE-HEE-HEE!
SPLATCH
SPLOTCH
PLOP
PLOP
PLOP
HAVE YOU SEEN MY FRIEND? THE FAT ONE?
NO, ASTERIX, I HAVEN'T SEEN OBELIX.
SCREEECH
?!
ASTERIX! YOU CALLED ME ASTERIX! SO, YOU'RE CURED!
FWUMPP
!!!
37B

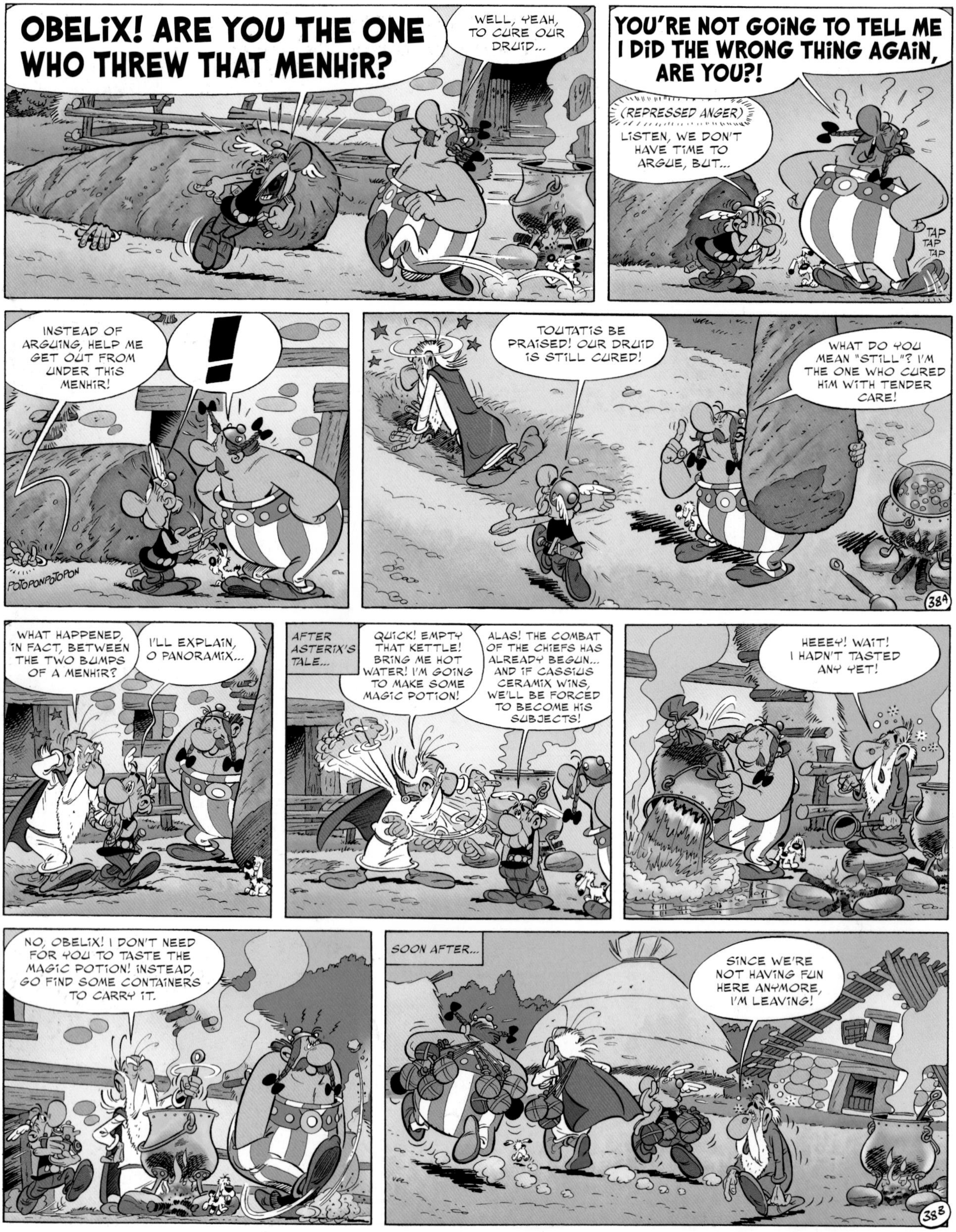
OBELIX! ARE YOU THE ONE WHO THREW THAT MENHIR?
WELL, YEAH, TO CURE OUR DRUID...
YOU'RE NOT GOING TO TELL ME I DID THE WRONG THING AGAIN, ARE YOU?!
(REPRESSED ANGER) LISTEN, WE DON'T HAVE TIME TO ARGUE, BUT...
TAP TAP TAP
INSTEAD OF ARGUING, HELP ME GET OUT FROM UNDER THIS MENHIR!
!
POTOPONPOTOPON
TOUTATIS BE PRAISED! OUR DRUID IS STILL CURED!
WHAT DO YOU MEAN "STILL"? I'M THE ONE WHO CURED HIM WITH TENDER CARE!
38A
WHAT HAPPENED, IN FACT, BETWEEN THE TWO BUMPS OF A MENHIR?
I'LL EXPLAIN, O PANORAMIX...
AFTER ASTERIX'S TALE...
QUICK! EMPTY THAT KETTLE! BRING ME HOT WATER! I'M GOING TO MAKE SOME MAGIC POTION!
ALAS! THE COMBAT OF THE CHIEFS HAS ALREADY BEGUN... AND IF CASSIUS CERAMIX WINS, WE'LL BE FORCED TO BECOME HIS SUBJECTS!
HEEEY! WAIT! I HADN'T TASTED ANY YET!
NO, OBELIX! I DON'T NEED FOR YOU TO TASTE THE MAGIC POTION! INSTEAD, GO FIND SOME CONTAINERS TO CARRY IT.
SOON AFTER...
SINCE WE'RE NOT HAVING FUN HERE ANYMORE, I'M LEAVING!
38B

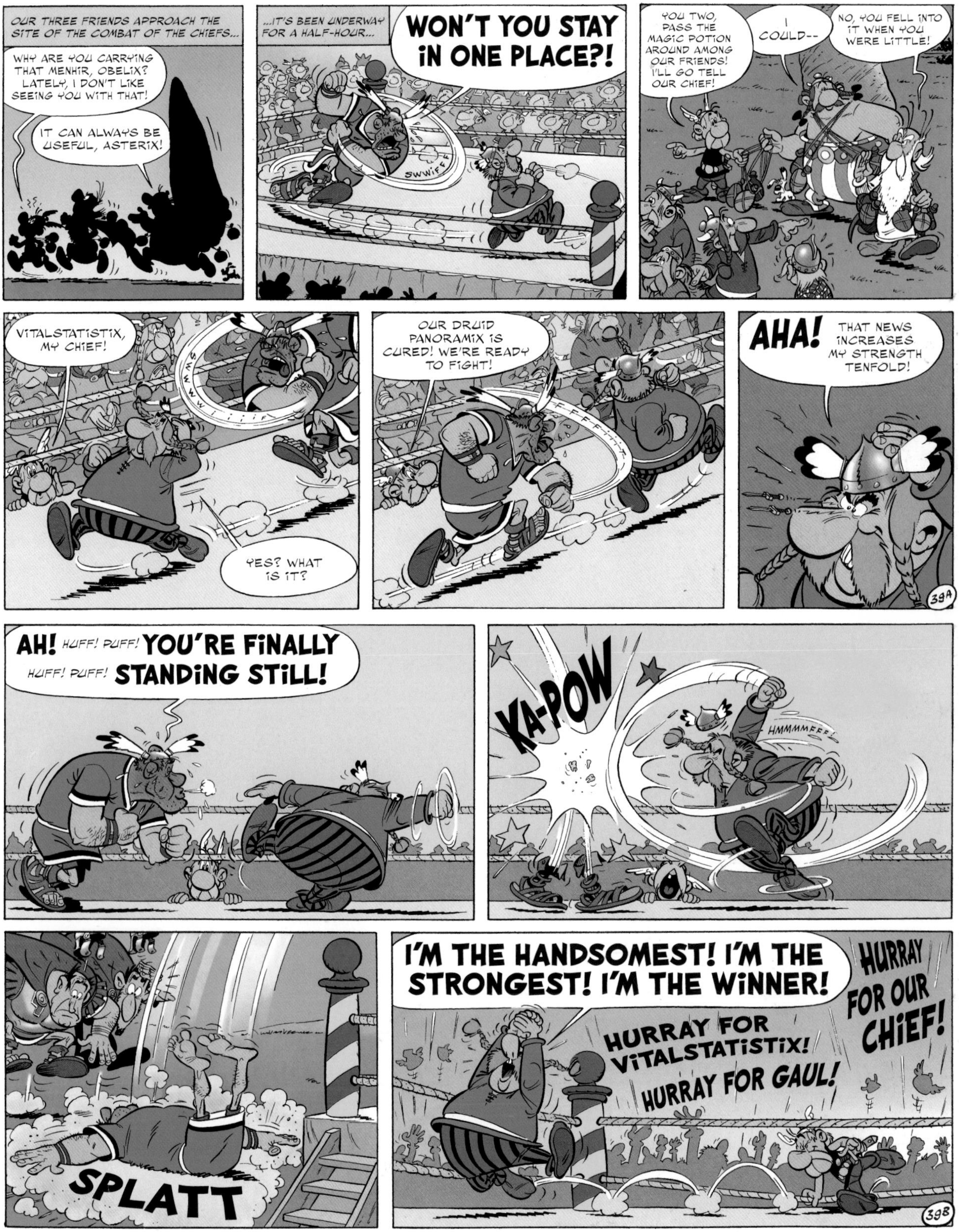

OUR THREE FRIENDS APPROACH THE SITE OF THE COMBAT OF THE CHIEFS...
WHY ARE YOU CARRYING THAT MENHIR, OBELIX? LATELY, I DON'T LIKE SEEING YOU WITH THAT!
IT CAN ALWAYS BE USEFUL, ASTERIX!
...IT'S BEEN UNDERWAY FOR A HALF-HOUR...
WON'T YOU STAY IN ONE PLACE?!
SWWIFF
YOU TWO, PASS THE MAGIC POTION AROUND AMONG OUR FRIENDS! I'LL GO TELL OUR CHIEF!
I COULD--
NO, YOU FELL INTO IT WHEN YOU WERE LITTLE!
VITALSTATISTIX, MY CHIEF!
YES? WHAT IS IT?
OUR DRUID PANORAMIX IS CURED! WE'RE READY TO FIGHT!
AHA! THAT NEWS INCREASES MY STRENGTH TENFOLD!
AH! HUFF! PUFF! YOU'RE FINALLY HUFF! PUFF! STANDING STILL!
KA-POW
HMMMMFFF!
SPLATT
I'M THE HANDSOMEST! I'M THE STRONGEST! I'M THE WINNER!
HURRAY FOR OUR CHIEF!
HURRAY FOR VITALSTATISTIX!
HURRAY FOR GAUL!

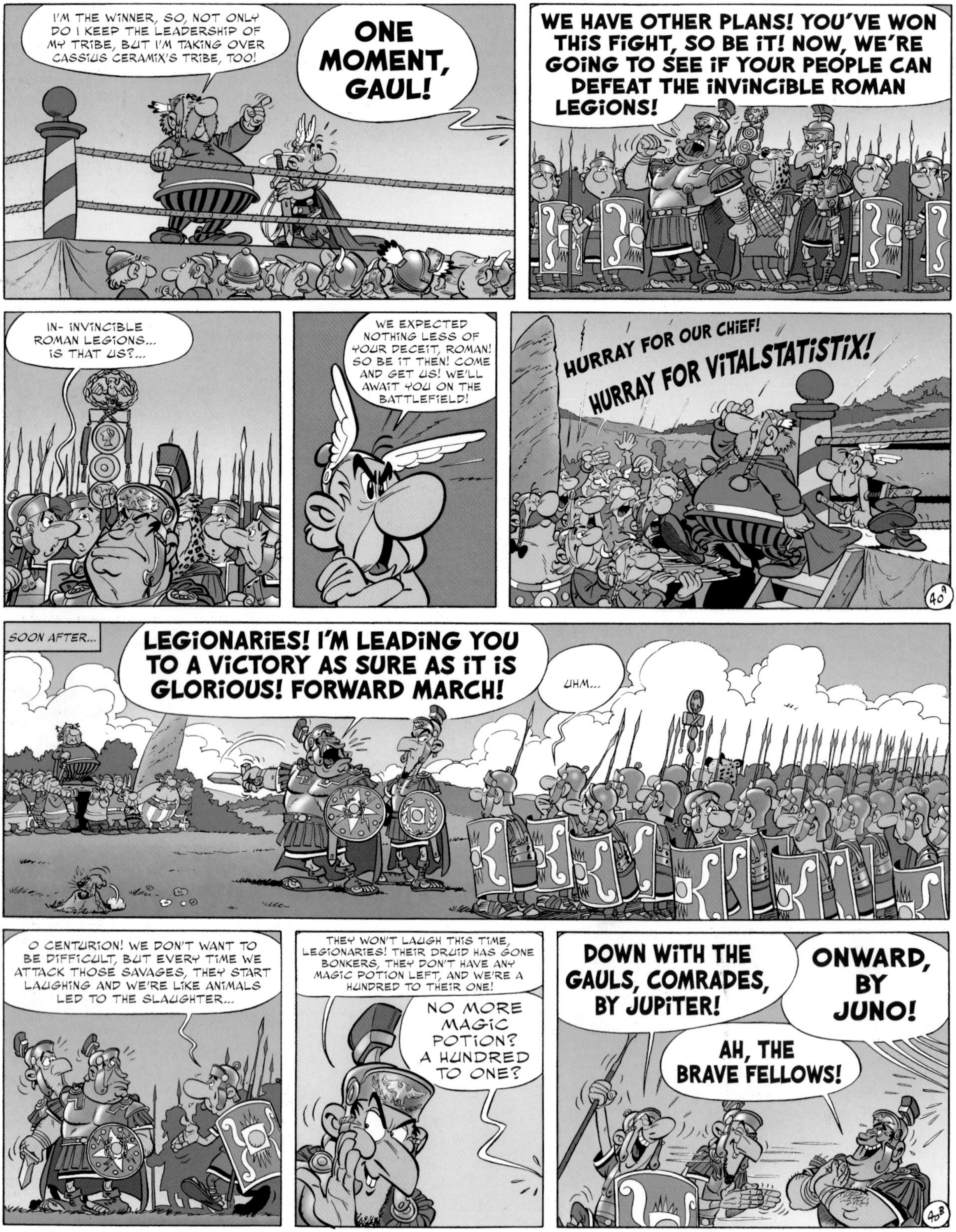

I'M THE WINNER, SO, NOT ONLY DO I KEEP THE LEADERSHIP OF MY TRIBE, BUT I'M TAKING OVER CASSIUS CERAMIX'S TRIBE, TOO!
ONE MOMENT, GAUL!
WE HAVE OTHER PLANS! YOU'VE WON THIS FIGHT, SO BE IT! NOW, WE'RE GOING TO SEE IF YOUR PEOPLE CAN DEFEAT THE INVINCIBLE ROMAN LEGIONS!
IN- INVINCIBLE ROMAN LEGIONS... IS THAT US?...
WE EXPECTED NOTHING LESS OF YOUR DECEIT, ROMAN! SO BE IT THEN! COME AND GET US! WE'LL AWAIT YOU ON THE BATTLEFIELD!
HURRAY FOR OUR CHIEF!
HURRAY FOR VITALSTATISTIX!
40A
SOON AFTER...
LEGIONARIES! I'M LEADING YOU TO A VICTORY AS SURE AS IT IS GLORIOUS! FORWARD MARCH!
UHM...
O CENTURION! WE DON'T WANT TO BE DIFFICULT, BUT EVERY TIME WE ATTACK THOSE SAVAGES, THEY START LAUGHING AND WE'RE LIKE ANIMALS LED TO THE SLAUGHTER...
THEY WON'T LAUGH THIS TIME, LEGIONARIES! THEIR DRUID HAS GONE BONKERS, THEY DON'T HAVE ANY MAGIC POTION LEFT, AND WE'RE A HUNDRED TO THEIR ONE!
NO MORE MAGIC POTION? A HUNDRED TO ONE?
DOWN WITH THE GAULS, COMRADES, BY JUPITER!
ONWARD, BY JUNO!
AH, THE BRAVE FELLOWS!
40B

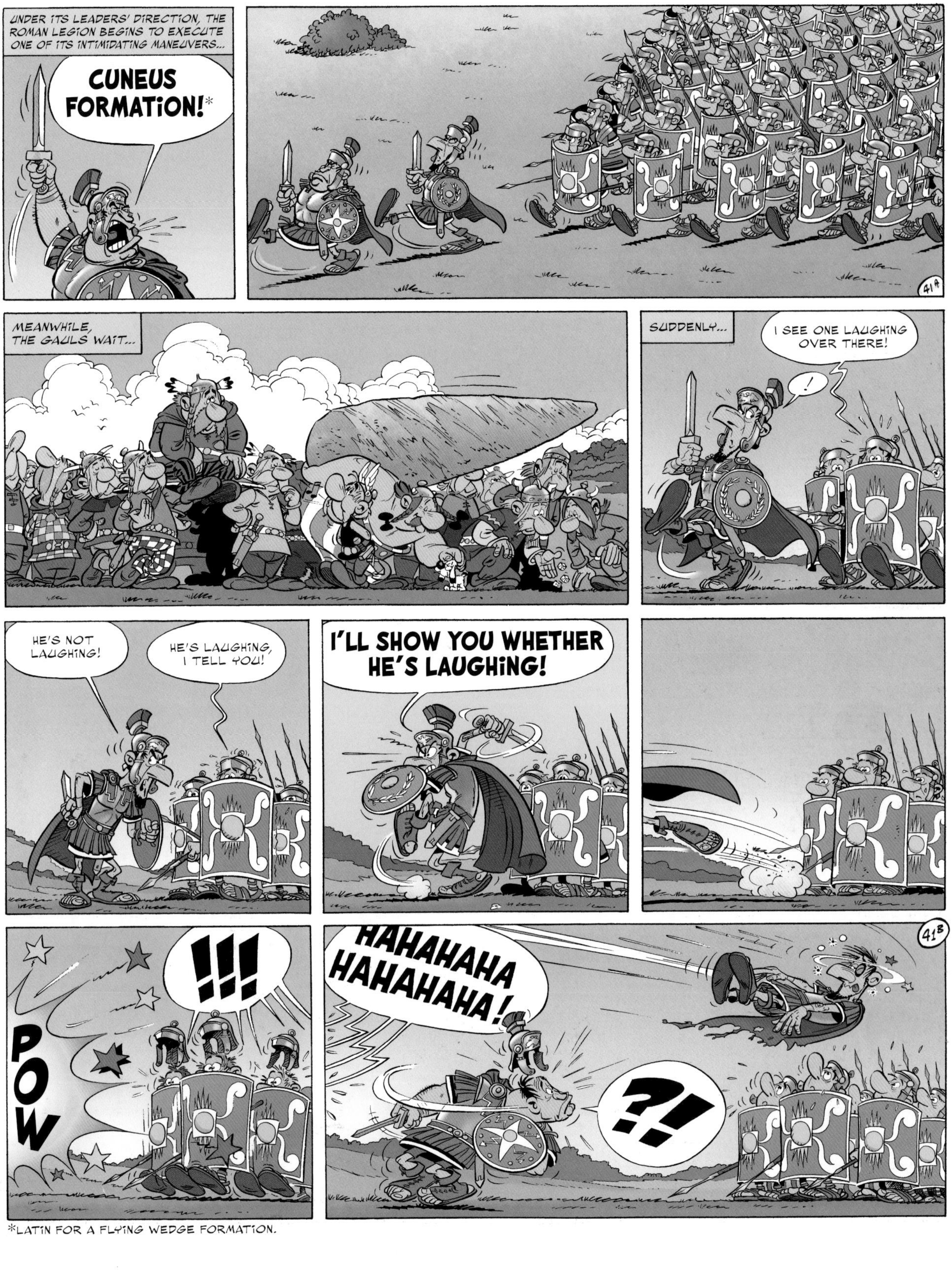
UNDER ITS LEADERS' DIRECTION, THE ROMAN LEGION BEGINS TO EXECUTE ONE OF ITS INTIMIDATING MANEUVERS...
CUNEUS FORMATION!*
MEANWHILE, THE GAULS WAIT...
SUDDENLY...
I SEE ONE LAUGHING OVER THERE!
!
HE'S NOT LAUGHING!
HE'S LAUGHING, I TELL YOU!
I'LL SHOW YOU WHETHER HE'S LAUGHING!
!!!
POW
HAHAHAHA HAHAHAHA!
?!

*LATIN FOR A FLYING WEDGE FORMATION.

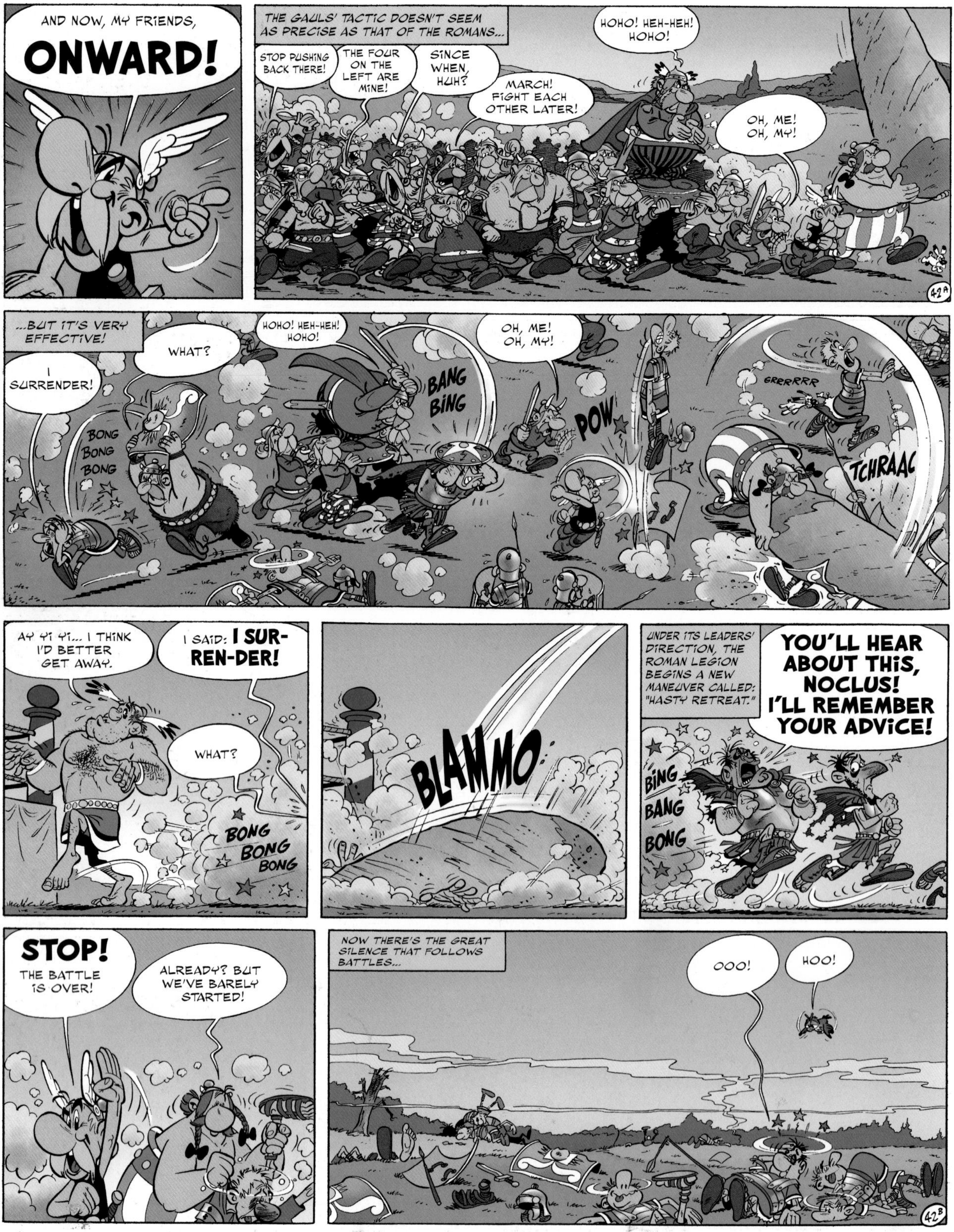
AND NOW, MY FRIENDS,
ONWARD!
THE GAULS' TACTIC DOESN'T SEEM AS PRECISE AS THAT OF THE ROMANS...
STOP PUSHING BACK THERE!
THE FOUR ON THE LEFT ARE MINE!
SINCE WHEN, HUH?
MARCH! FIGHT EACH OTHER LATER!
HOHO! HEH-HEH! HOHO!
OH, ME! OH, MY!
...BUT IT'S VERY EFFECTIVE!
WHAT?
I SURRENDER!
BONG BONG BONG
HOHO! HEH-HEH! HOHO!
BANG BING
OH, ME! OH, MY!
POW
GRRRRRR
TCHRAAC
AY YI YI... I THINK I'D BETTER GET AWAY.
I SAID: I SUR-REN-DER!
WHAT?
BONG BONG BONG
BLAMMO
UNDER ITS LEADERS' DIRECTION, THE ROMAN LEGION BEGINS A NEW MANEUVER CALLED: "HASTY RETREAT."
YOU'LL HEAR ABOUT THIS, NOCLUS! I'LL REMEMBER YOUR ADVICE!
BING BANG BONG
STOP! THE BATTLE IS OVER!
ALREADY? BUT WE'VE BARELY STARTED!
NOW THERE'S THE GREAT SILENCE THAT FOLLOWS BATTLES...
OOO!
HOO!

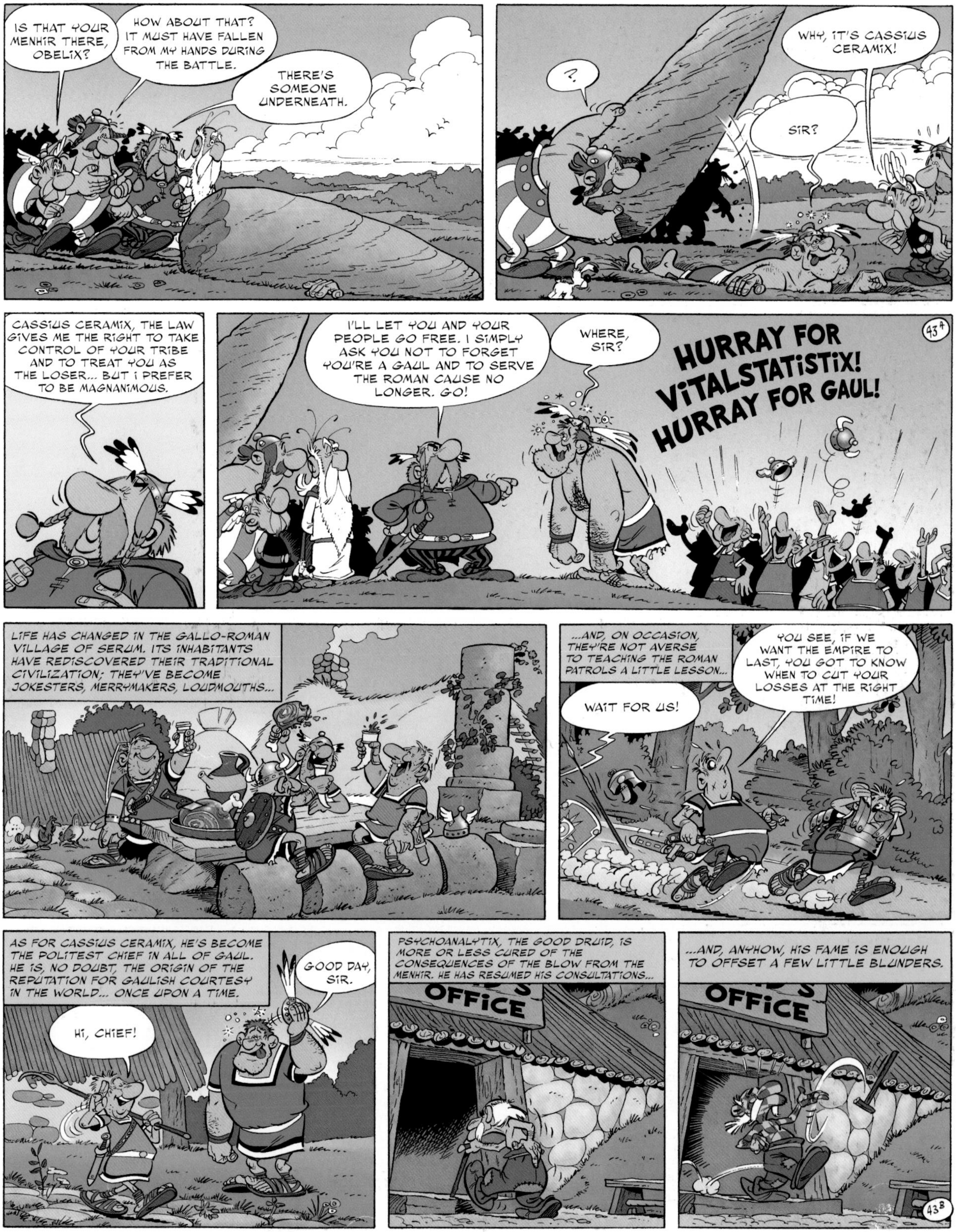
IS THAT YOUR MENHIR THERE, OBELIX?
HOW ABOUT THAT? IT MUST HAVE FALLEN FROM MY HANDS DURING THE BATTLE.
THERE'S SOMEONE UNDERNEATH.
?
WHY, IT'S CASSIUS CERAMIX!
SIR?
CASSIUS CERAMIX, THE LAW GIVES ME THE RIGHT TO TAKE CONTROL OF YOUR TRIBE AND TO TREAT YOU AS THE LOSER... BUT I PREFER TO BE MAGNANIMOUS.
I'LL LET YOU AND YOUR PEOPLE GO FREE. I SIMPLY ASK YOU NOT TO FORGET YOU'RE A GAUL AND TO SERVE THE ROMAN CAUSE NO LONGER. GO!
WHERE, SIR?
HURRAY FOR VITALSTATISTIX! HURRAY FOR GAUL!
43A
LIFE HAS CHANGED IN THE GALLO-ROMAN VILLAGE OF SERUM. ITS INHABITANTS HAVE REDISCOVERED THEIR TRADITIONAL CIVILIZATION; THEY'VE BECOME JOKESTERS, MERRYMAKERS, LOUDMOUTHS...
...AND, ON OCCASION, THEY'RE NOT AVERSE TO TEACHING THE ROMAN PATROLS A LITTLE LESSON...
WAIT FOR US!
YOU SEE, IF WE WANT THE EMPIRE TO LAST, YOU GOT TO KNOW WHEN TO CUT YOUR LOSSES AT THE RIGHT TIME!
AS FOR CASSIUS CERAMIX, HE'S BECOME THE POLITEST CHIEF IN ALL OF GAUL. HE IS, NO DOUBT, THE ORIGIN OF THE REPUTATION FOR GAULISH COURTESY IN THE WORLD... ONCE UPON A TIME.
GOOD DAY, SIR.
HI, CHIEF!
PSYCHOANALYTIX, THE GOOD DRUID, IS MORE OR LESS CURED OF THE CONSEQUENCES OF THE BLOW FROM THE MENHIR. HE HAS RESUMED HIS CONSULTATIONS...
OFFICE
...AND, ANYHOW, HIS FAME IS ENOUGH TO OFFSET A FEW LITTLE BLUNDERS.
OFFICE
43B

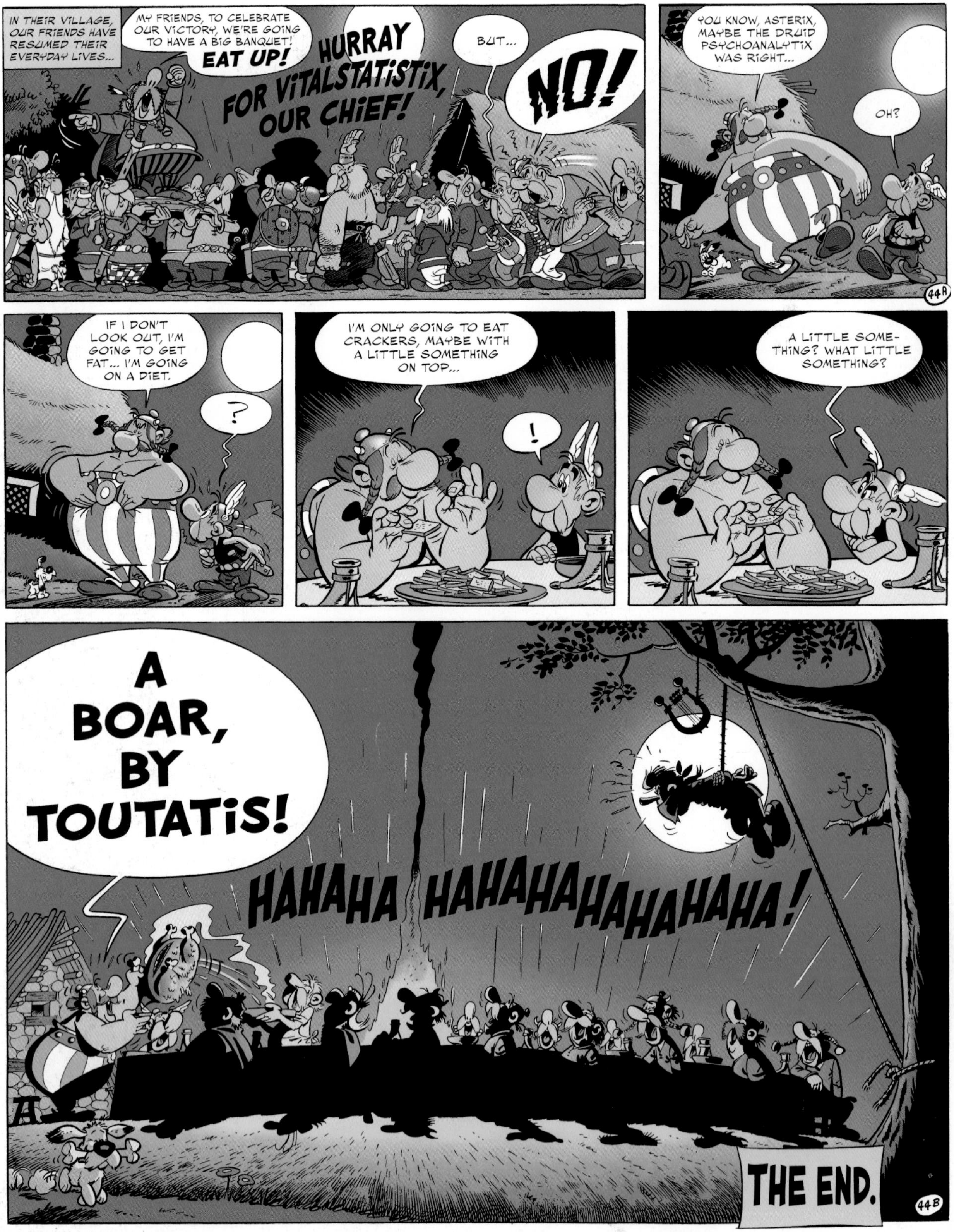

IN THEIR VILLAGE, OUR FRIENDS HAVE RESUMED THEIR EVERYDAY LIVES...
MY FRIENDS, TO CELEBRATE OUR VICTORY, WE'RE GOING TO HAVE A BIG BANQUET!
EAT UP!
HURRAY FOR VITALSTATISTIX, OUR CHIEF!
BUT...
NO!
YOU KNOW, ASTERIX, MAYBE THE DRUID PSYCHOANALYTIX WAS RIGHT...
OH?
44A
IF I DON'T LOOK OUT, I'M GOING TO GET FAT... I'M GOING ON A DIET.
?
I'M ONLY GOING TO EAT CRACKERS, MAYBE WITH A LITTLE SOMETHING ON TOP...
!
A LITTLE SOMETHING? WHAT LITTLE SOMETHING?
A BOAR, BY TOUTATIS!
HAHAHA HAHAHAHAHAHAHAHA!
THE END.
44B

R. GOSCINNY Asterix A. UDERZO

Asterix IN BRITAIN

Written by René GOSCINNY

Illustrated by Albert UDERZO

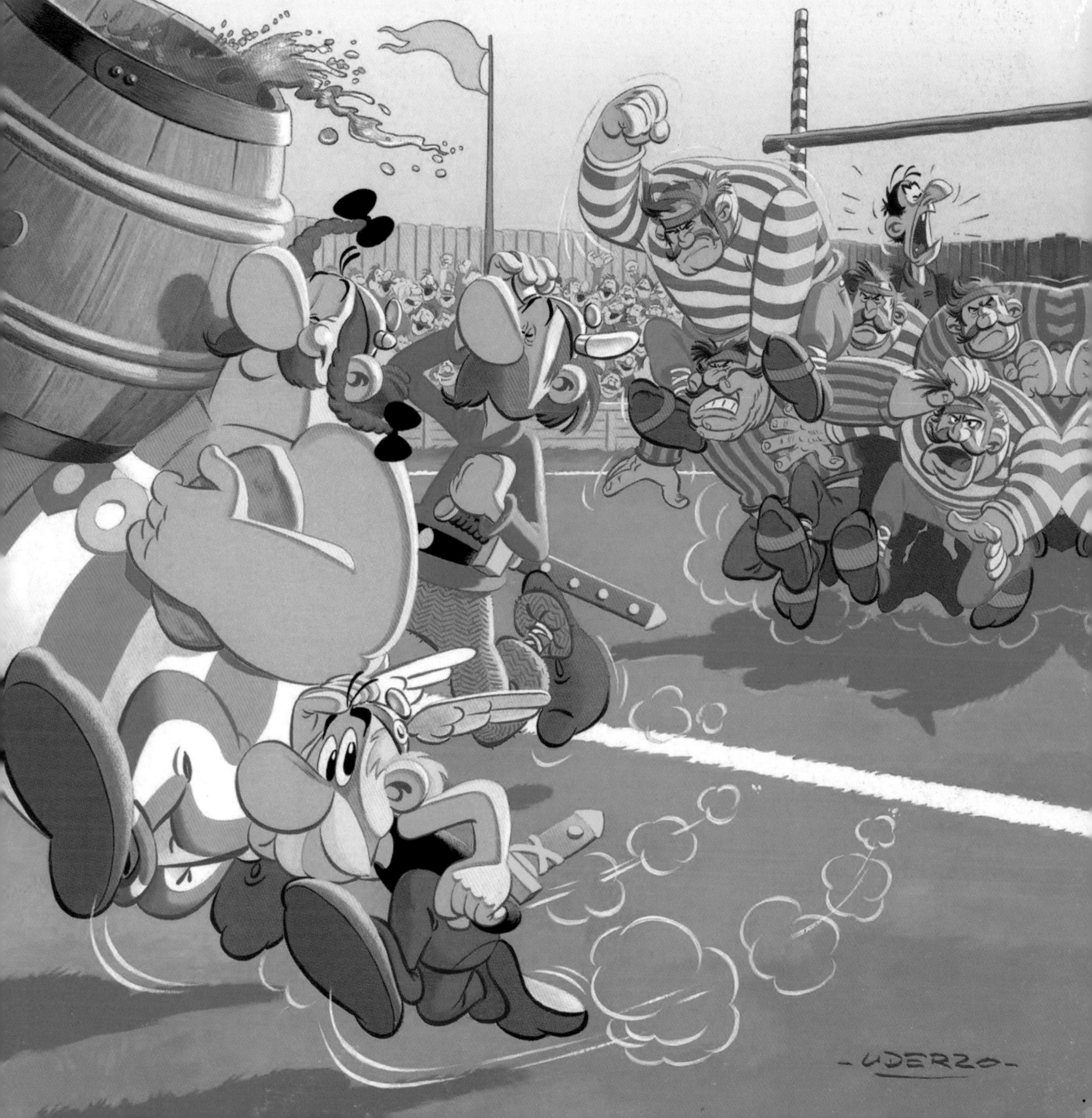
-UDERZO-

ASTERIX IN BRITAIN

Written by RENÉ GOSCINNY *and illustrated by* ALBERT UDERZO

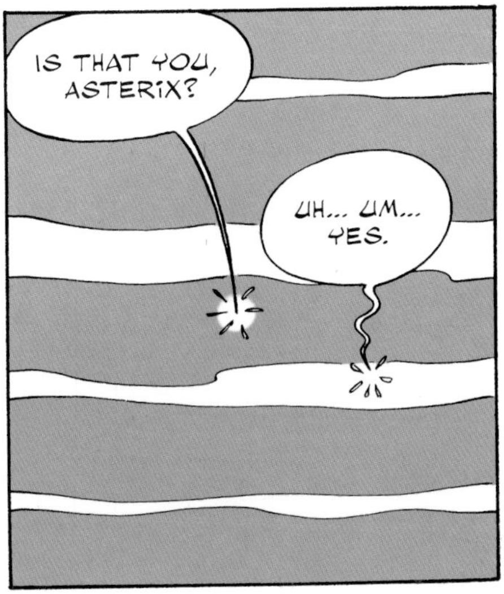
IS THAT YOU, ASTERIX?
UH... UM... YES.

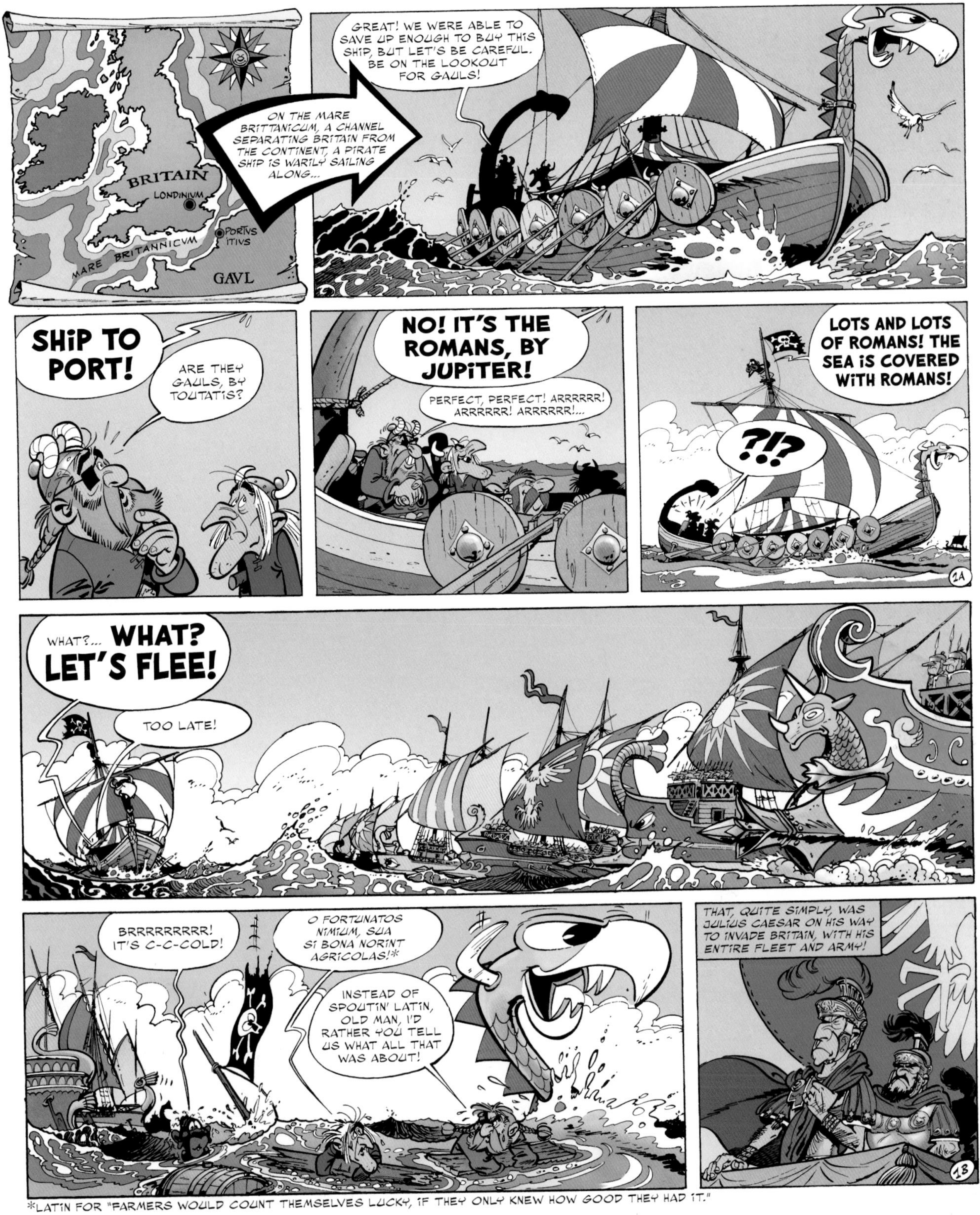

BRITAIN
LONDINIVM
PORTVS ITIVS
MARE BRITANNICVM
GAVL
ON THE MARE BRITTANICUM, A CHANNEL SEPARATING BRITAIN FROM THE CONTINENT, A PIRATE SHIP IS WARILY SAILING ALONG...
GREAT! WE WERE ABLE TO SAVE UP ENOUGH TO BUY THIS SHIP, BUT LET'S BE CAREFUL. BE ON THE LOOKOUT FOR GAULS!
SHIP TO PORT!
ARE THEY GAULS, BY TOUTATIS?
NO! IT'S THE ROMANS, BY JUPITER!
PERFECT, PERFECT! ARRRRRR! ARRRRRR! ARRRRRR!...
LOTS AND LOTS OF ROMANS! THE SEA IS COVERED WITH ROMANS!
?!?
WHAT?... WHAT? LET'S FLEE!
TOO LATE!
BRRRRRRRRR! IT'S C-C-COLD!
O FORTUNATOS NIMIUM, SUA SI BONA NORINT AGRICOLAS!*
INSTEAD OF SPOUTIN' LATIN, OLD MAN, I'D RATHER YOU TELL US WHAT ALL THAT WAS ABOUT!
THAT, QUITE SIMPLY, WAS JULIUS CAESAR ON HIS WAY TO INVADE BRITAIN, WITH HIS ENTIRE FLEET AND ARMY!

*LATIN FOR "FARMERS WOULD COUNT THEMSELVES LUCKY, IF THEY ONLY KNEW HOW GOOD THEY HAD IT."

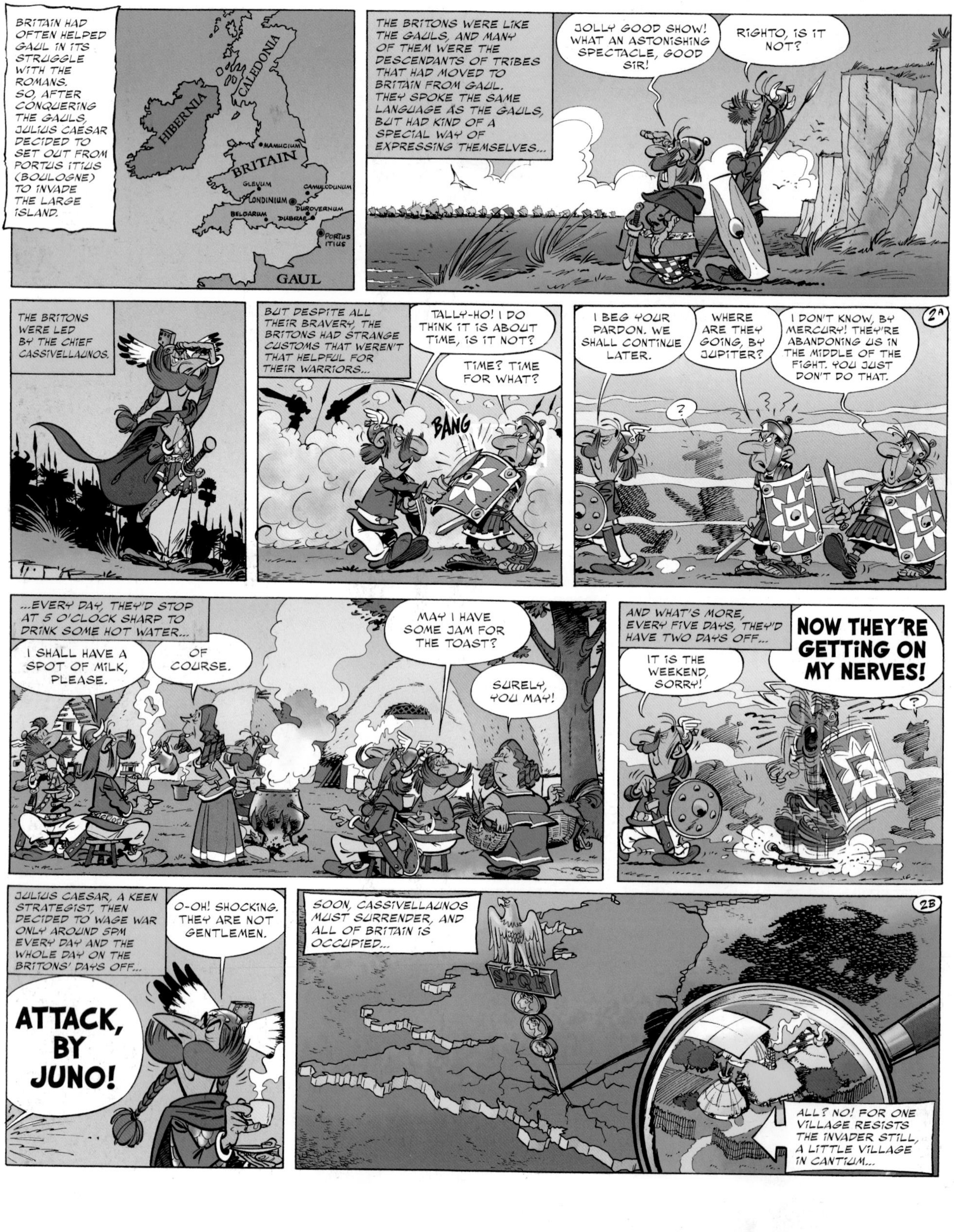
BRITAIN HAD OFTEN HELPED GAUL IN ITS STRUGGLE WITH THE ROMANS. SO, AFTER CONQUERING THE GAULS, JULIUS CAESAR DECIDED TO SET OUT FROM PORTUS ITIUS (BOULOGNE) TO INVADE THE LARGE ISLAND.
HIBERNIA
CALEDONIA
BRITAIN
MAMUCIUM
GLEVUM
LONDINIUM
CAMULODUNUM
DUROVERNUM
BELGARUM
DUBRAE
PORTUS ITIUS
GAUL
THE BRITONS WERE LIKE THE GAULS, AND MANY OF THEM WERE THE DESCENDANTS OF TRIBES THAT HAD MOVED TO BRITAIN FROM GAUL. THEY SPOKE THE SAME LANGUAGE AS THE GAULS, BUT HAD KIND OF A SPECIAL WAY OF EXPRESSING THEMSELVES...
JOLLY GOOD SHOW! WHAT AN ASTONISHING SPECTACLE, GOOD SIR!
RIGHTO, IS IT NOT?
THE BRITONS WERE LED BY THE CHIEF CASSIVELLAUNOS.
BUT DESPITE ALL THEIR BRAVERY, THE BRITONS HAD STRANGE CUSTOMS THAT WEREN'T THAT HELPFUL FOR THEIR WARRIORS...
TALLY-HO! I DO THINK IT IS ABOUT TIME, IS IT NOT?
BANG
TIME? TIME FOR WHAT?
2A
I BEG YOUR PARDON. WE SHALL CONTINUE LATER.
WHERE ARE THEY GOING, BY JUPITER?
I DON'T KNOW, BY MERCURY! THEY'RE ABANDONING US IN THE MIDDLE OF THE FIGHT. YOU JUST DON'T DO THAT.
...EVERY DAY, THEY'D STOP AT 5 O'CLOCK SHARP TO DRINK SOME HOT WATER...
I SHALL HAVE A SPOT OF MILK, PLEASE.
OF COURSE.
MAY I HAVE SOME JAM FOR THE TOAST?
SURELY, YOU MAY!
AND WHAT'S MORE, EVERY FIVE DAYS, THEY'D HAVE TWO DAYS OFF...
IT IS THE WEEKEND, SORRY!
NOW THEY'RE GETTING ON MY NERVES!
JULIUS CAESAR, A KEEN STRATEGIST, THEN DECIDED TO WAGE WAR ONLY AROUND 5PM EVERY DAY AND THE WHOLE DAY ON THE BRITONS' DAYS OFF...
O-OH! SHOCKING. THEY ARE NOT GENTLEMEN.
ATTACK, BY JUNO!
SOON, CASSIVELLAUNOS MUST SURRENDER, AND ALL OF BRITAIN IS OCCUPIED...
2B
SPQR
ALL? NO! FOR ONE VILLAGE RESISTS THE INVADER STILL, A LITTLE VILLAGE IN CANTIUM...

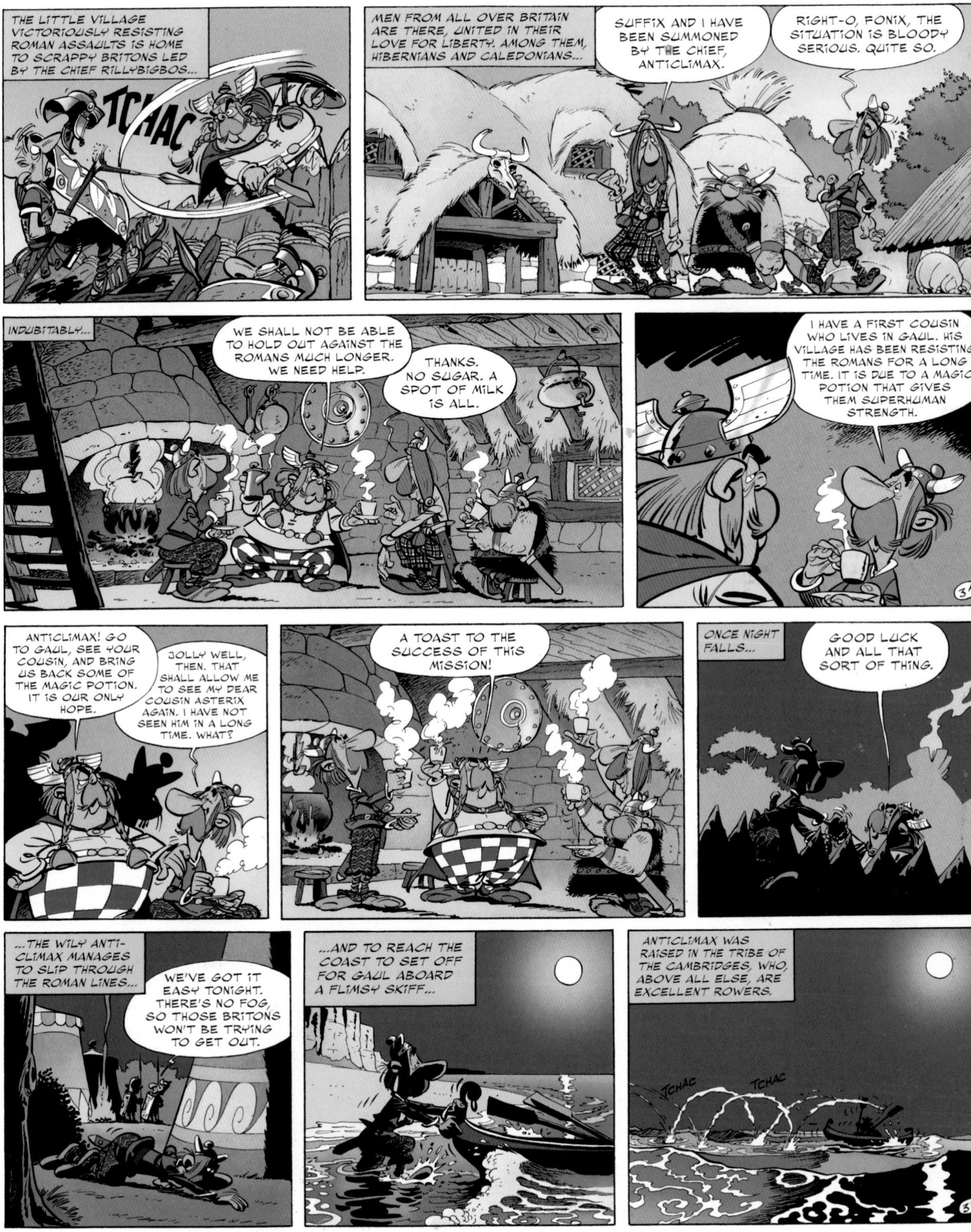

THE LITTLE VILLAGE VICTORIOUSLY RESISTING ROMAN ASSAULTS IS HOME TO SCRAPPY BRITONS LED BY THE CHIEF RILLYBIGBOS...
TCHAC
MEN FROM ALL OVER BRITAIN ARE THERE, UNITED IN THEIR LOVE FOR LIBERTY. AMONG THEM, HIBERNIANS AND CALEDONIANS...
SUFFIX AND I HAVE BEEN SUMMONED BY THE CHIEF, ANTICLIMAX.
RIGHT-O, FONIX, THE SITUATION IS BLOODY SERIOUS. QUITE SO.
INDUBITABLY...
WE SHALL NOT BE ABLE TO HOLD OUT AGAINST THE ROMANS MUCH LONGER. WE NEED HELP.
THANKS. NO SUGAR. A SPOT OF MILK IS ALL.
I HAVE A FIRST COUSIN WHO LIVES IN GAUL. HIS VILLAGE HAS BEEN RESISTING THE ROMANS FOR A LONG TIME. IT IS DUE TO A MAGIC POTION THAT GIVES THEM SUPERHUMAN STRENGTH.
3A
ANTICLIMAX! GO TO GAUL, SEE YOUR COUSIN, AND BRING US BACK SOME OF THE MAGIC POTION. IT IS OUR ONLY HOPE.
JOLLY WELL, THEN. THAT SHALL ALLOW ME TO SEE MY DEAR COUSIN ASTERIX AGAIN. I HAVE NOT SEEN HIM IN A LONG TIME. WHAT?
A TOAST TO THE SUCCESS OF THIS MISSION!
ONCE NIGHT FALLS...
GOOD LUCK AND ALL THAT SORT OF THING.
...THE WILY ANTICLIMAX MANAGES TO SLIP THROUGH THE ROMAN LINES...
WE'VE GOT IT EASY TONIGHT. THERE'S NO FOG, SO THOSE BRITONS WON'T BE TRYING TO GET OUT.
...AND TO REACH THE COAST TO SET OFF FOR GAUL ABOARD A FLIMSY SKIFF...
ANTICLIMAX WAS RAISED IN THE TRIBE OF THE CAMBRIDGES, WHO, ABOVE ALL ELSE, ARE EXCELLENT ROWERS.
TCHAC
TCHAC
3B

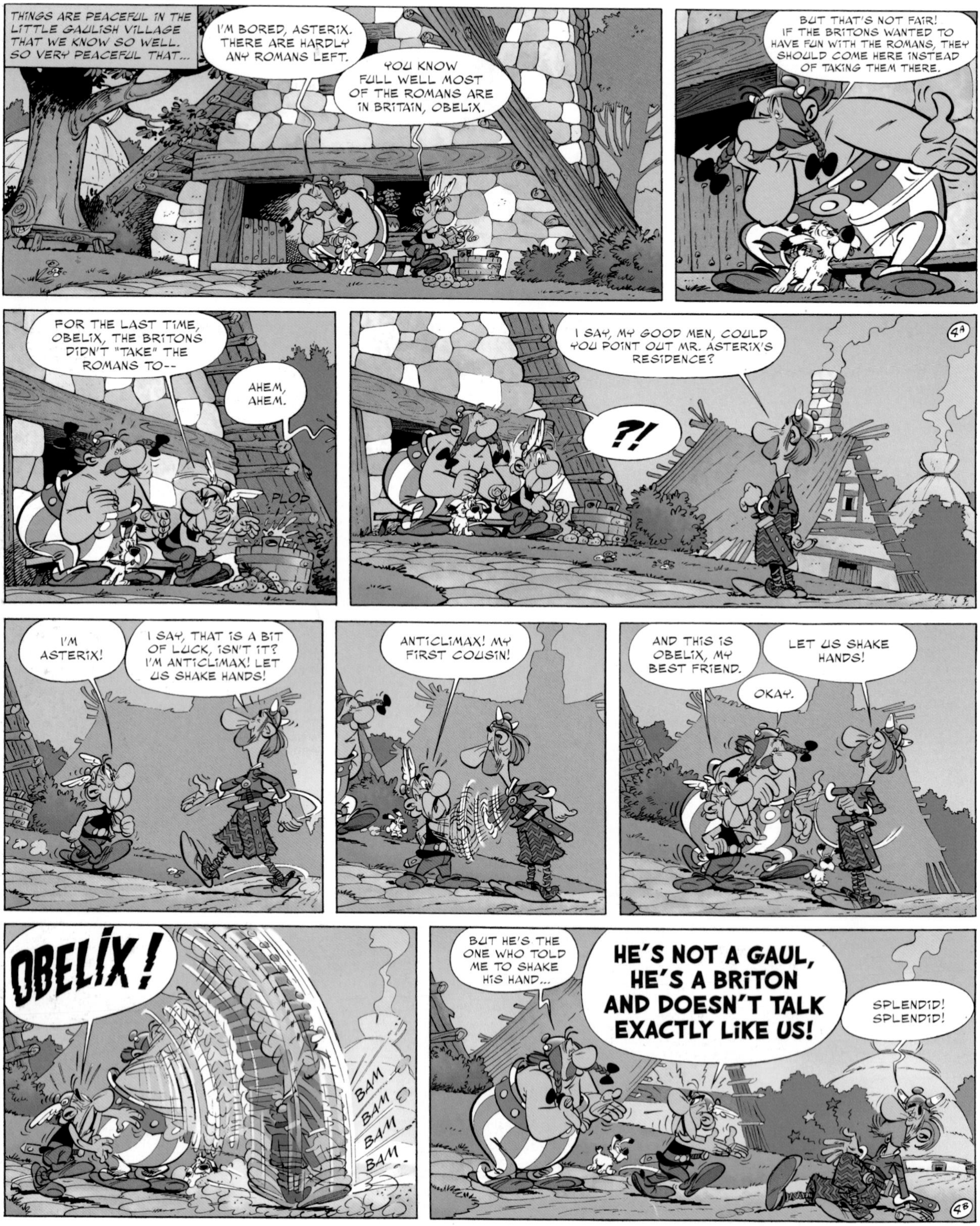

THINGS ARE PEACEFUL IN THE LITTLE GAULISH VILLAGE THAT WE KNOW SO WELL. SO VERY PEACEFUL THAT...
I'M BORED, ASTERIX. THERE ARE HARDLY ANY ROMANS LEFT.
YOU KNOW FULL WELL MOST OF THE ROMANS ARE IN BRITAIN, OBELIX.
BUT THAT'S NOT FAIR! IF THE BRITONS WANTED TO HAVE FUN WITH THE ROMANS, THEY SHOULD COME HERE INSTEAD OF TAKING THEM THERE.
FOR THE LAST TIME, OBELIX, THE BRITONS DIDN'T "TAKE" THE ROMANS TO--
AHEM, AHEM.
PLOD
I SAY, MY GOOD MEN, COULD YOU POINT OUT MR. ASTERIX'S RESIDENCE?
?!
I'M ASTERIX!
I SAY, THAT IS A BIT OF LUCK, ISN'T IT? I'M ANTICLIMAX! LET US SHAKE HANDS!
ANTICLIMAX! MY FIRST COUSIN!
AND THIS IS OBELIX, MY BEST FRIEND.
LET US SHAKE HANDS!
OKAY.
OBELIX!
BAM
BAM
BAM
BAM
BUT HE'S THE ONE WHO TOLD ME TO SHAKE HIS HAND...
HE'S NOT A GAUL, HE'S A BRITON AND DOESN'T TALK EXACTLY LIKE US!
SPLENDID! SPLENDID!

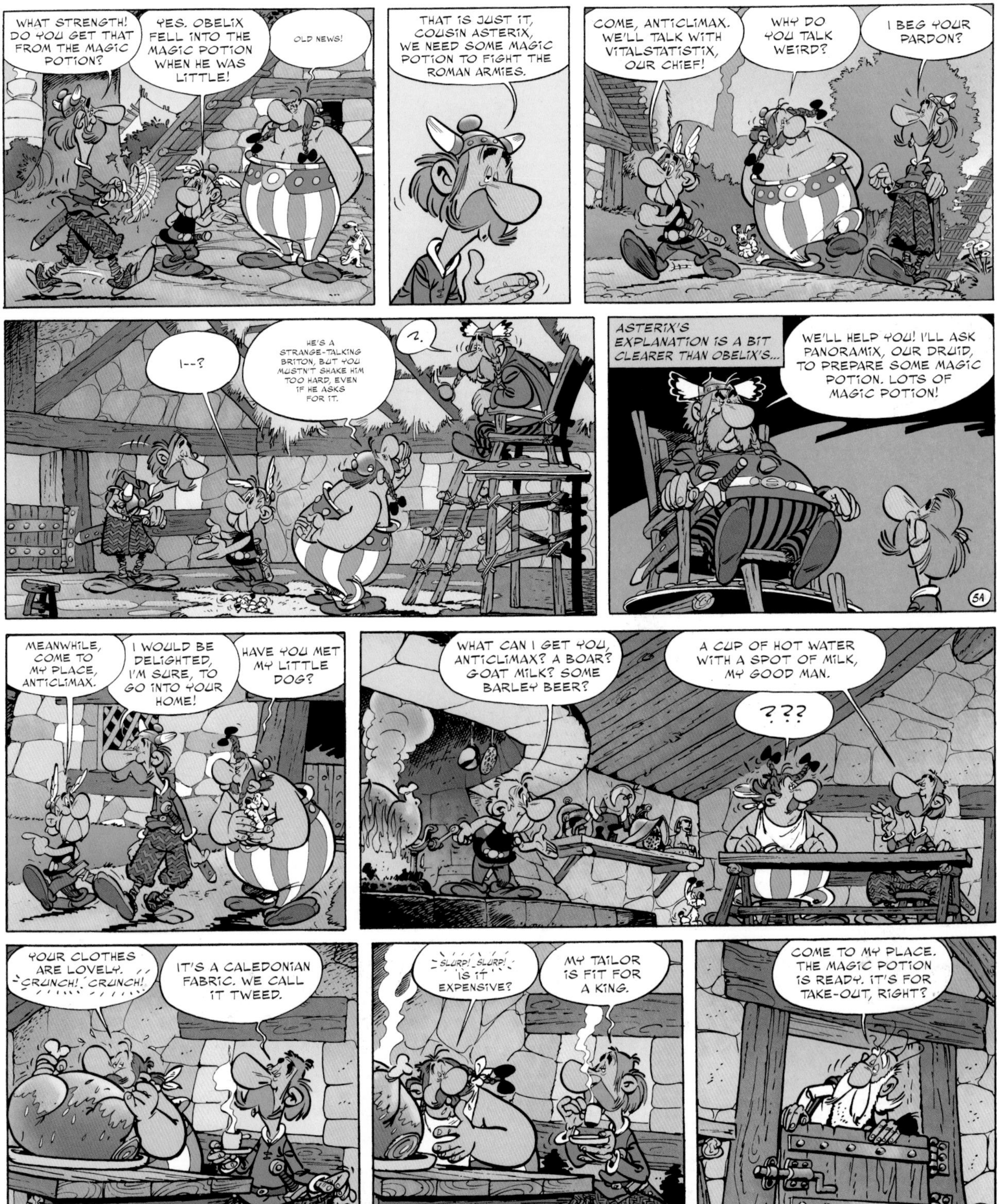
WHAT STRENGTH! DO YOU GET THAT FROM THE MAGIC POTION?
YES. OBELIX FELL INTO THE MAGIC POTION WHEN HE WAS LITTLE!
OLD NEWS!
THAT IS JUST IT, COUSIN ASTERIX, WE NEED SOME MAGIC POTION TO FIGHT THE ROMAN ARMIES.
COME, ANTICLIMAX. WE'LL TALK WITH VITALSTATISTIX, OUR CHIEF!
WHY DO YOU TALK WEIRD?
I BEG YOUR PARDON?
I--?
HE'S A STRANGE-TALKING BRITON, BUT YOU MUSTN'T SHAKE HIM TOO HARD, EVEN IF HE ASKS FOR IT.
?
ASTERIX'S EXPLANATION IS A BIT CLEARER THAN OBELIX'S...
WE'LL HELP YOU! I'LL ASK PANORAMIX, OUR DRUID, TO PREPARE SOME MAGIC POTION. LOTS OF MAGIC POTION!
5A
MEANWHILE, COME TO MY PLACE, ANTICLIMAX.
I WOULD BE DELIGHTED, I'M SURE, TO GO INTO YOUR HOME!
HAVE YOU MET MY LITTLE DOG?
WHAT CAN I GET YOU, ANTICLIMAX? A BOAR? GOAT MILK? SOME BARLEY BEER?
A CUP OF HOT WATER WITH A SPOT OF MILK, MY GOOD MAN.
???
YOUR CLOTHES ARE LOVELY. CRUNCH! CRUNCH!
IT'S A CALEDONIAN FABRIC. WE CALL IT TWEED.
SLURP! SLURP! IS IT EXPENSIVE?
MY TAILOR IS FIT FOR A KING.
COME TO MY PLACE. THE MAGIC POTION IS READY. IT'S FOR TAKE-OUT, RIGHT?
5B

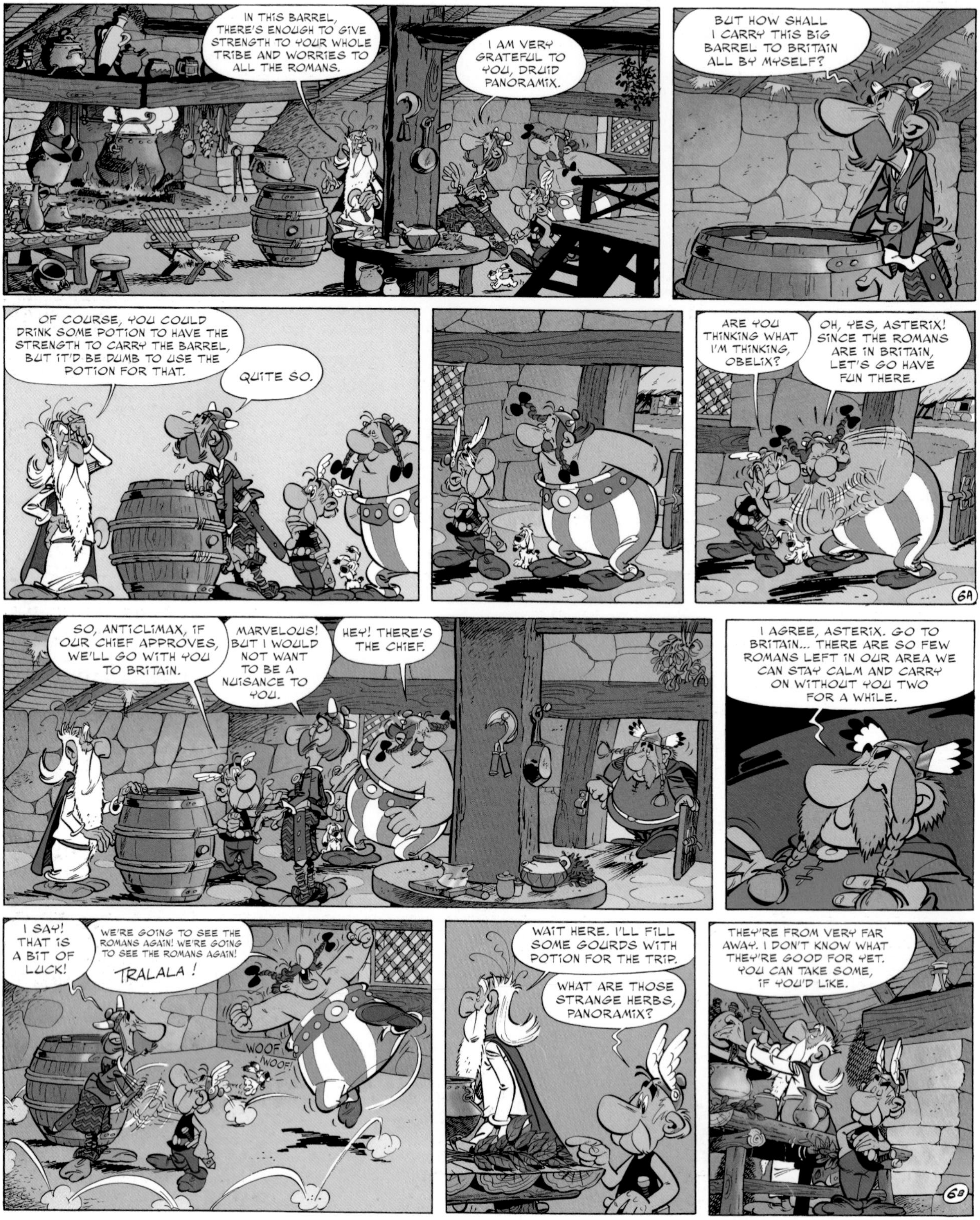

IN THIS BARREL, THERE'S ENOUGH TO GIVE STRENGTH TO YOUR WHOLE TRIBE AND WORRIES TO ALL THE ROMANS.
I AM VERY GRATEFUL TO YOU, DRUID PANORAMIX.
BUT HOW SHALL I CARRY THIS BIG BARREL TO BRITAIN ALL BY MYSELF?
OF COURSE, YOU COULD DRINK SOME POTION TO HAVE THE STRENGTH TO CARRY THE BARREL, BUT IT'D BE DUMB TO USE THE POTION FOR THAT.
QUITE SO.
ARE YOU THINKING WHAT I'M THINKING, OBELIX?
OH, YES, ASTERIX! SINCE THE ROMANS ARE IN BRITAIN, LET'S GO HAVE FUN THERE.
6A
SO, ANTICLIMAX, IF OUR CHIEF APPROVES, WE'LL GO WITH YOU TO BRITAIN.
MARVELOUS! BUT I WOULD NOT WANT TO BE A NUISANCE TO YOU.
HEY! THERE'S THE CHIEF.
I AGREE, ASTERIX. GO TO BRITAIN... THERE ARE SO FEW ROMANS LEFT IN OUR AREA WE CAN STAY CALM AND CARRY ON WITHOUT YOU TWO FOR A WHILE.
I SAY! THAT IS A BIT OF LUCK!
WE'RE GOING TO SEE THE ROMANS AGAIN! WE'RE GOING TO SEE THE ROMANS AGAIN!
TRALALA !
WOOF WOOF!
WAIT HERE. I'LL FILL SOME GOURDS WITH POTION FOR THE TRIP.
WHAT ARE THOSE STRANGE HERBS, PANORAMIX?
THEY'RE FROM VERY FAR AWAY. I DON'T KNOW WHAT THEY'RE GOOD FOR YET. YOU CAN TAKE SOME, IF YOU'D LIKE.
6B

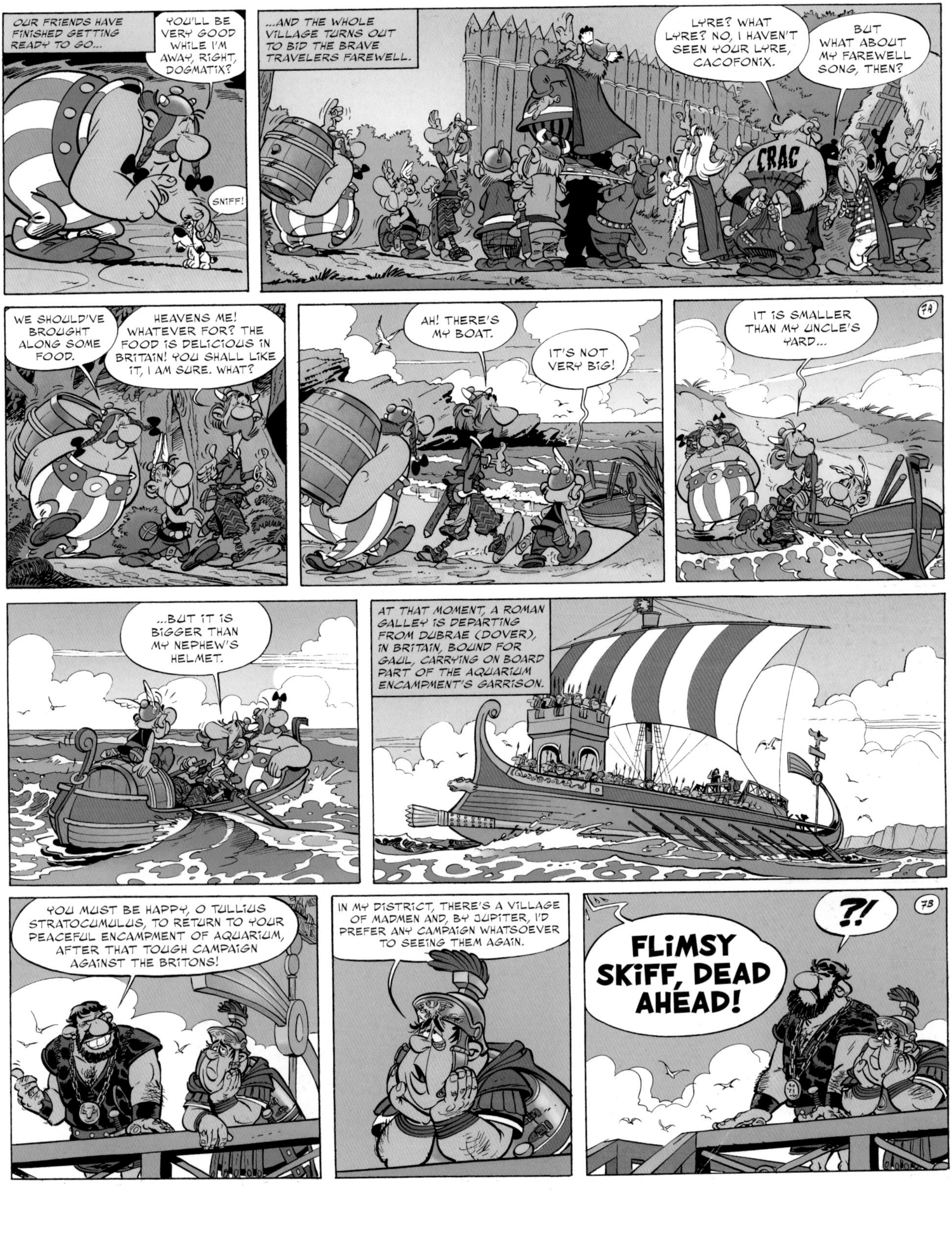

OUR FRIENDS HAVE FINISHED GETTING READY TO GO...
YOU'LL BE VERY GOOD WHILE I'M AWAY, RIGHT, DOGMATIX?
SNIFF!
...AND THE WHOLE VILLAGE TURNS OUT TO BID THE BRAVE TRAVELERS FAREWELL.
LYRE? WHAT LYRE? NO, I HAVEN'T SEEN YOUR LYRE, CACOFONIX.
BUT WHAT ABOUT MY FAREWELL SONG, THEN?
CRAC
WE SHOULD'VE BROUGHT ALONG SOME FOOD.
HEAVENS ME! WHATEVER FOR? THE FOOD IS DELICIOUS IN BRITAIN! YOU SHALL LIKE IT, I AM SURE. WHAT?
AH! THERE'S MY BOAT.
IT'S NOT VERY BIG!
IT IS SMALLER THAN MY UNCLE'S YARD...
...BUT IT IS BIGGER THAN MY NEPHEW'S HELMET.
AT THAT MOMENT, A ROMAN GALLEY IS DEPARTING FROM DUBRAE (DOVER), IN BRITAIN, BOUND FOR GAUL, CARRYING ON BOARD PART OF THE AQUARIUM ENCAMPMENT'S GARRISON.
YOU MUST BE HAPPY, O TULLIUS STRATOCUMULUS, TO RETURN TO YOUR PEACEFUL ENCAMPMENT OF AQUARIUM, AFTER THAT TOUGH CAMPAIGN AGAINST THE BRITONS!
IN MY DISTRICT, THERE'S A VILLAGE OF MADMEN AND, BY JUPITER, I'D PREFER ANY CAMPAIGN WHATSOEVER TO SEEING THEM AGAIN.
FLIMSY SKIFF, DEAD AHEAD!
?!

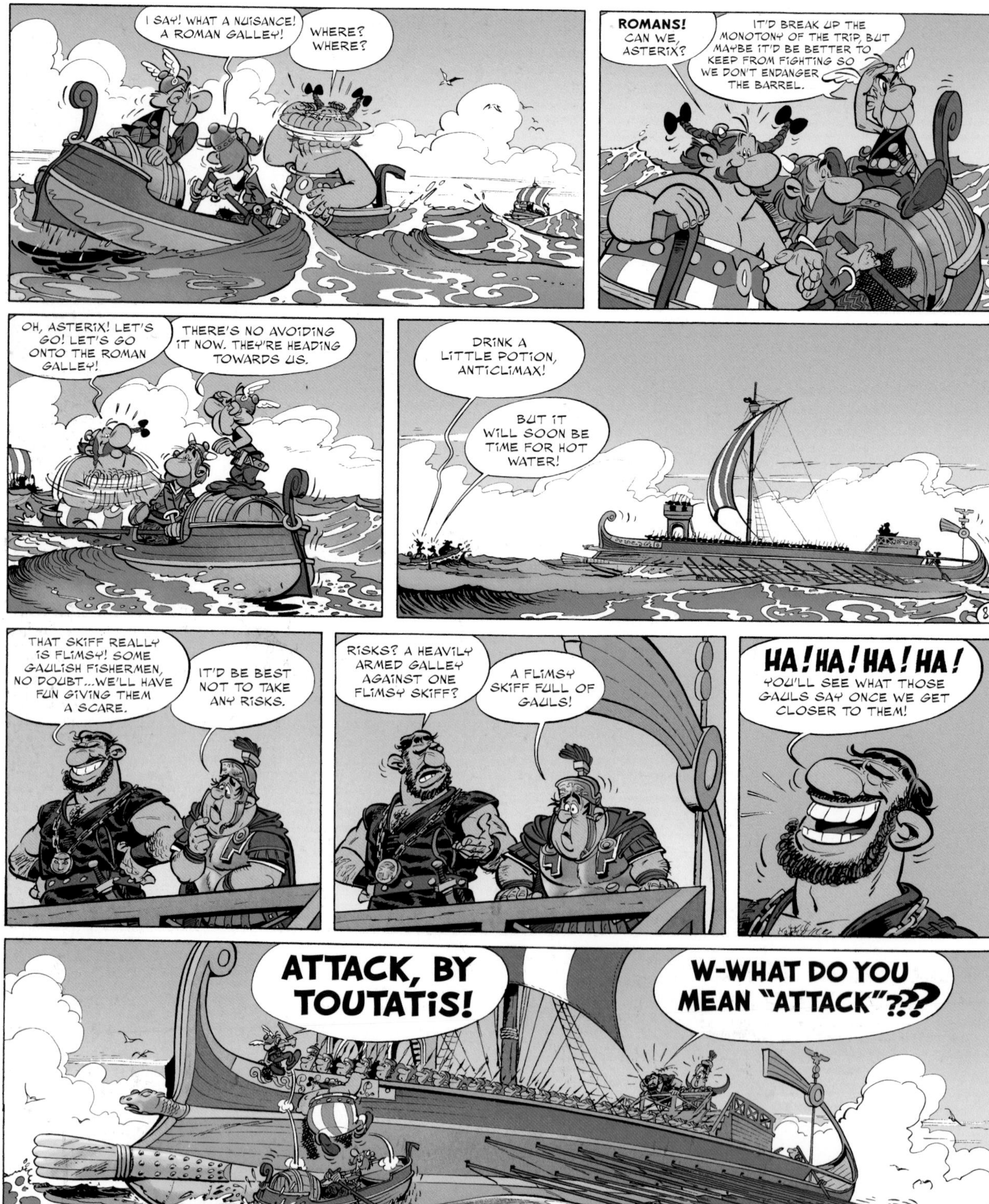
I SAY! WHAT A NUISANCE! A ROMAN GALLEY!
WHERE? WHERE?
ROMANS! CAN WE, ASTERIX?
IT'D BREAK UP THE MONOTONY OF THE TRIP, BUT MAYBE IT'D BE BETTER TO KEEP FROM FIGHTING SO WE DON'T ENDANGER THE BARREL.
OH, ASTERIX! LET'S GO! LET'S GO ONTO THE ROMAN GALLEY!
THERE'S NO AVOIDING IT NOW. THEY'RE HEADING TOWARDS US.
DRINK A LITTLE POTION, ANTICLIMAX!
BUT IT WILL SOON BE TIME FOR HOT WATER!
THAT SKIFF REALLY IS FLIMSY! SOME GAULISH FISHERMEN, NO DOUBT...WE'LL HAVE FUN GIVING THEM A SCARE.
IT'D BE BEST NOT TO TAKE ANY RISKS.
RISKS? A HEAVILY ARMED GALLEY AGAINST ONE FLIMSY SKIFF?
A FLIMSY SKIFF FULL OF GAULS!
HA! HA! HA! HA!
YOU'LL SEE WHAT THOSE GAULS SAY ONCE WE GET CLOSER TO THEM!
ATTACK, BY TOUTATIS!
W-WHAT DO YOU MEAN "ATTACK"???

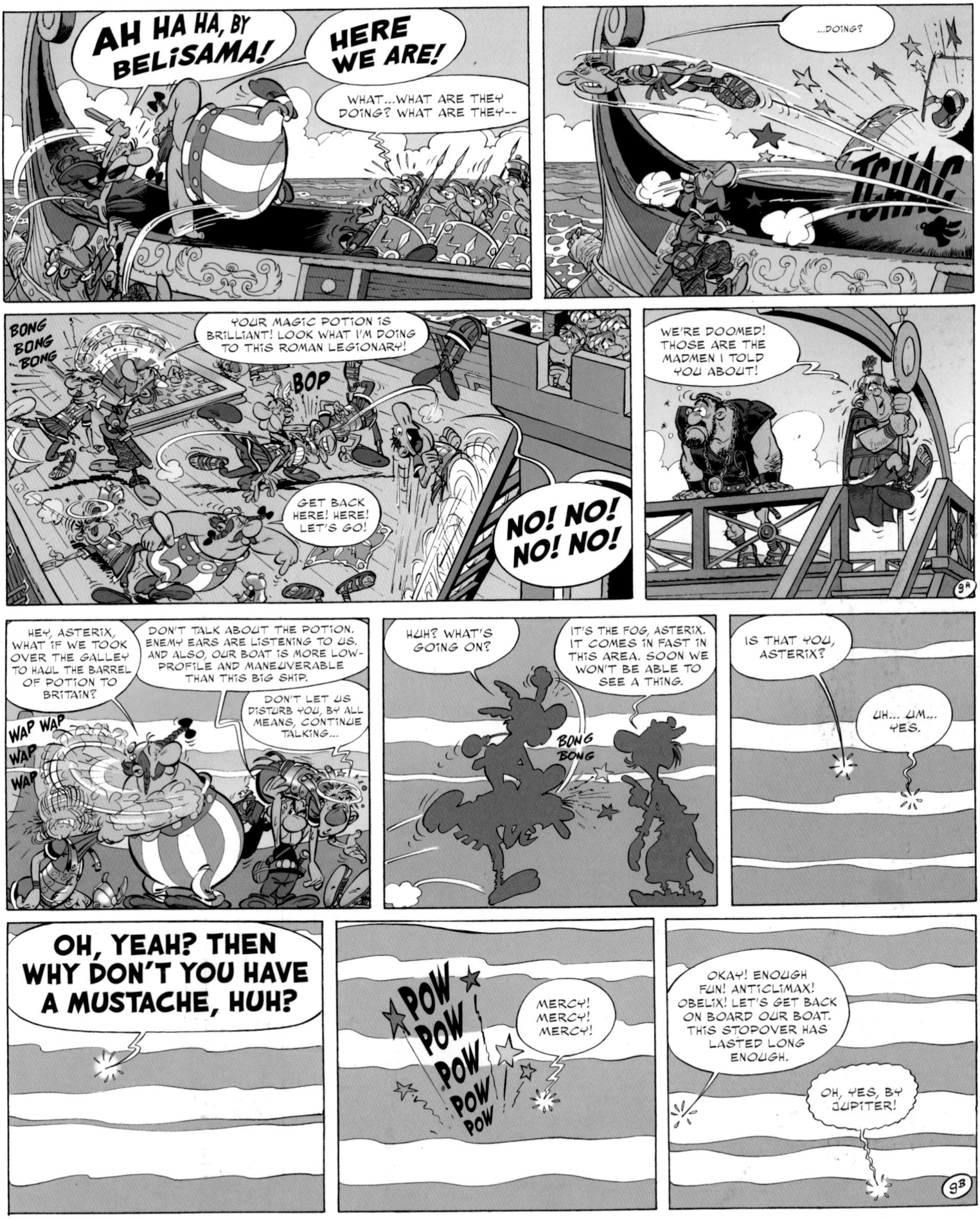
AH HA HA, BY BELISAMA!
HERE WE ARE!
WHAT...WHAT ARE THEY DOING? WHAT ARE THEY--
...DOING?
TCHAC
BONG BONG BONG
YOUR MAGIC POTION IS BRILLIANT! LOOK WHAT I'M DOING TO THIS ROMAN LEGIONARY!
BOP
GET BACK HERE! HERE! LET'S GO!
NO! NO! NO! NO!
WE'RE DOOMED! THOSE ARE THE MADMEN I TOLD YOU ABOUT!
HEY, ASTERIX, WHAT IF WE TOOK OVER THE GALLEY TO HAUL THE BARREL OF POTION TO BRITAIN?
DON'T TALK ABOUT THE POTION. ENEMY EARS ARE LISTENING TO US. AND ALSO, OUR BOAT IS MORE LOW-PROFILE AND MANEUVERABLE THAN THIS BIG SHIP.
DON'T LET US DISTURB YOU, BY ALL MEANS, CONTINUE TALKING...
WAP WAP WAP WAP
HUH? WHAT'S GOING ON?
IT'S THE FOG, ASTERIX. IT COMES IN FAST IN THIS AREA. SOON WE WON'T BE ABLE TO SEE A THING.
BONG BONG
IS THAT YOU, ASTERIX?
UH... UM... YES.
OH, YEAH? THEN WHY DON'T YOU HAVE A MUSTACHE, HUH?
POW POW POW POW POW
MERCY! MERCY! MERCY!
OKAY! ENOUGH FUN! ANTICLIMAX! OBELIX! LET'S GET BACK ON BOARD OUR BOAT. THIS STOPOVER HAS LASTED LONG ENOUGH.
OH, YES, BY JUPITER!

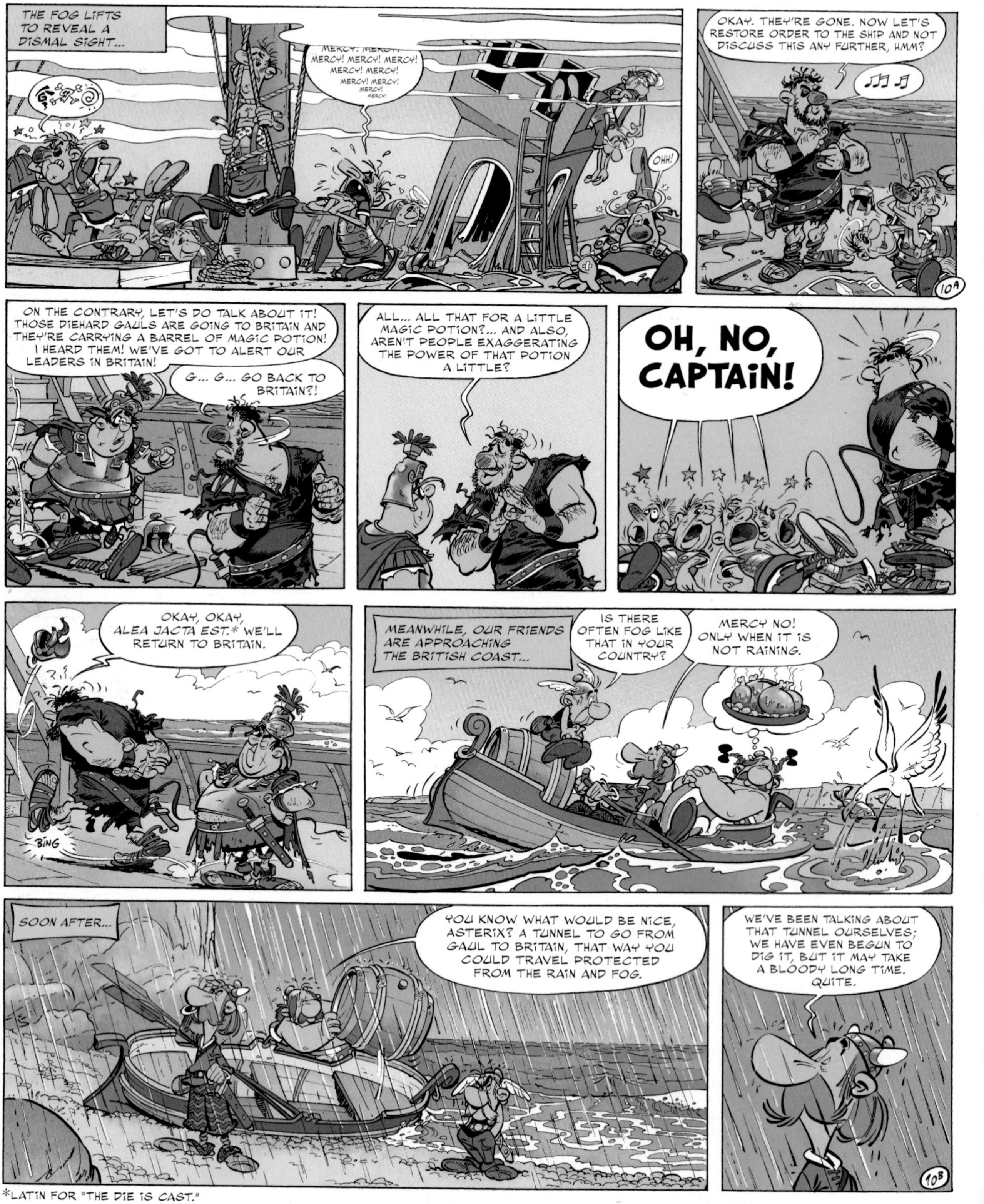
THE FOG LIFTS TO REVEAL A DISMAL SIGHT...
MERCY! MERCY! MERCY! MERCY! MERCY! MERCY! MERCY! MERCY! MERCY! MERCY!
OHH!
OKAY. THEY'RE GONE. NOW LET'S RESTORE ORDER TO THE SHIP AND NOT DISCUSS THIS ANY FURTHER, HMM?
10A
ON THE CONTRARY, LET'S DO TALK ABOUT IT! THOSE DIEHARD GAULS ARE GOING TO BRITAIN AND THEY'RE CARRYING A BARREL OF MAGIC POTION! I HEARD THEM! WE'VE GOT TO ALERT OUR LEADERS IN BRITAIN!
G... G... GO BACK TO BRITAIN?!
ALL... ALL THAT FOR A LITTLE MAGIC POTION?... AND ALSO, AREN'T PEOPLE EXAGGERATING THE POWER OF THAT POTION A LITTLE?
OH, NO, CAPTAIN!
OKAY, OKAY, ALEA JACTA EST.* WE'LL RETURN TO BRITAIN.
BING
MEANWHILE, OUR FRIENDS ARE APPROACHING THE BRITISH COAST...
IS THERE OFTEN FOG LIKE THAT IN YOUR COUNTRY?
MERCY NO! ONLY WHEN IT IS NOT RAINING.
SOON AFTER...
YOU KNOW WHAT WOULD BE NICE, ASTERIX? A TUNNEL TO GO FROM GAUL TO BRITAIN, THAT WAY YOU COULD TRAVEL PROTECTED FROM THE RAIN AND FOG.
WE'VE BEEN TALKING ABOUT THAT TUNNEL OURSELVES; WE HAVE EVEN BEGUN TO DIG IT, BUT IT MAY TAKE A BLOODY LONG TIME. QUITE.
10B

*LATIN FOR "THE DIE IS CAST."

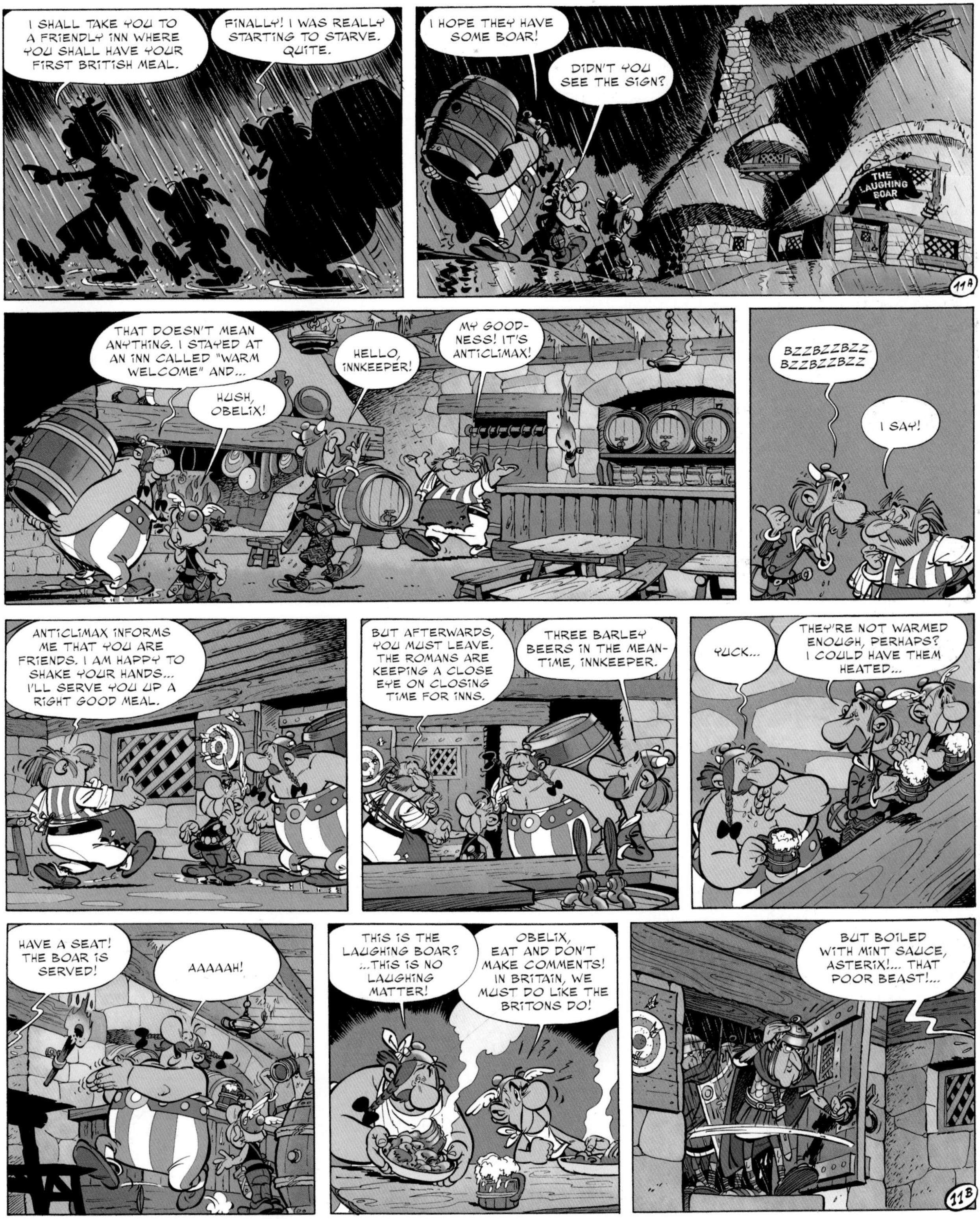
I SHALL TAKE YOU TO A FRIENDLY INN WHERE YOU SHALL HAVE YOUR FIRST BRITISH MEAL.
FINALLY! I WAS REALLY STARTING TO STARVE. QUITE.
I HOPE THEY HAVE SOME BOAR!
DIDN'T YOU SEE THE SIGN?
THE LAUGHING BOAR
11A
THAT DOESN'T MEAN ANYTHING. I STAYED AT AN INN CALLED "WARM WELCOME" AND...
HUSH, OBELIX!
HELLO, INNKEEPER!
MY GOODNESS! IT'S ANTICLIMAX!
BZZBZZBZZ. BZZBZZBZZ
I SAY!
ANTICLIMAX INFORMS ME THAT YOU ARE FRIENDS. I AM HAPPY TO SHAKE YOUR HANDS... I'LL SERVE YOU UP A RIGHT GOOD MEAL.
BUT AFTERWARDS, YOU MUST LEAVE. THE ROMANS ARE KEEPING A CLOSE EYE ON CLOSING TIME FOR INNS.
THREE BARLEY BEERS IN THE MEANTIME, INNKEEPER.
YUCK...
THEY'RE NOT WARMED ENOUGH, PERHAPS? I COULD HAVE THEM HEATED...
HAVE A SEAT! THE BOAR IS SERVED!
AAAAAH!
THIS IS THE LAUGHING BOAR? ...THIS IS NO LAUGHING MATTER!
OBELIX, EAT AND DON'T MAKE COMMENTS! IN BRITAIN, WE MUST DO LIKE THE BRITONS DO!
BUT BOILED WITH MINT SAUCE, ASTERIX!... THAT POOR BEAST!...
11B

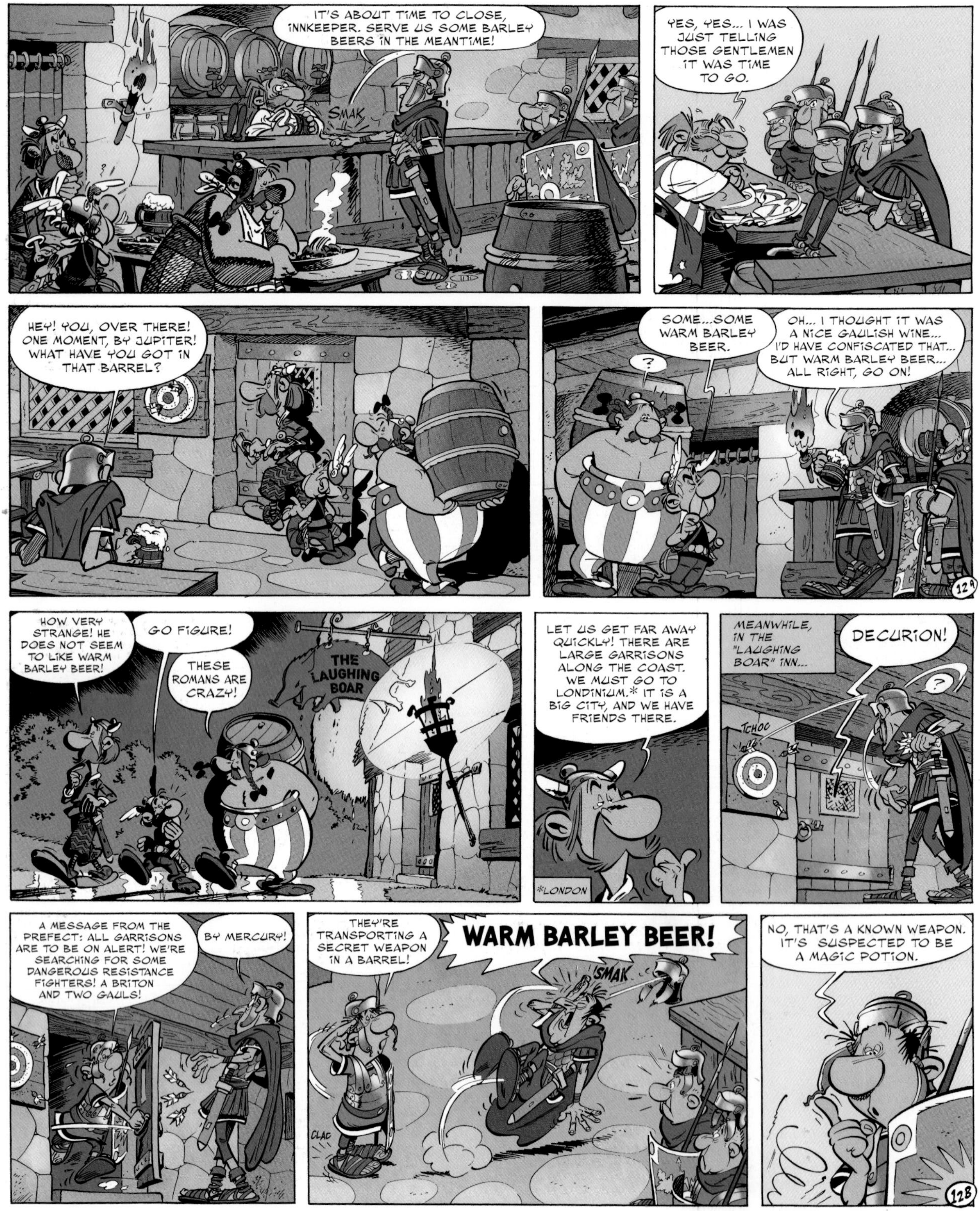

IT'S ABOUT TIME TO CLOSE, INNKEEPER. SERVE US SOME BARLEY BEERS IN THE MEANTIME!
SMAK
YES, YES... I WAS JUST TELLING THOSE GENTLEMEN IT WAS TIME TO GO.
HEY! YOU, OVER THERE! ONE MOMENT, BY JUPITER! WHAT HAVE YOU GOT IN THAT BARREL?
SOME...SOME WARM BARLEY BEER.
?
OH... I THOUGHT IT WAS A NICE GAULISH WINE... I'D HAVE CONFISCATED THAT... BUT WARM BARLEY BEER... ALL RIGHT, GO ON!
129
HOW VERY STRANGE! HE DOES NOT SEEM TO LIKE WARM BARLEY BEER!
GO FIGURE!
THESE ROMANS ARE CRAZY!
THE LAUGHING BOAR
LET US GET FAR AWAY QUICKLY! THERE ARE LARGE GARRISONS ALONG THE COAST. WE MUST GO TO LONDINIUM.* IT IS A BIG CITY, AND WE HAVE FRIENDS THERE.
*LONDON
MEANWHILE, IN THE "LAUGHING BOAR" INN...
DECURION!
?
TCHOC
A MESSAGE FROM THE PREFECT: ALL GARRISONS ARE TO BE ON ALERT! WE'RE SEARCHING FOR SOME DANGEROUS RESISTANCE FIGHTERS! A BRITON AND TWO GAULS!
BY MERCURY!
THEY'RE TRANSPORTING A SECRET WEAPON IN A BARREL!
WARM BARLEY BEER!
SMAK
CLAC
NO, THAT'S A KNOWN WEAPON. IT'S SUSPECTED TO BE A MAGIC POTION.
128

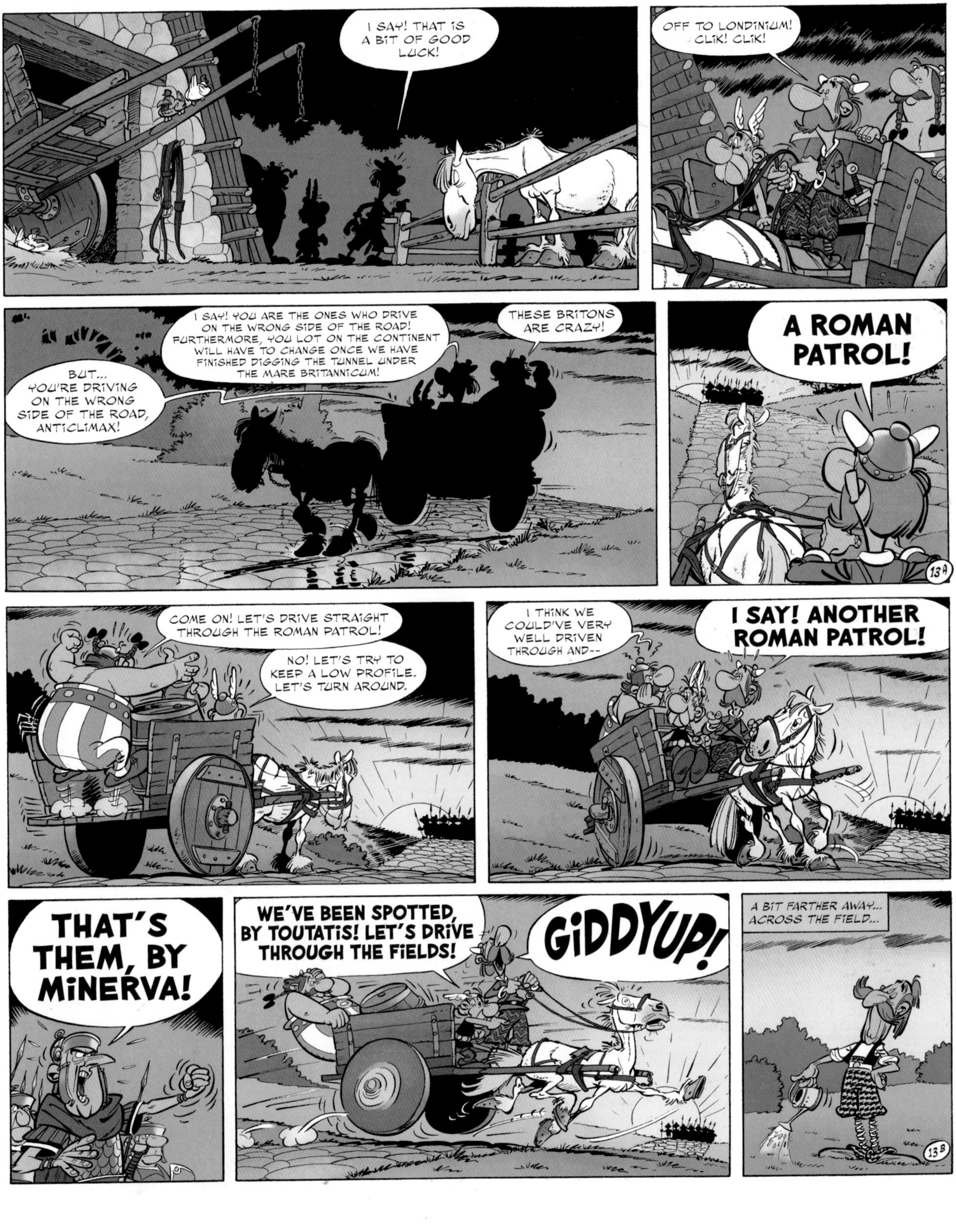
I SAY! THAT IS A BIT OF GOOD LUCK!
OFF TO LONDINIUM! CLIK! CLIK!
BUT... YOU'RE DRIVING ON THE WRONG SIDE OF THE ROAD, ANTICLIMAX!
I SAY! YOU ARE THE ONES WHO DRIVE ON THE WRONG SIDE OF THE ROAD! FURTHERMORE, YOU LOT ON THE CONTINENT WILL HAVE TO CHANGE ONCE WE HAVE FINISHED DIGGING THE TUNNEL UNDER THE MARE BRITANNICUM!
THESE BRITONS ARE CRAZY!
A ROMAN PATROL!
13A
COME ON! LET'S DRIVE STRAIGHT THROUGH THE ROMAN PATROL!
NO! LET'S TRY TO KEEP A LOW PROFILE. LET'S TURN AROUND.
I THINK WE COULD'VE VERY WELL DRIVEN THROUGH AND--
I SAY! ANOTHER ROMAN PATROL!
THAT'S THEM, BY MINERVA!
WE'VE BEEN SPOTTED, BY TOUTATIS! LET'S DRIVE THROUGH THE FIELDS!
GIDDYUP!
A BIT FARTHER AWAY... ACROSS THE FIELD...
13B

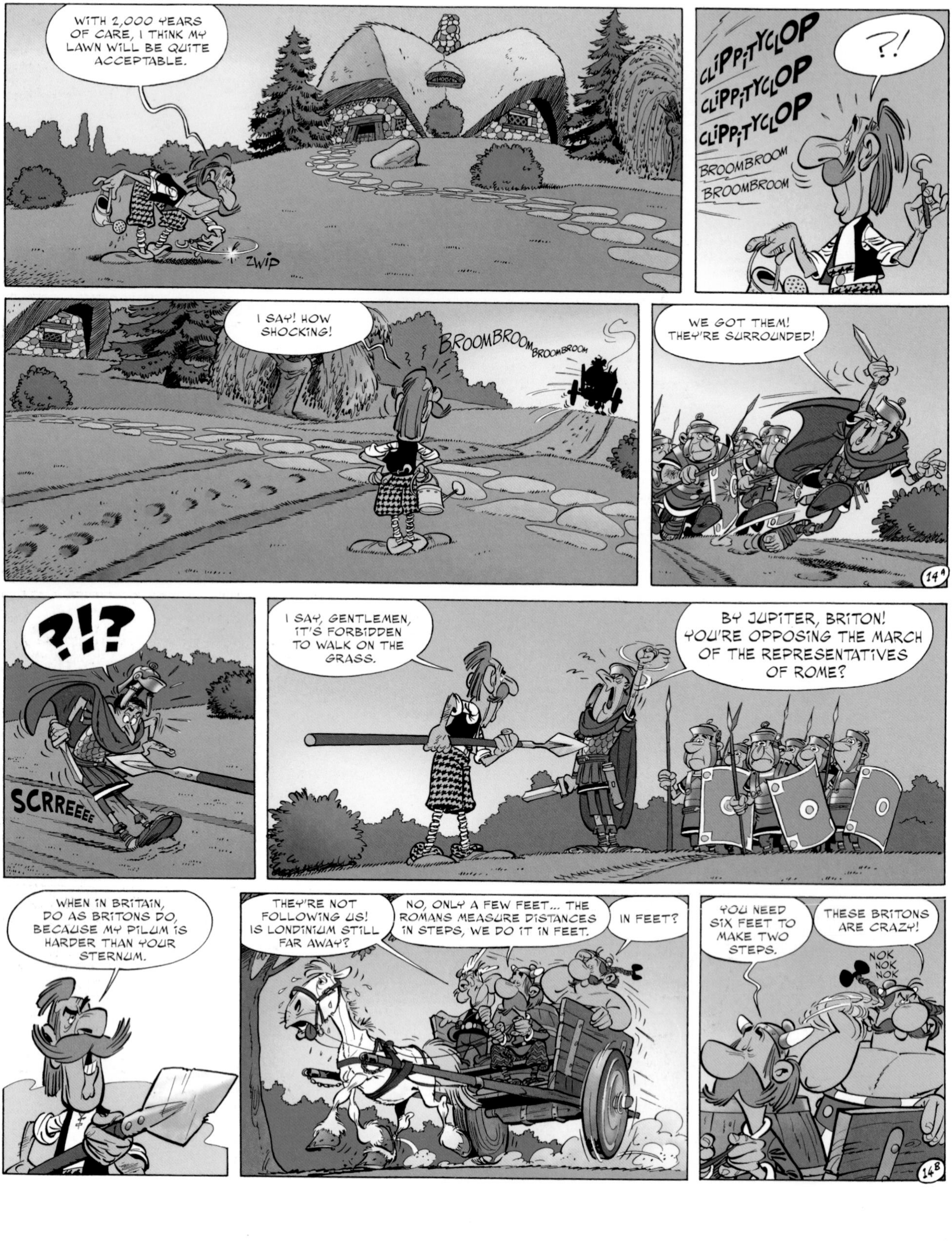
WITH 2,000 YEARS OF CARE, I THINK MY LAWN WILL BE QUITE ACCEPTABLE.
ZWIP
CLIPPITYCLOP
CLIPPITYCLOP
CLIPPITYCLOP
BROOMBROOM
BROOMBROOM
?!
I SAY! HOW SHOCKING!
BROOMBROOM
BROOMBROOM
WE GOT THEM! THEY'RE SURROUNDED!
14A
?!?
SCRREEEEE
I SAY, GENTLEMEN, IT'S FORBIDDEN TO WALK ON THE GRASS.
BY JUPITER, BRITON! YOU'RE OPPOSING THE MARCH OF THE REPRESENTATIVES OF ROME?
WHEN IN BRITAIN, DO AS BRITONS DO, BECAUSE MY PILUM IS HARDER THAN YOUR STERNUM.
THEY'RE NOT FOLLOWING US! IS LONDINIUM STILL FAR AWAY?
NO, ONLY A FEW FEET... THE ROMANS MEASURE DISTANCES IN STEPS, WE DO IT IN FEET.
IN FEET?
YOU NEED SIX FEET TO MAKE TWO STEPS.
THESE BRITONS ARE CRAZY!
NOK NOK NOK
14B

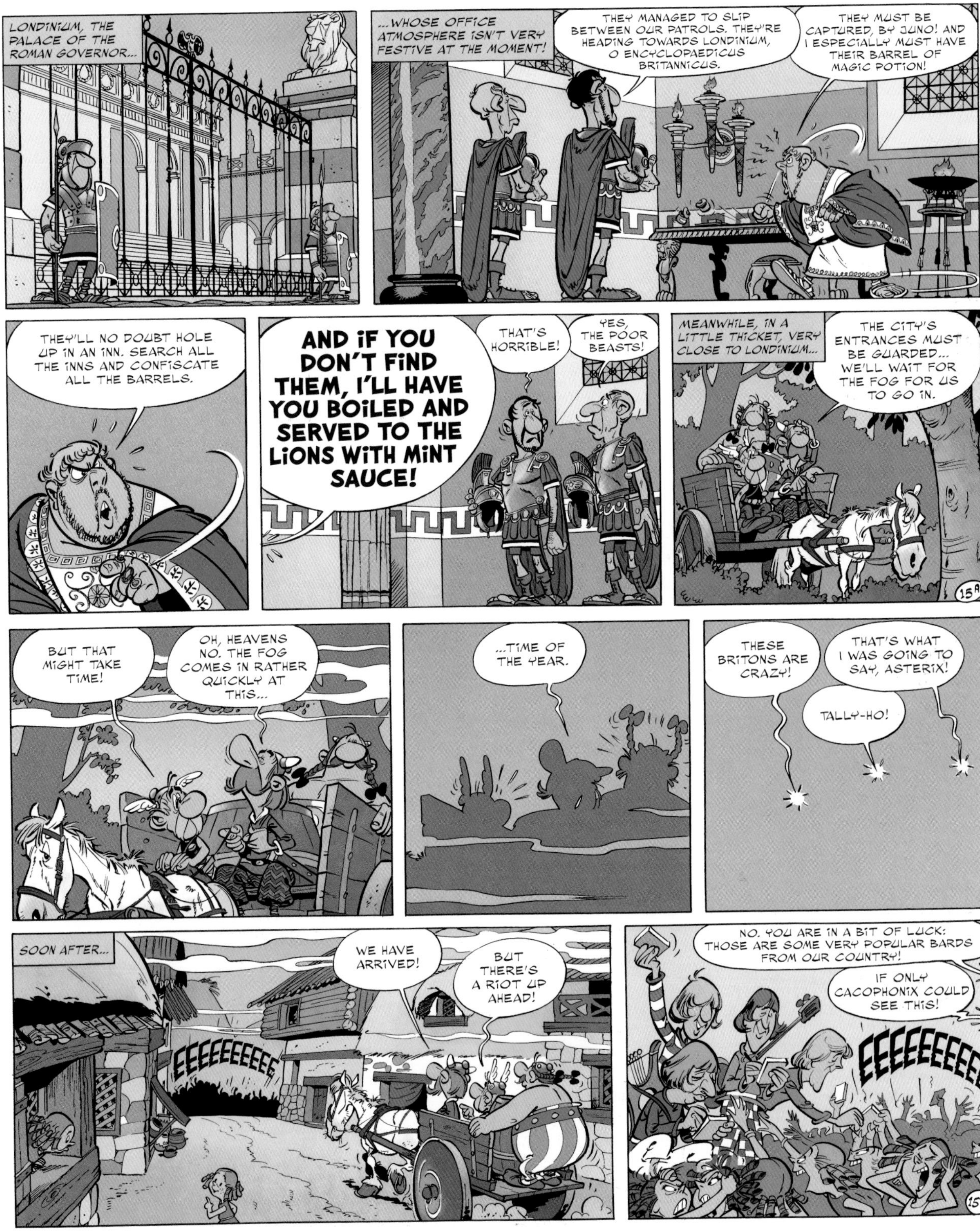
LONDINIUM, THE PALACE OF THE ROMAN GOVERNOR...
...WHOSE OFFICE ATMOSPHERE ISN'T VERY FESTIVE AT THE MOMENT!
THEY MANAGED TO SLIP BETWEEN OUR PATROLS. THEY'RE HEADING TOWARDS LONDINIUM, O ENCYCLOPAEDICUS BRITANNICUS.
THEY MUST BE CAPTURED, BY JUNO! AND I ESPECIALLY MUST HAVE THEIR BARREL OF MAGIC POTION!
THEY'LL NO DOUBT HOLE UP IN AN INN. SEARCH ALL THE INNS AND CONFISCATE ALL THE BARRELS.
AND IF YOU DON'T FIND THEM, I'LL HAVE YOU BOILED AND SERVED TO THE LIONS WITH MINT SAUCE!
THAT'S HORRIBLE!
YES, THE POOR BEASTS!
MEANWHILE, IN A LITTLE THICKET, VERY CLOSE TO LONDINIUM...
THE CITY'S ENTRANCES MUST BE GUARDED... WE'LL WAIT FOR THE FOG FOR US TO GO IN.
15A
BUT THAT MIGHT TAKE TIME!
OH, HEAVENS NO. THE FOG COMES IN RATHER QUICKLY AT THIS...
...TIME OF THE YEAR.
THESE BRITONS ARE CRAZY!
THAT'S WHAT I WAS GOING TO SAY, ASTERIX!
TALLY-HO!
SOON AFTER...
WE HAVE ARRIVED!
BUT THERE'S A RIOT UP AHEAD!
EEEEEEEEEE
NO. YOU ARE IN A BIT OF LUCK: THOSE ARE SOME VERY POPULAR BARDS FROM OUR COUNTRY!
IF ONLY CACOPHONIX COULD SEE THIS!
EEEEEEEEEE
15B

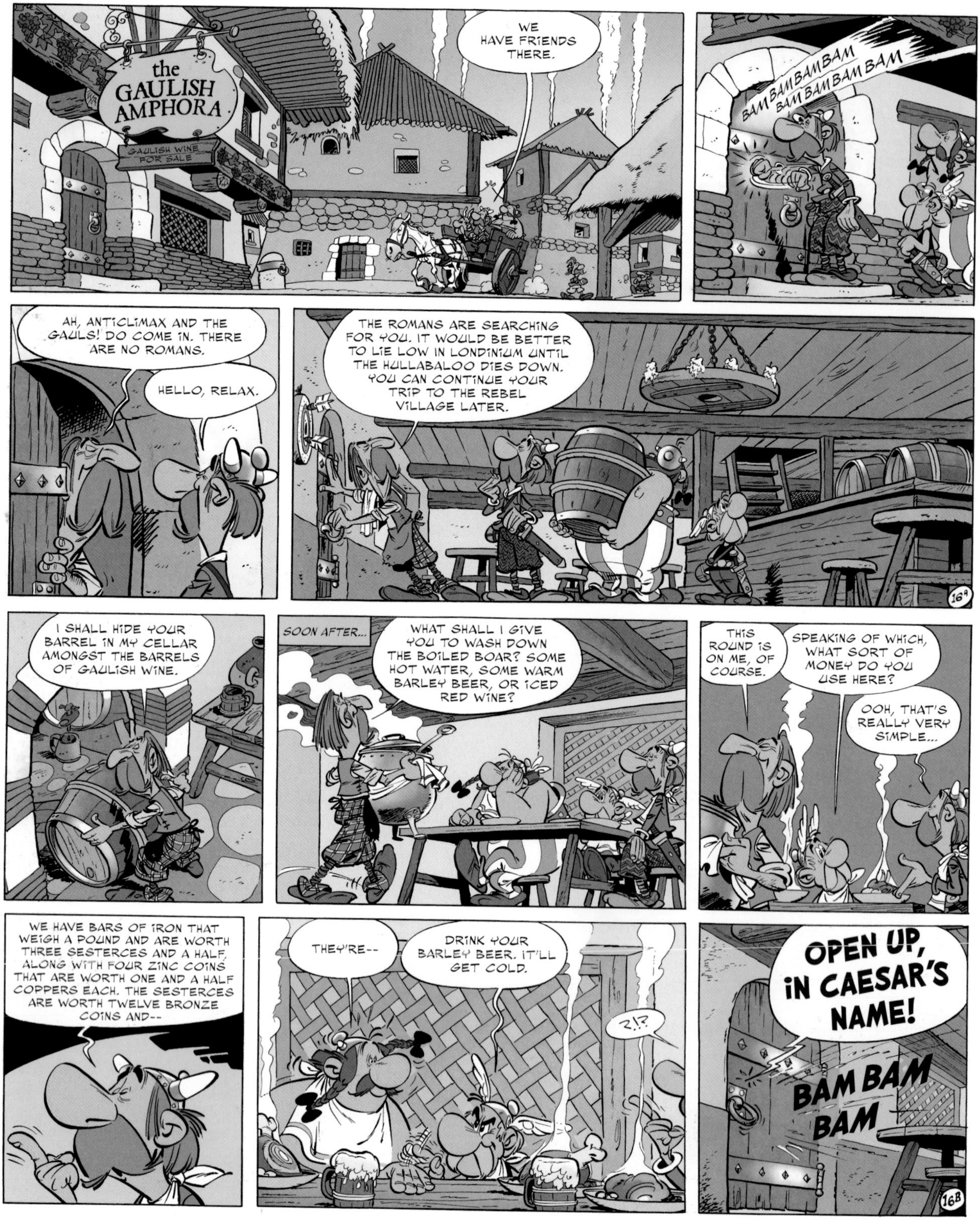
the GAULISH AMPHORA
GAULISH WINE FOR SALE
WE HAVE FRIENDS THERE.
BAM BAM BAM BAM
BAM BAM BAM BAM
AH, ANTICLIMAX AND THE GAULS! DO COME IN. THERE ARE NO ROMANS.
HELLO, RELAX.
THE ROMANS ARE SEARCHING FOR YOU. IT WOULD BE BETTER TO LIE LOW IN LONDINIUM UNTIL THE HULLABALOO DIES DOWN. YOU CAN CONTINUE YOUR TRIP TO THE REBEL VILLAGE LATER.
I SHALL HIDE YOUR BARREL IN MY CELLAR AMONGST THE BARRELS OF GAULISH WINE.
SOON AFTER...
WHAT SHALL I GIVE YOU TO WASH DOWN THE BOILED BOAR? SOME HOT WATER, SOME WARM BARLEY BEER, OR ICED RED WINE?
THIS ROUND IS ON ME, OF COURSE.
SPEAKING OF WHICH, WHAT SORT OF MONEY DO YOU USE HERE?
OOH, THAT'S REALLY VERY SIMPLE...
WE HAVE BARS OF IRON THAT WEIGH A POUND AND ARE WORTH THREE SESTERCES AND A HALF, ALONG WITH FOUR ZINC COINS THAT ARE WORTH ONE AND A HALF COPPERS EACH. THE SESTERCES ARE WORTH TWELVE BRONZE COINS AND--
THEY'RE--
DRINK YOUR BARLEY BEER. IT'LL GET COLD.
?!?
OPEN UP, IN CAESAR'S NAME!
BAM BAM BAM

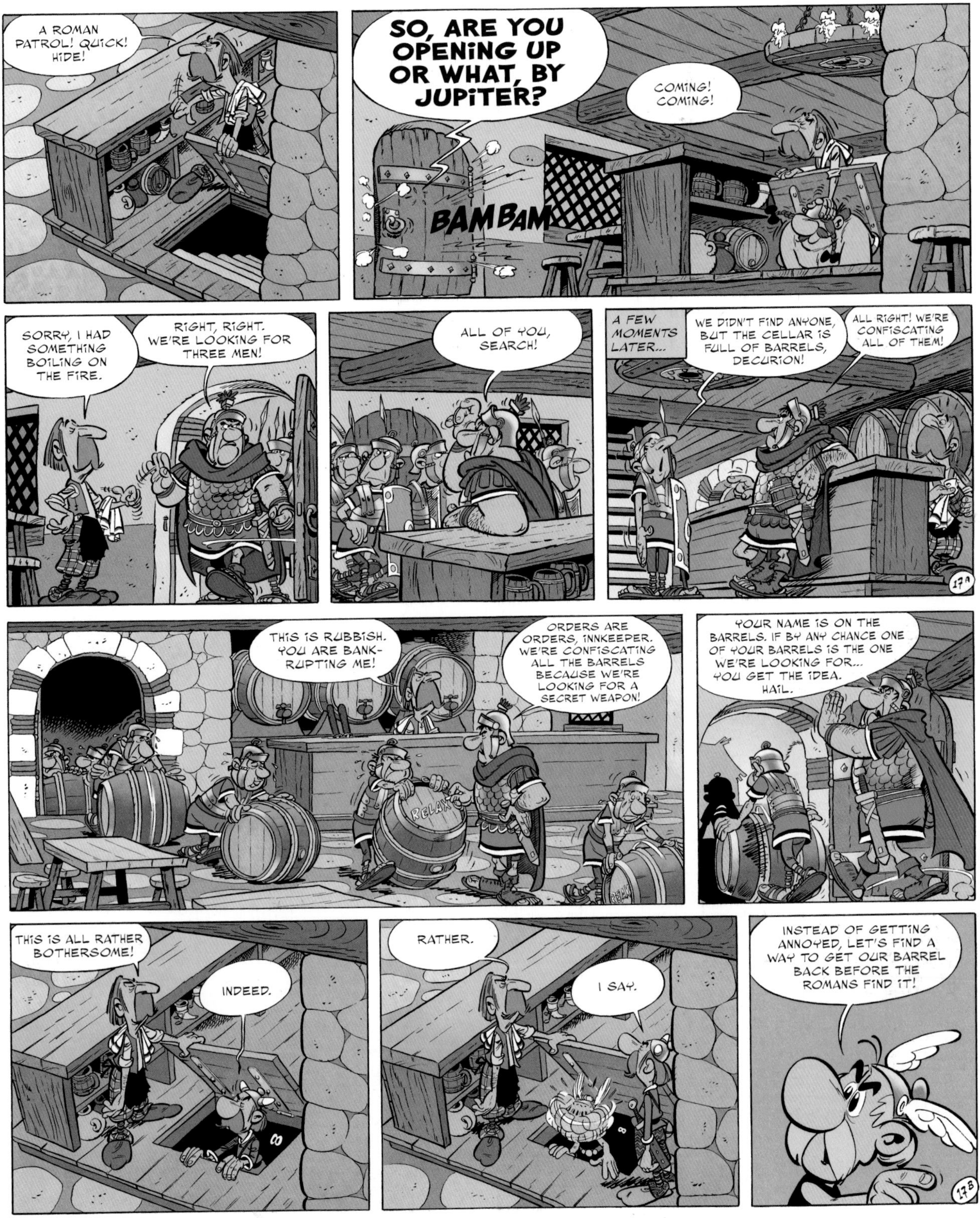

A ROMAN PATROL! QUICK! HIDE!
SO, ARE YOU OPENING UP OR WHAT, BY JUPITER?
BAM BAM
COMING! COMING!
SORRY, I HAD SOMETHING BOILING ON THE FIRE.
RIGHT, RIGHT. WE'RE LOOKING FOR THREE MEN!
ALL OF YOU, SEARCH!
A FEW MOMENTS LATER...
WE DIDN'T FIND ANYONE, BUT THE CELLAR IS FULL OF BARRELS, DECURION!
ALL RIGHT! WE'RE CONFISCATING ALL OF THEM!
THIS IS RUBBISH. YOU ARE BANK-RUPTING ME!
ORDERS ARE ORDERS, INNKEEPER. WE'RE CONFISCATING ALL THE BARRELS BECAUSE WE'RE LOOKING FOR A SECRET WEAPON!
RELAX
YOUR NAME IS ON THE BARRELS. IF BY ANY CHANCE ONE OF YOUR BARRELS IS THE ONE WE'RE LOOKING FOR... YOU GET THE IDEA. HAIL.
THIS IS ALL RATHER BOTHERSOME!
INDEED.
RATHER.
I SAY.
INSTEAD OF GETTING ANNOYED, LET'S FIND A WAY TO GET OUR BARREL BACK BEFORE THE ROMANS FIND IT!

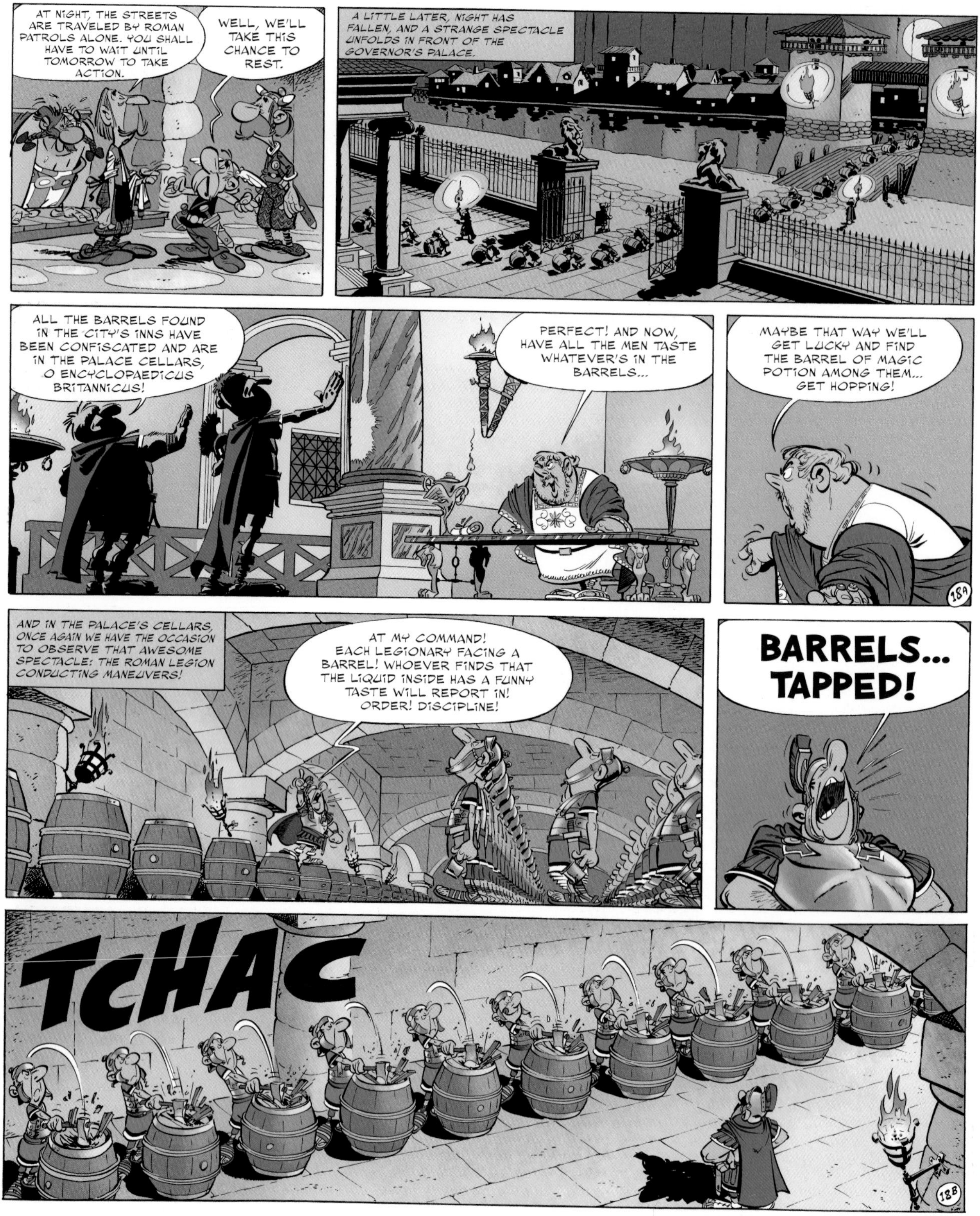

AT NIGHT, THE STREETS ARE TRAVELED BY ROMAN PATROLS ALONE. YOU SHALL HAVE TO WAIT UNTIL TOMORROW TO TAKE ACTION.
WELL, WE'LL TAKE THIS CHANCE TO REST.
A LITTLE LATER, NIGHT HAS FALLEN, AND A STRANGE SPECTACLE UNFOLDS IN FRONT OF THE GOVERNOR'S PALACE.
ALL THE BARRELS FOUND IN THE CITY'S INNS HAVE BEEN CONFISCATED AND ARE IN THE PALACE CELLARS, O ENCYCLOPAEDICUS BRITANNICUS!
PERFECT! AND NOW, HAVE ALL THE MEN TASTE WHATEVER'S IN THE BARRELS...
MAYBE THAT WAY WE'LL GET LUCKY AND FIND THE BARREL OF MAGIC POTION AMONG THEM... GET HOPPING!
18A
AND IN THE PALACE'S CELLARS, ONCE AGAIN WE HAVE THE OCCASION TO OBSERVE THAT AWESOME SPECTACLE: THE ROMAN LEGION CONDUCTING MANEUVERS!
AT MY COMMAND! EACH LEGIONARY FACING A BARREL! WHOEVER FINDS THAT THE LIQUID INSIDE HAS A FUNNY TASTE WILL REPORT IN! ORDER! DISCIPLINE!
BARRELS... TAPPED!
TCHAC
18B

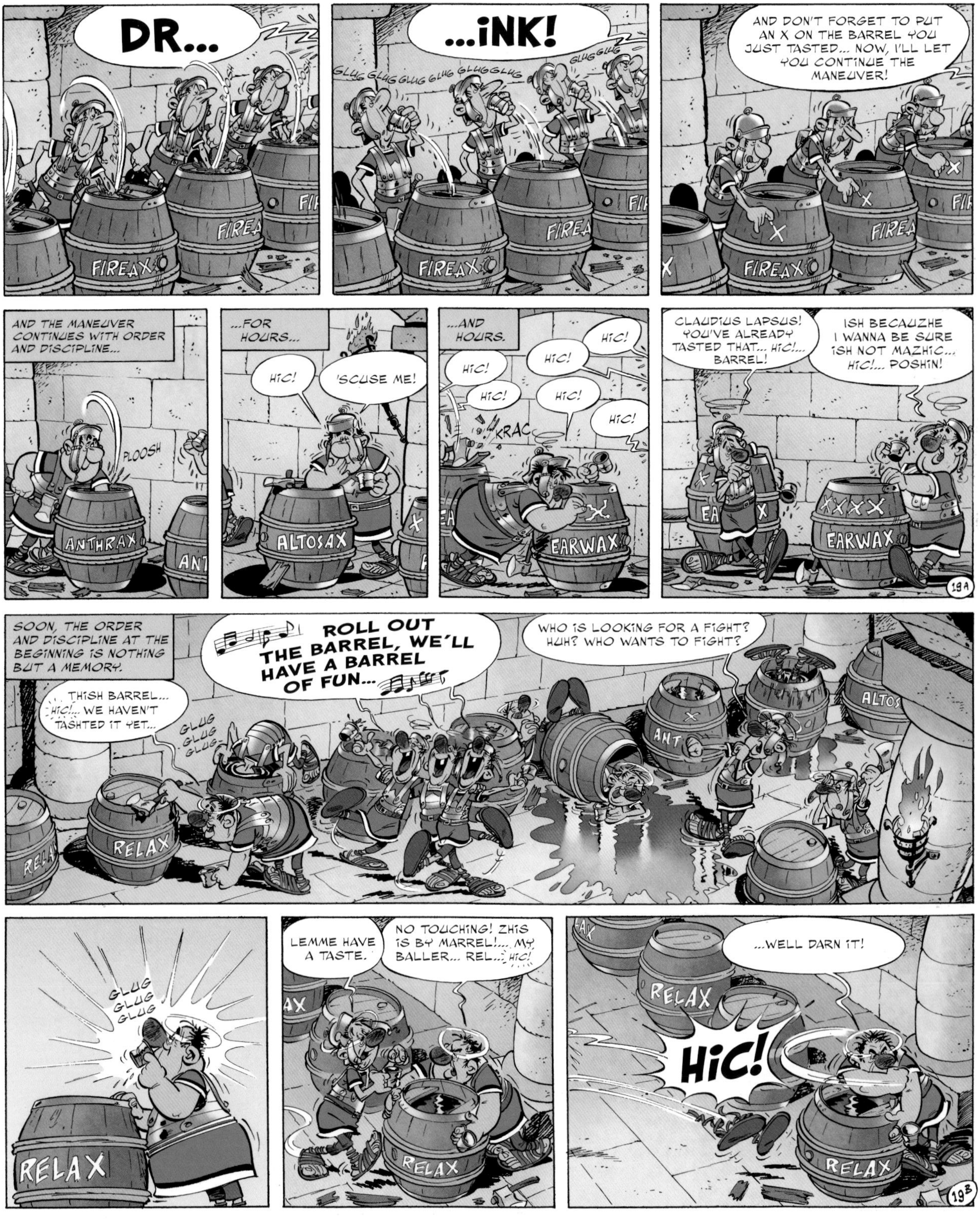
DR...
...iNK!
GLUG GLUG GLUG GLUG GLUG GLUG
AND DON'T FORGET TO PUT AN X ON THE BARREL YOU JUST TASTED... NOW, I'LL LET YOU CONTINUE THE MANEUVER!
FIREAX
AND THE MANEUVER CONTINUES WITH ORDER AND DISCIPLINE...
PLOOSH
ANTHRAX
...FOR HOURS...
HIC!
'SCUSE ME!
ALTOSAX
...AND HOURS.
HIC!
HIC!
HIC!
HIC!
HIC!
HIC!
KRAC
EARWAX
CLAUDIUS LAPSUS! YOU'VE ALREADY TASTED THAT... HIC!... BARREL!
ISH BECAUZHE I WANNA BE SURE ISH NOT MAZHIC... HIC!... POSHIN!
EARWAX
SOON, THE ORDER AND DISCIPLINE AT THE BEGINNING IS NOTHING BUT A MEMORY.
ROLL OUT THE BARREL, WE'LL HAVE A BARREL OF FUN...
WHO IS LOOKING FOR A FIGHT? HUH? WHO WANTS TO FIGHT?
THISH BARREL... HIC!... WE HAVEN'T TASHTED IT YET...
GLUG GLUG GLUG
RELAX
ANT
ALTOS
GLUG GLUG GLUG
RELAX
LEMME HAVE A TASTE.
NO TOUCHING! ZHIS IS BY MARREL!... MY BALLER... REL... HIC!
RELAX
...WELL DARN IT!
HIC!
RELAX

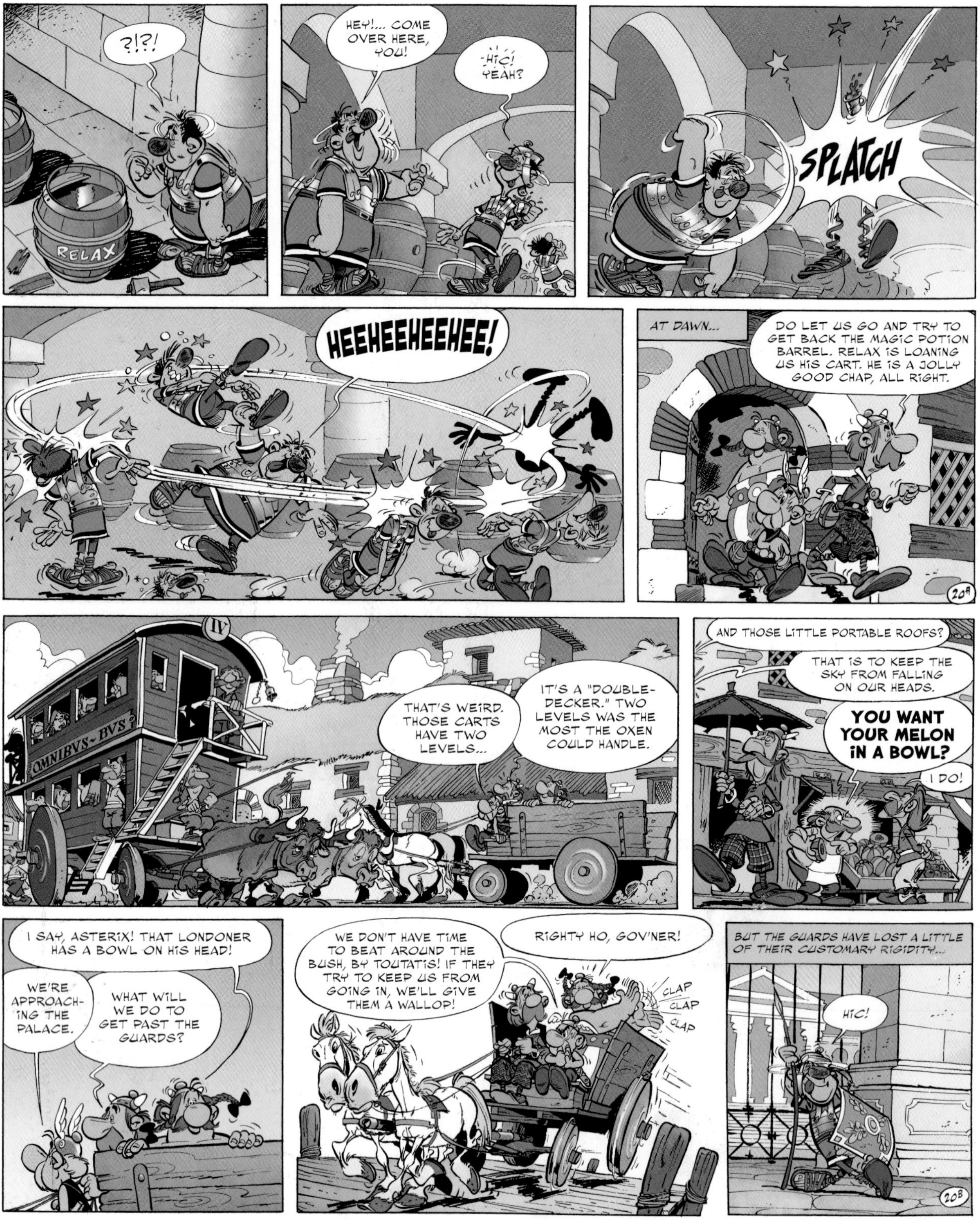
?!?!
HEY!... COME OVER HERE, YOU!
-HIC! YEAH?
SPLATCH
HEEHEEHEEHEE!
AT DAWN...
DO LET US GO AND TRY TO GET BACK THE MAGIC POTION BARREL. RELAX IS LOANING US HIS CART. HE IS A JOLLY GOOD CHAP, ALL RIGHT.
OMNIBVS-BVS
THAT'S WEIRD. THOSE CARTS HAVE TWO LEVELS...
IT'S A "DOUBLE-DECKER." TWO LEVELS WAS THE MOST THE OXEN COULD HANDLE.
AND THOSE LITTLE PORTABLE ROOFS?
THAT IS TO KEEP THE SKY FROM FALLING ON OUR HEADS.
YOU WANT YOUR MELON IN A BOWL?
I DO!
I SAY, ASTERIX! THAT LONDONER HAS A BOWL ON HIS HEAD!
WE'RE APPROACHING THE PALACE.
WHAT WILL WE DO TO GET PAST THE GUARDS?
WE DON'T HAVE TIME TO BEAT AROUND THE BUSH, BY TOUTATIS! IF THEY TRY TO KEEP US FROM GOING IN, WE'LL GIVE THEM A WALLOP!
RIGHTY HO, GOV'NER!
CLAP CLAP CLAP
BUT THE GUARDS HAVE LOST A LITTLE OF THEIR CUSTOMARY RIGIDITY...
HIC!

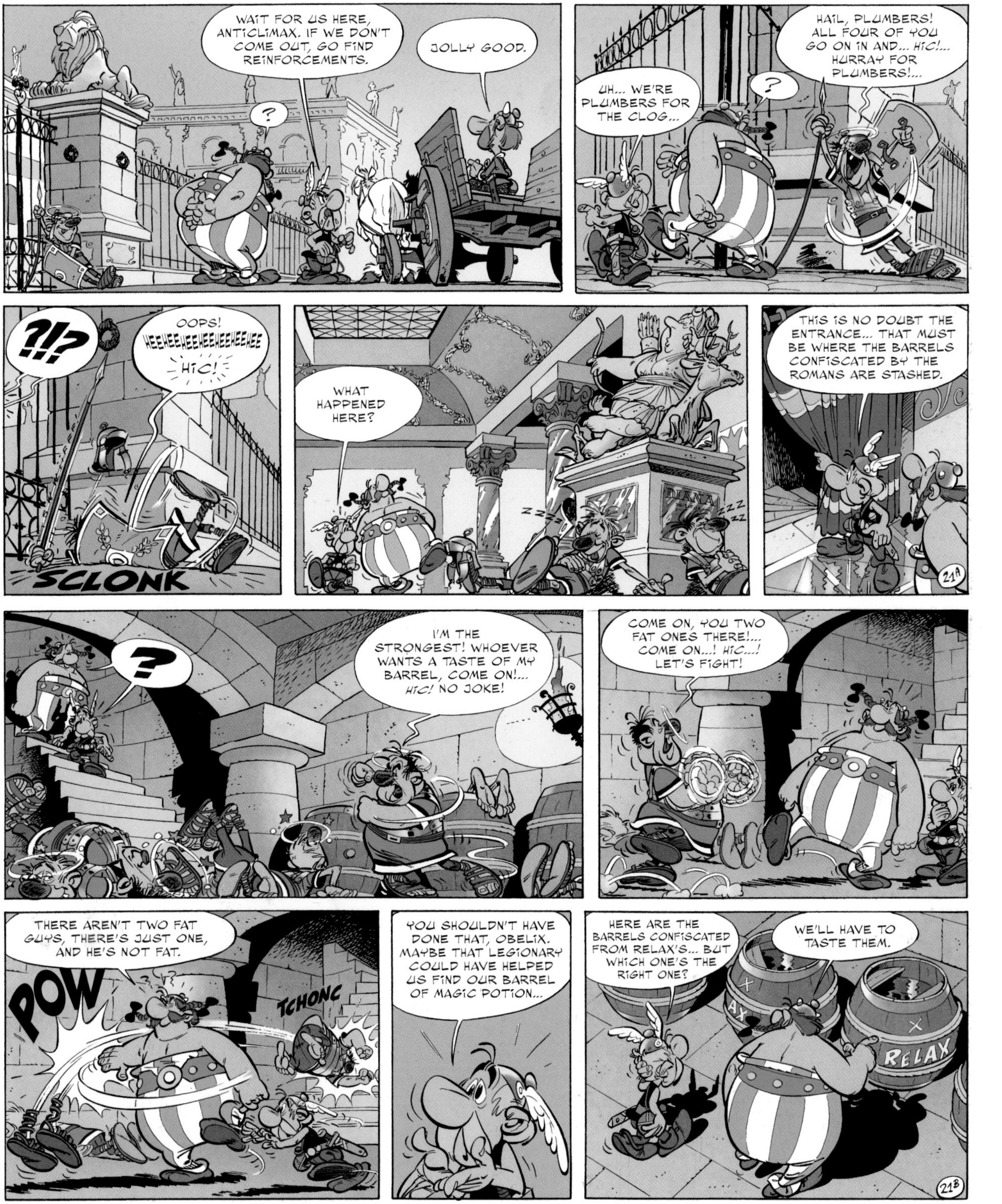
WAIT FOR US HERE, ANTICLIMAX. IF WE DON'T COME OUT, GO FIND REINFORCEMENTS.
?
JOLLY GOOD.
UH... WE'RE PLUMBERS FOR THE CLOG...
?
HAIL, PLUMBERS! ALL FOUR OF YOU GO ON IN AND... HIC!... HURRAY FOR PLUMBERS!...
?!?
OOPS! HEEHEEHEEHEEHEEHEEHEE HIC!
SCLONK
WHAT HAPPENED HERE?
DIANA
THIS IS NO DOUBT THE ENTRANCE... THAT MUST BE WHERE THE BARRELS CONFISCATED BY THE ROMANS ARE STASHED.
21A
?
I'M THE STRONGEST! WHOEVER WANTS A TASTE OF MY BARREL, COME ON!... HIC! NO JOKE!
COME ON, YOU TWO FAT ONES THERE!... COME ON...! HIC...! LET'S FIGHT!
THERE AREN'T TWO FAT GUYS, THERE'S JUST ONE, AND HE'S NOT FAT.
POW
TCHONC
YOU SHOULDN'T HAVE DONE THAT, OBELIX. MAYBE THAT LEGIONARY COULD HAVE HELPED US FIND OUR BARREL OF MAGIC POTION...
HERE ARE THE BARRELS CONFISCATED FROM RELAX'S... BUT WHICH ONE'S THE RIGHT ONE?
WE'LL HAVE TO TASTE THEM.
RELAX
21B

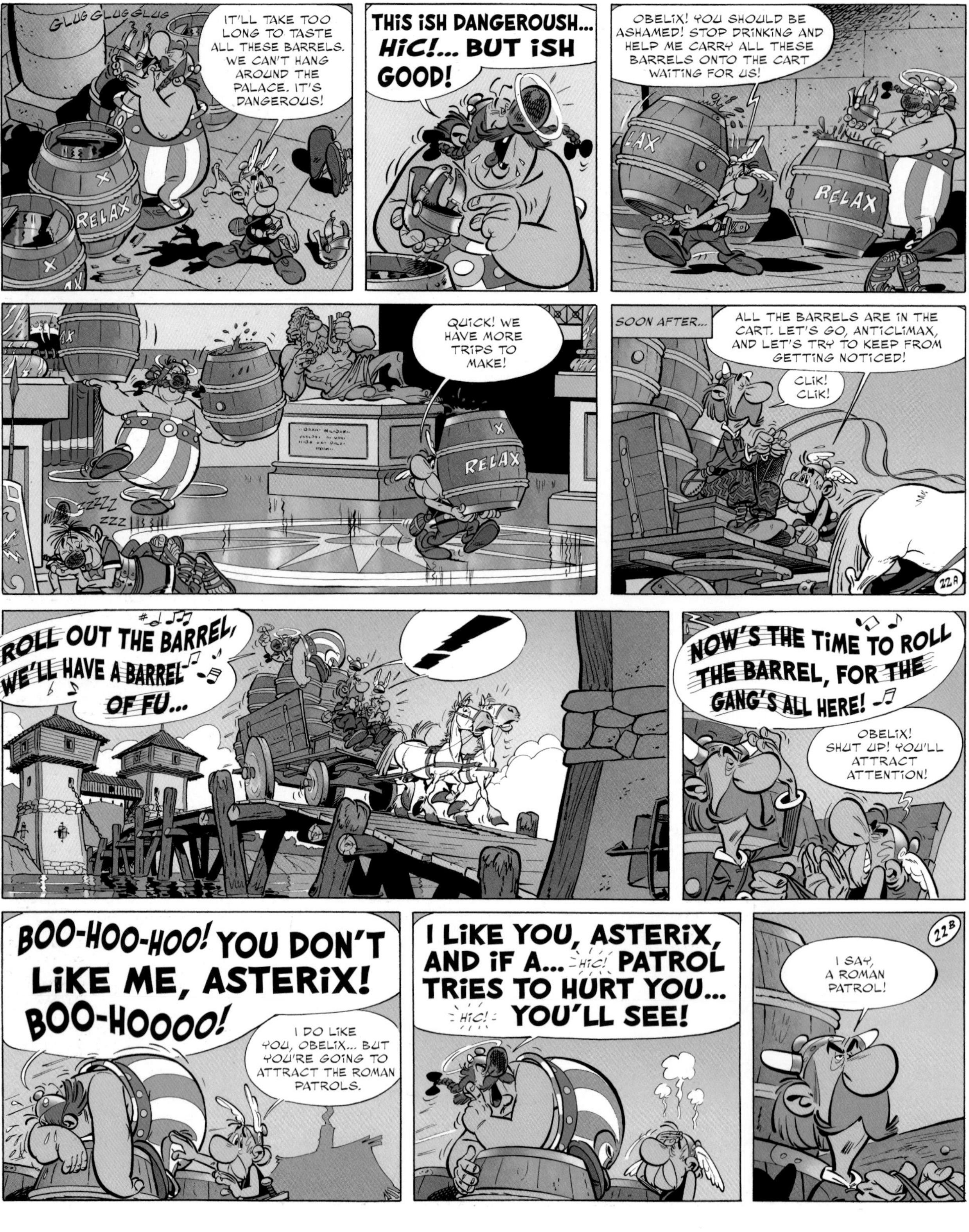
GLUG GLUG GLUG
IT'LL TAKE TOO LONG TO TASTE ALL THESE BARRELS. WE CAN'T HANG AROUND THE PALACE. IT'S DANGEROUS!
RELAX
THIS ISH DANGEROUSH... HIC!... BUT ISH GOOD!
OBELIX! YOU SHOULD BE ASHAMED! STOP DRINKING AND HELP ME CARRY ALL THESE BARRELS ONTO THE CART WAITING FOR US!
LAX
RELAX
QUICK! WE HAVE MORE TRIPS TO MAKE!
RELAX
ZZZZZ
ZZZ
SOON AFTER...
ALL THE BARRELS ARE IN THE CART. LET'S GO, ANTICLIMAX, AND LET'S TRY TO KEEP FROM GETTING NOTICED!
CLIK! CLIK!
22A
ROLL OUT THE BARREL, WE'LL HAVE A BARREL OF FU...
NOW'S THE TIME TO ROLL THE BARREL, FOR THE GANG'S ALL HERE!
OBELIX! SHUT UP! YOU'LL ATTRACT ATTENTION!
BOO-HOO-HOO! YOU DON'T LIKE ME, ASTERIX! BOO-HOOOO!
I DO LIKE YOU, OBELIX... BUT YOU'RE GOING TO ATTRACT THE ROMAN PATROLS.
I LIKE YOU, ASTERIX, AND IF A... HIC! PATROL TRIES TO HURT YOU... HIC! YOU'LL SEE!
22B
I SAY, A ROMAN PATROL!

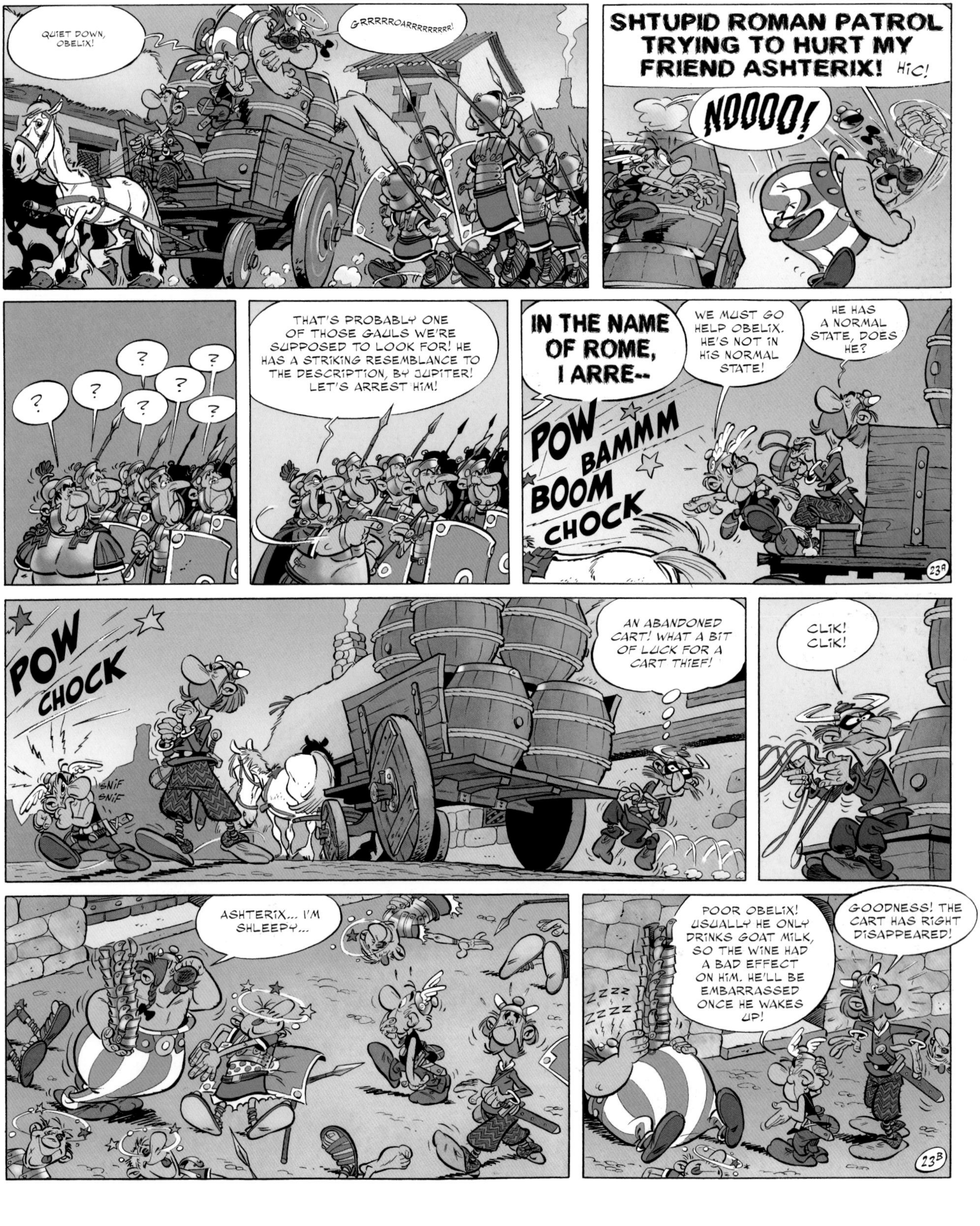
QUIET DOWN, OBELIX!
GRRRRROARRRRRRRR!
SHTUPID ROMAN PATROL TRYING TO HURT MY FRIEND ASHTERIX! HIC!
NOOOO!
?
THAT'S PROBABLY ONE OF THOSE GAULS WE'RE SUPPOSED TO LOOK FOR! HE HAS A STRIKING RESEMBLANCE TO THE DESCRIPTION, BY JUPITER! LET'S ARREST HIM!
IN THE NAME OF ROME, I ARRE--
WE MUST GO HELP OBELIX. HE'S NOT IN HIS NORMAL STATE!
HE HAS A NORMAL STATE, DOES HE?
POW BAMMM BOOM CHOCK
23A
POW CHOCK
SNIF SNIF
AN ABANDONED CART! WHAT A BIT OF LUCK FOR A CART THIEF!
CLIK! CLIK!
ASHTERIX... I'M SHLEEPY...
ZZZZ ZZZZ
POOR OBELIX! USUALLY HE ONLY DRINKS GOAT MILK, SO THE WINE HAD A BAD EFFECT ON HIM. HE'LL BE EMBARRASSED ONCE HE WAKES UP!
GOODNESS! THE CART HAS RIGHT DISAPPEARED!
23B

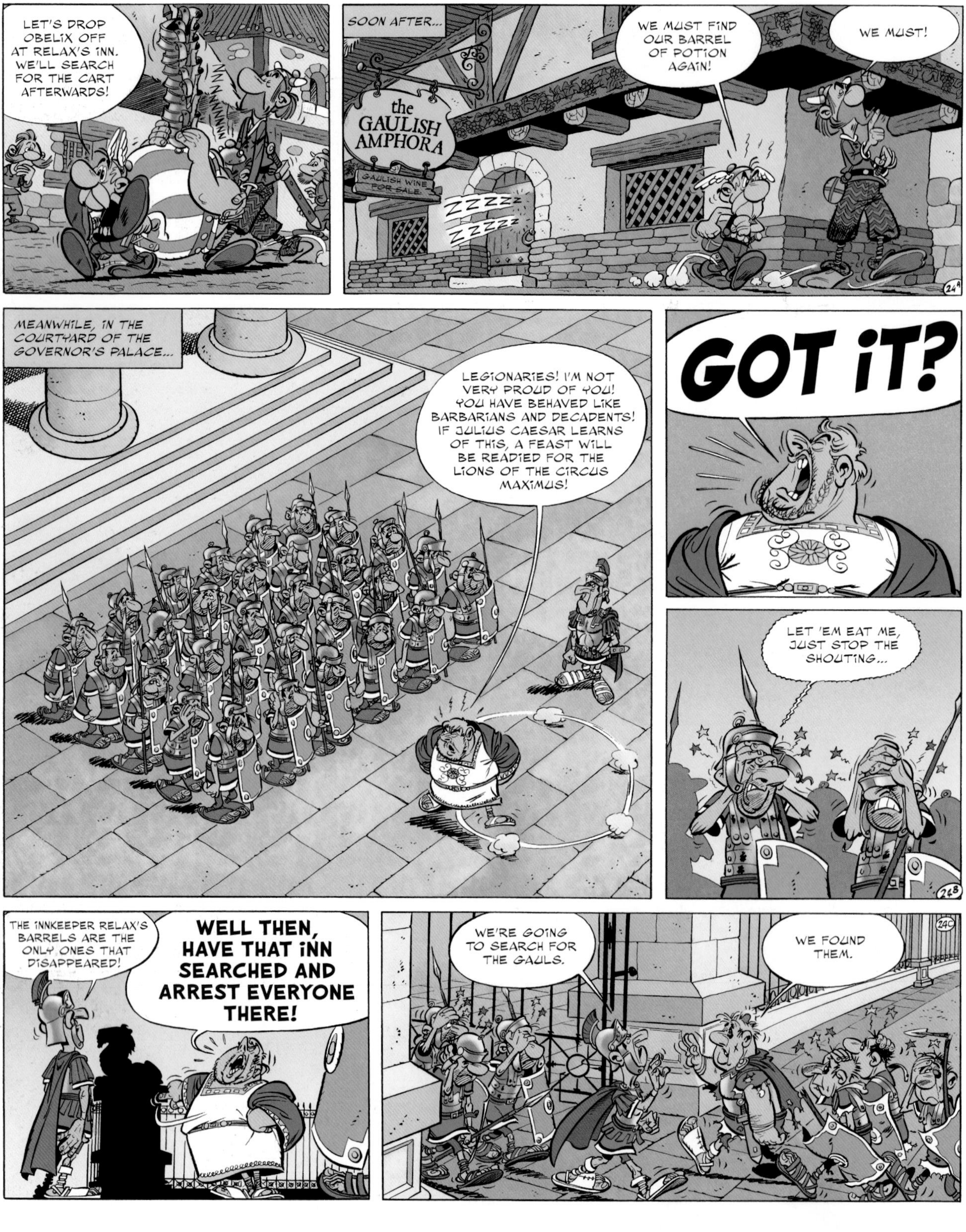
LET'S DROP OBELIX OFF AT RELAX'S INN. WE'LL SEARCH FOR THE CART AFTERWARDS!
ZZZZZZZZZ
SOON AFTER...
the GAULISH AMPHORA
GAULISH WINE FOR SALE
ZZZZZ
ZZZZZ
WE MUST FIND OUR BARREL OF POTION AGAIN!
WE MUST!
24A
MEANWHILE, IN THE COURTYARD OF THE GOVERNOR'S PALACE...
LEGIONARIES! I'M NOT VERY PROUD OF YOU! YOU HAVE BEHAVED LIKE BARBARIANS AND DECADENTS! IF JULIUS CAESAR LEARNS OF THIS, A FEAST WILL BE READIED FOR THE LIONS OF THE CIRCUS MAXIMUS!
GOT IT?
LET 'EM EAT ME, JUST STOP THE SHOUTING...
24B
THE INNKEEPER RELAX'S BARRELS ARE THE ONLY ONES THAT DISAPPEARED!
WELL THEN, HAVE THAT INN SEARCHED AND ARREST EVERYONE THERE!
24C
WE'RE GOING TO SEARCH FOR THE GAULS.
WE FOUND THEM.

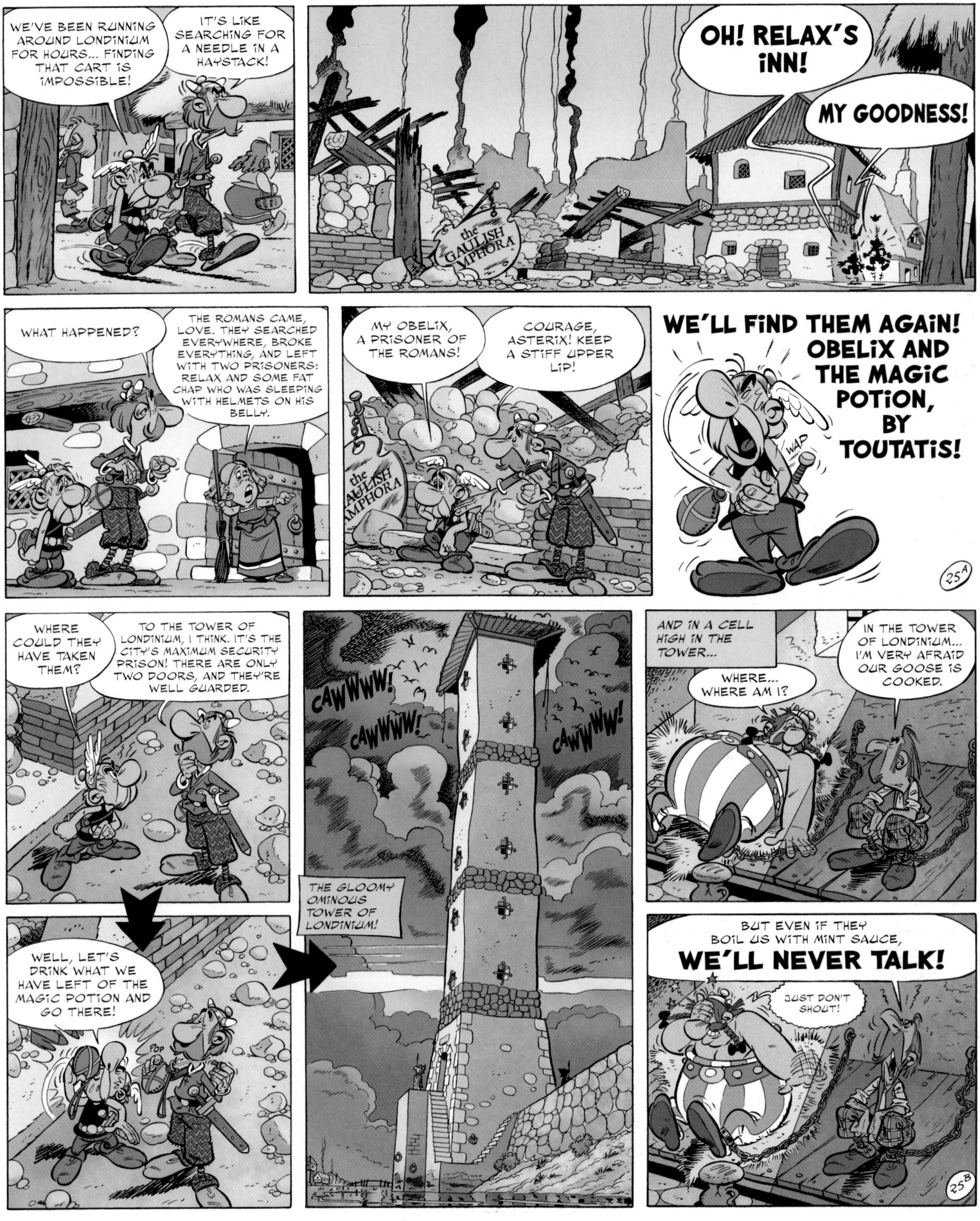

WE'VE BEEN RUNNING AROUND LONDINIUM FOR HOURS... FINDING THAT CART IS IMPOSSIBLE!
IT'S LIKE SEARCHING FOR A NEEDLE IN A HAYSTACK!
the GAULISH AMPHORA
OH! RELAX'S INN!
MY GOODNESS!
WHAT HAPPENED?
THE ROMANS CAME, LOVE. THEY SEARCHED EVERYWHERE, BROKE EVERYTHING, AND LEFT WITH TWO PRISONERS: RELAX AND SOME FAT CHAP WHO WAS SLEEPING WITH HELMETS ON HIS BELLY.
MY OBELIX, A PRISONER OF THE ROMANS!
COURAGE, ASTERIX! KEEP A STIFF UPPER LIP!
the GAULISH AMPHORA
WE'LL FIND THEM AGAIN! OBELIX AND THE MAGIC POTION, BY TOUTATIS!
WAP
25A
WHERE COULD THEY HAVE TAKEN THEM?
TO THE TOWER OF LONDINIUM, I THINK. IT'S THE CITY'S MAXIMUM SECURITY PRISON! THERE ARE ONLY TWO DOORS, AND THEY'RE WELL GUARDED.
WELL, LET'S DRINK WHAT WE HAVE LEFT OF THE MAGIC POTION AND GO THERE!
POP
CAWWWW!
CAWWWW!
CAWWWW!
THE GLOOMY OMINOUS TOWER OF LONDINIUM!
AND IN A CELL HIGH IN THE TOWER...
WHERE... WHERE AM I?
IN THE TOWER OF LONDINIUM... I'M VERY AFRAID OUR GOOSE IS COOKED.
BUT EVEN IF THEY BOIL US WITH MINT SAUCE, WE'LL NEVER TALK!
JUST DON'T SHOUT!
25B

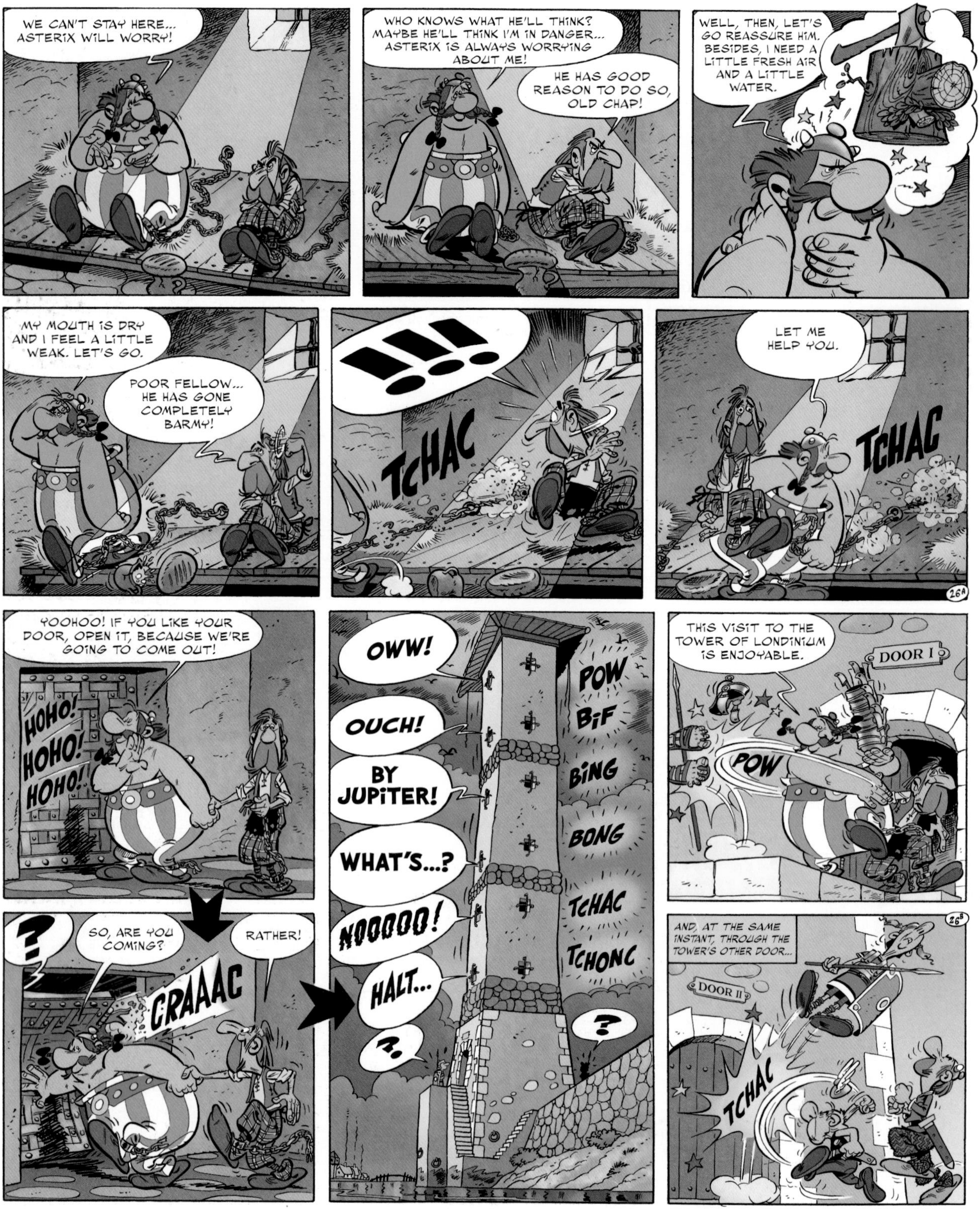

WE CAN'T STAY HERE... ASTERIX WILL WORRY!
WHO KNOWS WHAT HE'LL THINK? MAYBE HE'LL THINK I'M IN DANGER... ASTERIX IS ALWAYS WORRYING ABOUT ME!
HE HAS GOOD REASON TO DO SO, OLD CHAP!
WELL, THEN, LET'S GO REASSURE HIM. BESIDES, I NEED A LITTLE FRESH AIR AND A LITTLE WATER.
MY MOUTH IS DRY AND I FEEL A LITTLE WEAK. LET'S GO.
POOR FELLOW... HE HAS GONE COMPLETELY BARMY!
!!!
TCHAC
LET ME HELP YOU.
TCHAC
YOOHOO! IF YOU LIKE YOUR DOOR, OPEN IT, BECAUSE WE'RE GOING TO COME OUT!
HOHO! HOHO! HOHO!
?
SO, ARE YOU COMING?
RATHER!
CRAAAC
OWW!
OUCH!
BY JUPITER!
WHAT'S...?
NOOOOO!
HALT...
?
POW
BIF
BING
BONG
TCHAC
TCHONC
?
THIS VISIT TO THE TOWER OF LONDINIUM IS ENJOYABLE.
DOOR I
POW
AND, AT THE SAME INSTANT, THROUGH THE TOWER'S OTHER DOOR...
DOOR II
TCHAC

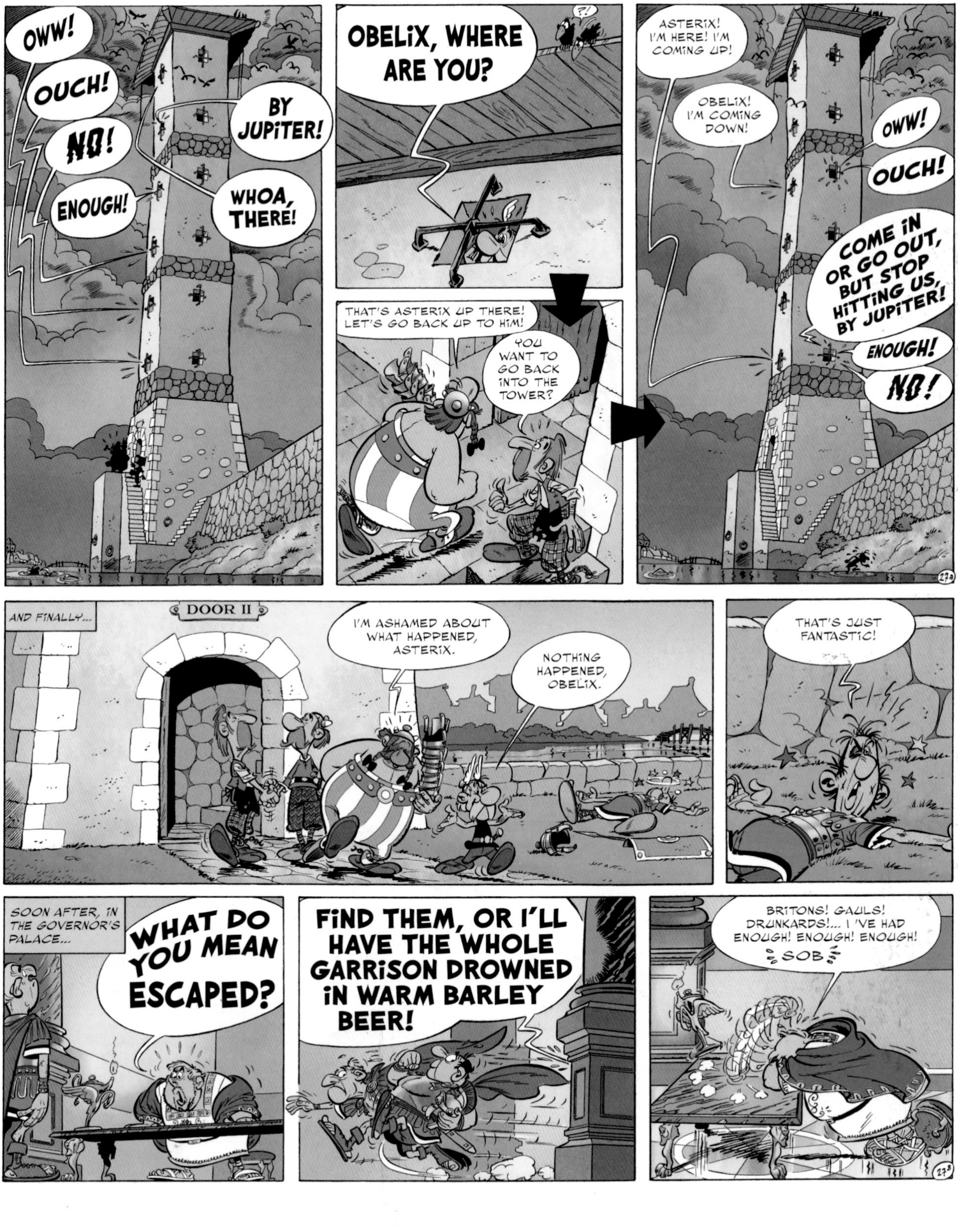
OWW!
OUCH!
NO!
ENOUGH!
BY JUPITER!
WHOA, THERE!
OBELIX, WHERE ARE YOU?
?!
THAT'S ASTERIX UP THERE! LET'S GO BACK UP TO HIM!
YOU WANT TO GO BACK INTO THE TOWER?
ASTERIX! I'M HERE! I'M COMING UP!
OBELIX! I'M COMING DOWN!
OWW!
OUCH!
COME IN OR GO OUT, BUT STOP HITTING US, BY JUPITER!
ENOUGH!
NO!
27A
AND FINALLY...
DOOR II
I'M ASHAMED ABOUT WHAT HAPPENED, ASTERIX.
NOTHING HAPPENED, OBELIX.
THAT'S JUST FANTASTIC!
SOON AFTER, IN THE GOVERNOR'S PALACE...
WHAT DO YOU MEAN ESCAPED?
FIND THEM, OR I'LL HAVE THE WHOLE GARRISON DROWNED IN WARM BARLEY BEER!
BRITONS! GAULS! DRUNKARDS!... I'VE HAD ENOUGH! ENOUGH! ENOUGH!
SOB

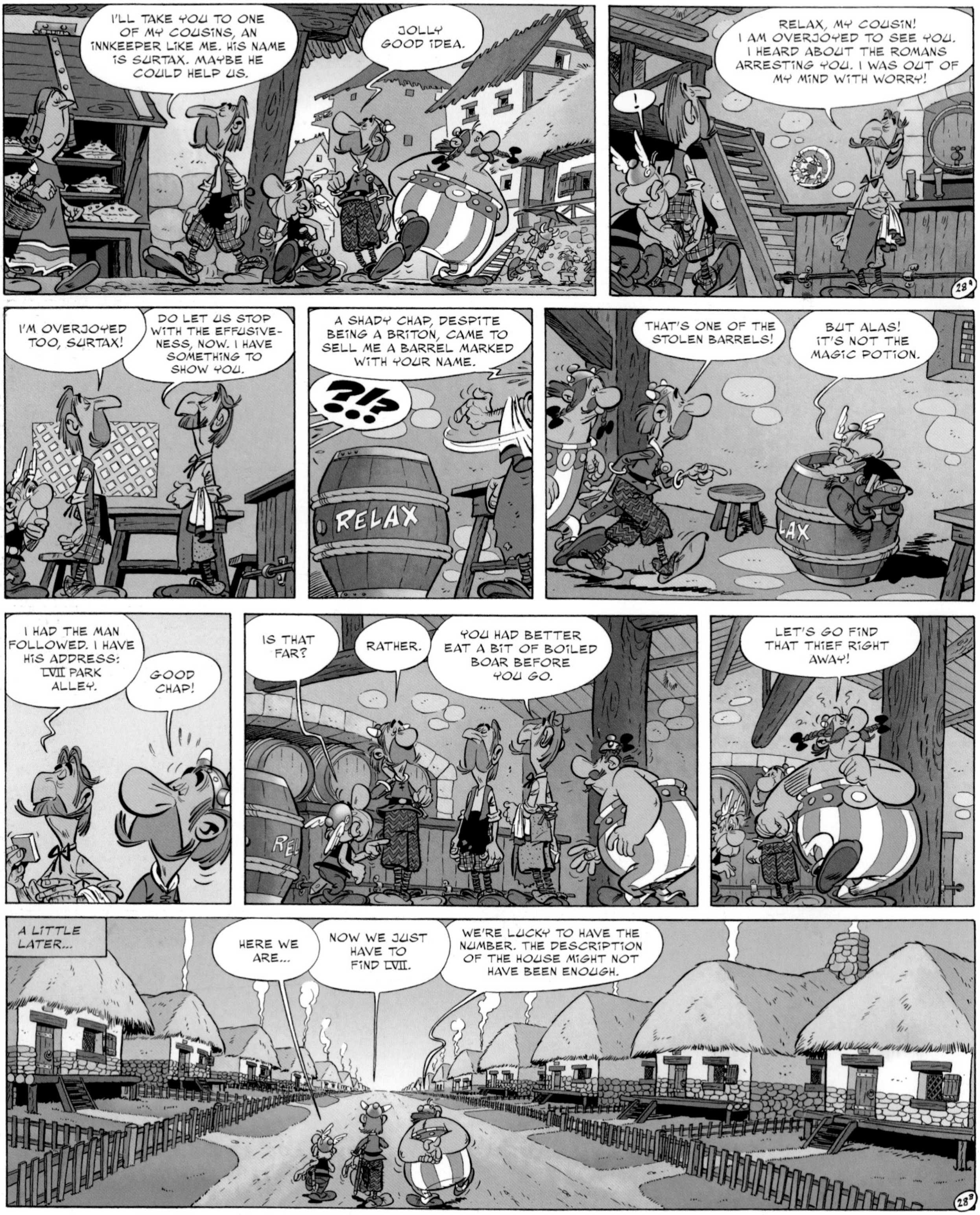
I'LL TAKE YOU TO ONE OF MY COUSINS, AN INNKEEPER LIKE ME. HIS NAME IS SURTAX. MAYBE HE COULD HELP US.
JOLLY GOOD IDEA.
!
RELAX, MY COUSIN! I AM OVERJOYED TO SEE YOU. I HEARD ABOUT THE ROMANS ARRESTING YOU. I WAS OUT OF MY MIND WITH WORRY!
I'M OVERJOYED TOO, SURTAX!
DO LET US STOP WITH THE EFFUSIVENESS, NOW. I HAVE SOMETHING TO SHOW YOU.
A SHADY CHAP, DESPITE BEING A BRITON, CAME TO SELL ME A BARREL MARKED WITH YOUR NAME.
?!?
RELAX
THAT'S ONE OF THE STOLEN BARRELS!
BUT ALAS! IT'S NOT THE MAGIC POTION.
LAX
I HAD THE MAN FOLLOWED. I HAVE HIS ADDRESS: LVII PARK ALLEY.
GOOD CHAP!
IS THAT FAR?
RATHER.
YOU HAD BETTER EAT A BIT OF BOILED BOAR BEFORE YOU GO.
REL
LET'S GO FIND THAT THIEF RIGHT AWAY!
A LITTLE LATER...
HERE WE ARE...
NOW WE JUST HAVE TO FIND LVII.
WE'RE LUCKY TO HAVE THE NUMBER. THE DESCRIPTION OF THE HOUSE MIGHT NOT HAVE BEEN ENOUGH.

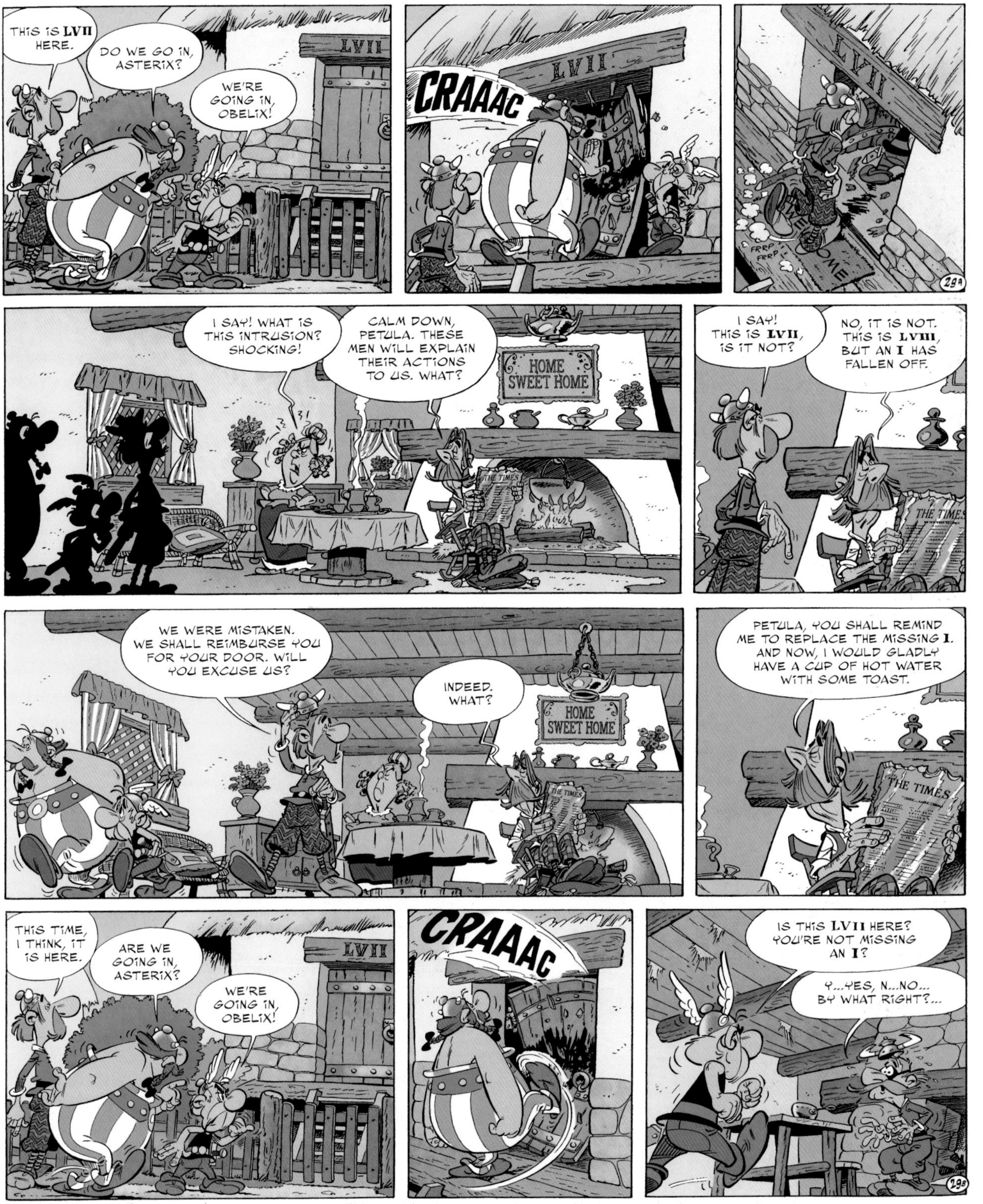
THIS IS LVII HERE.
DO WE GO IN, ASTERIX?
WE'RE GOING IN, OBELIX!
LVII
CRAAAC
LVII
LVII
FRRP FRRP
29A
I SAY! WHAT IS THIS INTRUSION? SHOCKING!
CALM DOWN, PETULA. THESE MEN WILL EXPLAIN THEIR ACTIONS TO US. WHAT?
HOME SWEET HOME
THE TIMES
I SAY! THIS IS LVII, IS IT NOT?
NO, IT IS NOT. THIS IS LVIII, BUT AN I HAS FALLEN OFF.
THE TIMES
WE WERE MISTAKEN. WE SHALL REIMBURSE YOU FOR YOUR DOOR. WILL YOU EXCUSE US?
INDEED. WHAT?
HOME SWEET HOME
THE TIMES
PETULA, YOU SHALL REMIND ME TO REPLACE THE MISSING I. AND NOW, I WOULD GLADLY HAVE A CUP OF HOT WATER WITH SOME TOAST.
THE TIMES
THIS TIME, I THINK, IT IS HERE.
ARE WE GOING IN, ASTERIX?
WE'RE GOING IN, OBELIX!
LVII
CRAAAC
IS THIS LVII HERE? YOU'RE NOT MISSING AN I?
Y...YES, N...NO... BY WHAT RIGHT?...
29B

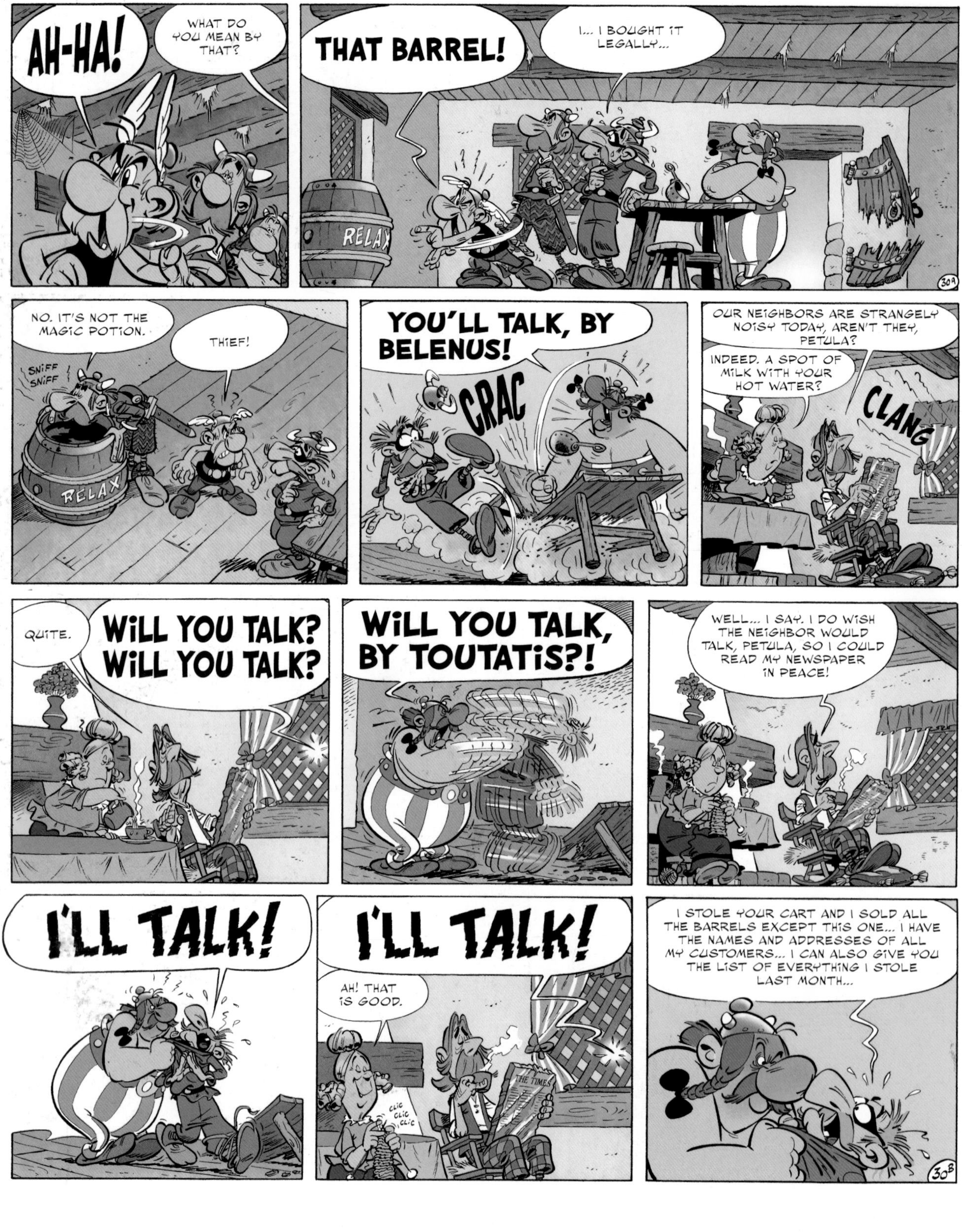
AH-HA!
WHAT DO YOU MEAN BY THAT?
THAT BARREL!
I... I BOUGHT IT LEGALLY...
RELAX
30A
NO. IT'S NOT THE MAGIC POTION.
SNIFF SNIFF
THIEF!
RELAX
YOU'LL TALK, BY BELENUS!
CRAC
OUR NEIGHBORS ARE STRANGELY NOISY TODAY, AREN'T THEY, PETULA?
INDEED. A SPOT OF MILK WITH YOUR HOT WATER?
CLANG
QUITE.
WILL YOU TALK? WILL YOU TALK?
WILL YOU TALK, BY TOUTATIS?!
WELL... I SAY. I DO WISH THE NEIGHBOR WOULD TALK, PETULA, SO I COULD READ MY NEWSPAPER IN PEACE!
I'LL TALK!
I'LL TALK!
AH! THAT IS GOOD.
CLIC CLIC CLIC
THE TIMES
I STOLE YOUR CART AND I SOLD ALL THE BARRELS EXCEPT THIS ONE... I HAVE THE NAMES AND ADDRESSES OF ALL MY CUSTOMERS... I CAN ALSO GIVE YOU THE LIST OF EVERYTHING I STOLE LAST MONTH...
30B

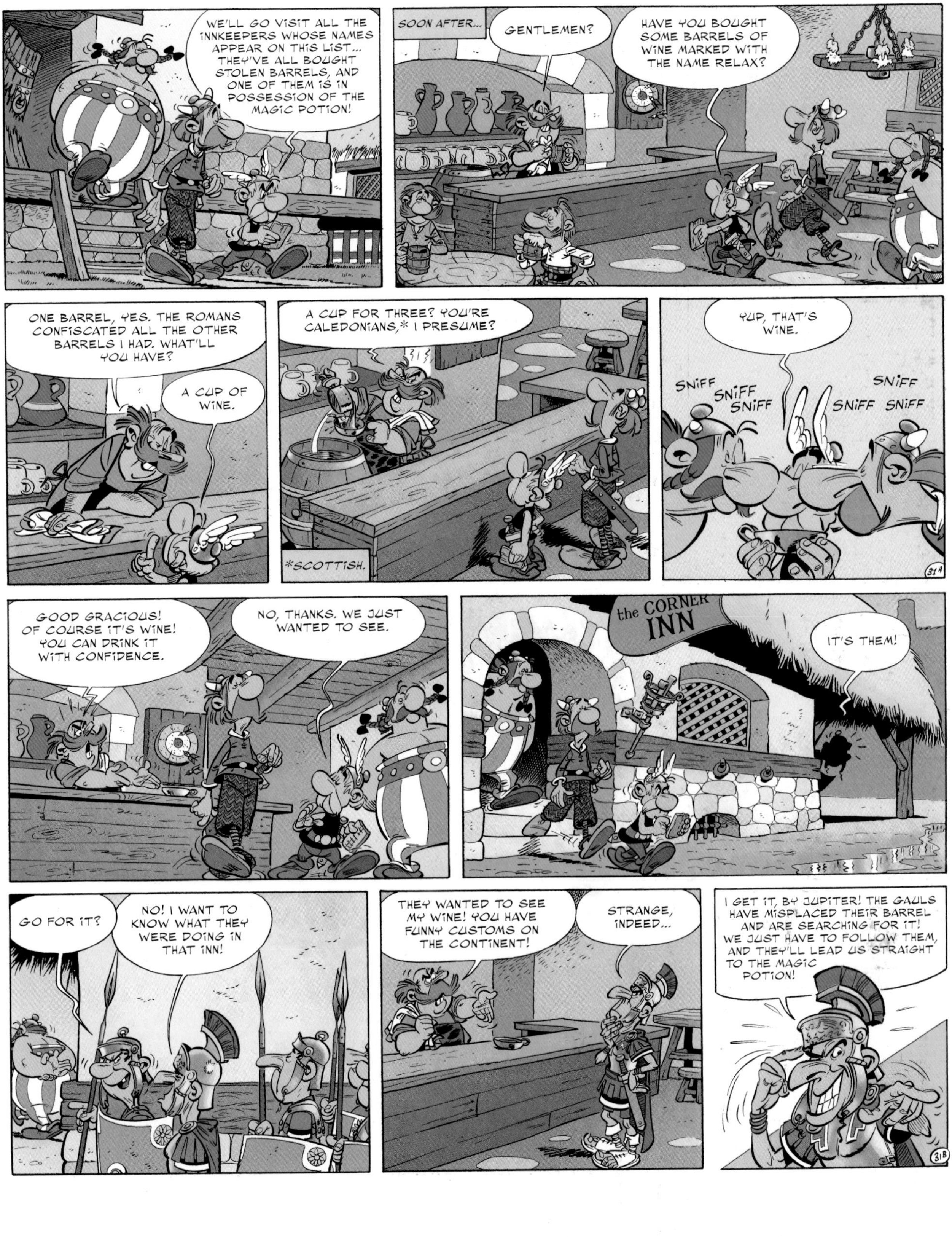
WE'LL GO VISIT ALL THE INNKEEPERS WHOSE NAMES APPEAR ON THIS LIST... THEY'VE ALL BOUGHT STOLEN BARRELS, AND ONE OF THEM IS IN POSSESSION OF THE MAGIC POTION!
SOON AFTER...
GENTLEMEN?
HAVE YOU BOUGHT SOME BARRELS OF WINE MARKED WITH THE NAME RELAX?
ONE BARREL, YES. THE ROMANS CONFISCATED ALL THE OTHER BARRELS I HAD. WHAT'LL YOU HAVE?
A CUP OF WINE.
A CUP FOR THREE? YOU'RE CALEDONIANS,* I PRESUME?
*SCOTTISH.
YUP, THAT'S WINE.
SNIFF SNIFF SNIFF
SNIFF SNIFF SNIFF
GOOD GRACIOUS! OF COURSE IT'S WINE! YOU CAN DRINK IT WITH CONFIDENCE.
NO, THANKS. WE JUST WANTED TO SEE.
the CORNER INN
IT'S THEM!
GO FOR IT?
NO! I WANT TO KNOW WHAT THEY WERE DOING IN THAT INN!
THEY WANTED TO SEE MY WINE! YOU HAVE FUNNY CUSTOMS ON THE CONTINENT!
STRANGE, INDEED...
I GET IT, BY JUPITER! THE GAULS HAVE MISPLACED THEIR BARREL AND ARE SEARCHING FOR IT! WE JUST HAVE TO FOLLOW THEM, AND THEY'LL LEAD US STRAIGHT TO THE MAGIC POTION!

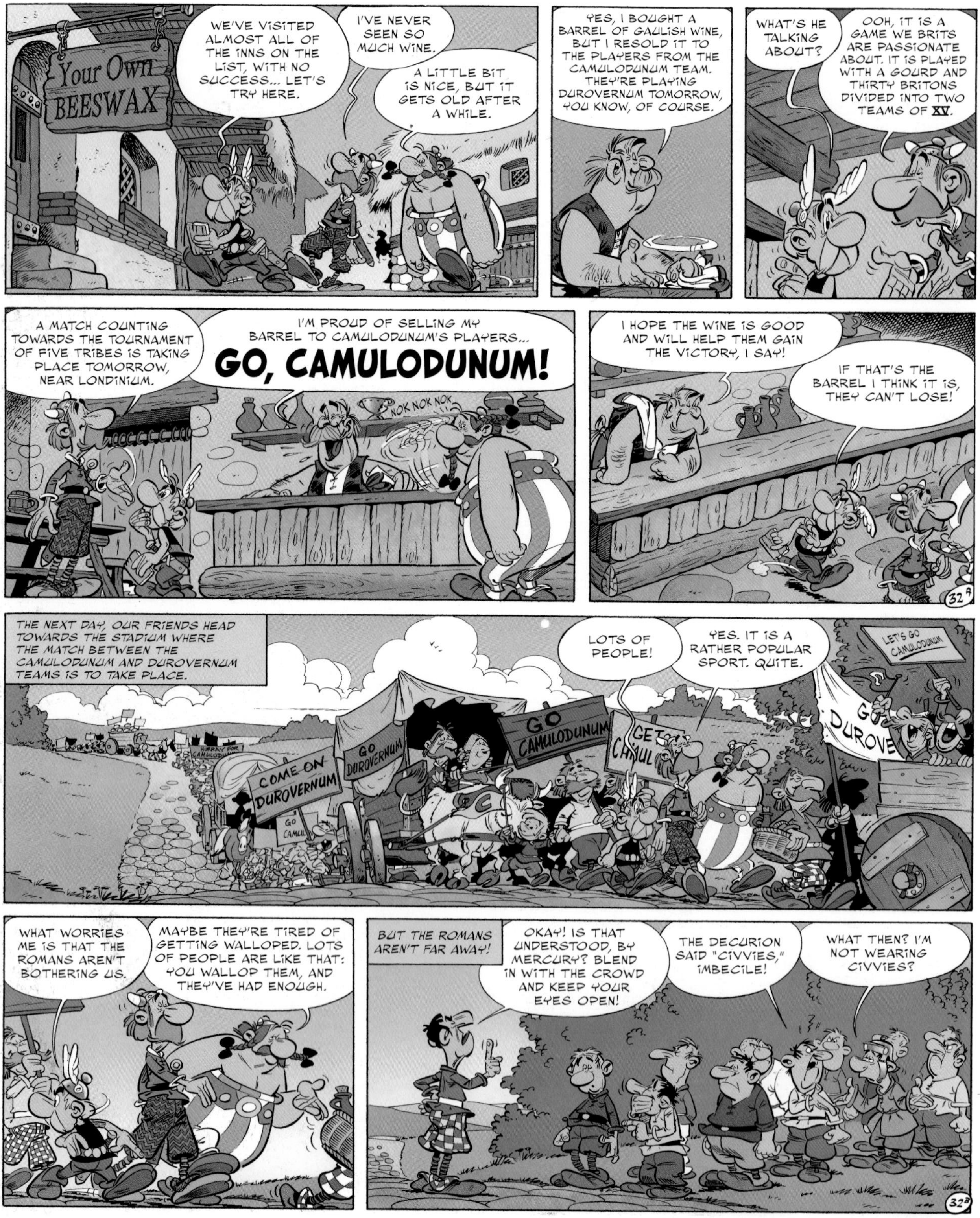

Your Own BEESWAX
WE'VE VISITED ALMOST ALL OF THE INNS ON THE LIST, WITH NO SUCCESS... LET'S TRY HERE.
I'VE NEVER SEEN SO MUCH WINE.
A LITTLE BIT IS NICE, BUT IT GETS OLD AFTER A WHILE.
YES, I BOUGHT A BARREL OF GAULISH WINE, BUT I RESOLD IT TO THE PLAYERS FROM THE CAMULODUNUM TEAM. THEY'RE PLAYING DUROVERNUM TOMORROW, YOU KNOW, OF COURSE.
WHAT'S HE TALKING ABOUT?
OOH, IT IS A GAME WE BRITS ARE PASSIONATE ABOUT. IT IS PLAYED WITH A GOURD AND THIRTY BRITONS DIVIDED INTO TWO TEAMS OF XV.
A MATCH COUNTING TOWARDS THE TOURNAMENT OF FIVE TRIBES IS TAKING PLACE TOMORROW, NEAR LONDINIUM.
I'M PROUD OF SELLING MY BARREL TO CAMULODUNUM'S PLAYERS... GO, CAMULODUNUM!
NOK NOK NOK
I HOPE THE WINE IS GOOD AND WILL HELP THEM GAIN THE VICTORY, I SAY!
IF THAT'S THE BARREL I THINK IT IS, THEY CAN'T LOSE!
THE NEXT DAY, OUR FRIENDS HEAD TOWARDS THE STADIUM WHERE THE MATCH BETWEEN THE CAMULODUNUM AND DUROVERNUM TEAMS IS TO TAKE PLACE.
LOTS OF PEOPLE!
YES. IT IS A RATHER POPULAR SPORT. QUITE.
LET'S GO CAMULODUNUM
GO CAMULODUNUM
GO DUROVERNUM
COME ON DUROVERNUM
WHAT WORRIES ME IS THAT THE ROMANS AREN'T BOTHERING US.
MAYBE THEY'RE TIRED OF GETTING WALLOPED. LOTS OF PEOPLE ARE LIKE THAT: YOU WALLOP THEM, AND THEY'VE HAD ENOUGH.
BUT THE ROMANS AREN'T FAR AWAY!
OKAY! IS THAT UNDERSTOOD, BY MERCURY? BLEND IN WITH THE CROWD AND KEEP YOUR EYES OPEN!
THE DECURION SAID "CIVVIES," IMBECILE!
WHAT THEN? I'M NOT WEARING CIVVIES?

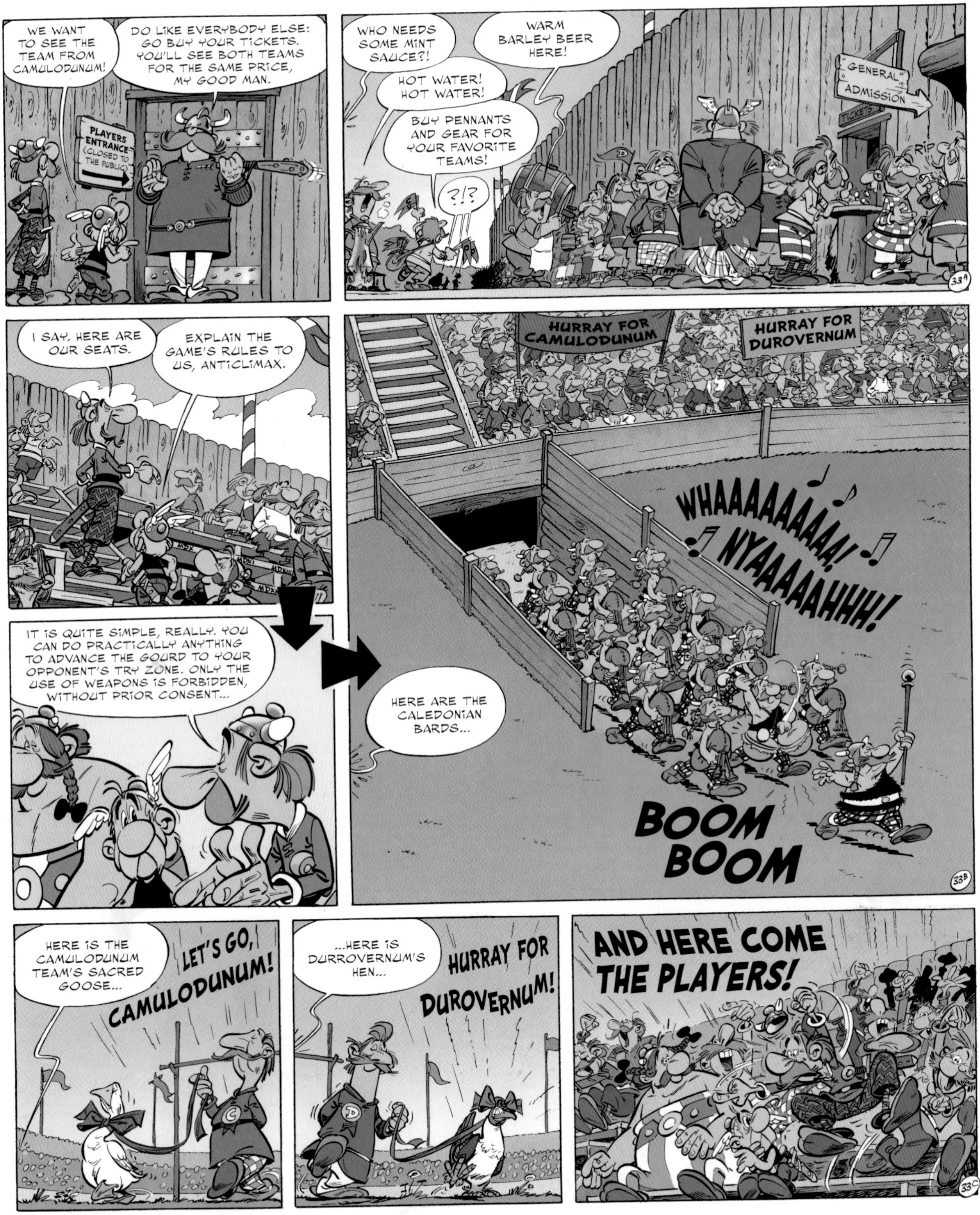
WE WANT TO SEE THE TEAM FROM CAMULODUNUM!
DO LIKE EVERYBODY ELSE: GO BUY YOUR TICKETS. YOU'LL SEE BOTH TEAMS FOR THE SAME PRICE, MY GOOD MAN.
PLAYERS ENTRANCE (CLOSED TO THE PUBLIC)
WHO NEEDS SOME MINT SAUCE?!
WARM BARLEY BEER HERE!
HOT WATER! HOT WATER!
BUY PENNANTS AND GEAR FOR YOUR FAVORITE TEAMS!
?!?
GENERAL ADMISSION
TICKETS
RIP
I SAY. HERE ARE OUR SEATS.
EXPLAIN THE GAME'S RULES TO US, ANTICLIMAX.
HURRAY FOR CAMULODUNUM
HURRAY FOR DUROVERNUM
WHAAAAAAAAA! NYAAAAAHHH!
IT IS QUITE SIMPLE, REALLY. YOU CAN DO PRACTICALLY ANYTHING TO ADVANCE THE GOURD TO YOUR OPPONENT'S TRY ZONE. ONLY THE USE OF WEAPONS IS FORBIDDEN, WITHOUT PRIOR CONSENT...
HERE ARE THE CALEDONIAN BARDS...
BOOM BOOM
HERE IS THE CAMULODUNUM TEAM'S SACRED GOOSE...
LET'S GO, CAMULODUNUM!
...HERE IS DURROVERNUM'S HEN...
HURRAY FOR DUROVERNUM!
AND HERE COME THE PLAYERS!

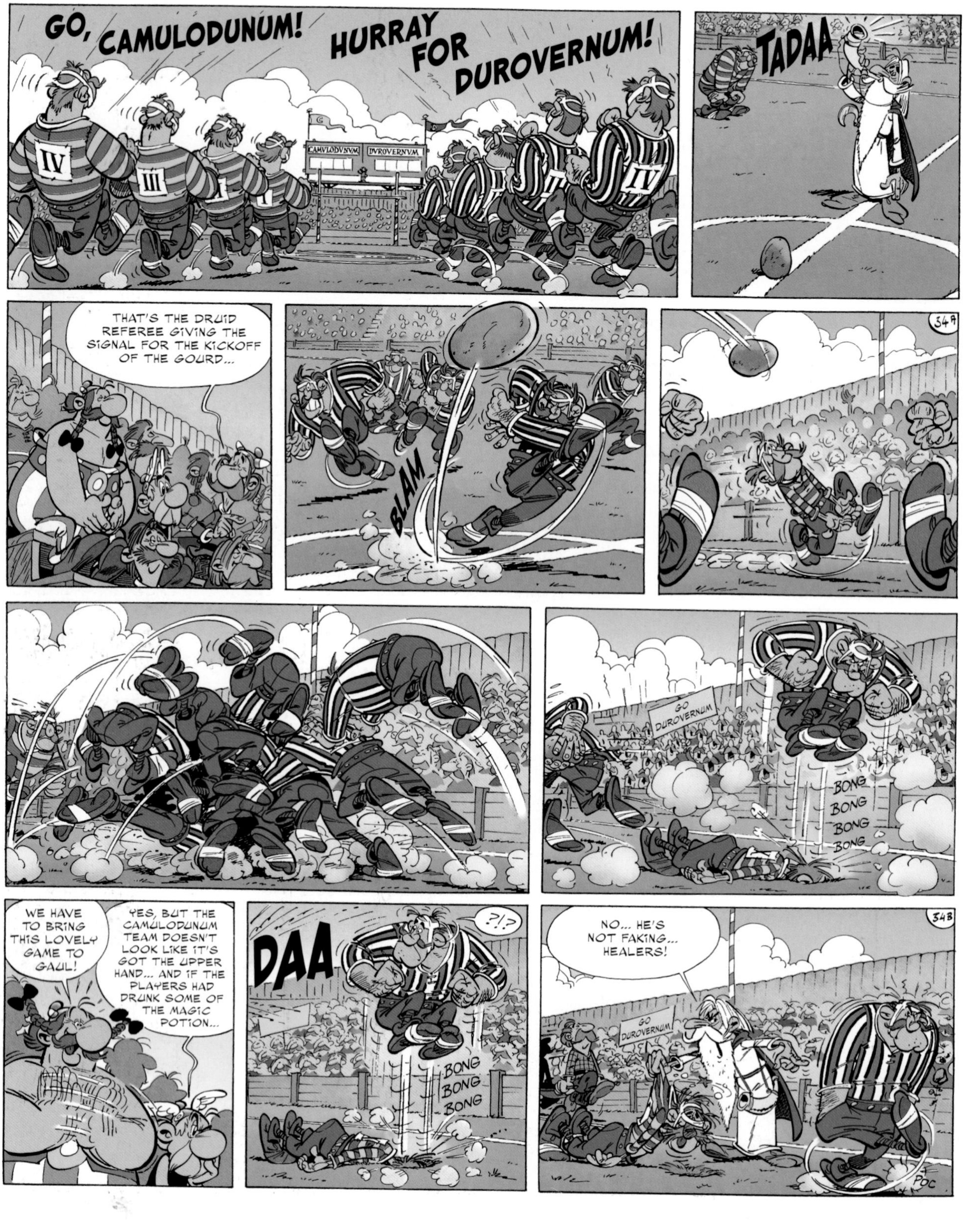
GO, CAMULODUNUM!
HURRAY FOR DUROVERNUM!
CAMVLODVNVM
DVROVERNVM
IV
III
IV
TADAA
THAT'S THE DRUID REFEREE GIVING THE SIGNAL FOR THE KICKOFF OF THE GOURD...
BLAM
34A
GO DUROVERNUM
BONG
BONG
BONG
BONG
WE HAVE TO BRING THIS LOVELY GAME TO GAUL!
YES, BUT THE CAMULODUNUM TEAM DOESN'T LOOK LIKE IT'S GOT THE UPPER HAND... AND IF THE PLAYERS HAD DRUNK SOME OF THE MAGIC POTION...
DAA
?!?
BONG
BONG
BONG
NO... HE'S NOT FAKING... HEALERS!
34B
GO DUROVERNUM
POC

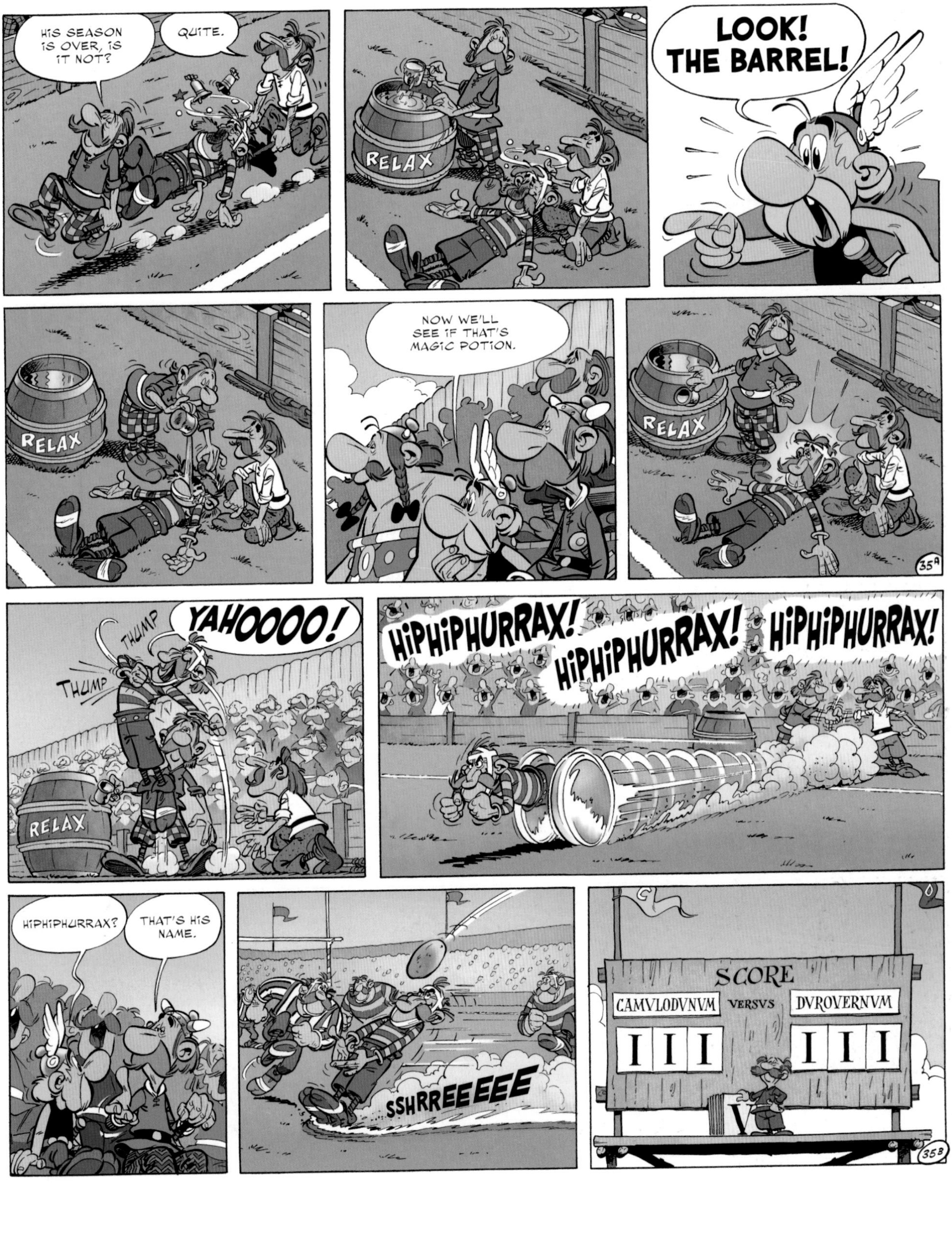
HIS SEASON IS OVER, IS IT NOT?
QUITE.
RELAX
LOOK! THE BARREL!
RELAX
NOW WE'LL SEE IF THAT'S MAGIC POTION.
RELAX
35A
THUMP
THUMP
YAHOOOO!
RELAX
HIPHIPHURRAX!
HIPHIPHURRAX!
HIPHIPHURRAX!
HIPHIPHURRAX?
THAT'S HIS NAME.
SSHRREEEEE
SCORE
CAMVLODVNVM
VERSVS
DVROVERNVM
III
III
V
35B

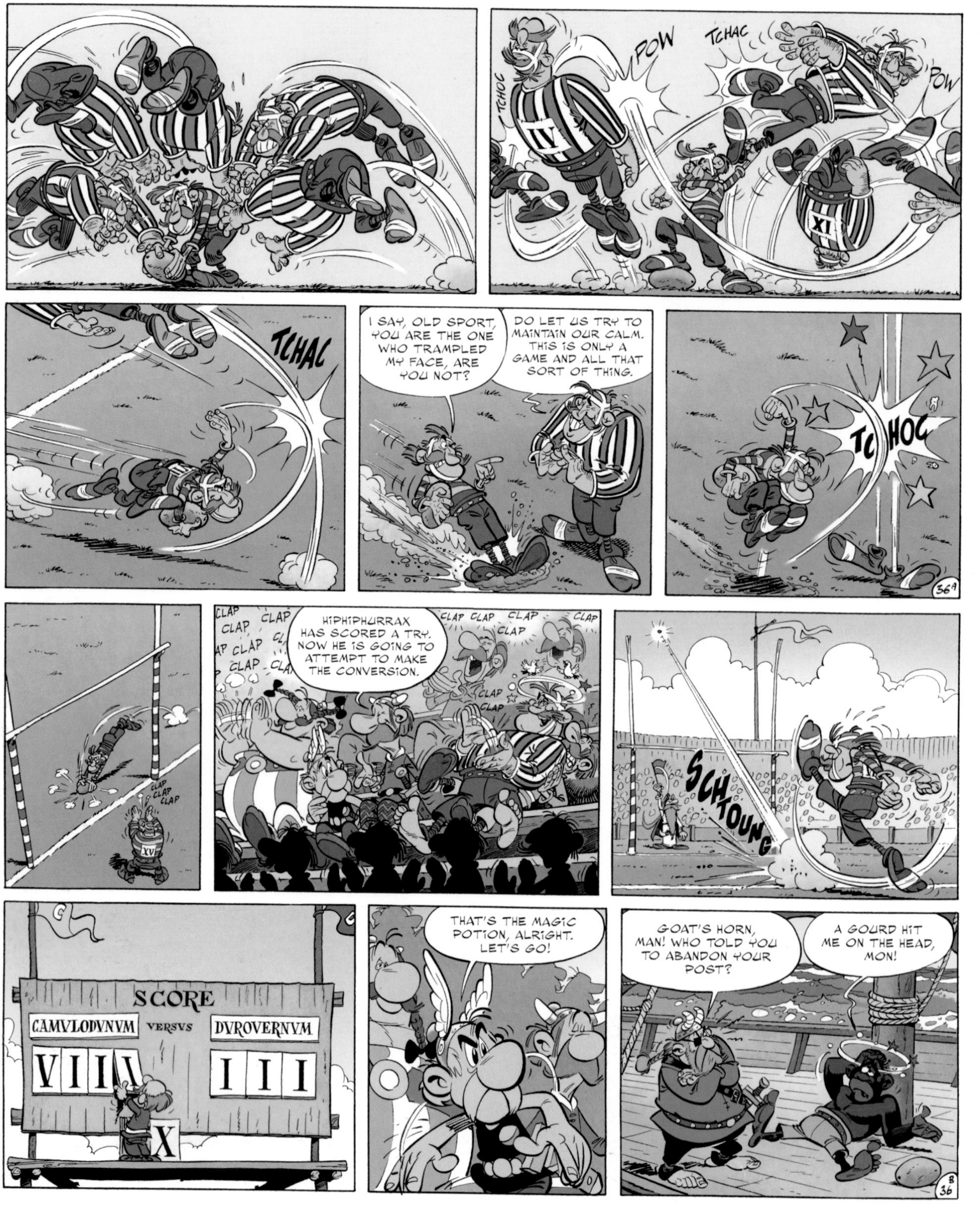
POW
TCHAC
TCHOC
POW
TCHAC
I SAY, OLD SPORT, YOU ARE THE ONE WHO TRAMPLED MY FACE, ARE YOU NOT?
DO LET US TRY TO MAINTAIN OUR CALM. THIS IS ONLY A GAME AND ALL THAT SORT OF THING.
TCHOC
36A
CLAP CLAP CLAP
HIPHIPHURRAX HAS SCORED A TRY. NOW HE IS GOING TO ATTEMPT TO MAKE THE CONVERSION.
CLAP CLAP CLAP CLAP
SCHTOUNG
SCORE
CAMVLODVNVM VERSVS DVROVERNVM
VIII
III
X
THAT'S THE MAGIC POTION, ALRIGHT. LET'S GO!
GOAT'S HORN, MAN! WHO TOLD YOU TO ABANDON YOUR POST?
A GOURD HIT ME ON THE HEAD, MON!
B 36

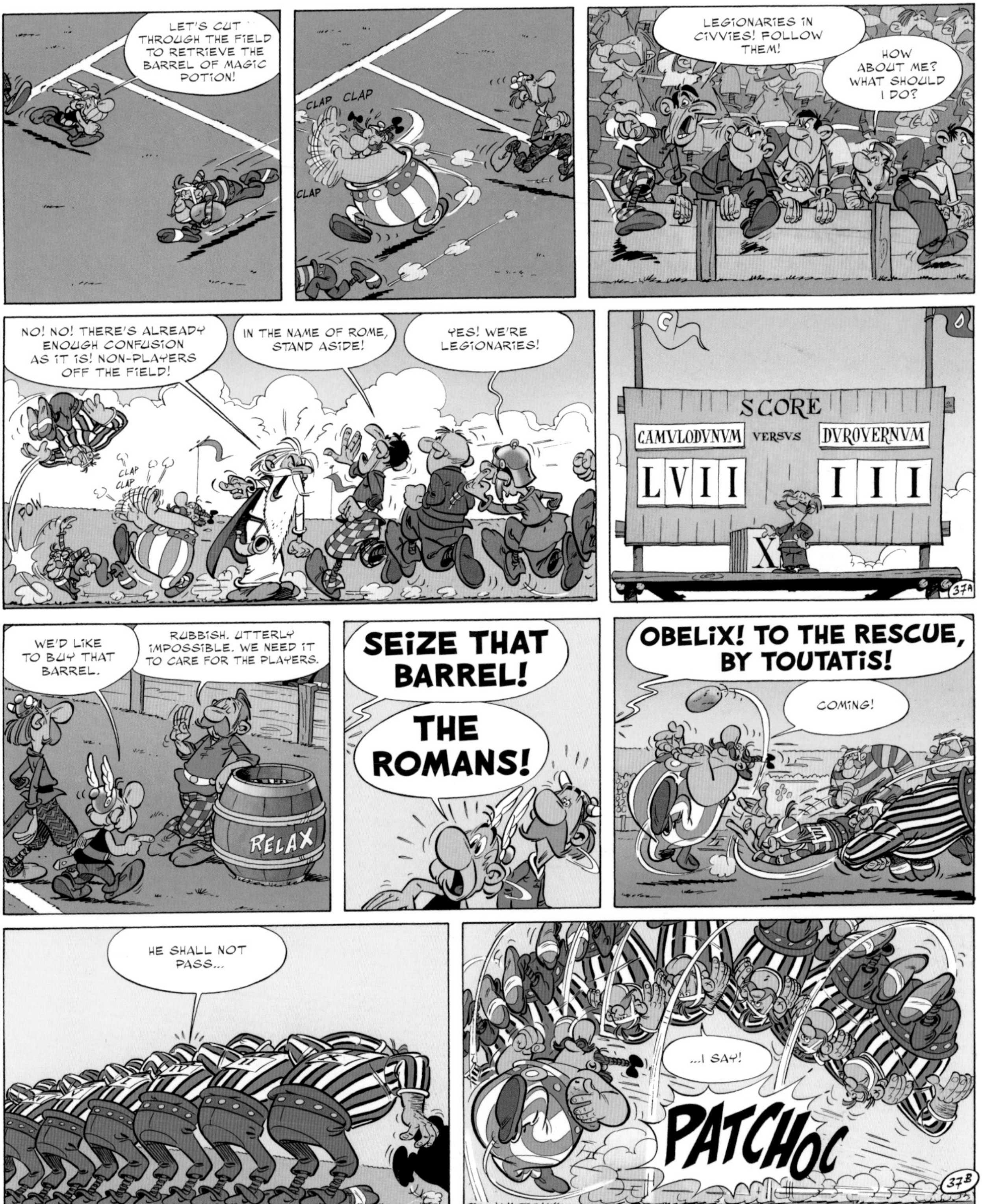
LET'S CUT THROUGH THE FIELD TO RETRIEVE THE BARREL OF MAGIC POTION!
CLAP CLAP
CLAP
LEGIONARIES IN CIVVIES! FOLLOW THEM!
HOW ABOUT ME? WHAT SHOULD I DO?
NO! NO! THERE'S ALREADY ENOUGH CONFUSION AS IT IS! NON-PLAYERS OFF THE FIELD!
IN THE NAME OF ROME, STAND ASIDE!
YES! WE'RE LEGIONARIES!
CLAP CLAP
POW
SCORE
CAMVLODVNVM VERSVS DVROVERNVM
LVII III
X
37A
WE'D LIKE TO BUY THAT BARREL.
RUBBISH. UTTERLY IMPOSSIBLE. WE NEED IT TO CARE FOR THE PLAYERS.
RELAX
SEIZE THAT BARREL!
THE ROMANS!
OBELIX! TO THE RESCUE, BY TOUTATIS!
COMING!
HE SHALL NOT PASS...
...I SAY!
PATCHOC
37B

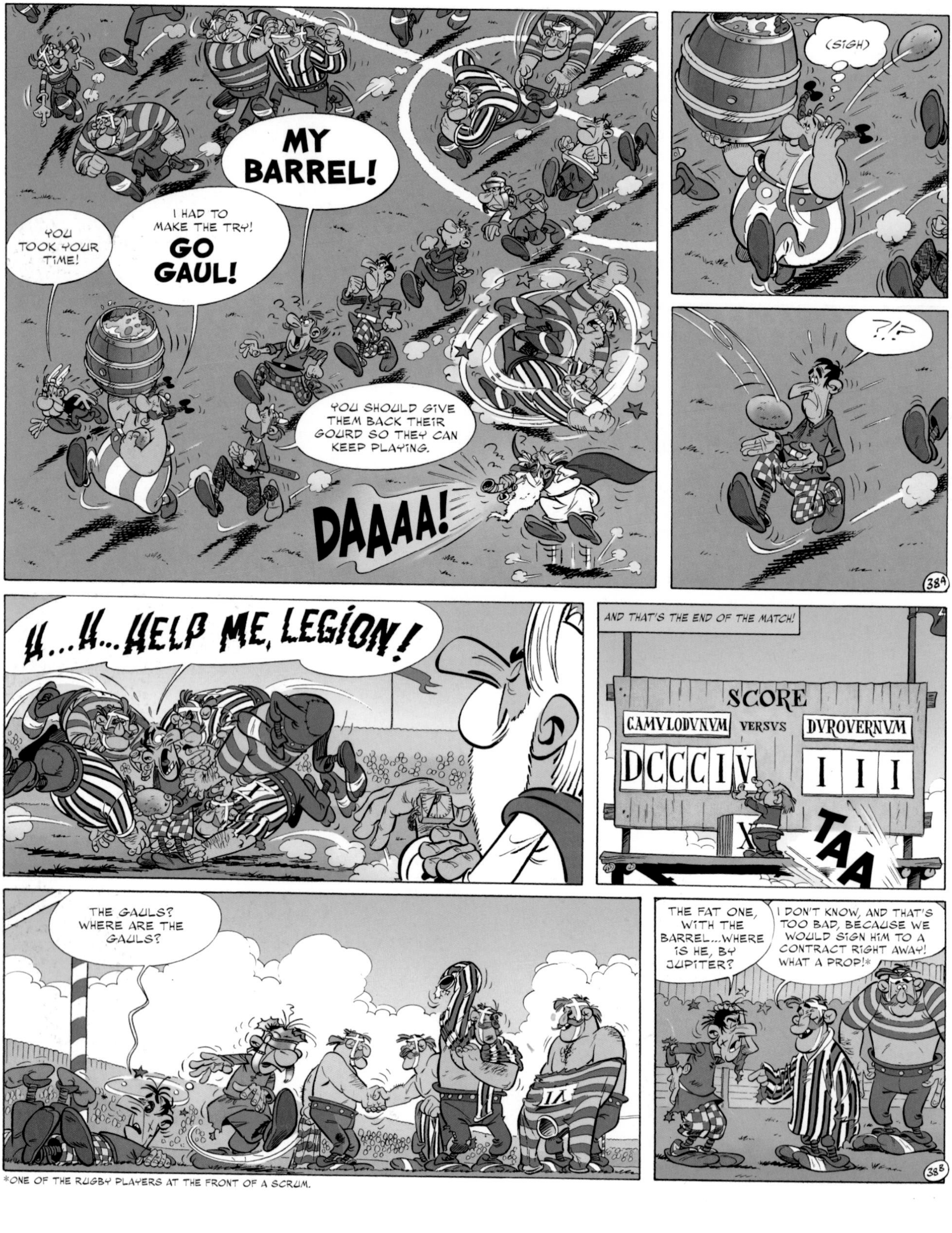
MY BARREL!
YOU TOOK YOUR TIME!
I HAD TO MAKE THE TRY! GO GAUL!
YOU SHOULD GIVE THEM BACK THEIR GOURD SO THEY CAN KEEP PLAYING.
DAAAA!
(SIGH)
?!?
H... H... HELP ME, LEGION!
AND THAT'S THE END OF THE MATCH!
SCORE
CAMVLODVNVM VERSVS DVROVERNVM
DCCCIV
III
TAA
THE GAULS? WHERE ARE THE GAULS?
THE FAT ONE, WITH THE BARREL... WHERE IS HE, BY JUPITER?
I DON'T KNOW, AND THAT'S TOO BAD, BECAUSE WE WOULD SIGN HIM TO A CONTRACT RIGHT AWAY! WHAT A PROP!*

*ONE OF THE RUGBY PLAYERS AT THE FRONT OF A SCRUM.

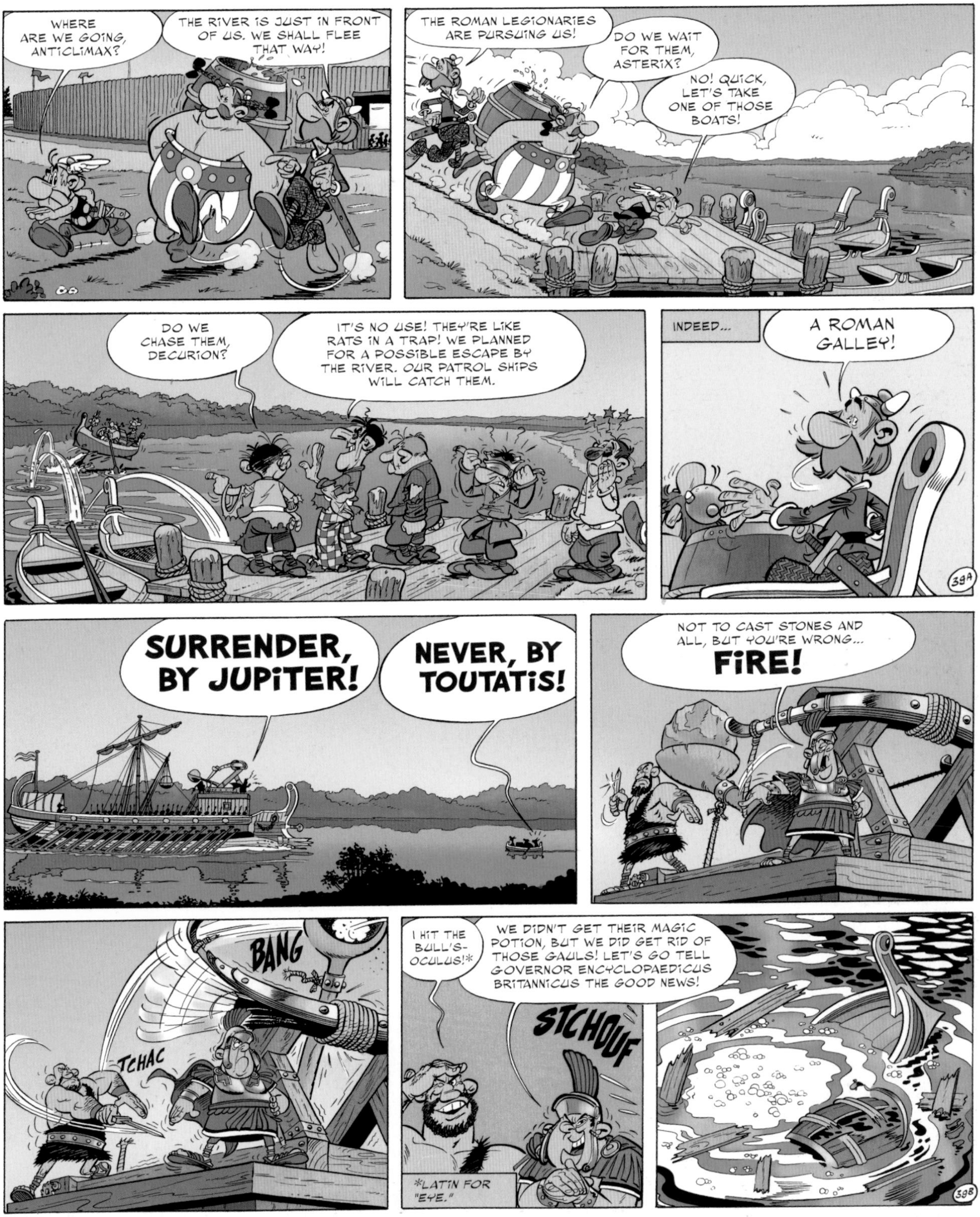
WHERE ARE WE GOING, ANTICLIMAX?
THE RIVER IS JUST IN FRONT OF US. WE SHALL FLEE THAT WAY!
THE ROMAN LEGIONARIES ARE PURSUING US!
DO WE WAIT FOR THEM, ASTERIX?
NO! QUICK, LET'S TAKE ONE OF THOSE BOATS!
DO WE CHASE THEM, DECURION?
IT'S NO USE! THEY'RE LIKE RATS IN A TRAP! WE PLANNED FOR A POSSIBLE ESCAPE BY THE RIVER. OUR PATROL SHIPS WILL CATCH THEM.
INDEED...
A ROMAN GALLEY!
39A
SURRENDER, BY JUPITER!
NEVER, BY TOUTATIS!
NOT TO CAST STONES AND ALL, BUT YOU'RE WRONG... FIRE!
BANG
TCHAC
I HIT THE BULL'S-OCULUS!*
WE DIDN'T GET THEIR MAGIC POTION, BUT WE DID GET RID OF THOSE GAULS! LET'S GO TELL GOVERNOR ENCYCLOPAEDICUS BRITANNICUS THE GOOD NEWS!
STCHOUF
*LATIN FOR "EYE."
39B

THEY'RE GOING AWAY. WE CAN MAKE FOR THE RIVERBANK.

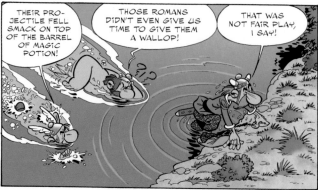

THEIR PROJECTILE FELL SMACK ON TOP OF THE BARREL OF MAGIC POTION!

THOSE ROMANS DIDN'T EVEN GIVE US TIME TO GIVE THEM A WALLOP!

THAT WAS NOT FAIR PLAY, I SAY!

DON'T BE DOWN, GOOD OLD OBELIX. WE'LL GO HELP ANTICLIMAX IN HIS VILLAGE TO FIGHT THE ROMANS, EVEN WITHOUT MAGIC POTION.

YOU SHALL BE WELCOME. THAT IS FOR CERTAIN.

SNIFF SNIFF

PAT PAT PAT

AND THUS, WITHOUT BEING BOTHERED BY THE ROMANS, WHO THINK THEY'RE DEAD, OUR THREE FRIENDS HEAD FOR THAT LITTLE VILLAGE IN CANTIUM, WHICH IS STILL RESISTING THE INVADER. AS FOR THE MAGIC POTION, IT DISSOLVED IN THE MURKY WATERS OF THE THAMES...

40⁴

...WHICH WILL CAUSE ANGLERS TO EXPERIENCE SOME UNUSUAL EMOTIONS THAT SEASON...

I SAY! I GOT A BITE!

...BECAUSE THE TINIEST FISH PUT THE ANGLERS IN THE DRINK...

...A DRINK OF WHICH LETS THE DUNKED ANGLERS SILENCE THE ONES WHO THOUGHT THE INCIDENT WAS FUNNY.

KAPOW

A FEW DAYS LATER, OUR FRIENDS ARRIVE IN ANTICLIMAX'S VILLAGE, WHERE THEY'RE WELCOMED BY THE CHIEF RILLYBIGBOS AND HIS MAIN SUBORDINATES: SUFFIX AND FONIX...

YOU MANAGED TO CROSS ENEMY LINES?

YES, THEY SEEM TO BE VERY SURE OF THEMSELVES. WE WERE ONLY QUESTIONED BY ONE SINGLE PATROL!

AND YET, I DIDN'T HAVE IT IN MY HEART TO LAUGH.

40ᴮ

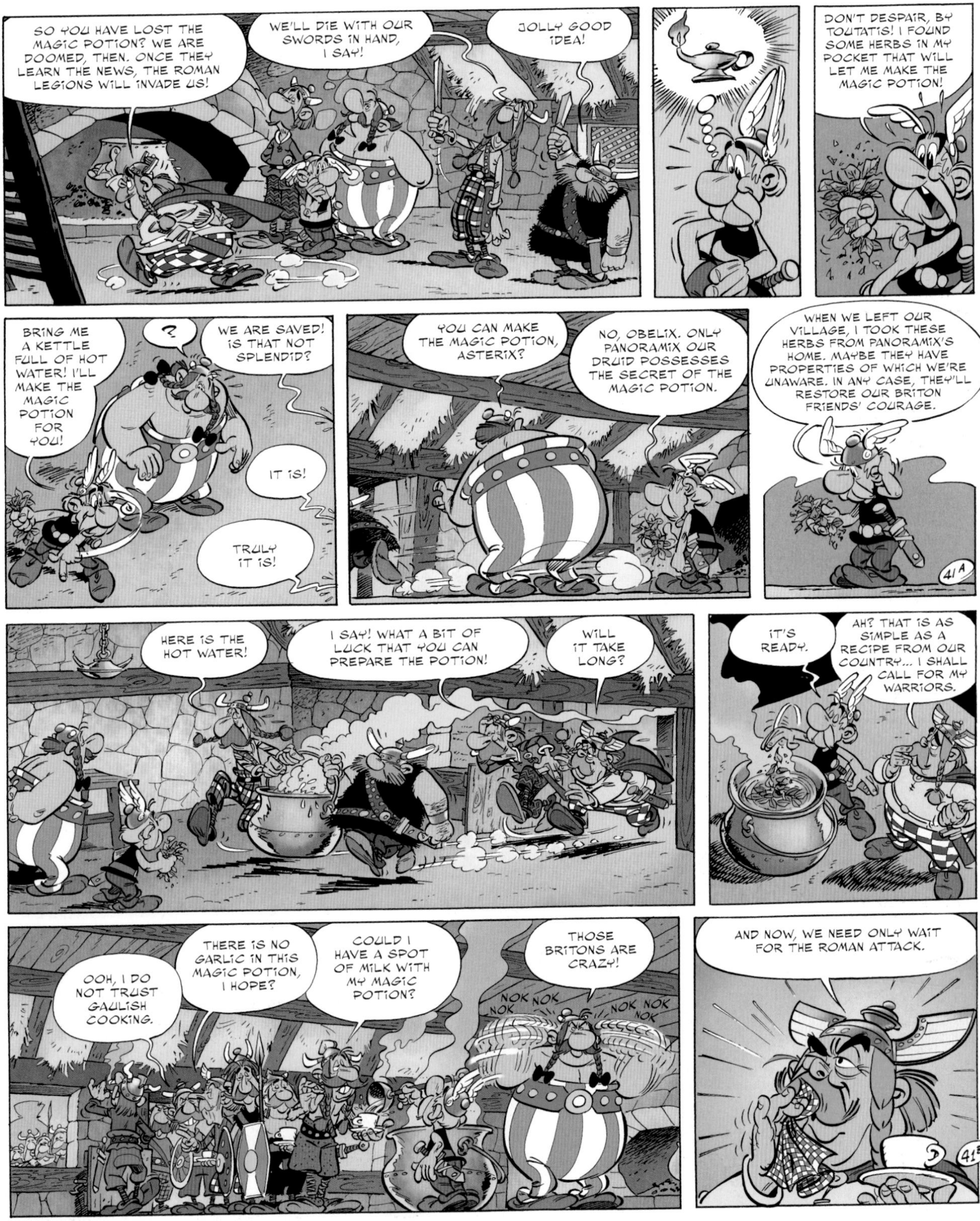
SO YOU HAVE LOST THE MAGIC POTION? WE ARE DOOMED, THEN. ONCE THEY LEARN THE NEWS, THE ROMAN LEGIONS WILL INVADE US!
WE'LL DIE WITH OUR SWORDS IN HAND, I SAY!
JOLLY GOOD IDEA!
DON'T DESPAIR, BY TOUTATIS! I FOUND SOME HERBS IN MY POCKET THAT WILL LET ME MAKE THE MAGIC POTION!
BRING ME A KETTLE FULL OF HOT WATER! I'LL MAKE THE MAGIC POTION FOR YOU!
?
WE ARE SAVED! IS THAT NOT SPLENDID?
IT IS!
TRULY IT IS!
YOU CAN MAKE THE MAGIC POTION, ASTERIX?
NO, OBELIX. ONLY PANORAMIX OUR DRUID POSSESSES THE SECRET OF THE MAGIC POTION.
WHEN WE LEFT OUR VILLAGE, I TOOK THESE HERBS FROM PANORAMIX'S HOME. MAYBE THEY HAVE PROPERTIES OF WHICH WE'RE UNAWARE. IN ANY CASE, THEY'LL RESTORE OUR BRITON FRIENDS' COURAGE.
41A
HERE IS THE HOT WATER!
I SAY! WHAT A BIT OF LUCK THAT YOU CAN PREPARE THE POTION!
WILL IT TAKE LONG?
IT'S READY.
AH? THAT IS AS SIMPLE AS A RECIPE FROM OUR COUNTRY... I SHALL CALL FOR MY WARRIORS.
OOH, I DO NOT TRUST GAULISH COOKING.
THERE IS NO GARLIC IN THIS MAGIC POTION, I HOPE?
COULD I HAVE A SPOT OF MILK WITH MY MAGIC POTION?
THOSE BRITONS ARE CRAZY!
NOK NOK NOK NOK NOK NOK
AND NOW, WE NEED ONLY WAIT FOR THE ROMAN ATTACK.
41B

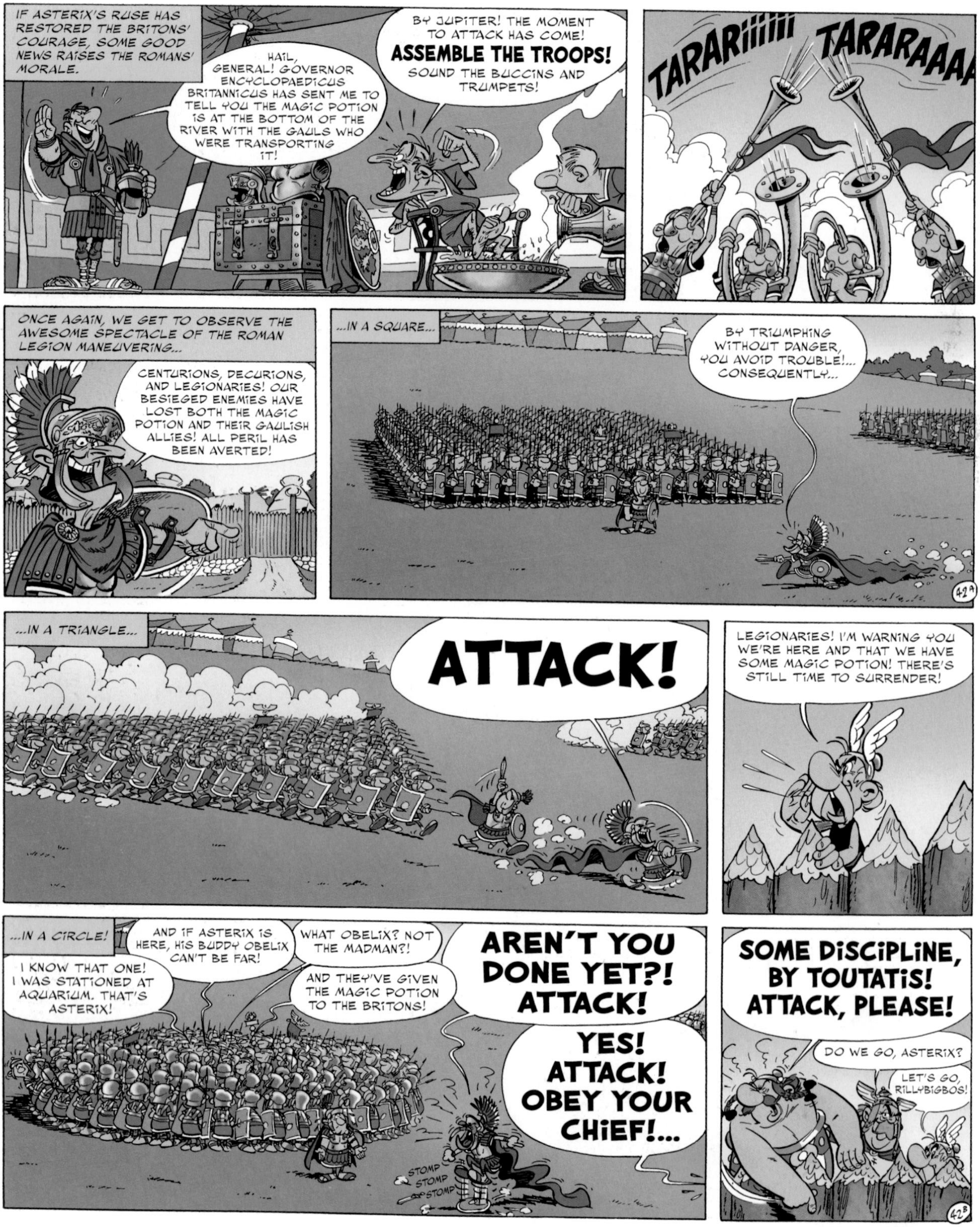

IF ASTERIX'S RUSE HAS RESTORED THE BRITONS' COURAGE, SOME GOOD NEWS RAISES THE ROMANS' MORALE.
HAIL, GENERAL! GOVERNOR ENCYCLOPAEDICUS BRITANNICUS HAS SENT ME TO TELL YOU THE MAGIC POTION IS AT THE BOTTOM OF THE RIVER WITH THE GAULS WHO WERE TRANSPORTING IT!
BY JUPITER! THE MOMENT TO ATTACK HAS COME! ASSEMBLE THE TROOPS! SOUND THE BUCCINS AND TRUMPETS!
TARARIIIIII TARARAAAA
ONCE AGAIN, WE GET TO OBSERVE THE AWESOME SPECTACLE OF THE ROMAN LEGION MANEUVERING...
CENTURIONS, DECURIONS, AND LEGIONARIES! OUR BESIEGED ENEMIES HAVE LOST BOTH THE MAGIC POTION AND THEIR GAULISH ALLIES! ALL PERIL HAS BEEN AVERTED!
...IN A SQUARE...
BY TRIUMPHING WITHOUT DANGER, YOU AVOID TROUBLE!... CONSEQUENTLY...
42A
...IN A TRIANGLE...
ATTACK!
LEGIONARIES! I'M WARNING YOU WE'RE HERE AND THAT WE HAVE SOME MAGIC POTION! THERE'S STILL TIME TO SURRENDER!
...IN A CIRCLE!
I KNOW THAT ONE! I WAS STATIONED AT AQUARIUM. THAT'S ASTERIX!
AND IF ASTERIX IS HERE, HIS BUDDY OBELIX CAN'T BE FAR!
WHAT OBELIX? NOT THE MADMAN?!
AND THEY'VE GIVEN THE MAGIC POTION TO THE BRITONS!
AREN'T YOU DONE YET?! ATTACK!
YES! ATTACK! OBEY YOUR CHIEF!...
STOMP STOMP STOMP
SOME DISCIPLINE, BY TOUTATIS! ATTACK, PLEASE!
DO WE GO, ASTERIX?
LET'S GO, RILLYBIGBOS!
42B

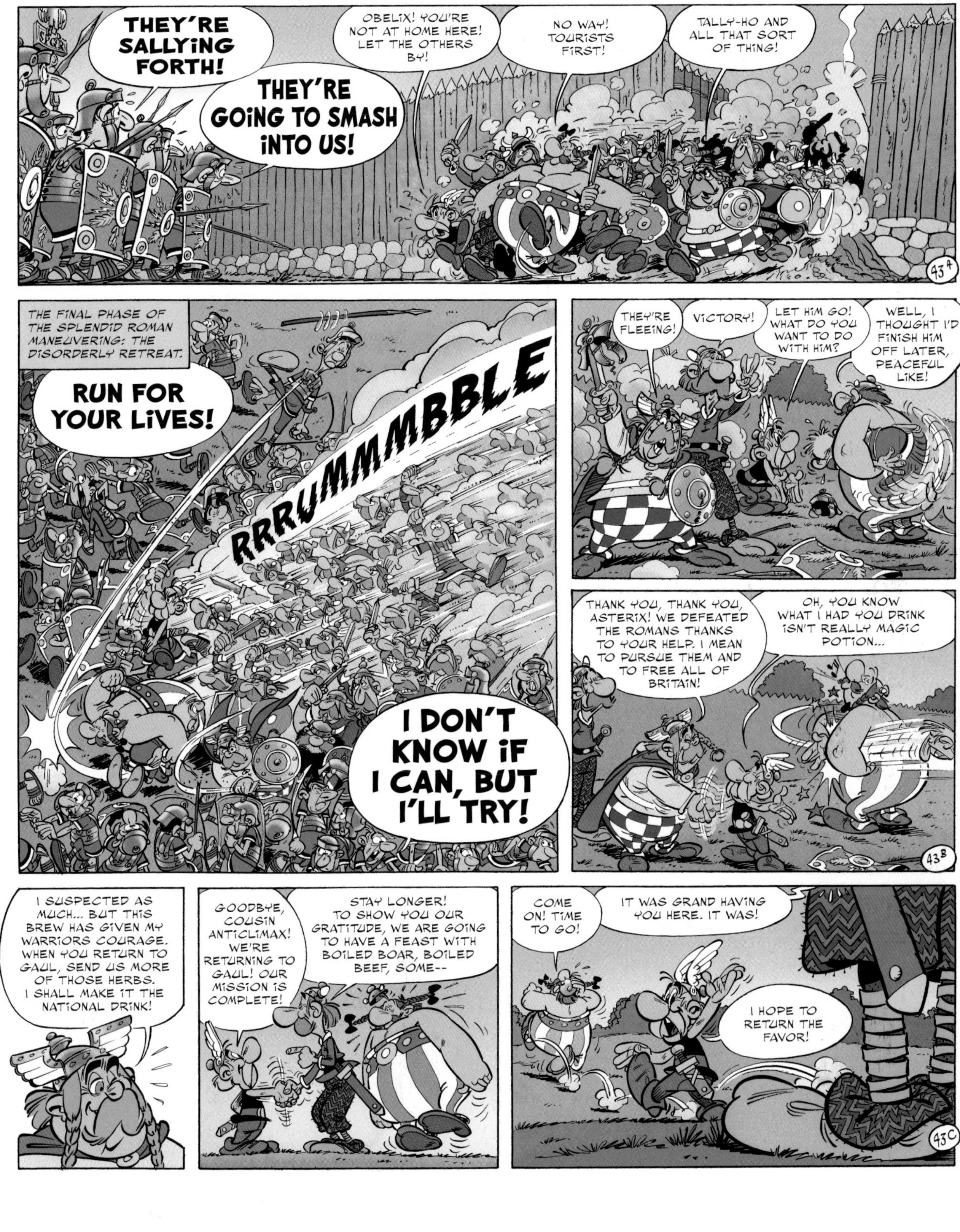
THEY'RE SALLYING FORTH!
THEY'RE GOING TO SMASH INTO US!
OBELIX! YOU'RE NOT AT HOME HERE! LET THE OTHERS BY!
NO WAY! TOURISTS FIRST!
TALLY-HO AND ALL THAT SORT OF THING!
43A
THE FINAL PHASE OF THE SPLENDID ROMAN MANEUVERING: THE DISORDERLY RETREAT.
RUN FOR YOUR LIVES!
RRRUMMMBBLE
I DON'T KNOW IF I CAN, BUT I'LL TRY!
THEY'RE FLEEING!
VICTORY!
LET HIM GO! WHAT DO YOU WANT TO DO WITH HIM?
WELL, I THOUGHT I'D FINISH HIM OFF LATER, PEACEFUL LIKE!
THANK YOU, THANK YOU, ASTERIX! WE DEFEATED THE ROMANS THANKS TO YOUR HELP. I MEAN TO PURSUE THEM AND TO FREE ALL OF BRITAIN!
OH, YOU KNOW WHAT I HAD YOU DRINK ISN'T REALLY MAGIC POTION...
43B
I SUSPECTED AS MUCH... BUT THIS BREW HAS GIVEN MY WARRIORS COURAGE. WHEN YOU RETURN TO GAUL, SEND US MORE OF THOSE HERBS. I SHALL MAKE IT THE NATIONAL DRINK!
GOODBYE, COUSIN ANTICLIMAX! WE'RE RETURNING TO GAUL! OUR MISSION IS COMPLETE!
STAY LONGER! TO SHOW YOU OUR GRATITUDE, WE ARE GOING TO HAVE A FEAST WITH BOILED BOAR, BOILED BEEF, SOME--
COME ON! TIME TO GO!
IT WAS GRAND HAVING YOU HERE. IT WAS!
I HOPE TO RETURN THE FAVOR!
43C

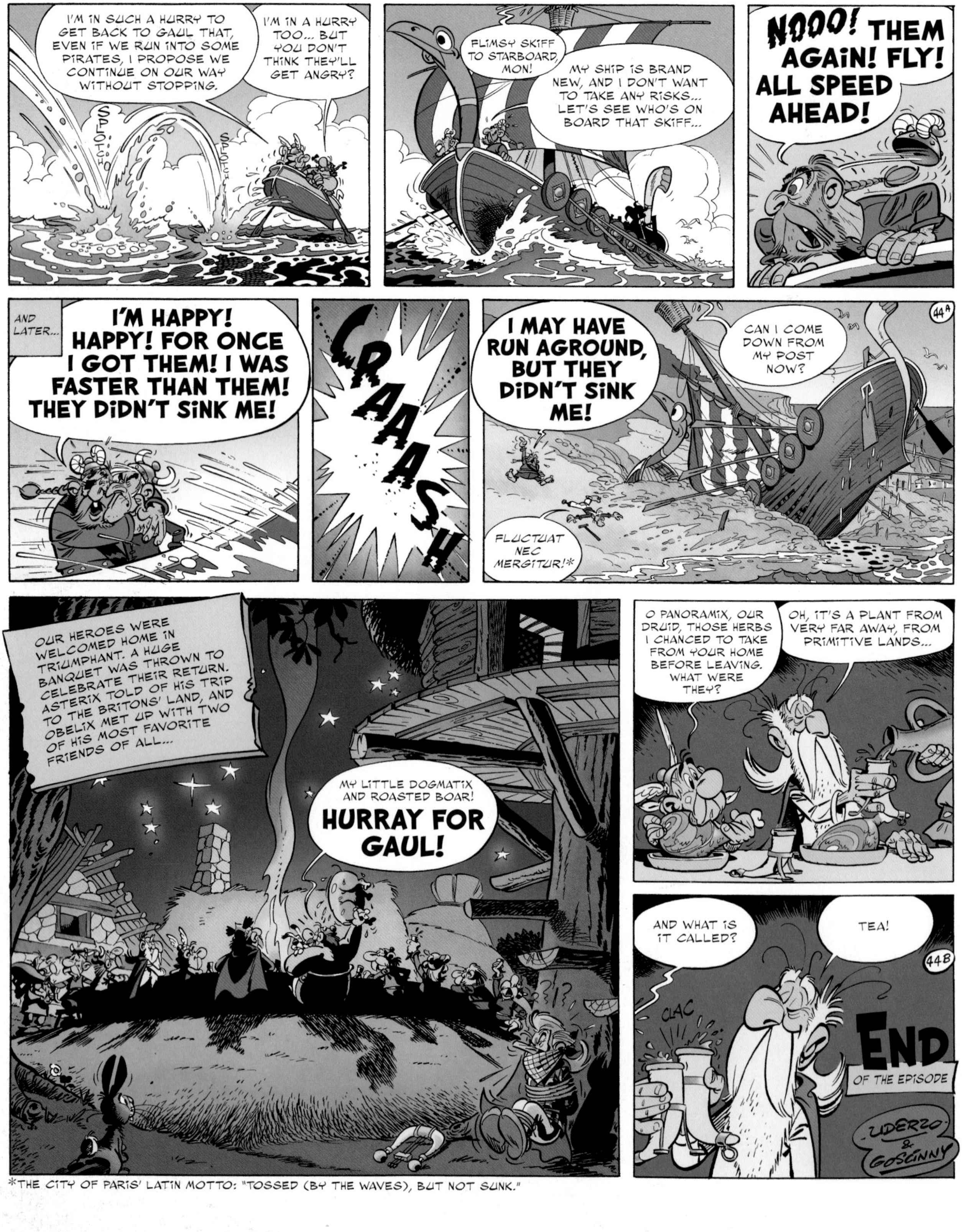
I'M IN SUCH A HURRY TO GET BACK TO GAUL THAT, EVEN IF WE RUN INTO SOME PIRATES, I PROPOSE WE CONTINUE ON OUR WAY WITHOUT STOPPING.
I'M IN A HURRY TOO... BUT YOU DON'T THINK THEY'LL GET ANGRY?
SPLOTCH
SPLOTCH
FLIMSY SKIFF TO STARBOARD, MON!
MY SHIP IS BRAND NEW, AND I DON'T WANT TO TAKE ANY RISKS... LET'S SEE WHO'S ON BOARD THAT SKIFF...
NOOO! THEM AGAIN! FLY! ALL SPEED AHEAD!
AND LATER...
I'M HAPPY! HAPPY! FOR ONCE I GOT THEM! I WAS FASTER THAN THEM! THEY DIDN'T SINK ME!
CRAAASH
I MAY HAVE RUN AGROUND, BUT THEY DIDN'T SINK ME!
CAN I COME DOWN FROM MY POST NOW?
44A
FLUCTUAT NEC MERGITUR!*
OUR HEROES WERE WELCOMED HOME IN TRIUMPHANT. A HUGE BANQUET WAS THROWN TO CELEBRATE THEIR RETURN. ASTERIX TOLD OF HIS TRIP TO THE BRITONS' LAND, AND OBELIX MET UP WITH TWO OF HIS MOST FAVORITE FRIENDS OF ALL...
MY LITTLE DOGMATIX AND ROASTED BOAR! HURRAY FOR GAUL!
O PANORAMIX, OUR DRUID, THOSE HERBS I CHANCED TO TAKE FROM YOUR HOME BEFORE LEAVING. WHAT WERE THEY?
OH, IT'S A PLANT FROM VERY FAR AWAY, FROM PRIMITIVE LANDS...
AND WHAT IS IT CALLED?
TEA!
44B
CLAC
END
OF THE EPISODE
UDERZO & GOSCINNY

*THE CITY OF PARIS' LATIN MOTTO: "TOSSED (BY THE WAVES), BUT NOT SUNK."

R. GOSCINNY **ASTERIX** A. UDERZO

ASTERIX AND THE NORMANS

Written by René GOSCINNY

Illustrated by Albert UDERZO

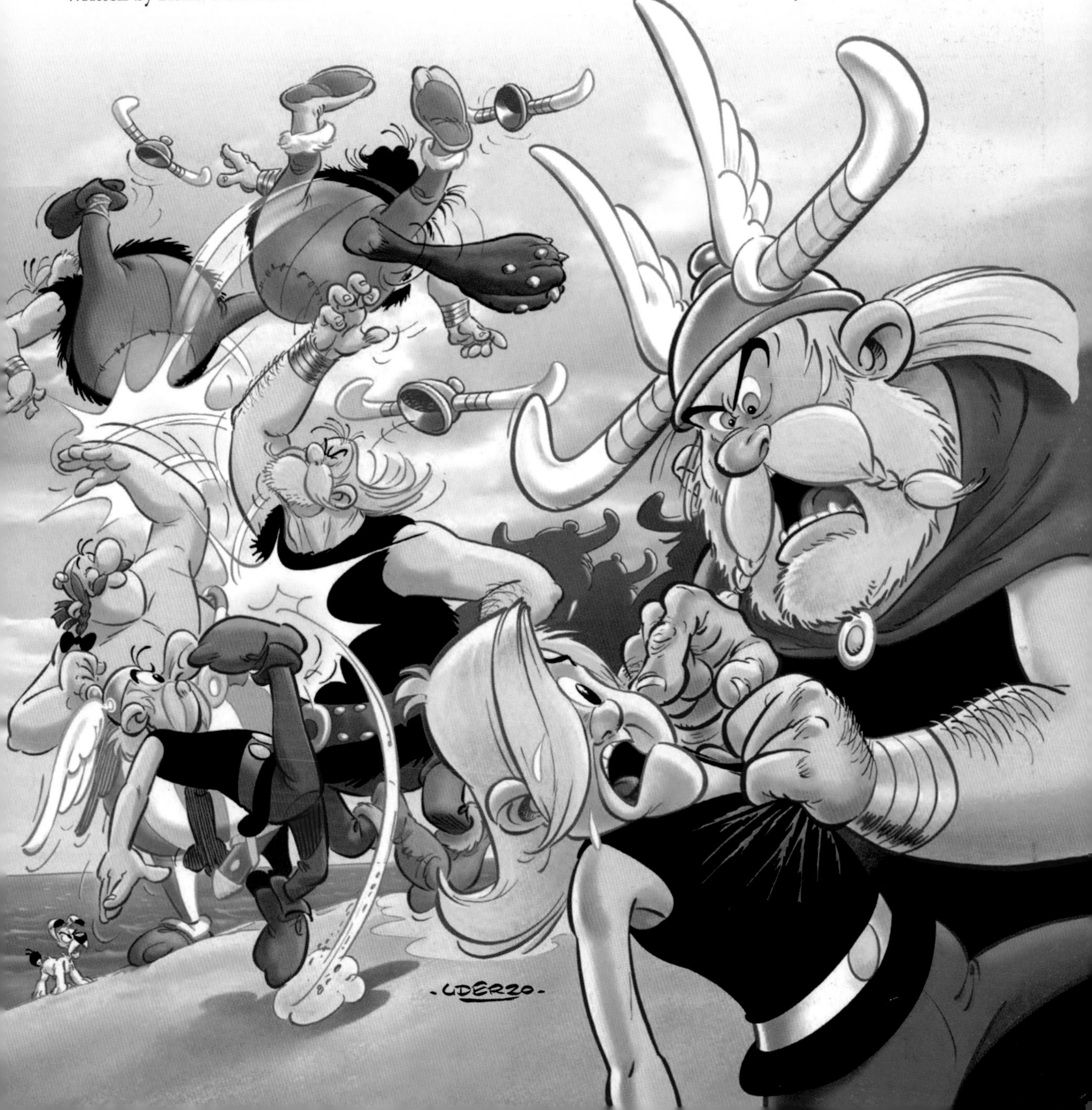
UDERZO

ASTERIX AND THE NORMANS

Written by RENÉ GOSCINNY *and illustrated by* ALBERT UDERZO

IT'S THE BEGINNING OF A PEACEFUL DAY IN THE LITTLE VILLAGE WE KNOW SO WELL...

HONEY! I FINALLY GOT THE SEERS AND WARLOCKS CATALOG!

HEY! THAT'S PNEUMATIX, THE MAILMAN!

NOTHING FOR US, PNEUMATIX?

NO! THE ONLY THING I HAVE LEFT IS A MESSAGE FOR CHIEF VITALSTATISTIX.

WE'LL GO WITH YOU.

MAIL

CAN I SEND MENHIRS BY MAIL?

YES, BUT BY REGISTERED MAIL, SO THEY DON'T GET LOST AT THE SORTING CENTER.

A LETTER FROM LUTETIA FOR YOU, O CHIEF VITALSTATISTIX.

AH! IT'S PROBABLY MY BROTHER, DOUBLEHELIX, WHO SENT IT... BUT HE DOESN'T ENGRAVE OFTEN.

OH!

NOTHING GRAVE IN THE ENGRAVING, I HOPE?

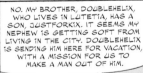

NO. MY BROTHER, DOUBLEHELIX, WHO LIVES IN LUTETIA, HAS A SON, JUSTFORKIX. IT SEEMS MY NEPHEW IS GETTING SOFT FROM LIVING IN THE CITY. DOUBLEHELIX IS SENDING HIM HERE FOR VACATION, WITH A MISSION FOR US TO MAKE A MAN OUT OF HIM.

WELL, I'M COUNTING ON YOU, MY FRIENDS!

WHEN WE'RE DONE WITH HIM, HE'LL HUNT BOARS WITH HIS BARE FISTS!

OH? IS THERE ANY OTHER WAY?

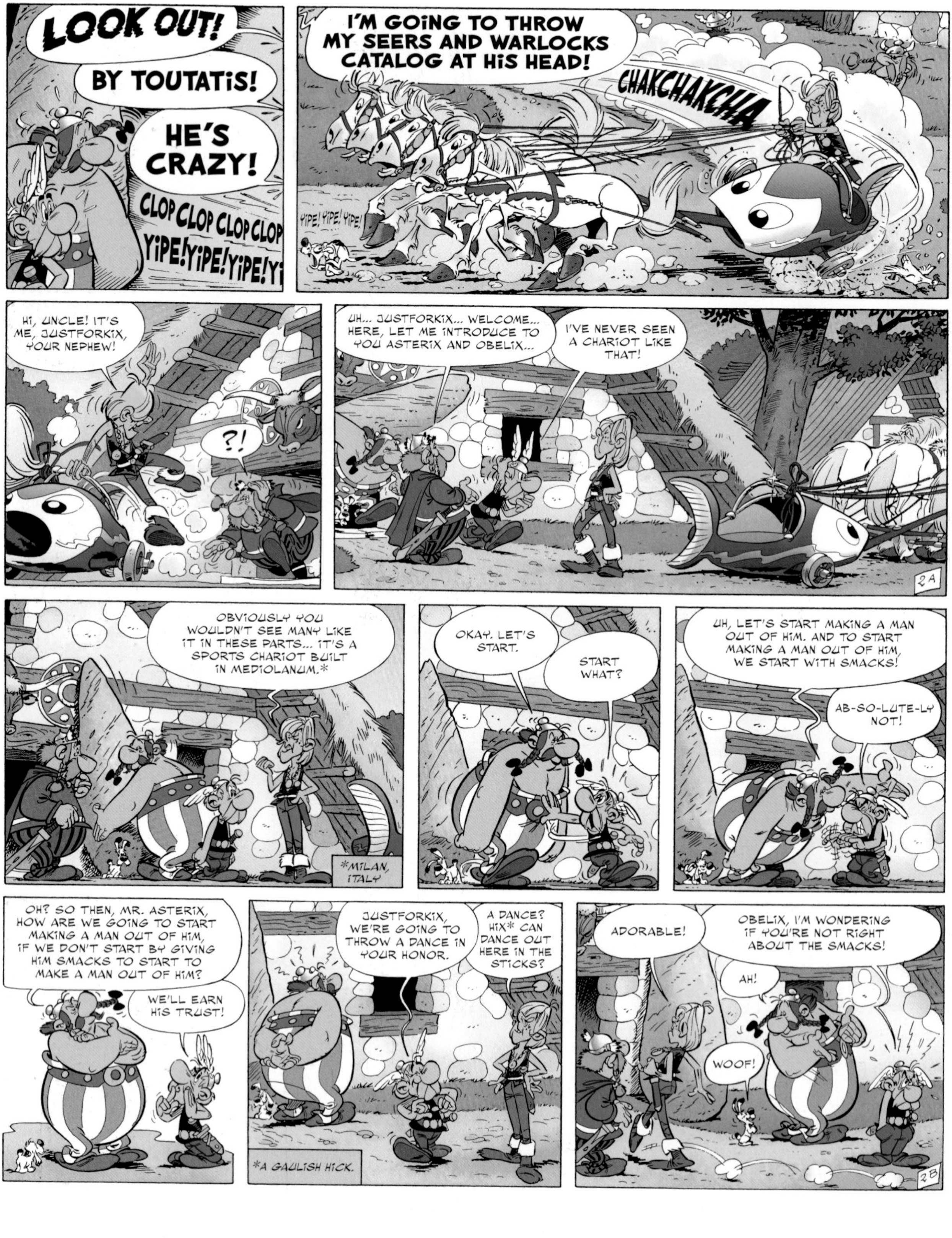
LOOK OUT!
BY TOUTATIS!
HE'S CRAZY!
CLOP CLOP CLOP CLOP
YIPE! YIPE! YIPE!
I'M GOING TO THROW MY SEERS AND WARLOCKS CATALOG AT HIS HEAD!
CHAKCHAKCHA
YIPE! YIPE! YIPE!
HI, UNCLE! IT'S ME, JUSTFORKIX, YOUR NEPHEW!
?!
UH... JUSTFORKIX... WELCOME... HERE, LET ME INTRODUCE TO YOU ASTERIX AND OBELIX...
I'VE NEVER SEEN A CHARIOT LIKE THAT!
OBVIOUSLY YOU WOULDN'T SEE MANY LIKE IT IN THESE PARTS... IT'S A SPORTS CHARIOT BUILT IN MEDIOLANUM.*
*MILAN, ITALY
OKAY. LET'S START.
START WHAT?
UH, LET'S START MAKING A MAN OUT OF HIM. AND TO START MAKING A MAN OUT OF HIM, WE START WITH SMACKS!
AB-SO-LUTE-LY NOT!
OH? SO THEN, MR. ASTERIX, HOW ARE WE GOING TO START MAKING A MAN OUT OF HIM, IF WE DON'T START BY GIVING HIM SMACKS TO START TO MAKE A MAN OUT OF HIM?
WE'LL EARN HIS TRUST!
JUSTFORKIX, WE'RE GOING TO THROW A DANCE IN YOUR HONOR.
A DANCE? HIX* CAN DANCE OUT HERE IN THE STICKS?
*A GAULISH HICK.
ADORABLE!
OBELIX, I'M WONDERING IF YOU'RE NOT RIGHT ABOUT THE SMACKS!
AH!
WOOF!

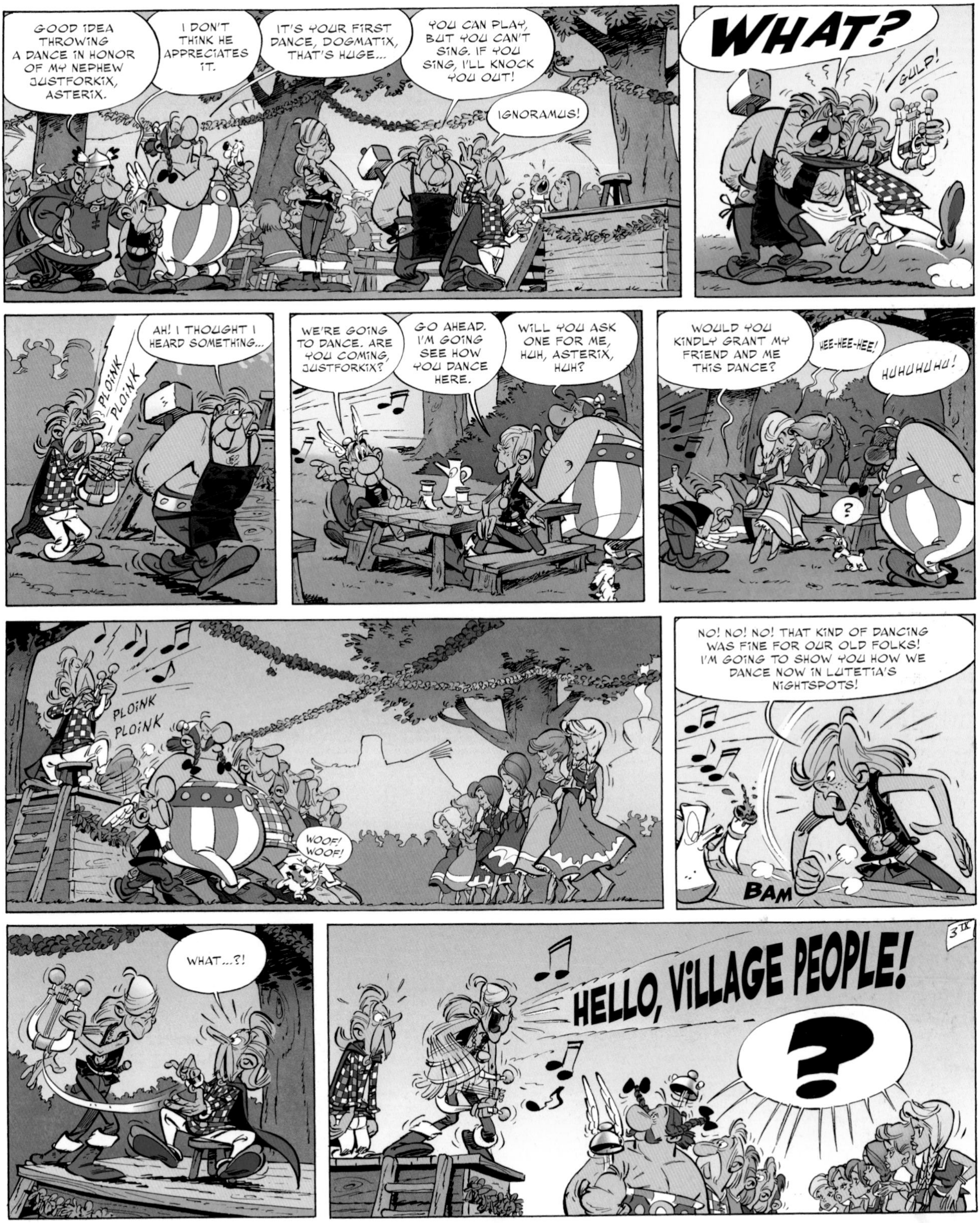
GOOD IDEA THROWING A DANCE IN HONOR OF MY NEPHEW JUSTFORKIX, ASTERIX.
I DON'T THINK HE APPRECIATES IT.
IT'S YOUR FIRST DANCE, DOGMATIX, THAT'S HUGE...
YOU CAN PLAY, BUT YOU CAN'T SING. IF YOU SING, I'LL KNOCK YOU OUT!
IGNORAMUS!
WHAT?
GULP!
PLOINK PLOINK
AH! I THOUGHT I HEARD SOMETHING...
WE'RE GOING TO DANCE. ARE YOU COMING, JUSTFORKIX?
GO AHEAD. I'M GOING SEE HOW YOU DANCE HERE.
WILL YOU ASK ONE FOR ME, HUH, ASTERIX, HUH?
WOULD YOU KINDLY GRANT MY FRIEND AND ME THIS DANCE?
HEE-HEE-HEE!
HUHUHUHU!
?
PLOINK PLOINK
WOOF! WOOF!
NO! NO! NO! THAT KIND OF DANCING WAS FINE FOR OUR OLD FOLKS! I'M GOING TO SHOW YOU HOW WE DANCE NOW IN LUTETIA'S NIGHTSPOTS!
BAM
WHAT...?!
HELLO, VILLAGE PEOPLE!
?

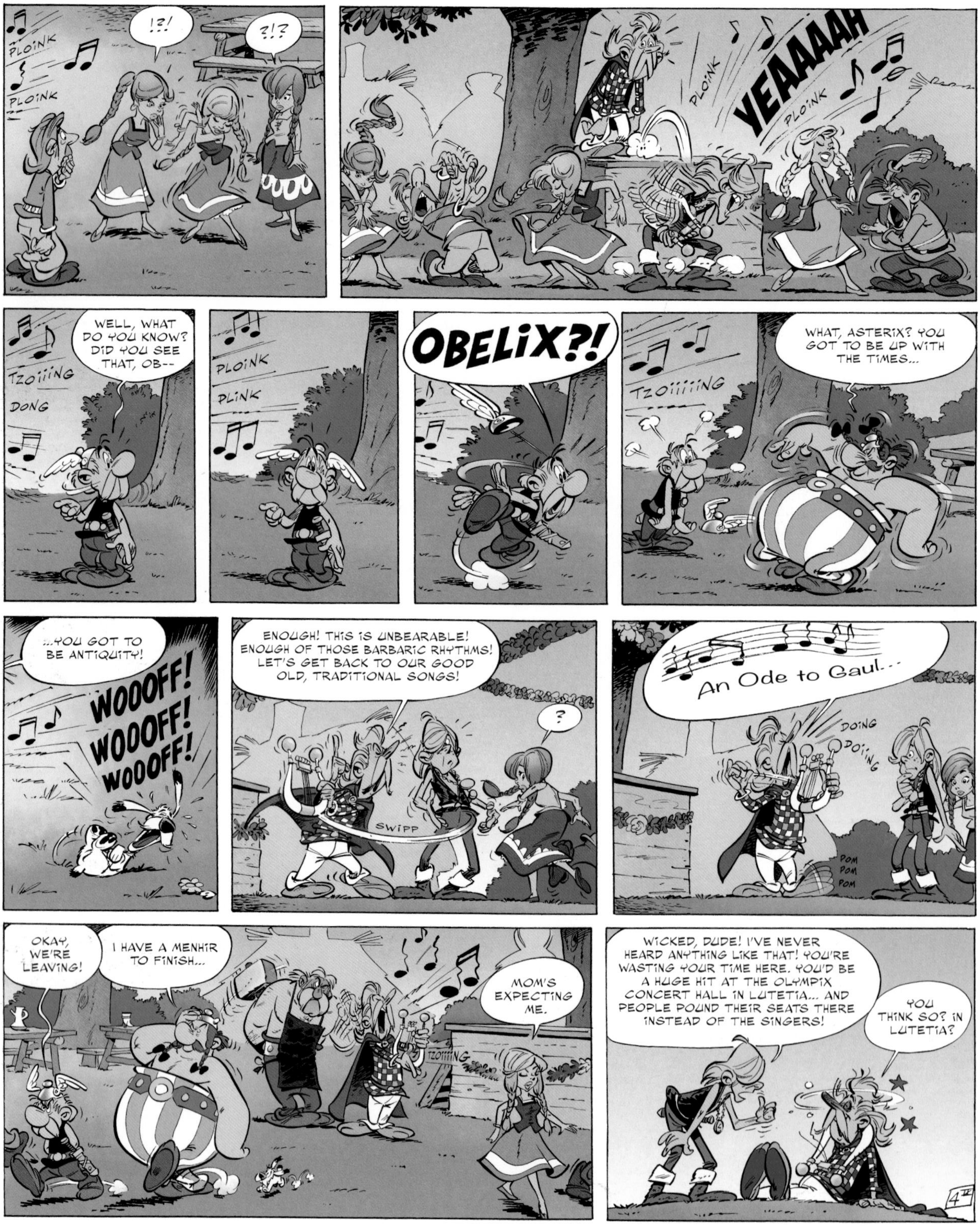
PLOINK
PLOINK
!?!
?!?
PLOINK
YEAAAAH
PLOINK
WELL, WHAT DO YOU KNOW? DID YOU SEE THAT, OB--
TZOiiiiNG
DONG
PLOiNK
PLiNK
OBELiX?!
WHAT, ASTERIX? YOU GOT TO BE UP WITH THE TIMES...
TZOiiiiiNG
...YOU GOT TO BE ANTIQUITY!
WOOOFF! WOOOFF! WOOOFF!
ENOUGH! THIS IS UNBEARABLE! ENOUGH OF THOSE BARBARIC RHYTHMS! LET'S GET BACK TO OUR GOOD OLD, TRADITIONAL SONGS!
?
SWIPP
An Ode to Gaul...
DOiNG
DOiNG
POM POM POM
OKAY, WE'RE LEAVING!
I HAVE A MENHIR TO FINISH...
MOM'S EXPECTING ME.
TZOiiiiNG
WICKED, DUDE! I'VE NEVER HEARD ANYTHING LIKE THAT! YOU'RE WASTING YOUR TIME HERE. YOU'D BE A HUGE HIT AT THE OLYMPIX CONCERT HALL IN LUTETIA... AND PEOPLE POUND THEIR SEATS THERE INSTEAD OF THE SINGERS!
YOU THINK SO? IN LUTETIA?

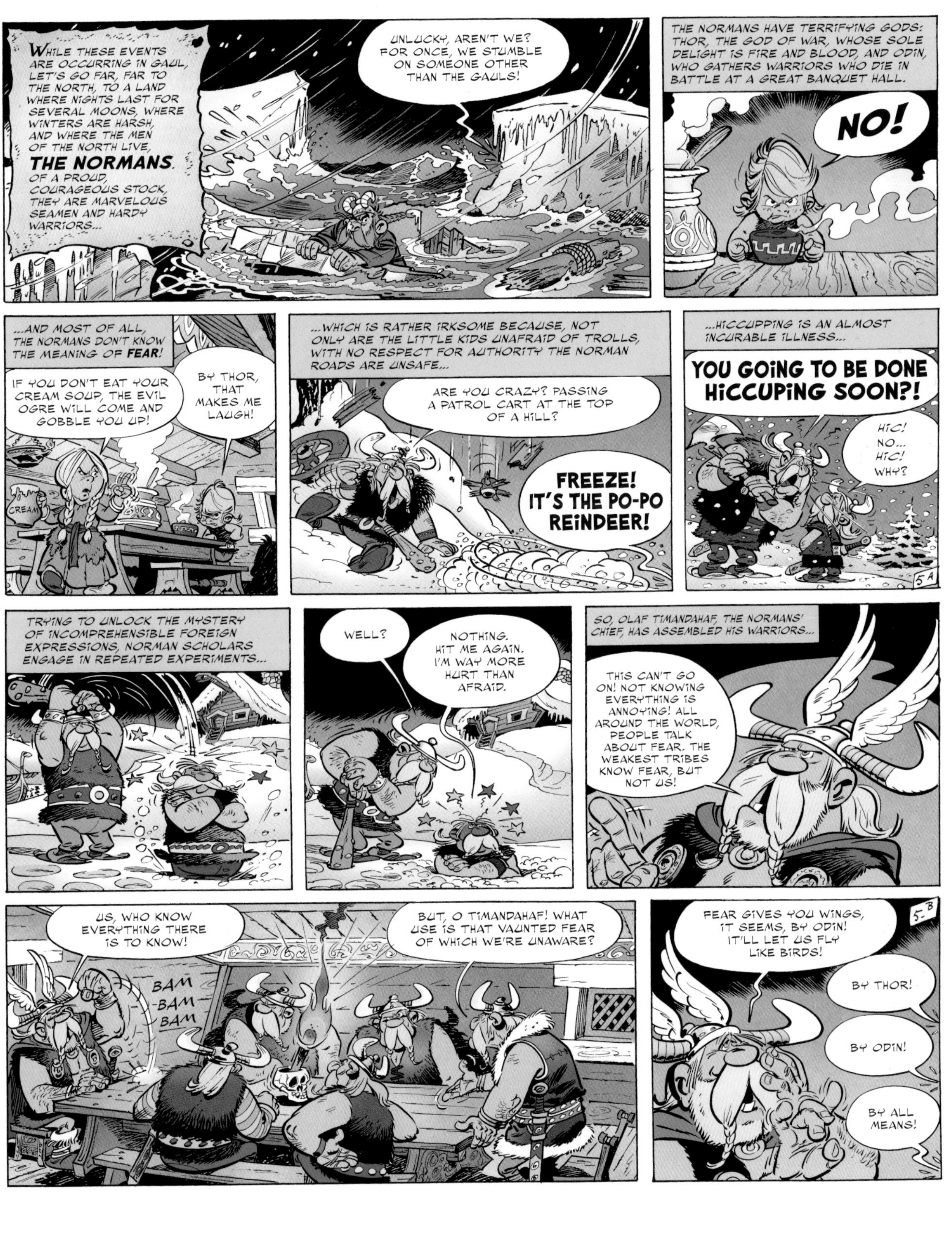
WHILE THESE EVENTS ARE OCCURRING IN GAUL, LET'S GO FAR, FAR TO THE NORTH, TO A LAND WHERE NIGHTS LAST FOR SEVERAL MOONS, WHERE WINTERS ARE HARSH, AND WHERE THE MEN OF THE NORTH LIVE, THE NORMANS. OF A PROUD, COURAGEOUS STOCK, THEY ARE MARVELOUS SEAMEN AND HARDY WARRIORS...
UNLUCKY, AREN'T WE? FOR ONCE, WE STUMBLE ON SOMEONE OTHER THAN THE GAULS!
THE NORMANS HAVE TERRIFYING GODS: THOR, THE GOD OF WAR, WHOSE SOLE DELIGHT IS FIRE AND BLOOD, AND ODIN, WHO GATHERS WARRIORS WHO DIE IN BATTLE AT A GREAT BANQUET HALL.
NO!
...AND MOST OF ALL, THE NORMANS DON'T KNOW THE MEANING OF FEAR!
IF YOU DON'T EAT YOUR CREAM SOUP, THE EVIL OGRE WILL COME AND GOBBLE YOU UP!
BY THOR, THAT MAKES ME LAUGH!
CREAM
...WHICH IS RATHER IRKSOME BECAUSE, NOT ONLY ARE THE LITTLE KIDS UNAFRAID OF TROLLS, WITH NO RESPECT FOR AUTHORITY THE NORMAN ROADS ARE UNSAFE...
ARE YOU CRAZY? PASSING A PATROL CART AT THE TOP OF A HILL?
FREEZE! IT'S THE PO-PO REINDEER!
...HICCUPPING IS AN ALMOST INCURABLE ILLNESS...
YOU GOING TO BE DONE HICCUPING SOON?!
HIC! NO... HIC! WHY?
5A
TRYING TO UNLOCK THE MYSTERY OF INCOMPREHENSIBLE FOREIGN EXPRESSIONS, NORMAN SCHOLARS ENGAGE IN REPEATED EXPERIMENTS...
WELL?
NOTHING. HIT ME AGAIN. I'M WAY MORE HURT THAN AFRAID.
SO, OLAF TIMANDAHAF, THE NORMANS' CHIEF, HAS ASSEMBLED HIS WARRIORS...
THIS CAN'T GO ON! NOT KNOWING EVERYTHING IS ANNOYING! ALL AROUND THE WORLD, PEOPLE TALK ABOUT FEAR. THE WEAKEST TRIBES KNOW FEAR, BUT NOT US!
US, WHO KNOW EVERYTHING THERE IS TO KNOW!
BAM BAM BAM
BUT, O TIMANDAHAF! WHAT USE IS THAT VAUNTED FEAR OF WHICH WE'RE UNAWARE?
5B
FEAR GIVES YOU WINGS, IT SEEMS, BY ODIN! IT'LL LET US FLY LIKE BIRDS!
BY THOR!
BY ODIN!
BY ALL MEANS!

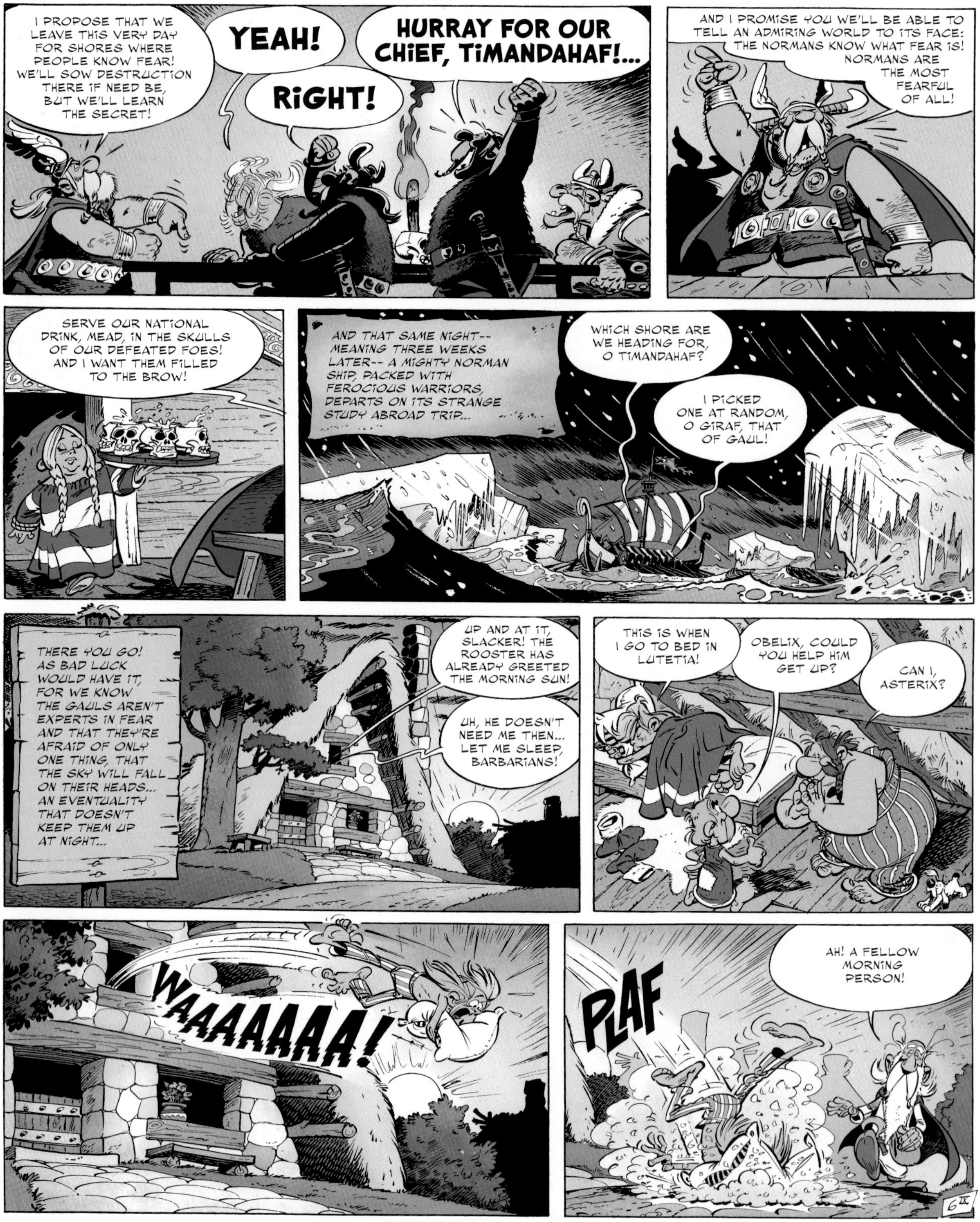

I PROPOSE THAT WE LEAVE THIS VERY DAY FOR SHORES WHERE PEOPLE KNOW FEAR! WE'LL SOW DESTRUCTION THERE IF NEED BE, BUT WE'LL LEARN THE SECRET!
YEAH!
RIGHT!
HURRAY FOR OUR CHIEF, TIMANDAHAF!...
AND I PROMISE YOU WE'LL BE ABLE TO TELL AN ADMIRING WORLD TO ITS FACE: THE NORMANS KNOW WHAT FEAR IS! NORMANS ARE THE MOST FEARFUL OF ALL!
SERVE OUR NATIONAL DRINK, MEAD, IN THE SKULLS OF OUR DEFEATED FOES! AND I WANT THEM FILLED TO THE BROW!
AND THAT SAME NIGHT-- MEANING THREE WEEKS LATER-- A MIGHTY NORMAN SHIP, PACKED WITH FEROCIOUS WARRIORS, DEPARTS ON ITS STRANGE STUDY ABROAD TRIP...
WHICH SHORE ARE WE HEADING FOR, O TIMANDAHAF?
I PICKED ONE AT RANDOM, O GIRAF, THAT OF GAUL!
THERE YOU GO! AS BAD LUCK WOULD HAVE IT, FOR WE KNOW THE GAULS AREN'T EXPERTS IN FEAR AND THAT THEY'RE AFRAID OF ONLY ONE THING, THAT THE SKY WILL FALL ON THEIR HEADS... AN EVENTUALITY THAT DOESN'T KEEP THEM UP AT NIGHT...
UP AND AT IT, SLACKER! THE ROOSTER HAS ALREADY GREETED THE MORNING SUN!
UH, HE DOESN'T NEED ME THEN... LET ME SLEEP, BARBARIANS!
THIS IS WHEN I GO TO BED IN LUTETIA!
OBELIX, COULD YOU HELP HIM GET UP?
CAN I, ASTERIX?
WAAAAAAA!
PLAF
AH! A FELLOW MORNING PERSON!

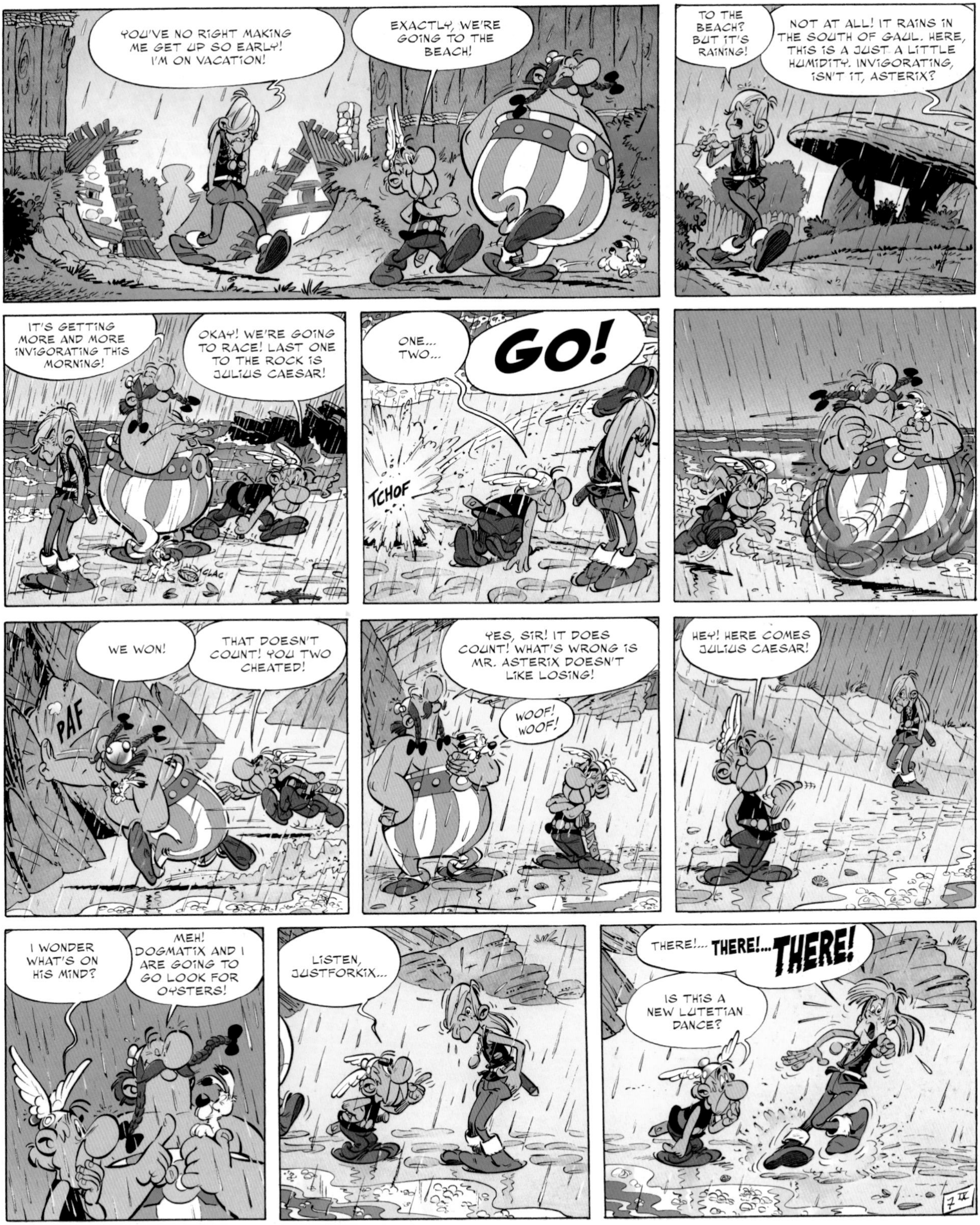
YOU'VE NO RIGHT MAKING ME GET UP SO EARLY! I'M ON VACATION!
EXACTLY, WE'RE GOING TO THE BEACH!
TO THE BEACH? BUT IT'S RAINING!
NOT AT ALL! IT RAINS IN THE SOUTH OF GAUL. HERE, THIS IS A JUST A LITTLE HUMIDITY. INVIGORATING, ISN'T IT, ASTERIX?
IT'S GETTING MORE AND MORE INVIGORATING THIS MORNING!
OKAY! WE'RE GOING TO RACE! LAST ONE TO THE ROCK IS JULIUS CAESAR!
GLAG
ONE... TWO...
GO!
TCHOF
WE WON!
THAT DOESN'T COUNT! YOU TWO CHEATED!
PAF
YES, SIR! IT DOES COUNT! WHAT'S WRONG IS MR. ASTERIX DOESN'T LIKE LOSING!
WOOF! WOOF!
HEY! HERE COMES JULIUS CAESAR!
I WONDER WHAT'S ON HIS MIND?
MEH! DOGMATIX AND I ARE GOING TO GO LOOK FOR OYSTERS!
LISTEN, JUSTFORKIX...
THERE!... THERE!... THERE!
IS THIS A NEW LUTETIAN DANCE?

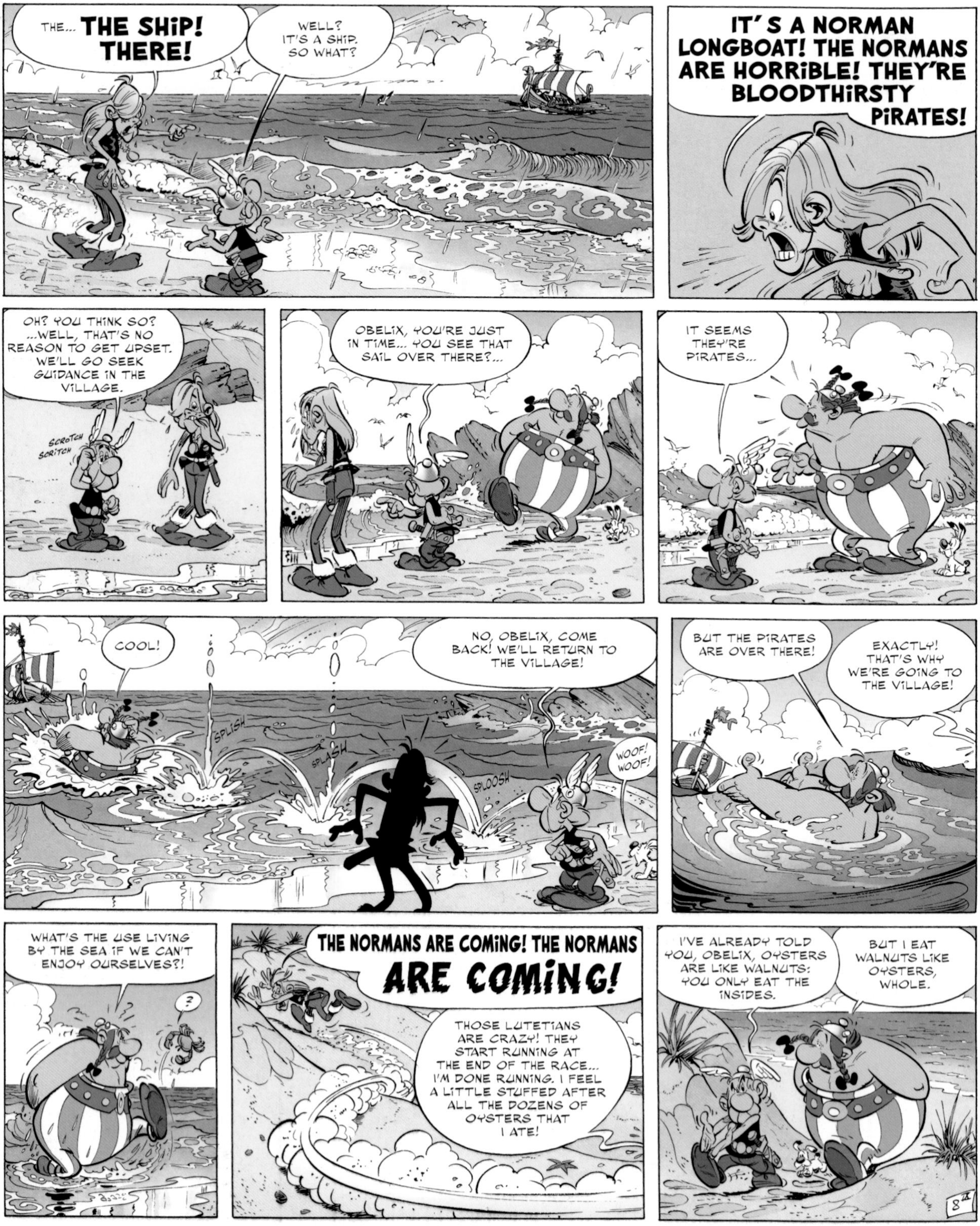
THE... THE SHIP! THERE!
WELL? IT'S A SHIP. SO WHAT?
IT'S A NORMAN LONGBOAT! THE NORMANS ARE HORRIBLE! THEY'RE BLOODTHIRSTY PIRATES!
OH? YOU THINK SO? ...WELL, THAT'S NO REASON TO GET UPSET. WE'LL GO SEEK GUIDANCE IN THE VILLAGE.
SCRATCH SCRITCH
OBELIX, YOU'RE JUST IN TIME... YOU SEE THAT SAIL OVER THERE?...
IT SEEMS THEY'RE PIRATES...
COOL!
SPLISH
SPLASH
SPLOOSH
NO, OBELIX, COME BACK! WE'LL RETURN TO THE VILLAGE!
WOOF! WOOF!
BUT THE PIRATES ARE OVER THERE!
EXACTLY! THAT'S WHY WE'RE GOING TO THE VILLAGE!
WHAT'S THE USE LIVING BY THE SEA IF WE CAN'T ENJOY OURSELVES?!
?
THE NORMANS ARE COMING! THE NORMANS ARE COMING!
THOSE LUTETIANS ARE CRAZY! THEY START RUNNING AT THE END OF THE RACE... I'M DONE RUNNING. I FEEL A LITTLE STUFFED AFTER ALL THE DOZENS OF OYSTERS THAT I ATE!
I'VE ALREADY TOLD YOU, OBELIX, OYSTERS ARE LIKE WALNUTS: YOU ONLY EAT THE INSIDES.
BUT I EAT WALNUTS LIKE OYSTERS, WHOLE.
8A

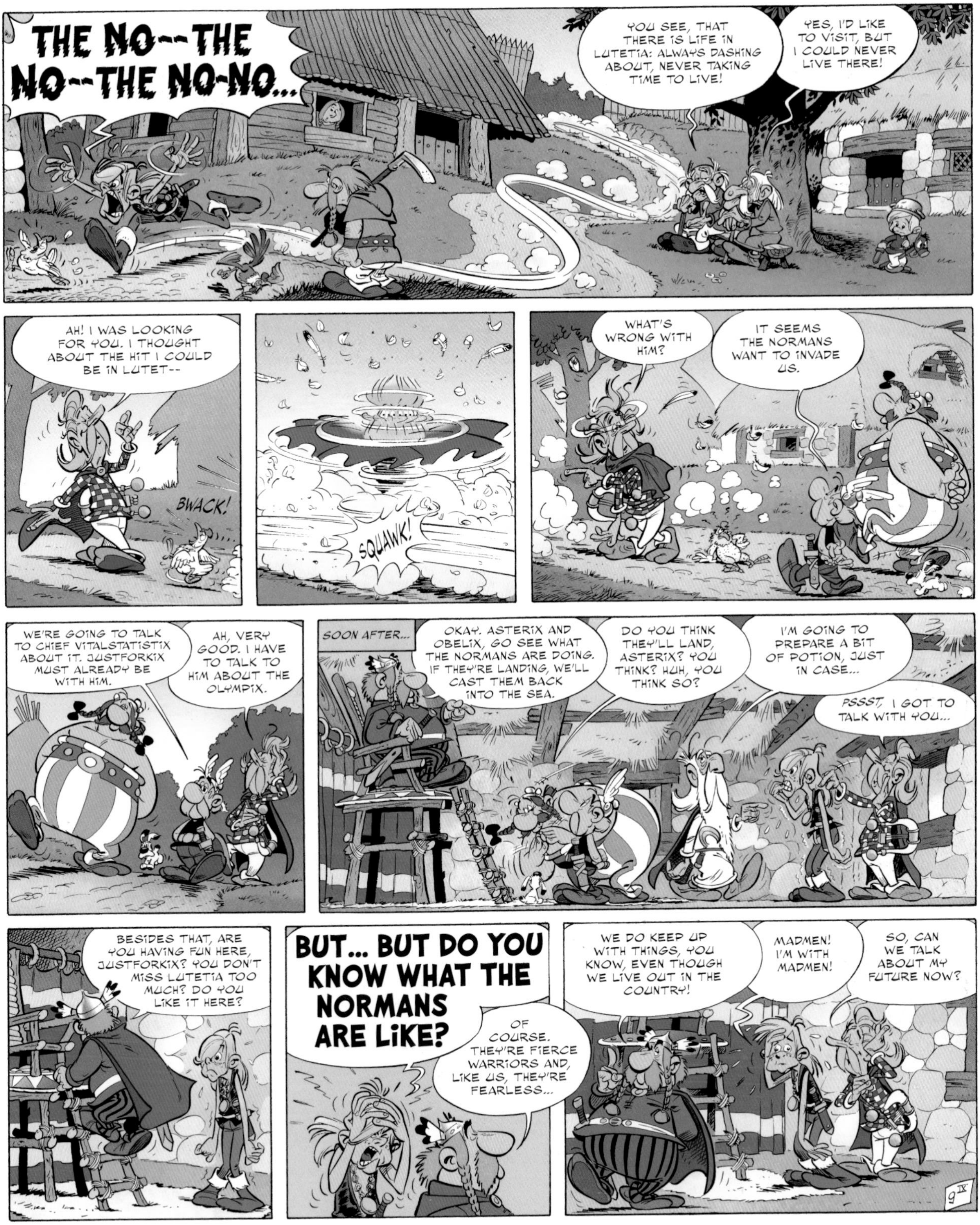
THE NO--THE NO--THE NO-NO...
YOU SEE, THAT THERE IS LIFE IN LUTETIA: ALWAYS DASHING ABOUT, NEVER TAKING TIME TO LIVE!
YES, I'D LIKE TO VISIT, BUT I COULD NEVER LIVE THERE!
AH! I WAS LOOKING FOR YOU. I THOUGHT ABOUT THE HIT I COULD BE IN LUTET--
BWACK!
SQUAWK!
WHAT'S WRONG WITH HIM?
IT SEEMS THE NORMANS WANT TO INVADE US.
WE'RE GOING TO TALK TO CHIEF VITALSTATISTIX ABOUT IT. JUSTFORKIX MUST ALREADY BE WITH HIM.
AH, VERY GOOD. I HAVE TO TALK TO HIM ABOUT THE OLYMPIX.
SOON AFTER...
OKAY. ASTERIX AND OBELIX, GO SEE WHAT THE NORMANS ARE DOING. IF THEY'RE LANDING, WE'LL CAST THEM BACK INTO THE SEA.
DO YOU THINK THEY'LL LAND, ASTERIX? YOU THINK? HUH, YOU THINK SO?
I'M GOING TO PREPARE A BIT OF POTION, JUST IN CASE...
PSSST, I GOT TO TALK WITH YOU...
BESIDES THAT, ARE YOU HAVING FUN HERE, JUSTFORKIX? YOU DON'T MISS LUTETIA TOO MUCH? DO YOU LIKE IT HERE?
BUT... BUT DO YOU KNOW WHAT THE NORMANS ARE LIKE?
OF COURSE. THEY'RE FIERCE WARRIORS AND, LIKE US, THEY'RE FEARLESS...
WE DO KEEP UP WITH THINGS, YOU KNOW, EVEN THOUGH WE LIVE OUT IN THE COUNTRY!
MADMEN! I'M WITH MADMEN!
SO, CAN WE TALK ABOUT MY FUTURE NOW?

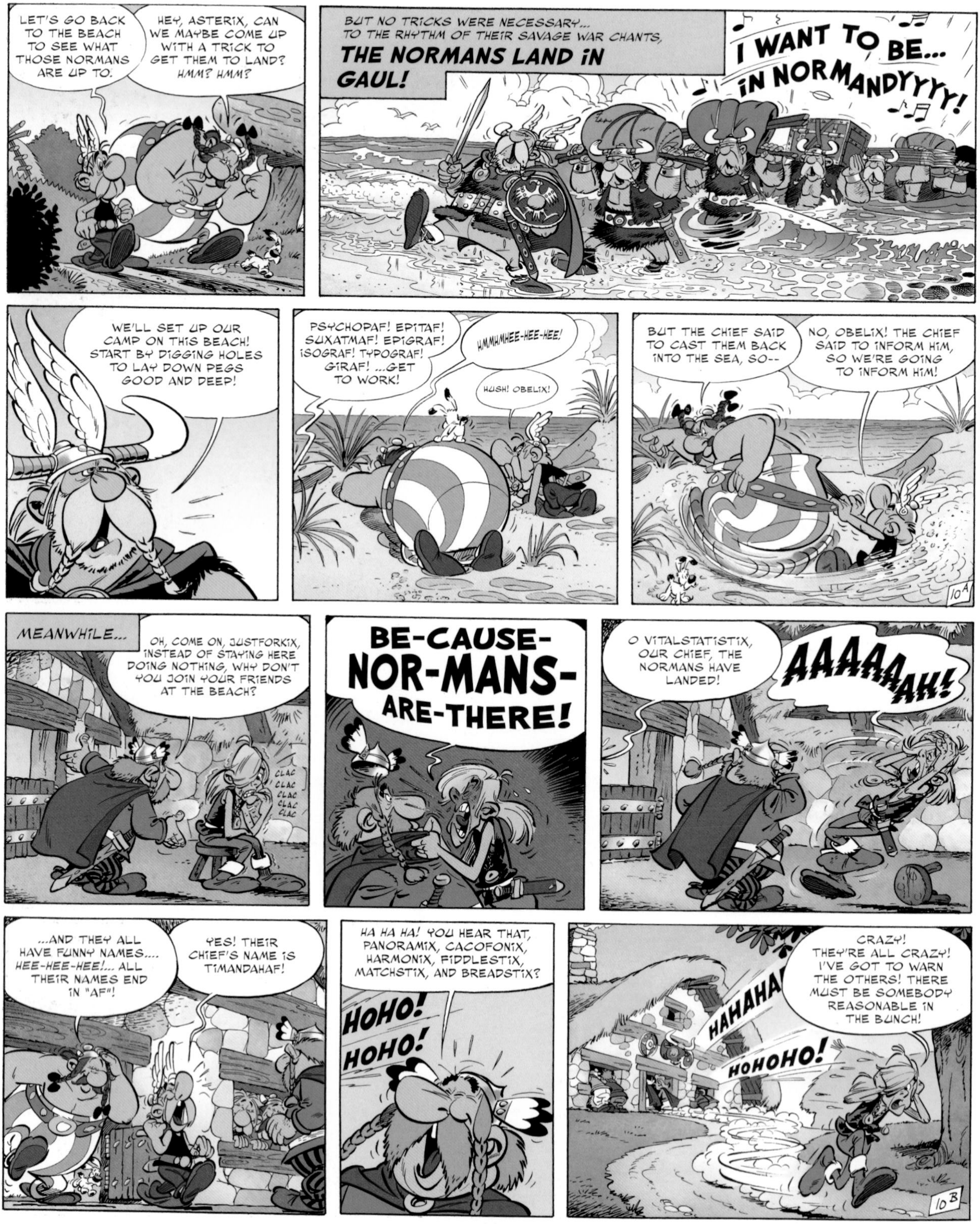
LET'S GO BACK TO THE BEACH TO SEE WHAT THOSE NORMANS ARE UP TO.
HEY, ASTERIX, CAN WE MAYBE COME UP WITH A TRICK TO GET THEM TO LAND? HMM? HMM?
BUT NO TRICKS WERE NECESSARY... TO THE RHYTHM OF THEIR SAVAGE WAR CHANTS, THE NORMANS LAND IN GAUL!
I WANT TO BE... IN NORMANDYYYY!
WE'LL SET UP OUR CAMP ON THIS BEACH! START BY DIGGING HOLES TO LAY DOWN PEGS GOOD AND DEEP!
PSYCHOPAF! EPITAF! SUXATMAF! EPIGRAF! ISOGRAF! TYPOGRAF! GIRAF! ...GET TO WORK!
HMMHMHEE-HEE-HEE!
HUSH! OBELIX!
BUT THE CHIEF SAID TO CAST THEM BACK INTO THE SEA, SO--
NO, OBELIX! THE CHIEF SAID TO INFORM HIM, SO WE'RE GOING TO INFORM HIM!
10A
MEANWHILE...
OH, COME ON, JUSTFORKIX, INSTEAD OF STAYING HERE DOING NOTHING, WHY DON'T YOU JOIN YOUR FRIENDS AT THE BEACH?
CLAC CLAC CLAC CLAC CLAC
BE-CAUSE- NOR-MANS- ARE-THERE!
O VITALSTATISTIX, OUR CHIEF, THE NORMANS HAVE LANDED!
AAAAAAH!
...AND THEY ALL HAVE FUNNY NAMES.... HEE-HEE-HEE!... ALL THEIR NAMES END IN "AF"!
YES! THEIR CHIEF'S NAME IS TIMANDAHAF!
HA HA HA! YOU HEAR THAT, PANORAMIX, CACOFONIX, HARMONIX, FIDDLESTIX, MATCHSTIX, AND BREADSTIX?
HOHO! HOHO!
HAHAHA
HOHOHO!
CRAZY! THEY'RE ALL CRAZY! I'VE GOT TO WARN THE OTHERS! THERE MUST BE SOMEBODY REASONABLE IN THE BUNCH!
10B

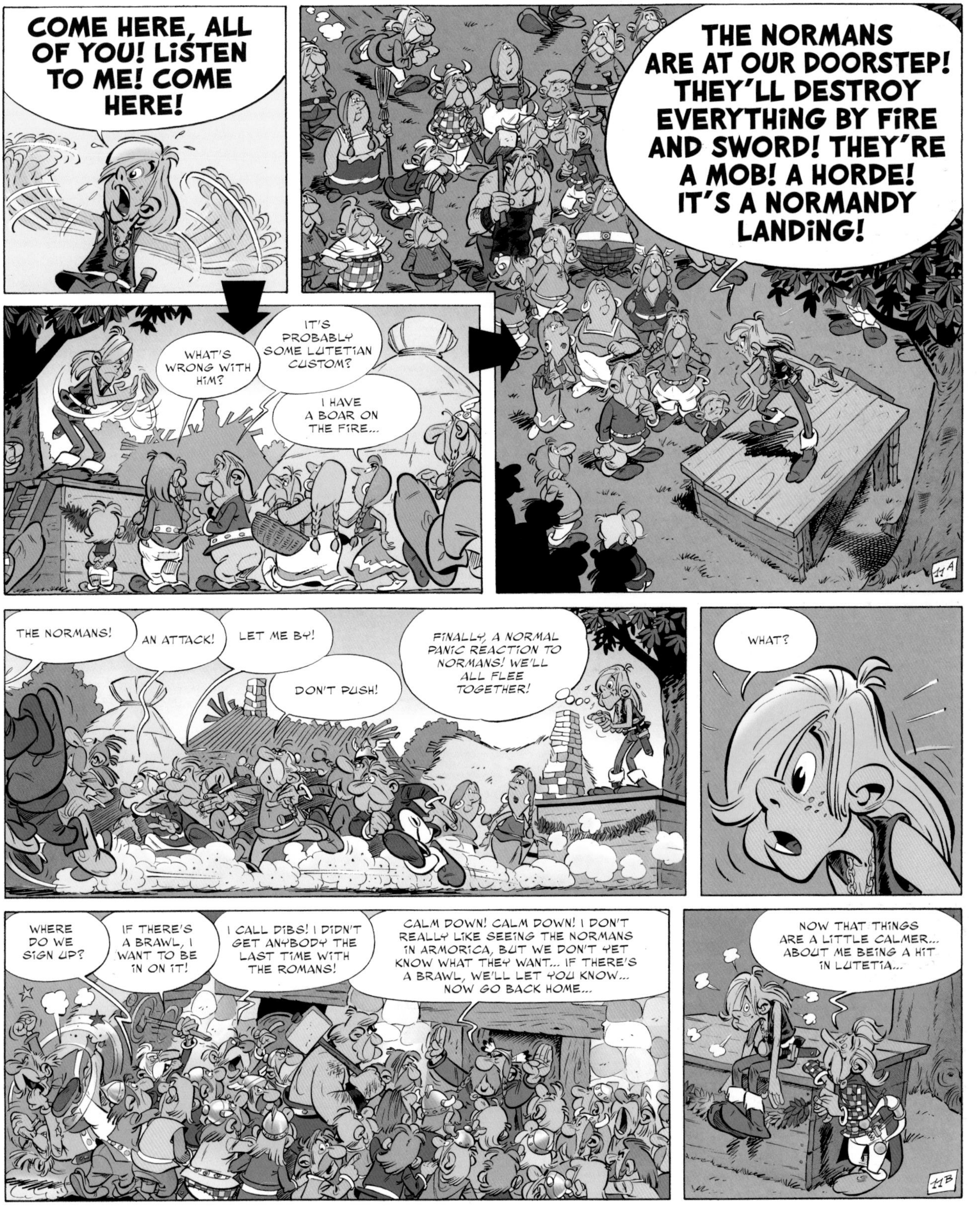
COME HERE, ALL OF YOU! LISTEN TO ME! COME HERE!
THE NORMANS ARE AT OUR DOORSTEP! THEY'LL DESTROY EVERYTHING BY FIRE AND SWORD! THEY'RE A MOB! A HORDE! IT'S A NORMANDY LANDING!
WHAT'S WRONG WITH HIM?
IT'S PROBABLY SOME LUTETIAN CUSTOM?
I HAVE A BOAR ON THE FIRE...
11A
THE NORMANS!
AN ATTACK!
LET ME BY!
DON'T PUSH!
FINALLY, A NORMAL PANIC REACTION TO NORMANS! WE'LL ALL FLEE TOGETHER!
WHAT?
WHERE DO WE SIGN UP?
IF THERE'S A BRAWL, I WANT TO BE IN ON IT!
I CALL DIBS! I DIDN'T GET ANYBODY THE LAST TIME WITH THE ROMANS!
CALM DOWN! CALM DOWN! I DON'T REALLY LIKE SEEING THE NORMANS IN ARMORICA, BUT WE DON'T YET KNOW WHAT THEY WANT... IF THERE'S A BRAWL, WE'LL LET YOU KNOW... NOW GO BACK HOME...
NOW THAT THINGS ARE A LITTLE CALMER... ABOUT ME BEING A HIT IN LUTETIA...
11B

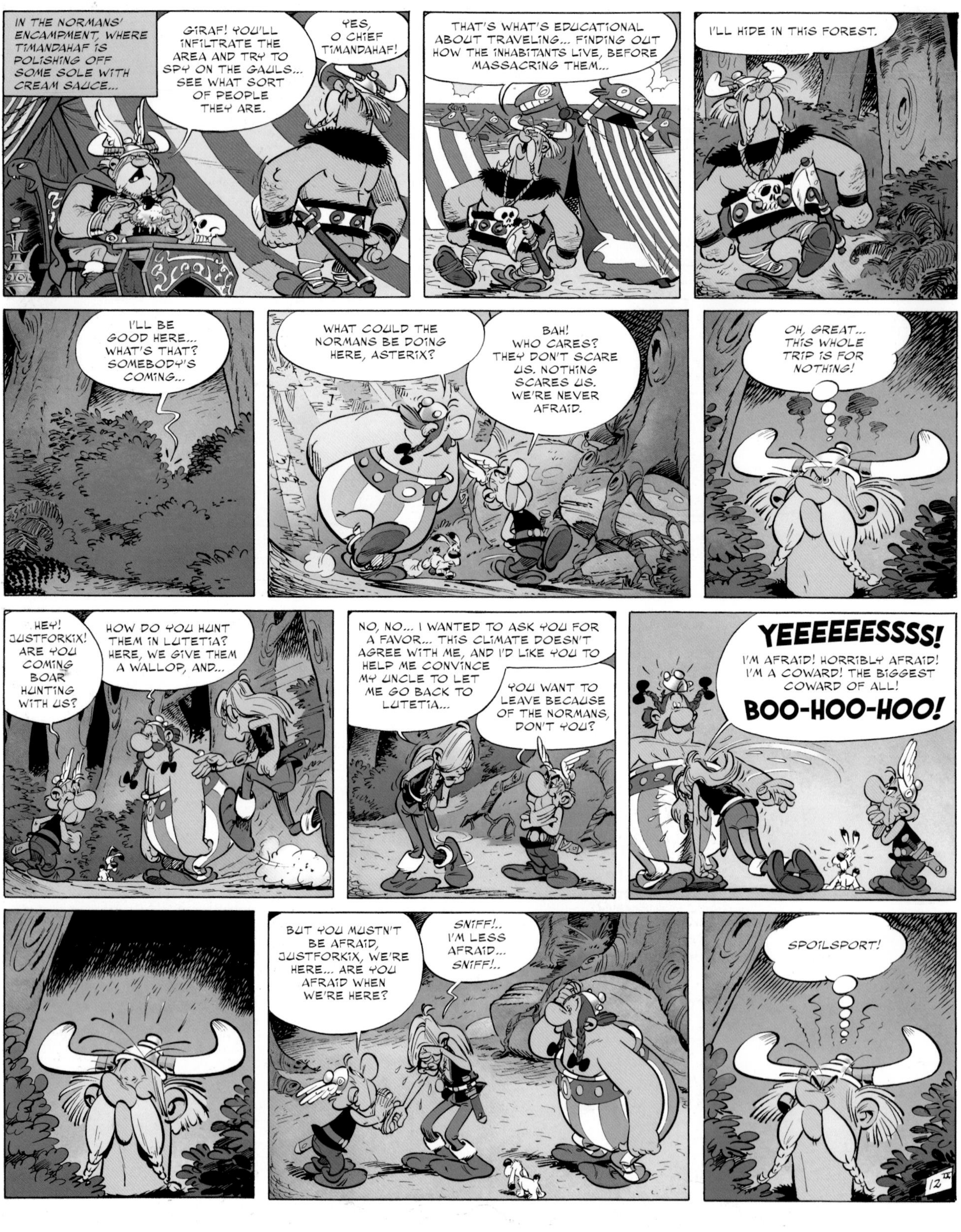
IN THE NORMANS' ENCAMPMENT, WHERE TIMANDAHAF IS POLISHING OFF SOME SOLE WITH CREAM SAUCE...
GIRAF! YOU'LL INFILTRATE THE AREA AND TRY TO SPY ON THE GAULS... SEE WHAT SORT OF PEOPLE THEY ARE.
YES, O CHIEF TIMANDAHAF!
THAT'S WHAT'S EDUCATIONAL ABOUT TRAVELING... FINDING OUT HOW THE INHABITANTS LIVE, BEFORE MASSACRING THEM...
I'LL HIDE IN THIS FOREST.
I'LL BE GOOD HERE... WHAT'S THAT? SOMEBODY'S COMING...
WHAT COULD THE NORMANS BE DOING HERE, ASTERIX?
BAH! WHO CARES? THEY DON'T SCARE US. NOTHING SCARES US. WE'RE NEVER AFRAID.
OH, GREAT... THIS WHOLE TRIP IS FOR NOTHING!
HEY! JUSTFORKIX! ARE YOU COMING BOAR HUNTING WITH US?
HOW DO YOU HUNT THEM IN LUTETIA? HERE, WE GIVE THEM A WALLOP, AND...
NO, NO... I WANTED TO ASK YOU FOR A FAVOR... THIS CLIMATE DOESN'T AGREE WITH ME, AND I'D LIKE YOU TO HELP ME CONVINCE MY UNCLE TO LET ME GO BACK TO LUTETIA...
YOU WANT TO LEAVE BECAUSE OF THE NORMANS, DON'T YOU?
YEEEEEESSSS!
I'M AFRAID! HORRIBLY AFRAID! I'M A COWARD! THE BIGGEST COWARD OF ALL!
BOO-HOO-HOO!
BUT YOU MUSTN'T BE AFRAID, JUSTFORKIX, WE'RE HERE... ARE YOU AFRAID WHEN WE'RE HERE?
SNIFF!.. I'M LESS AFRAID... SNIFF!..
SPOILSPORT!
12

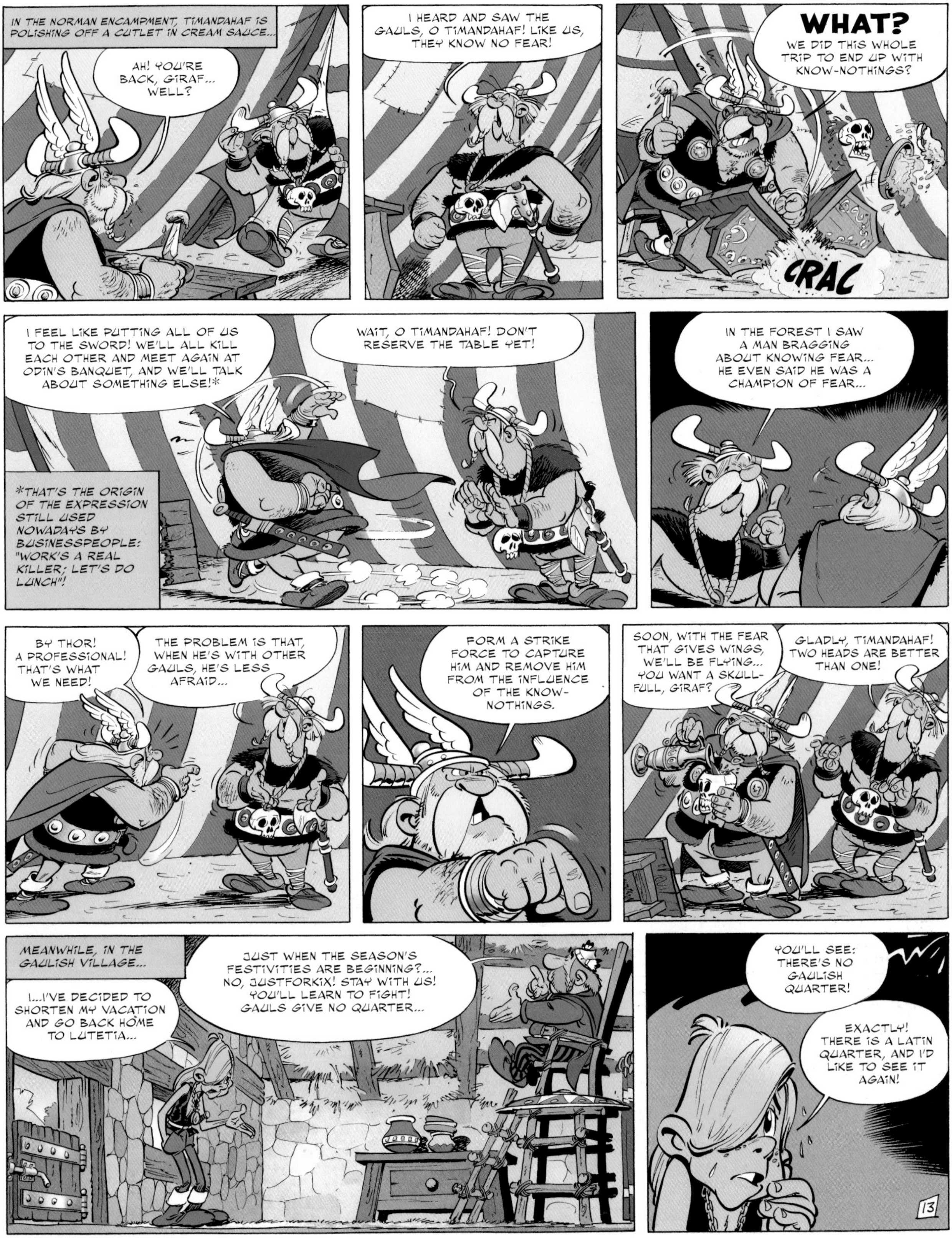

IN THE NORMAN ENCAMPMENT, TIMANDAHAF IS POLISHING OFF A CUTLET IN CREAM SAUCE...
AH! YOU'RE BACK, GIRAF... WELL?
I HEARD AND SAW THE GAULS, O TIMANDAHAF! LIKE US, THEY KNOW NO FEAR!
WHAT?
WE DID THIS WHOLE TRIP TO END UP WITH KNOW-NOTHINGS?
CRAC
I FEEL LIKE PUTTING ALL OF US TO THE SWORD! WE'LL ALL KILL EACH OTHER AND MEET AGAIN AT ODIN'S BANQUET, AND WE'LL TALK ABOUT SOMETHING ELSE!*
WAIT, O TIMANDAHAF! DON'T RESERVE THE TABLE YET!
*THAT'S THE ORIGIN OF THE EXPRESSION STILL USED NOWADAYS BY BUSINESSPEOPLE: "WORK'S A REAL KILLER; LET'S DO LUNCH"!
IN THE FOREST I SAW A MAN BRAGGING ABOUT KNOWING FEAR... HE EVEN SAID HE WAS A CHAMPION OF FEAR...
BY THOR! A PROFESSIONAL! THAT'S WHAT WE NEED!
THE PROBLEM IS THAT, WHEN HE'S WITH OTHER GAULS, HE'S LESS AFRAID...
FORM A STRIKE FORCE TO CAPTURE HIM AND REMOVE HIM FROM THE INFLUENCE OF THE KNOW-NOTHINGS.
SOON, WITH THE FEAR THAT GIVES WINGS, WE'LL BE FLYING... YOU WANT A SKULL-FULL, GIRAF?
GLADLY, TIMANDAHAF! TWO HEADS ARE BETTER THAN ONE!
MEANWHILE, IN THE GAULISH VILLAGE...
I...I'VE DECIDED TO SHORTEN MY VACATION AND GO BACK HOME TO LUTETIA...
JUST WHEN THE SEASON'S FESTIVITIES ARE BEGINNING?... NO, JUSTFORKIX! STAY WITH US! YOU'LL LEARN TO FIGHT! GAULS GIVE NO QUARTER...
YOU'LL SEE: THERE'S NO GAULISH QUARTER!
EXACTLY! THERE IS A LATIN QUARTER, AND I'D LIKE TO SEE IT AGAIN!
13

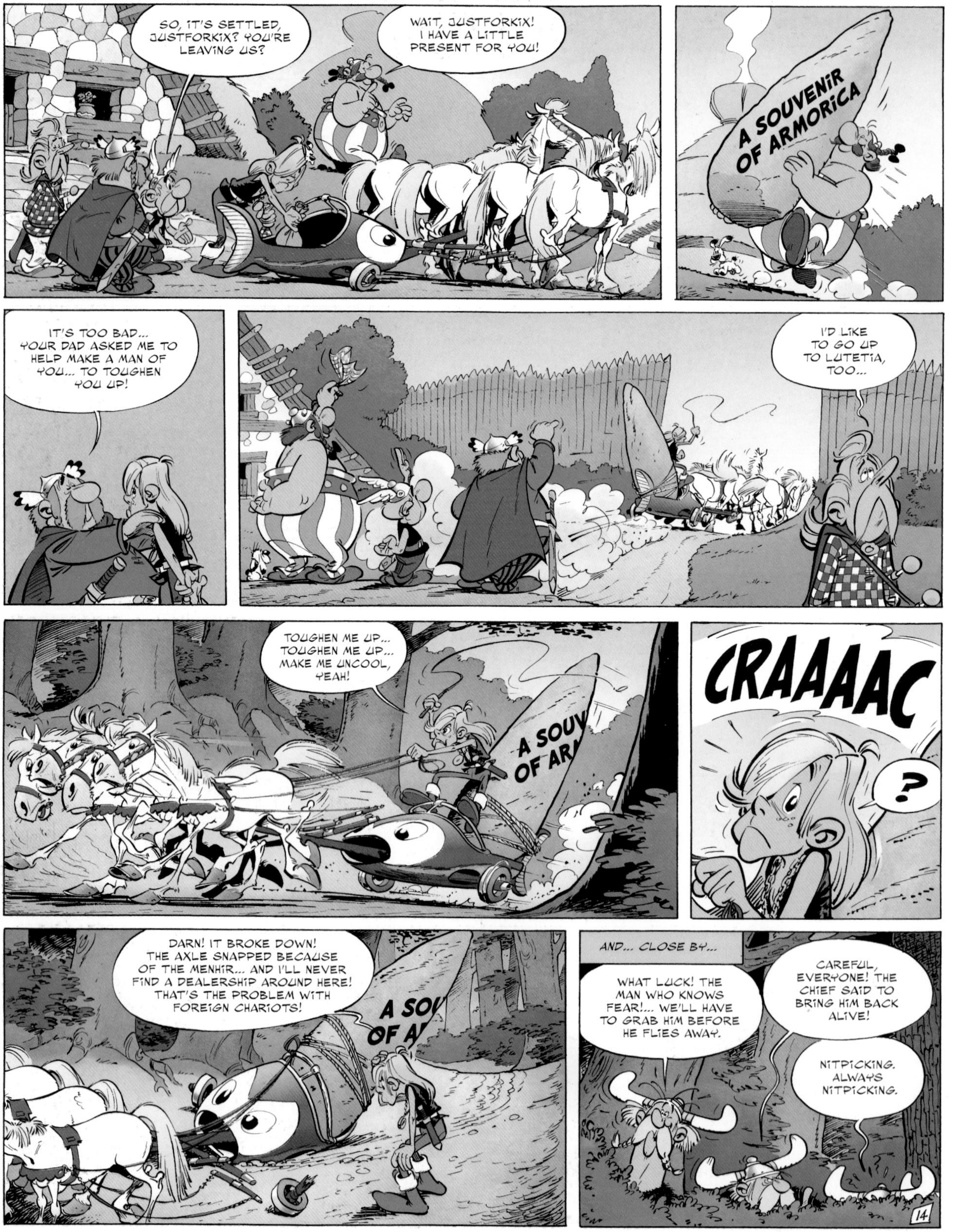
SO, IT'S SETTLED, JUSTFORKIX? YOU'RE LEAVING US?
WAIT, JUSTFORKIX! I HAVE A LITTLE PRESENT FOR YOU!
A SOUVENIR OF ARMORICA
IT'S TOO BAD... YOUR DAD ASKED ME TO HELP MAKE A MAN OF YOU... TO TOUGHEN YOU UP!
I'D LIKE TO GO UP TO LUTETIA, TOO...
TOUGHEN ME UP... TOUGHEN ME UP... MAKE ME UNCOOL, YEAH!
CRAAAAC
?
DARN! IT BROKE DOWN! THE AXLE SNAPPED BECAUSE OF THE MENHIR... AND I'LL NEVER FIND A DEALERSHIP AROUND HERE! THAT'S THE PROBLEM WITH FOREIGN CHARIOTS!
AND... CLOSE BY...
WHAT LUCK! THE MAN WHO KNOWS FEAR!... WE'LL HAVE TO GRAB HIM BEFORE HE FLIES AWAY.
CAREFUL, EVERYONE! THE CHIEF SAID TO BRING HIM BACK ALIVE!
NITPICKING. ALWAYS NITPICKING.
14

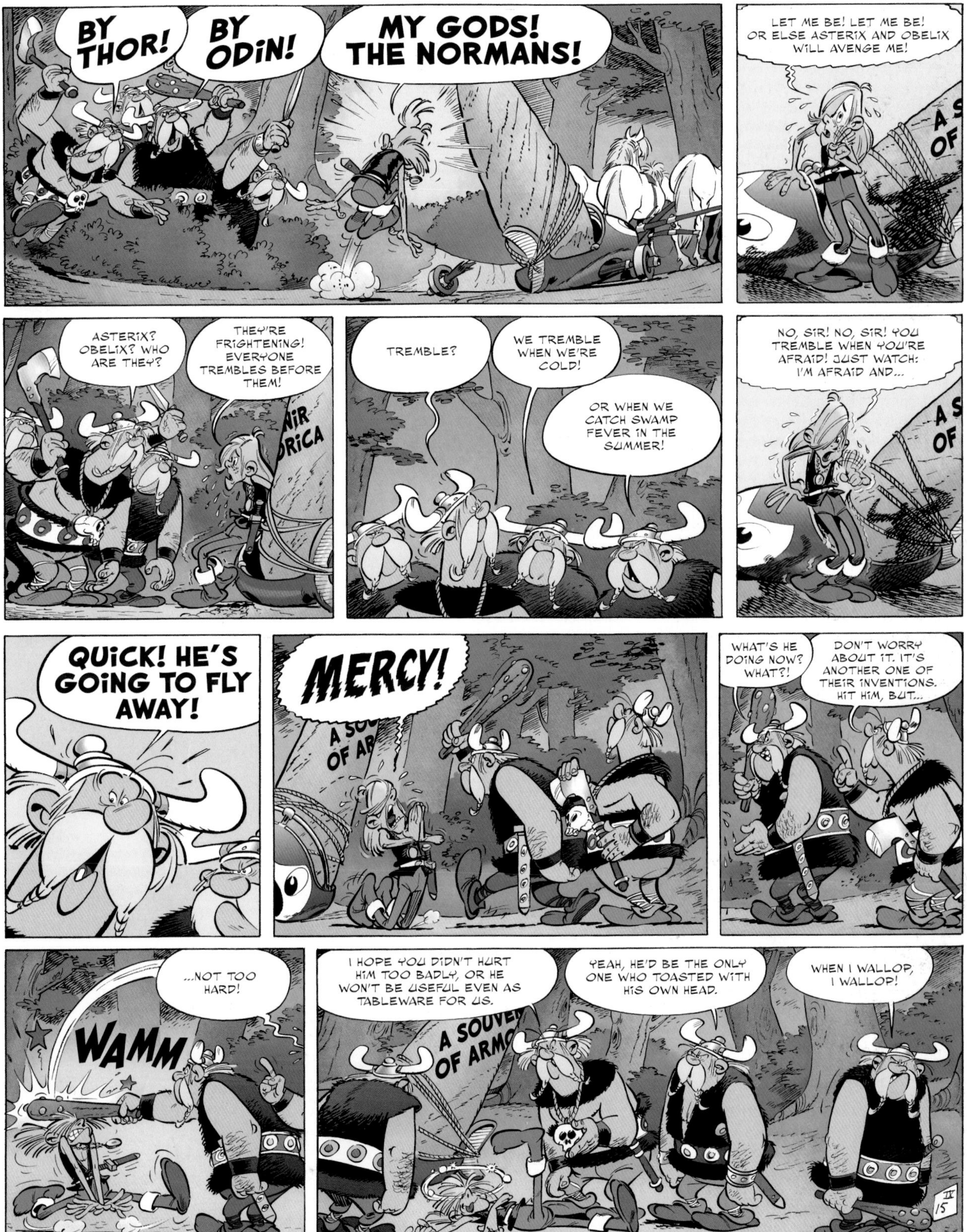
BY THOR!
BY ODIN!
MY GODS! THE NORMANS!
LET ME BE! LET ME BE! OR ELSE ASTERIX AND OBELIX WILL AVENGE ME!
ASTERIX? OBELIX? WHO ARE THEY?
THEY'RE FRIGHTENING! EVERYONE TREMBLES BEFORE THEM!
TREMBLE?
WE TREMBLE WHEN WE'RE COLD!
OR WHEN WE CATCH SWAMP FEVER IN THE SUMMER!
NO, SIR! NO, SIR! YOU TREMBLE WHEN YOU'RE AFRAID! JUST WATCH: I'M AFRAID AND...
QUICK! HE'S GOING TO FLY AWAY!
MERCY!
WHAT'S HE DOING NOW? WHAT?!
DON'T WORRY ABOUT IT. IT'S ANOTHER ONE OF THEIR INVENTIONS. HIT HIM, BUT...
...NOT TOO HARD!
WAMM
I HOPE YOU DIDN'T HURT HIM TOO BADLY, OR HE WON'T BE USEFUL EVEN AS TABLEWARE FOR US.
YEAH, HE'D BE THE ONLY ONE WHO TOASTED WITH HIS OWN HEAD.
WHEN I WALLOP, I WALLOP!

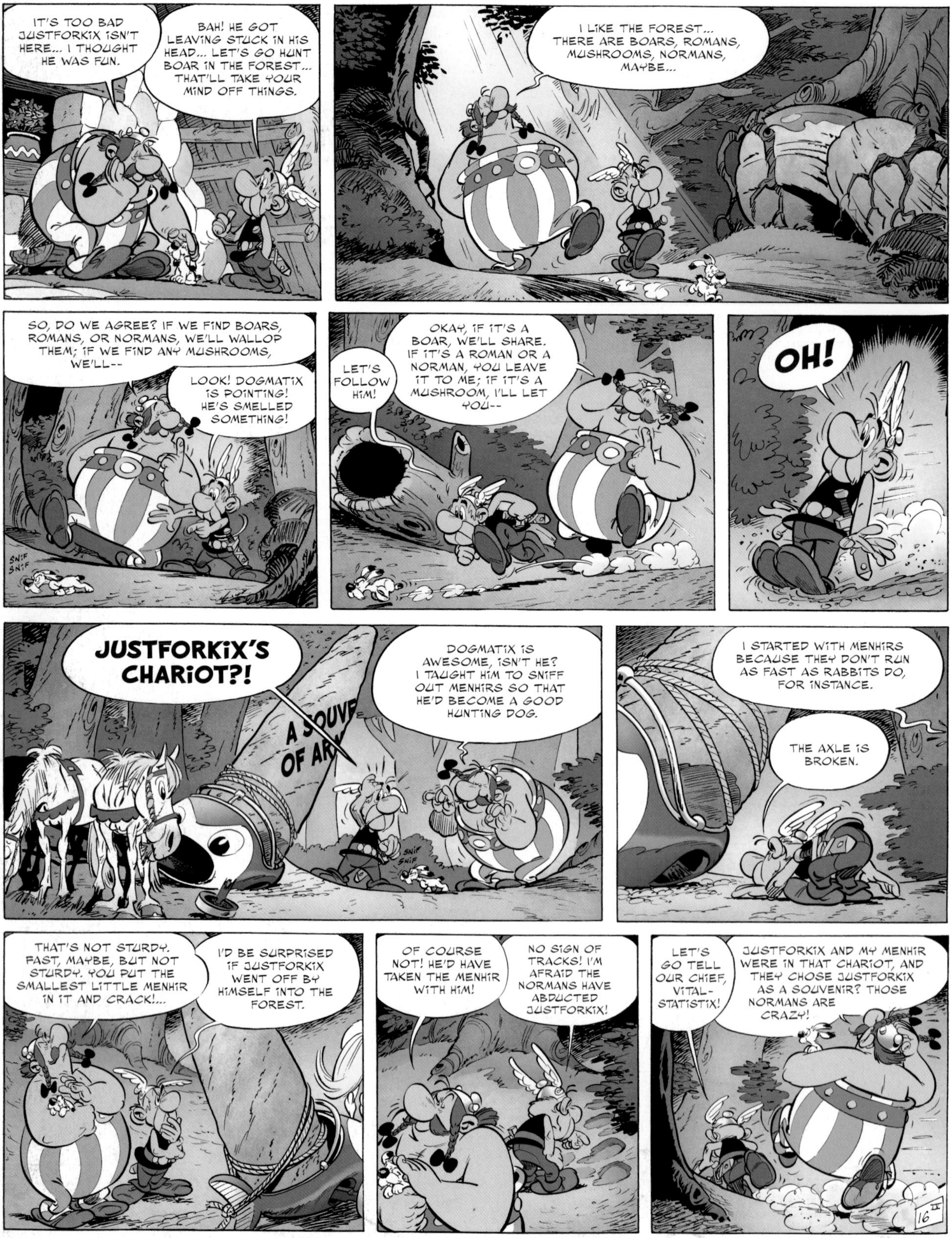
IT'S TOO BAD JUSTFORKIX ISN'T HERE... I THOUGHT HE WAS FUN.
BAH! HE GOT LEAVING STUCK IN HIS HEAD... LET'S GO HUNT BOAR IN THE FOREST... THAT'LL TAKE YOUR MIND OFF THINGS.
I LIKE THE FOREST... THERE ARE BOARS, ROMANS, MUSHROOMS, NORMANS, MAYBE...
SO, DO WE AGREE? IF WE FIND BOARS, ROMANS, OR NORMANS, WE'LL WALLOP THEM; IF WE FIND ANY MUSHROOMS, WE'LL--
LOOK! DOGMATIX IS POINTING! HE'S SMELLED SOMETHING!
SNIF SNIF
LET'S FOLLOW HIM!
OKAY, IF IT'S A BOAR, WE'LL SHARE. IF IT'S A ROMAN OR A NORMAN, YOU LEAVE IT TO ME; IF IT'S A MUSHROOM, I'LL LET YOU--
OH!
JUSTFORKIX'S CHARIOT?!
A SOUVE OF AR
DOGMATIX IS AWESOME, ISN'T HE? I TAUGHT HIM TO SNIFF OUT MENHIRS SO THAT HE'D BECOME A GOOD HUNTING DOG.
SNIF SNIF
I STARTED WITH MENHIRS BECAUSE THEY DON'T RUN AS FAST AS RABBITS DO, FOR INSTANCE.
THE AXLE IS BROKEN.
THAT'S NOT STURDY. FAST, MAYBE, BUT NOT STURDY. YOU PUT THE SMALLEST LITTLE MENHIR IN IT AND CRACK!...
I'D BE SURPRISED IF JUSTFORKIX WENT OFF BY HIMSELF INTO THE FOREST.
OF COURSE NOT! HE'D HAVE TAKEN THE MENHIR WITH HIM!
NO SIGN OF TRACKS! I'M AFRAID THE NORMANS HAVE ABDUCTED JUSTFORKIX!
LET'S GO TELL OUR CHIEF, VITAL-STATISTIX!
JUSTFORKIX AND MY MENHIR WERE IN THAT CHARIOT, AND THEY CHOSE JUSTFORKIX AS A SOUVENIR? THOSE NORMANS ARE CRAZY!
16

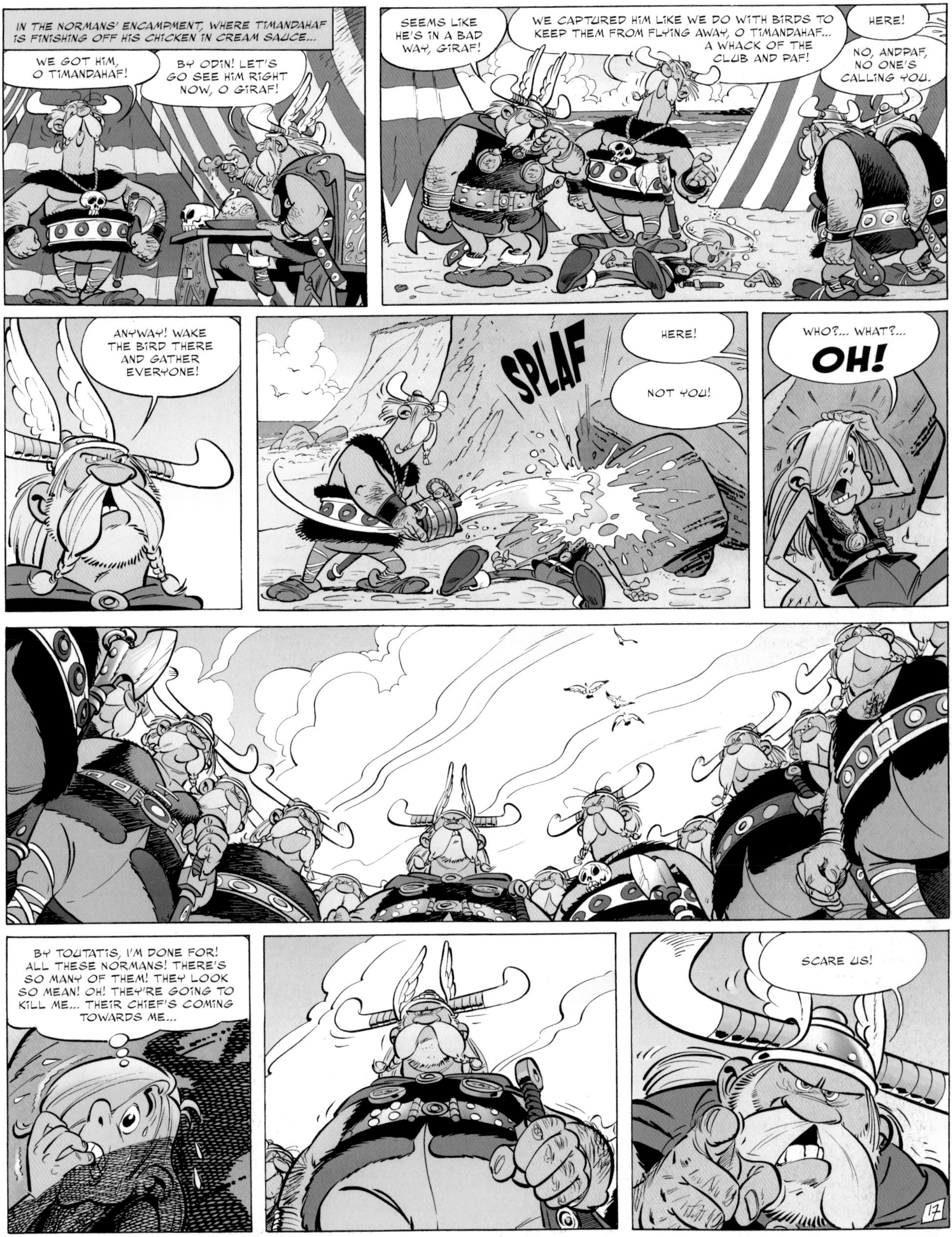
IN THE NORMANS' ENCAMPMENT, WHERE TIMANDAHAF IS FINISHING OFF HIS CHICKEN IN CREAM SAUCE...
WE GOT HIM, O TIMANDAHAF!
BY ODIN! LET'S GO SEE HIM RIGHT NOW, O GIRAF!
SEEMS LIKE HE'S IN A BAD WAY, GIRAF!
WE CAPTURED HIM LIKE WE DO WITH BIRDS TO KEEP THEM FROM FLYING AWAY, O TIMANDAHAF... A WHACK OF THE CLUB AND PAF!
HERE!
NO, ANDPAF, NO ONE'S CALLING YOU.
ANYWAY! WAKE THE BIRD THERE AND GATHER EVERYONE!
SPLAF
HERE!
NOT YOU!
WHO?... WHAT?...
OH!
BY TOUTATIS, I'M DONE FOR! ALL THESE NORMANS! THERE'S SO MANY OF THEM! THEY LOOK SO MEAN! OH! THEY'RE GOING TO KILL ME... THEIR CHIEF'S COMING TOWARDS ME...
SCARE US!
17

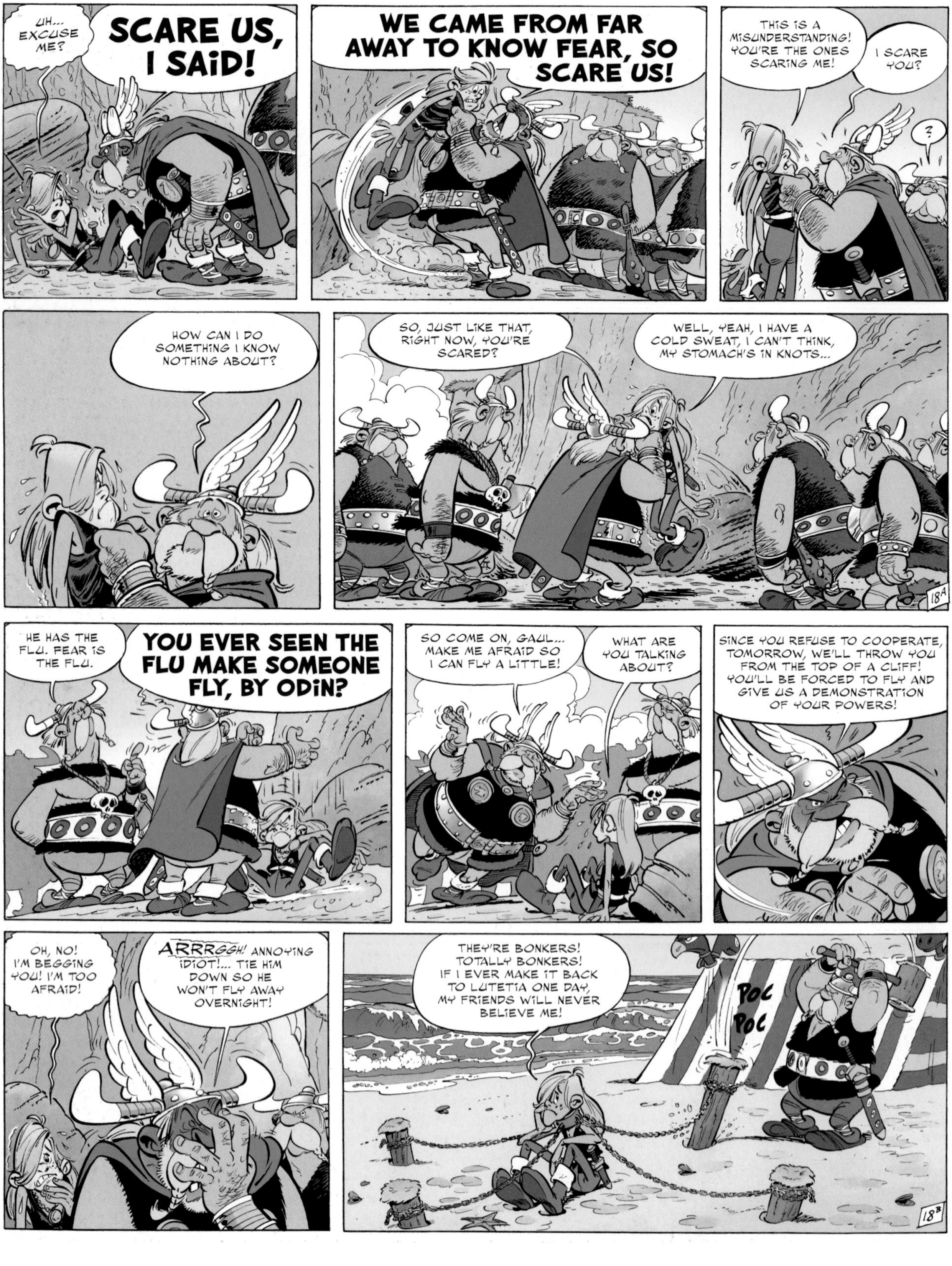
UH... EXCUSE ME?
SCARE US, I SAID!
WE CAME FROM FAR AWAY TO KNOW FEAR, SO SCARE US!
THIS IS A MISUNDERSTANDING! YOU'RE THE ONES SCARING ME!
I SCARE YOU?
?
HOW CAN I DO SOMETHING I KNOW NOTHING ABOUT?
SO, JUST LIKE THAT, RIGHT NOW, YOU'RE SCARED?
WELL, YEAH, I HAVE A COLD SWEAT, I CAN'T THINK, MY STOMACH'S IN KNOTS...
18A
HE HAS THE FLU. FEAR IS THE FLU.
YOU EVER SEEN THE FLU MAKE SOMEONE FLY, BY ODIN?
SO COME ON, GAUL... MAKE ME AFRAID SO I CAN FLY A LITTLE!
WHAT ARE YOU TALKING ABOUT?
SINCE YOU REFUSE TO COOPERATE, TOMORROW, WE'LL THROW YOU FROM THE TOP OF A CLIFF! YOU'LL BE FORCED TO FLY AND GIVE US A DEMONSTRATION OF YOUR POWERS!
OH, NO! I'M BEGGING YOU! I'M TOO AFRAID!
ARRRGGH! ANNOYING IDIOT!... TIE HIM DOWN SO HE WON'T FLY AWAY OVERNIGHT!
THEY'RE BONKERS! TOTALLY BONKERS! IF I EVER MAKE IT BACK TO LUTETIA ONE DAY, MY FRIENDS WILL NEVER BELIEVE ME!
POC
POC
18B

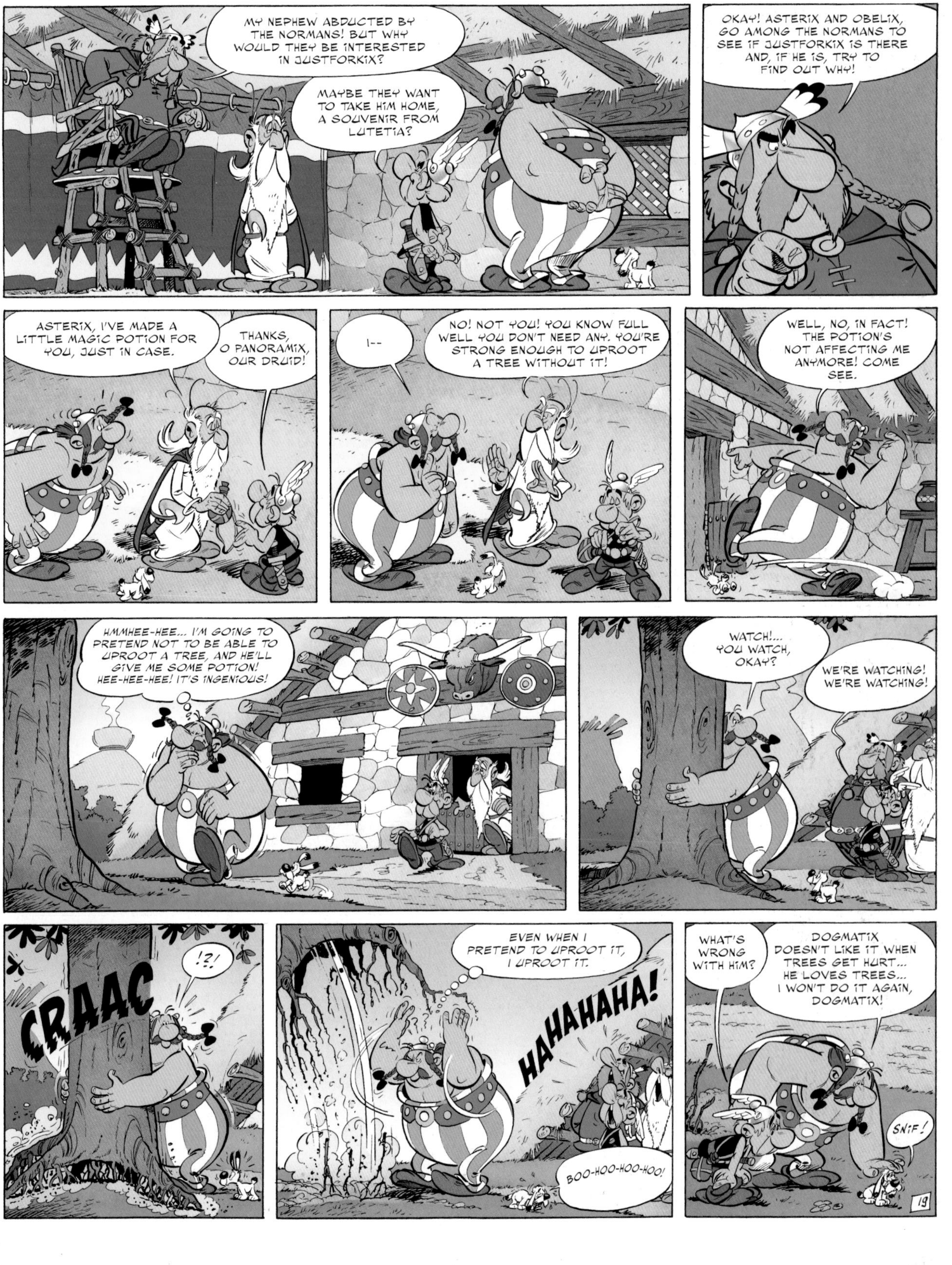

MY NEPHEW ABDUCTED BY THE NORMANS! BUT WHY WOULD THEY BE INTERESTED IN JUSTFORKIX?
MAYBE THEY WANT TO TAKE HIM HOME, A SOUVENIR FROM LUTETIA?
OKAY! ASTERIX AND OBELIX, GO AMONG THE NORMANS TO SEE IF JUSTFORKIX IS THERE AND, IF HE IS, TRY TO FIND OUT WHY!
ASTERIX, I'VE MADE A LITTLE MAGIC POTION FOR YOU, JUST IN CASE.
THANKS, O PANORAMIX, OUR DRUID!
I--
NO! NOT YOU! YOU KNOW FULL WELL YOU DON'T NEED ANY. YOU'RE STRONG ENOUGH TO UPROOT A TREE WITHOUT IT!
WELL, NO, IN FACT! THE POTION'S NOT AFFECTING ME ANYMORE! COME SEE.
HMMHEE-HEE... I'M GOING TO PRETEND NOT TO BE ABLE TO UPROOT A TREE, AND HE'LL GIVE ME SOME POTION! HEE-HEE-HEE! IT'S INGENIOUS!
WATCH!... YOU WATCH, OKAY?
WE'RE WATCHING! WE'RE WATCHING!
CRAAC
!?!
EVEN WHEN I PRETEND TO UPROOT IT, I UPROOT IT.
HAHAHAHA!
BOO-HOO-HOO-HOO!
WHAT'S WRONG WITH HIM?
DOGMATIX DOESN'T LIKE IT WHEN TREES GET HURT... HE LOVES TREES... I WON'T DO IT AGAIN, DOGMATIX!
SNIF!
19

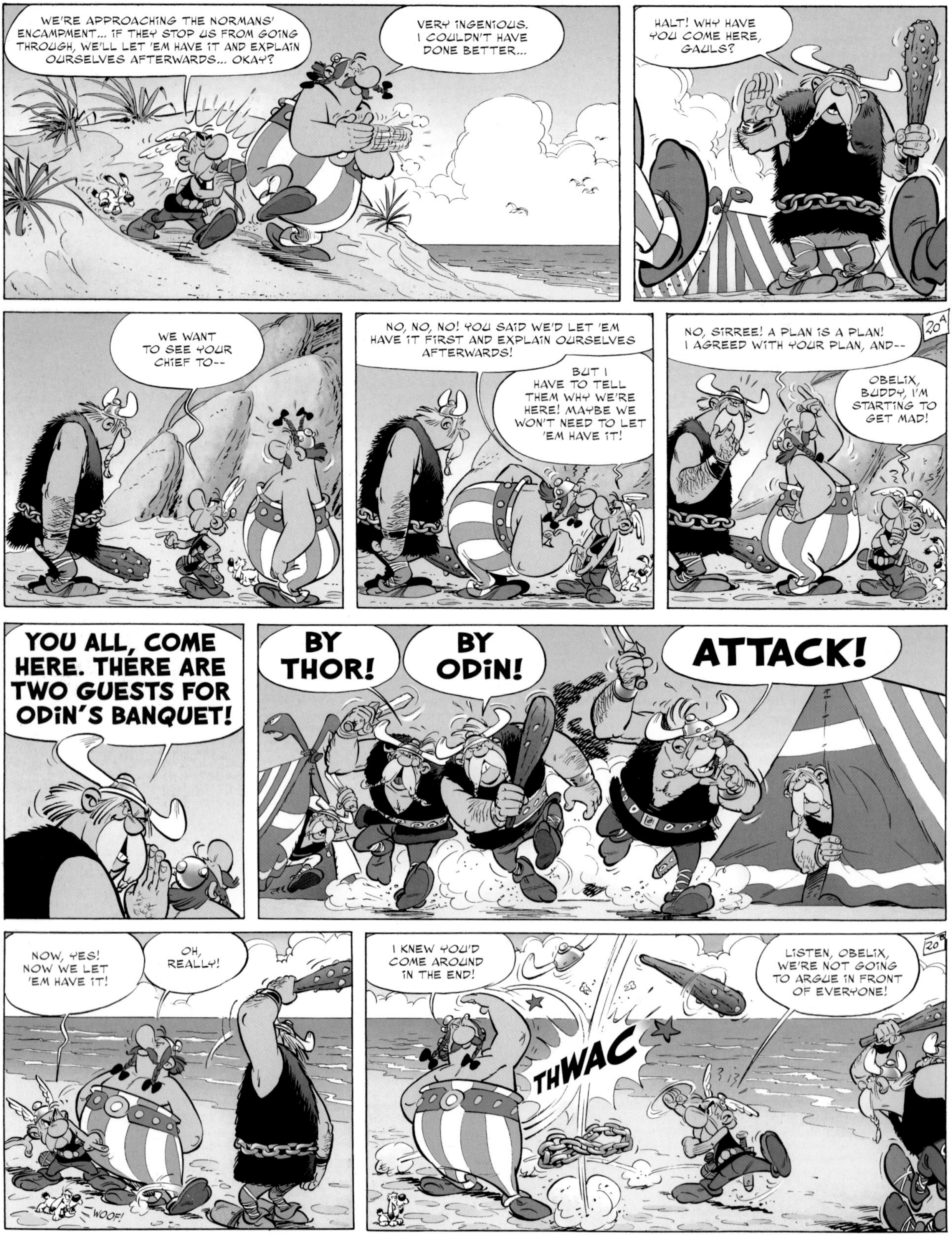
WE'RE APPROACHING THE NORMANS' ENCAMPMENT... IF THEY STOP US FROM GOING THROUGH, WE'LL LET 'EM HAVE IT AND EXPLAIN OURSELVES AFTERWARDS... OKAY?
VERY INGENIOUS. I COULDN'T HAVE DONE BETTER...
HALT! WHY HAVE YOU COME HERE, GAULS?
WE WANT TO SEE YOUR CHIEF TO--
NO, NO, NO! YOU SAID WE'D LET 'EM HAVE IT FIRST AND EXPLAIN OURSELVES AFTERWARDS!
BUT I HAVE TO TELL THEM WHY WE'RE HERE! MAYBE WE WON'T NEED TO LET 'EM HAVE IT!
NO, SIRREE! A PLAN IS A PLAN! I AGREED WITH YOUR PLAN, AND--
20A
OBELIX, BUDDY, I'M STARTING TO GET MAD!
YOU ALL, COME HERE. THERE ARE TWO GUESTS FOR ODIN'S BANQUET!
BY THOR!
BY ODIN!
ATTACK!
NOW, YES! NOW WE LET 'EM HAVE IT!
OH, REALLY!
WOOF!
I KNEW YOU'D COME AROUND IN THE END!
20B
LISTEN, OBELIX, WE'RE NOT GOING TO ARGUE IN FRONT OF EVERYONE!
THWAC

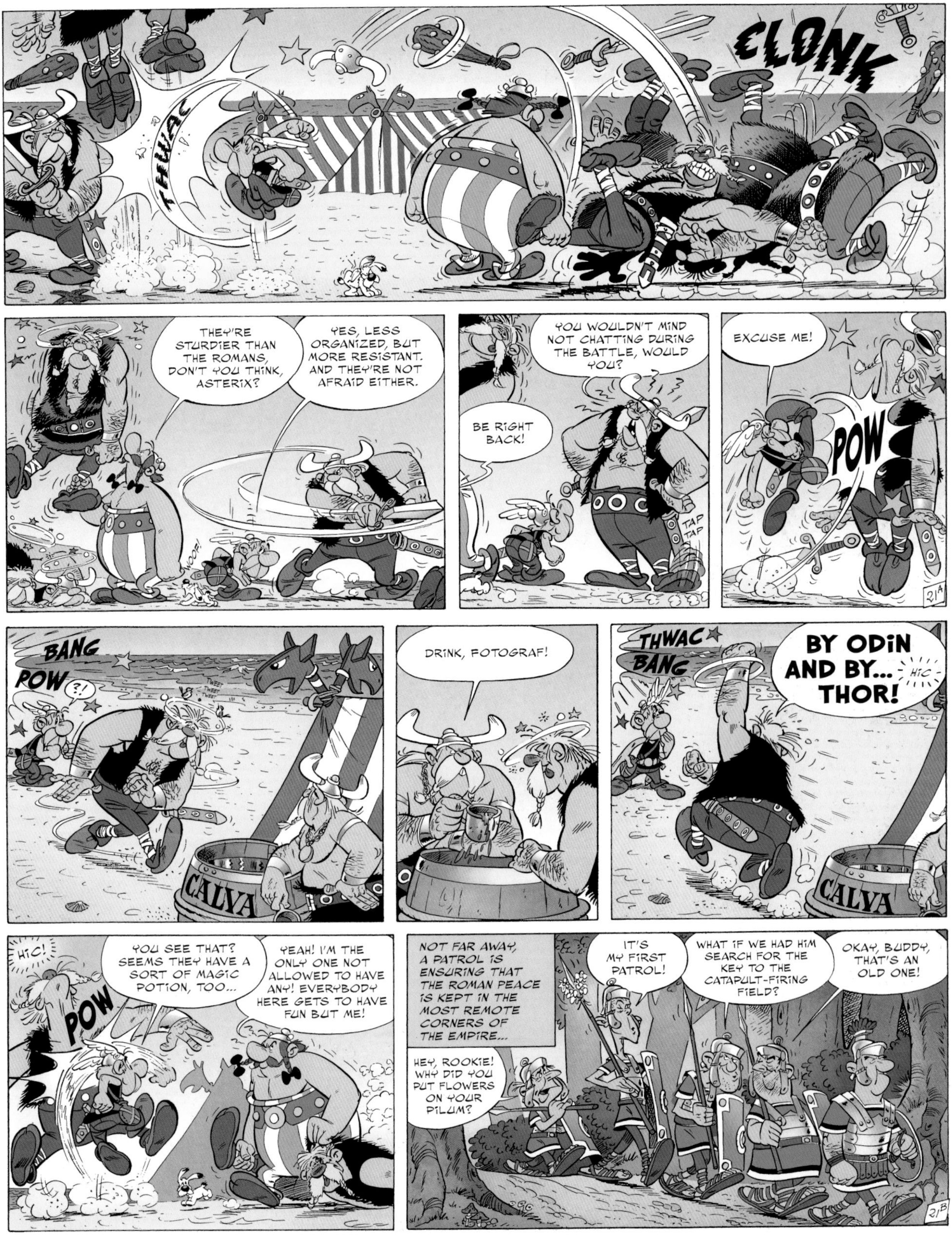
THWAC
CLONK
THEY'RE STURDIER THAN THE ROMANS, DON'T YOU THINK, ASTERIX?
YES, LESS ORGANIZED, BUT MORE RESISTANT. AND THEY'RE NOT AFRAID EITHER.
WOOF!
YOU WOULDN'T MIND NOT CHATTING DURING THE BATTLE, WOULD YOU?
BE RIGHT BACK!
TAP TAP
EXCUSE ME!
POW
21A
BANG
POW
?!
CALVA
DRINK, FOTOGRAF!
THWAC
BANG
BY ODIN AND BY... THOR!
HIC
CALVA
HIC!
POW
YOU SEE THAT? SEEMS THEY HAVE A SORT OF MAGIC POTION, TOO...
YEAH! I'M THE ONLY ONE NOT ALLOWED TO HAVE ANY! EVERYBODY HERE GETS TO HAVE FUN BUT ME!
NOT FAR AWAY, A PATROL IS ENSURING THAT THE ROMAN PEACE IS KEPT IN THE MOST REMOTE CORNERS OF THE EMPIRE...
HEY, ROOKIE! WHY DID YOU PUT FLOWERS ON YOUR PILUM?
IT'S MY FIRST PATROL!
WHAT IF WE HAD HIM SEARCH FOR THE KEY TO THE CATAPULT-FIRING FIELD?
OKAY, BUDDY, THAT'S AN OLD ONE!
21B

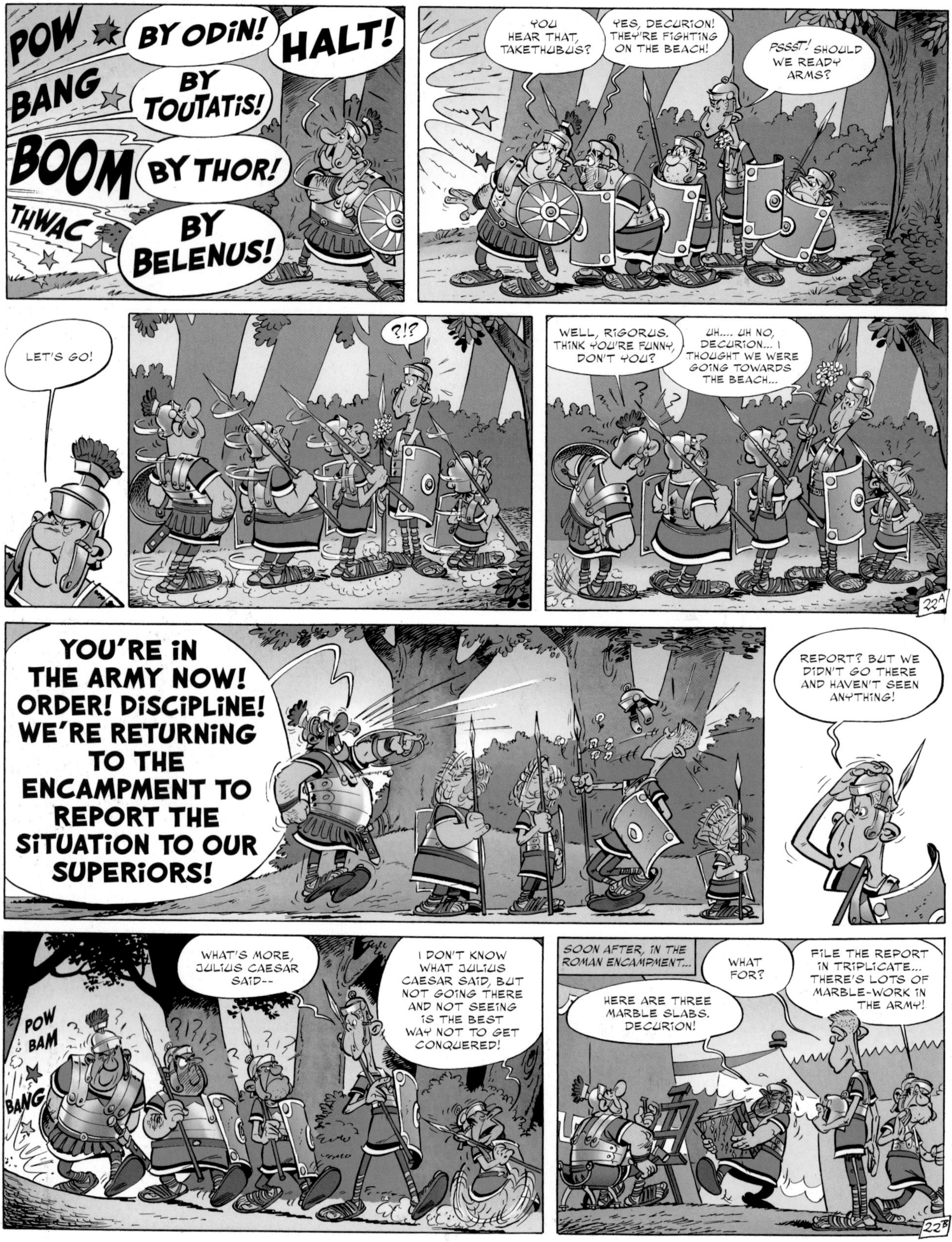
POW
BY ODIN!
BANG
BY TOUTATIS!
BOOM
BY THOR!
THWAC
BY BELENUS!
HALT!
YOU HEAR THAT, TAKETHUBUS?
YES, DECURION! THEY'RE FIGHTING ON THE BEACH!
PSSST! SHOULD WE READY ARMS?
LET'S GO!
?!?
WELL, RIGORUS. THINK YOU'RE FUNNY, DON'T YOU?
UH.... UH NO, DECURION... I THOUGHT WE WERE GOING TOWARDS THE BEACH...
22A
YOU'RE IN THE ARMY NOW! ORDER! DISCIPLINE! WE'RE RETURNING TO THE ENCAMPMENT TO REPORT THE SITUATION TO OUR SUPERIORS!
REPORT? BUT WE DIDN'T GO THERE AND HAVEN'T SEEN ANYTHING!
POW
BAM
BANG
WHAT'S MORE, JULIUS CAESAR SAID--
I DON'T KNOW WHAT JULIUS CAESAR SAID, BUT NOT GOING THERE AND NOT SEEING IS THE BEST WAY NOT TO GET CONQUERED!
SOON AFTER, IN THE ROMAN ENCAMPMENT...
HERE ARE THREE MARBLE SLABS, DECURION!
WHAT FOR?
FILE THE REPORT IN TRIPLICATE... THERE'S LOTS OF MARBLE-WORK IN THE ARMY!
22B

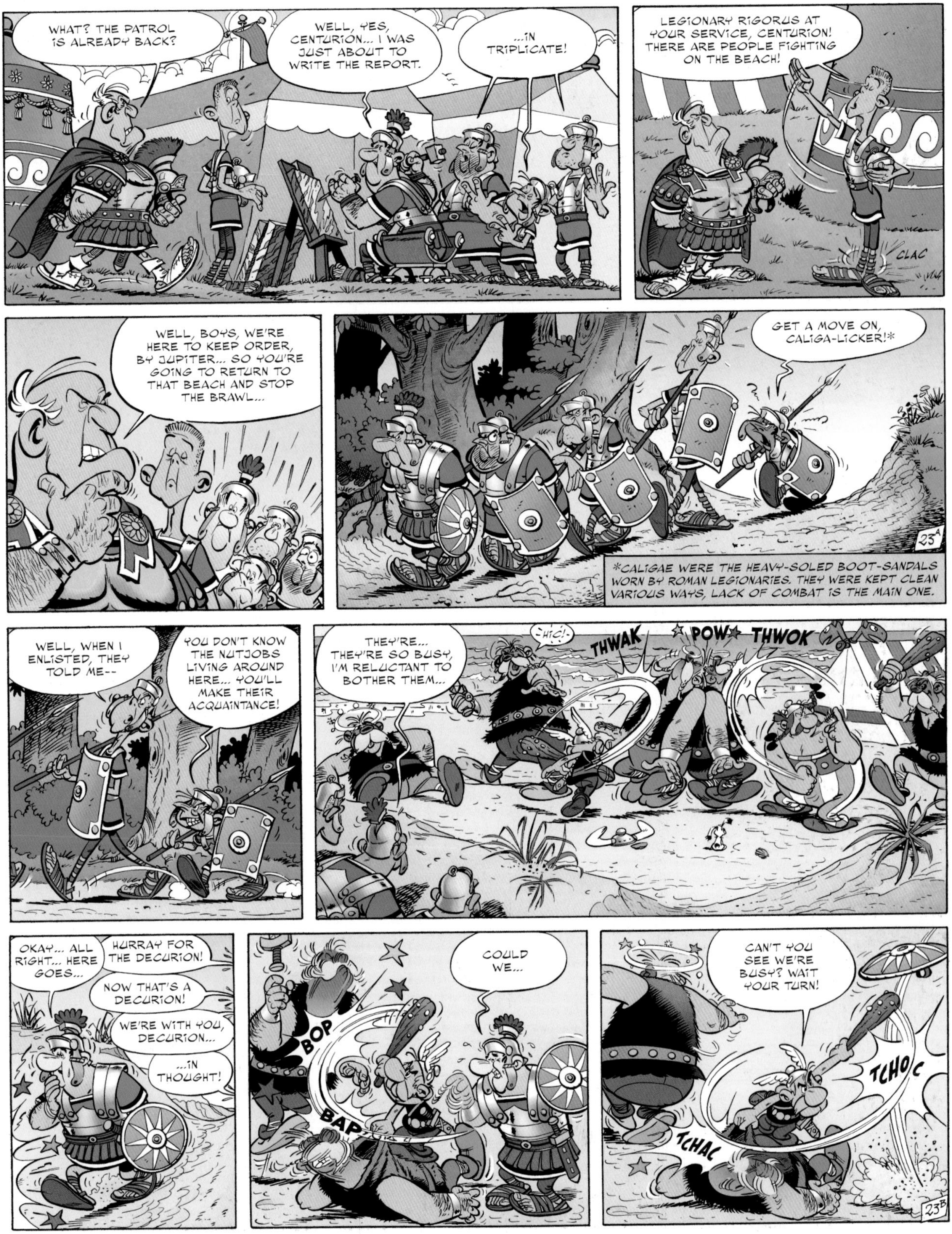
WHAT? THE PATROL IS ALREADY BACK?
WELL, YES, CENTURION... I WAS JUST ABOUT TO WRITE THE REPORT.
...IN TRIPLICATE!
LEGIONARY RIGORUS AT YOUR SERVICE, CENTURION! THERE ARE PEOPLE FIGHTING ON THE BEACH!
CLAC
WELL, BOYS, WE'RE HERE TO KEEP ORDER, BY JUPITER... SO YOU'RE GOING TO RETURN TO THAT BEACH AND STOP THE BRAWL...
GET A MOVE ON, CALIGA-LICKER!*
23A
*CALIGAE WERE THE HEAVY-SOLED BOOT-SANDALS WORN BY ROMAN LEGIONARIES. THEY WERE KEPT CLEAN VARIOUS WAYS, LACK OF COMBAT IS THE MAIN ONE.
WELL, WHEN I ENLISTED, THEY TOLD ME--
YOU DON'T KNOW THE NUTJOBS LIVING AROUND HERE... YOU'LL MAKE THEIR ACQUAINTANCE!
THEY'RE... THEY'RE SO BUSY, I'M RELUCTANT TO BOTHER THEM...
HIC!
THWAK
POW
THWOK
OKAY... ALL RIGHT... HERE GOES...
HURRAY FOR THE DECURION!
NOW THAT'S A DECURION!
WE'RE WITH YOU, DECURION...
...IN THOUGHT!
COULD WE...
BOP
BAP
CAN'T YOU SEE WE'RE BUSY? WAIT YOUR TURN!
TCHOC
TCHAC
23B

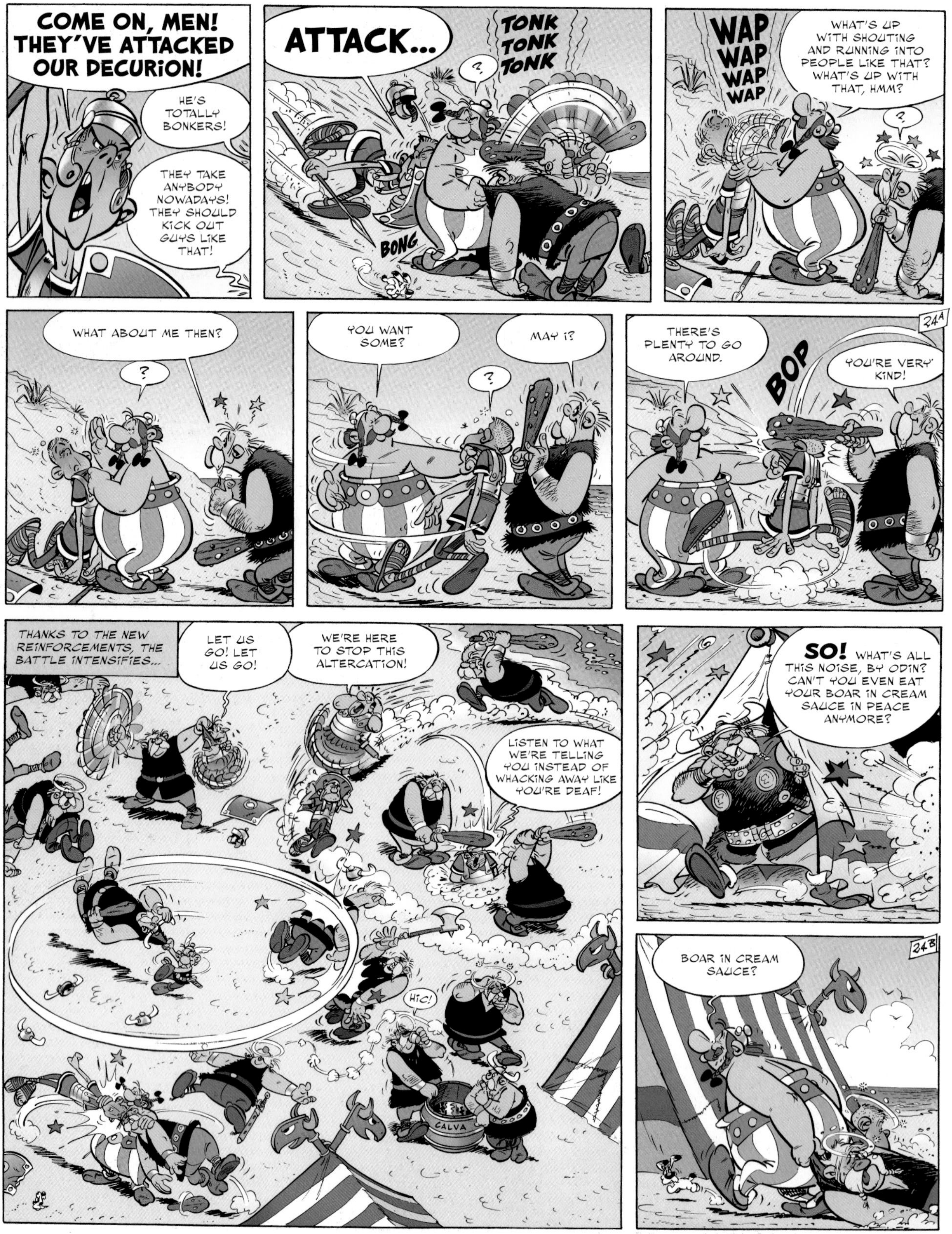
COME ON, MEN! THEY'VE ATTACKED OUR DECURION!
HE'S TOTALLY BONKERS!
THEY TAKE ANYBODY NOWADAYS! THEY SHOULD KICK OUT GUYS LIKE THAT!
ATTACK...
TONK TONK TONK
?
BONG
WAP WAP WAP WAP
WHAT'S UP WITH SHOUTING AND RUNNING INTO PEOPLE LIKE THAT? WHAT'S UP WITH THAT, HMM?
?
WHAT ABOUT ME THEN?
?
YOU WANT SOME?
MAY I?
?
24A
THERE'S PLENTY TO GO AROUND.
BOP
YOU'RE VERY KIND!
THANKS TO THE NEW REINFORCEMENTS, THE BATTLE INTENSIFIES...
LET US GO! LET US GO!
WE'RE HERE TO STOP THIS ALTERCATION!
LISTEN TO WHAT WE'RE TELLING YOU INSTEAD OF WHACKING AWAY LIKE YOU'RE DEAF!
HIC!
CALVA
SO! WHAT'S ALL THIS NOISE, BY ODIN? CAN'T YOU EVEN EAT YOUR BOAR IN CREAM SAUCE IN PEACE ANYMORE?
24B
BOAR IN CREAM SAUCE?

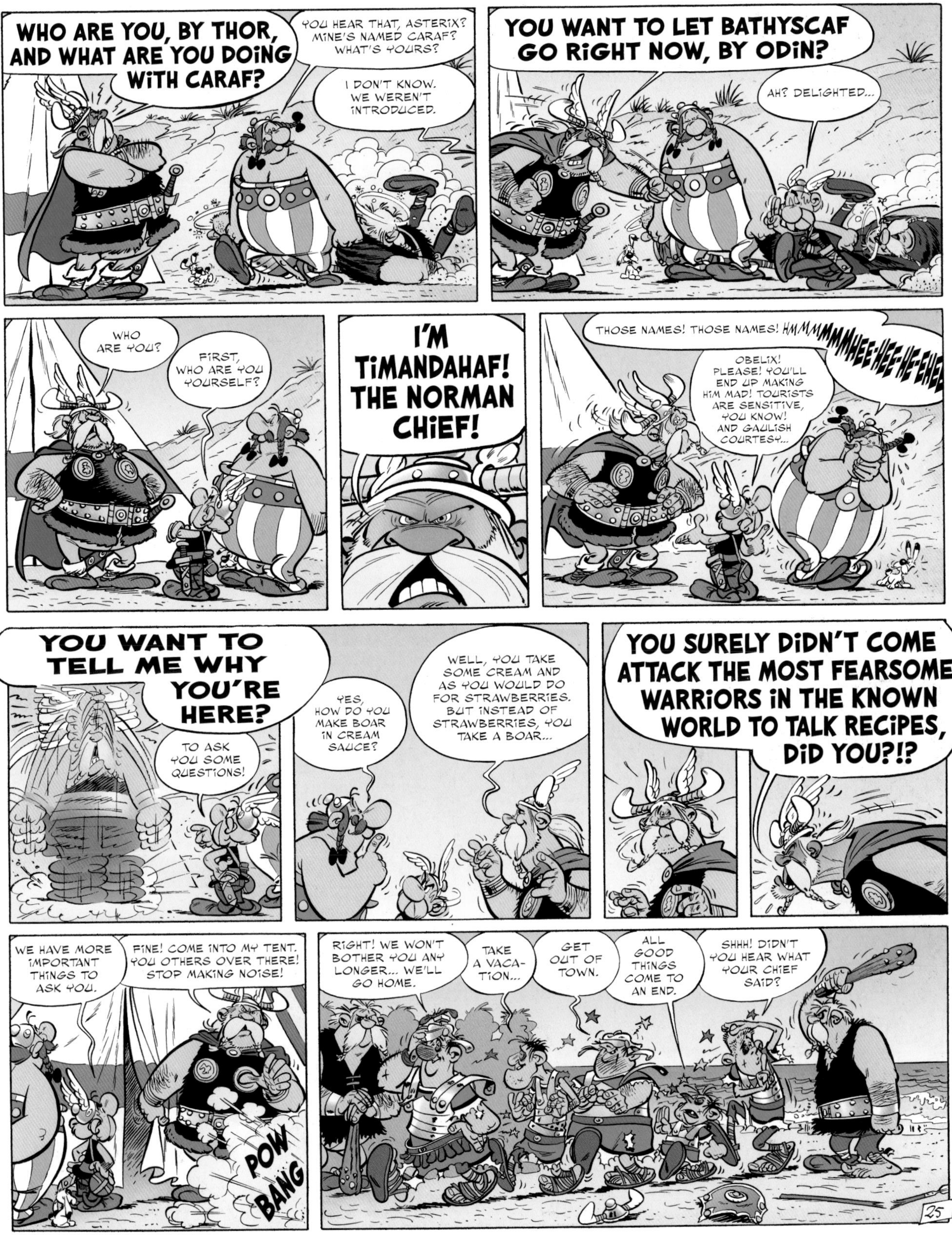

WHO ARE YOU, BY THOR, AND WHAT ARE YOU DOING WITH CARAF?
YOU HEAR THAT, ASTERIX? MINE'S NAMED CARAF? WHAT'S YOURS?
I DON'T KNOW. WE WEREN'T INTRODUCED.
YOU WANT TO LET BATHYSCAF GO RIGHT NOW, BY ODIN?
AH? DELIGHTED...
WHO ARE YOU?
FIRST, WHO ARE YOU YOURSELF?
I'M TIMANDAHAF! THE NORMAN CHIEF!
THOSE NAMES! THOSE NAMES! HMMMMMMHEE-HEE-HE-EHEE
OBELIX! PLEASE! YOU'LL END UP MAKING HIM MAD! TOURISTS ARE SENSITIVE, YOU KNOW! AND GAULISH COURTESY...
YOU WANT TO TELL ME WHY YOU'RE HERE?
TO ASK YOU SOME QUESTIONS!
YES, HOW DO YOU MAKE BOAR IN CREAM SAUCE?
WELL, YOU TAKE SOME CREAM AND AS YOU WOULD DO FOR STRAWBERRIES. BUT INSTEAD OF STRAWBERRIES, YOU TAKE A BOAR...
YOU SURELY DIDN'T COME ATTACK THE MOST FEARSOME WARRIORS IN THE KNOWN WORLD TO TALK RECIPES, DID YOU?!?
WE HAVE MORE IMPORTANT THINGS TO ASK YOU.
FINE! COME INTO MY TENT. YOU OTHERS OVER THERE! STOP MAKING NOISE!
POW
BANG
RIGHT! WE WON'T BOTHER YOU ANY LONGER... WE'LL GO HOME.
TAKE A VACATION...
GET OUT OF TOWN.
ALL GOOD THINGS COME TO AN END.
SHHH! DIDN'T YOU HEAR WHAT YOUR CHIEF SAID?
25

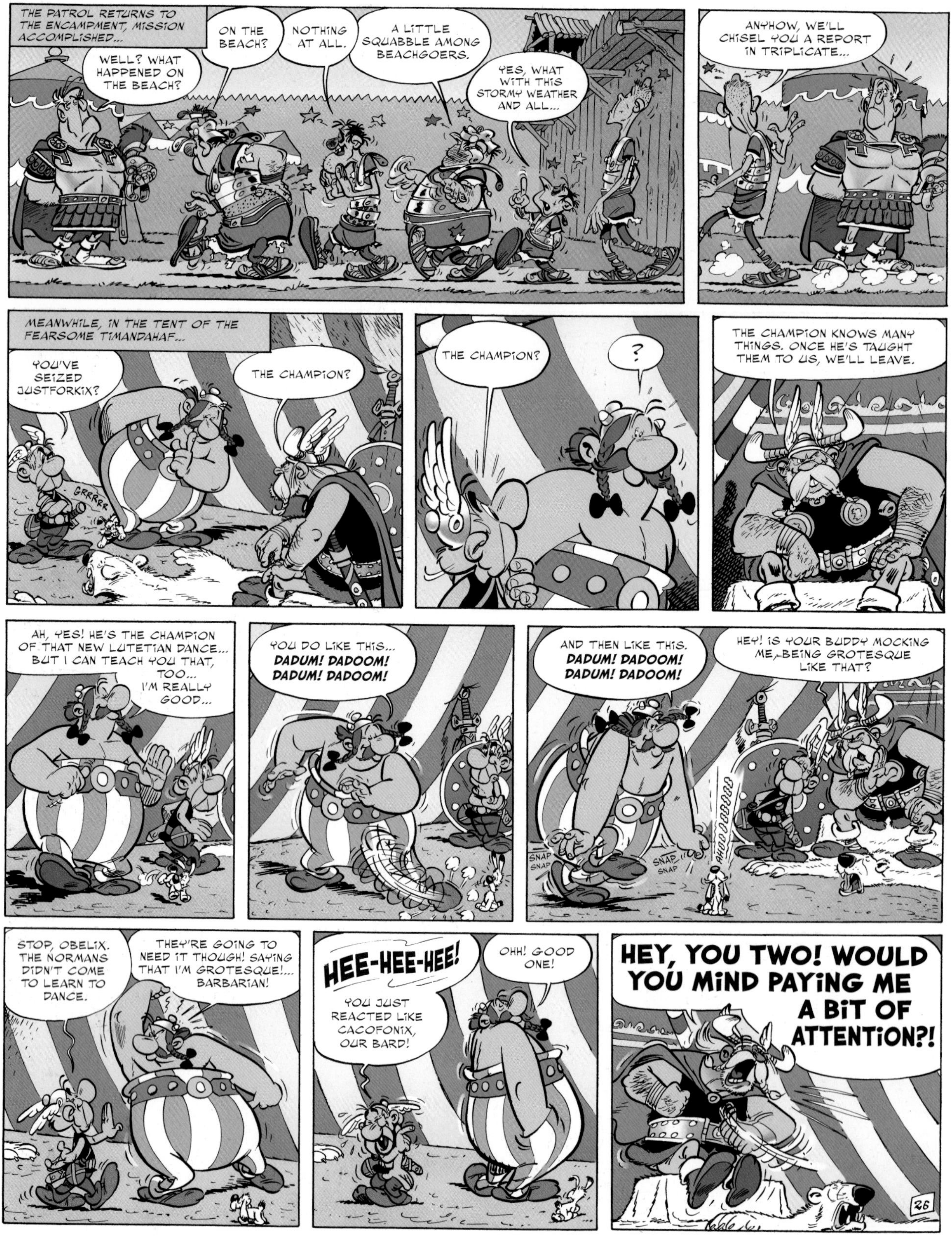

THE PATROL RETURNS TO THE ENCAMPMENT, MISSION ACCOMPLISHED...
WELL? WHAT HAPPENED ON THE BEACH?
ON THE BEACH?
NOTHING AT ALL.
A LITTLE SQUABBLE AMONG BEACHGOERS.
YES, WHAT WITH THIS STORMY WEATHER AND ALL...
ANYHOW, WE'LL CHISEL YOU A REPORT IN TRIPLICATE...
MEANWHILE, IN THE TENT OF THE FEARSOME TIMANDAHAF...
YOU'VE SEIZED JUSTFORKIX?
GRRRRR
THE CHAMPION?
THE CHAMPION?
?
THE CHAMPION KNOWS MANY THINGS. ONCE HE'S TAUGHT THEM TO US, WE'LL LEAVE.
AH, YES! HE'S THE CHAMPION OF THAT NEW LUTETIAN DANCE... BUT I CAN TEACH YOU THAT, TOO... I'M REALLY GOOD...
YOU DO LIKE THIS... DADUM! DADOOM! DADUM! DADOOM!
AND THEN LIKE THIS. DADUM! DADOOM! DADUM! DADOOM!
HEY! IS YOUR BUDDY MOCKING ME, BEING GROTESQUE LIKE THAT?
SNAP SNAP
SNAP SNAP
STOP, OBELIX. THE NORMANS DIDN'T COME TO LEARN TO DANCE.
THEY'RE GOING TO NEED IT THOUGH! SAYING THAT I'M GROTESQUE!... BARBARIAN!
HEE-HEE-HEE!
YOU JUST REACTED LIKE CACOFONIX, OUR BARD!
OHH! GOOD ONE!
HEY, YOU TWO! WOULD YOU MIND PAYING ME A BIT OF ATTENTION?!
26

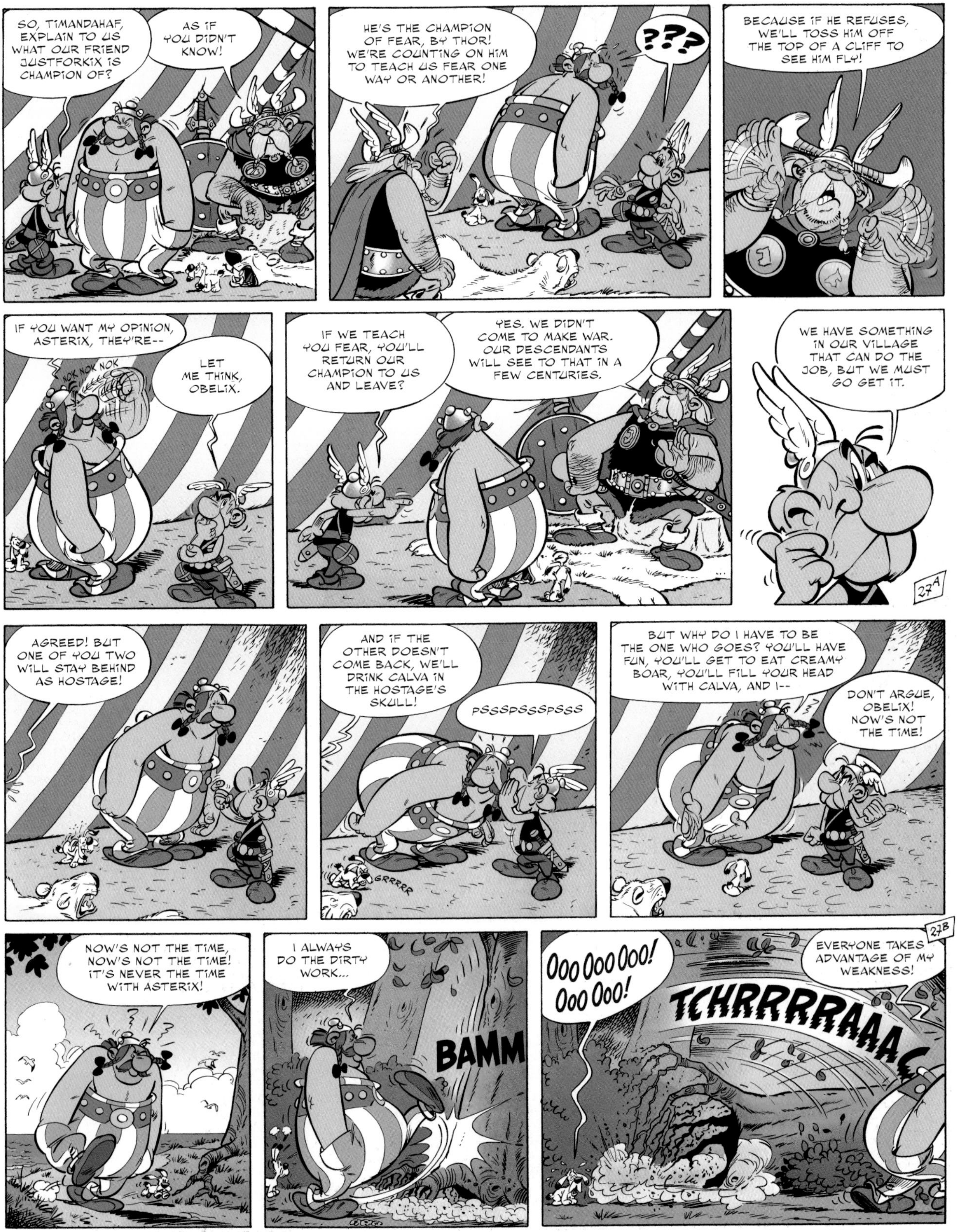
SO, TIMANDAHAF, EXPLAIN TO US WHAT OUR FRIEND JUSTFORKIX IS CHAMPION OF?
AS IF YOU DIDN'T KNOW!
HE'S THE CHAMPION OF FEAR, BY THOR! WE'RE COUNTING ON HIM TO TEACH US FEAR ONE WAY OR ANOTHER!
???
BECAUSE IF HE REFUSES, WE'LL TOSS HIM OFF THE TOP OF A CLIFF TO SEE HIM FLY!
IF YOU WANT MY OPINION, ASTERIX, THEY'RE--
NOK NOK NOK
LET ME THINK, OBELIX.
IF WE TEACH YOU FEAR, YOU'LL RETURN OUR CHAMPION TO US AND LEAVE?
YES. WE DIDN'T COME TO MAKE WAR. OUR DESCENDANTS WILL SEE TO THAT IN A FEW CENTURIES.
WE HAVE SOMETHING IN OUR VILLAGE THAT CAN DO THE JOB, BUT WE MUST GO GET IT.
27A
AGREED! BUT ONE OF YOU TWO WILL STAY BEHIND AS HOSTAGE!
AND IF THE OTHER DOESN'T COME BACK, WE'LL DRINK CALVA IN THE HOSTAGE'S SKULL!
PSSSPSSSPSSS
GRRRRR
BUT WHY DO I HAVE TO BE THE ONE WHO GOES? YOU'LL HAVE FUN, YOU'LL GET TO EAT CREAMY BOAR, YOU'LL FILL YOUR HEAD WITH CALVA, AND I--
DON'T ARGUE, OBELIX! NOW'S NOT THE TIME!
NOW'S NOT THE TIME, NOW'S NOT THE TIME! IT'S NEVER THE TIME WITH ASTERIX!
I ALWAYS DO THE DIRTY WORK...
BAMM
27B
OOO OOO OOO! OOO OOO!
EVERYONE TAKES ADVANTAGE OF MY WEAKNESS!
TCHRRRRAAAC

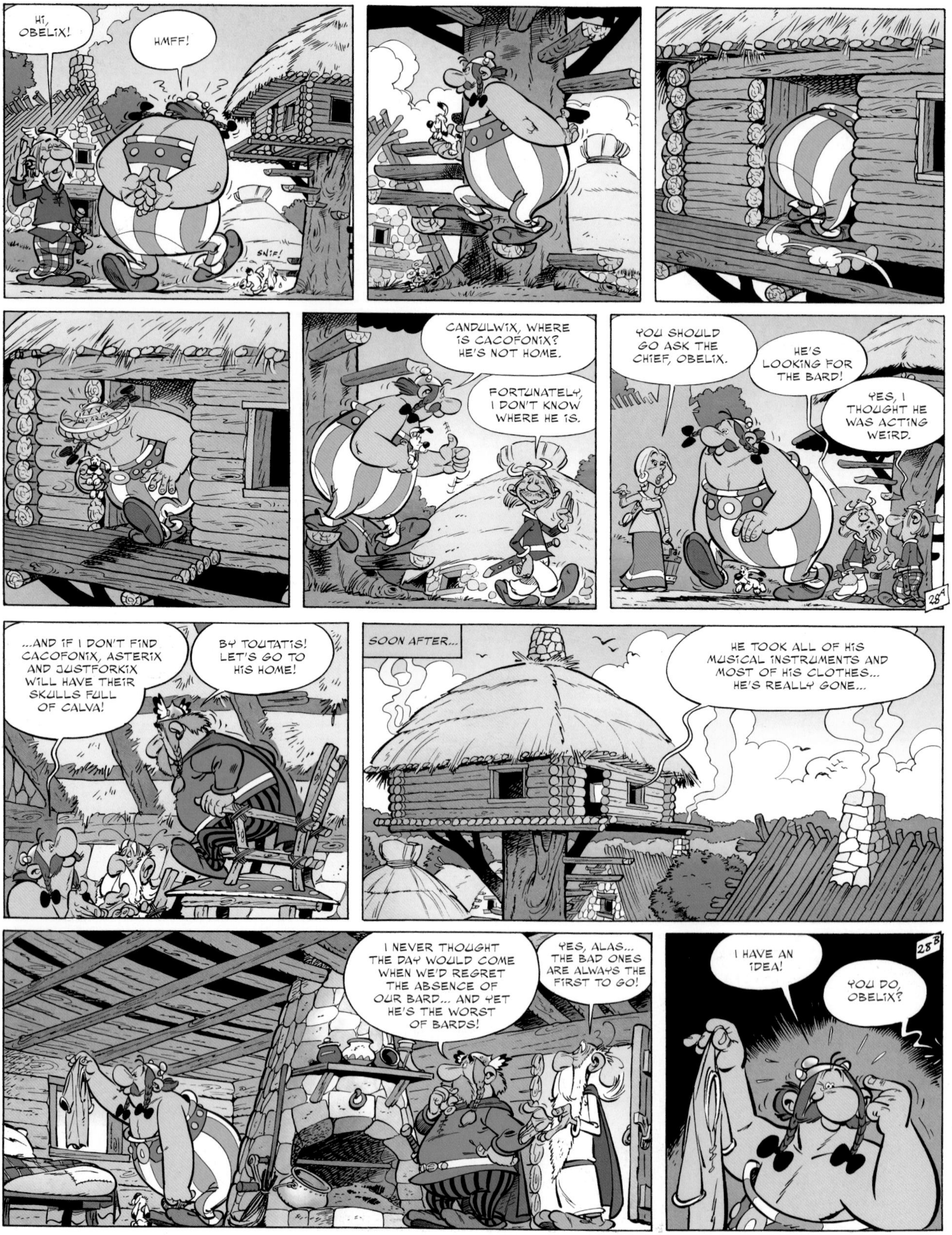
HI, OBELIX!
HMFF!
SNIF!
CANDULWIX, WHERE IS CACOFONIX? HE'S NOT HOME.
FORTUNATELY, I DON'T KNOW WHERE HE IS.
YOU SHOULD GO ASK THE CHIEF, OBELIX.
HE'S LOOKING FOR THE BARD!
YES, I THOUGHT HE WAS ACTING WEIRD.
28A
...AND IF I DON'T FIND CACOFONIX, ASTERIX AND JUSTFORKIX WILL HAVE THEIR SKULLS FULL OF CALVA!
BY TOUTATIS! LET'S GO TO HIS HOME!
SOON AFTER...
HE TOOK ALL OF HIS MUSICAL INSTRUMENTS AND MOST OF HIS CLOTHES... HE'S REALLY GONE...
I NEVER THOUGHT THE DAY WOULD COME WHEN WE'D REGRET THE ABSENCE OF OUR BARD... AND YET HE'S THE WORST OF BARDS!
YES, ALAS... THE BAD ONES ARE ALWAYS THE FIRST TO GO!
28B
I HAVE AN IDEA!
YOU DO, OBELIX?

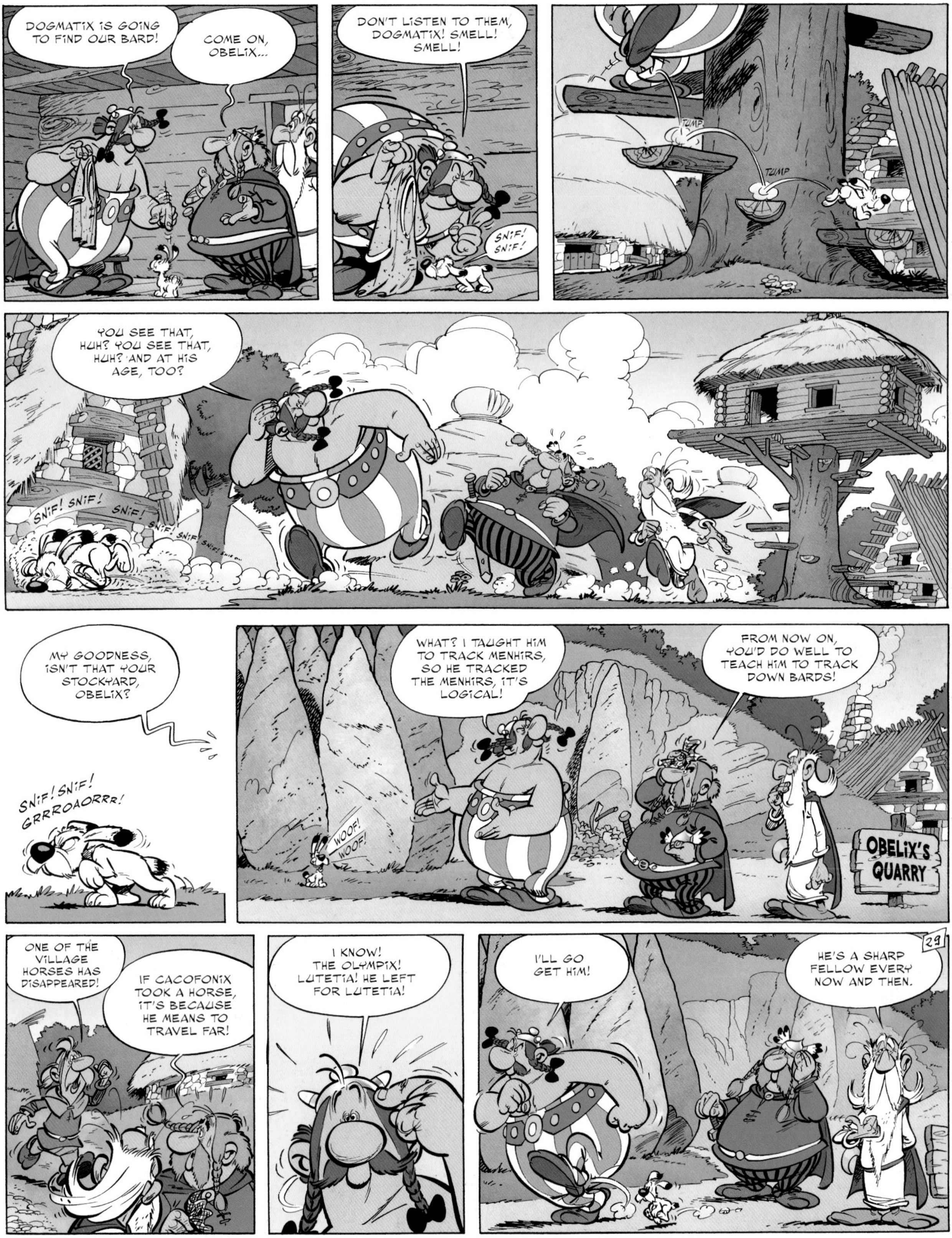
DOGMATIX IS GOING TO FIND OUR BARD!
COME ON, OBELIX...
DON'T LISTEN TO THEM, DOGMATIX! SMELL! SMELL!
SNIF! SNIF!
TUMP
TUMP
YOU SEE THAT, HUH? YOU SEE THAT, HUH? AND AT HIS AGE, TOO?
SNIF! SNIF! SNIF! SNIF! SNIF!
MY GOODNESS, ISN'T THAT YOUR STOCKYARD, OBELIX?
SNIF! SNIF! GRRROAORRR!
WHAT? I TAUGHT HIM TO TRACK MENHIRS, SO HE TRACKED THE MENHIRS, IT'S LOGICAL!
FROM NOW ON, YOU'D DO WELL TO TEACH HIM TO TRACK DOWN BARDS!
WOOF! WOOF!
OBELIX'S QUARRY
ONE OF THE VILLAGE HORSES HAS DISAPPEARED!
IF CACOFONIX TOOK A HORSE, IT'S BECAUSE HE MEANS TO TRAVEL FAR!
I KNOW! THE OLYMPIX! LUTETIA! HE LEFT FOR LUTETIA!
I'LL GO GET HIM!
29
HE'S A SHARP FELLOW EVERY NOW AND THEN.

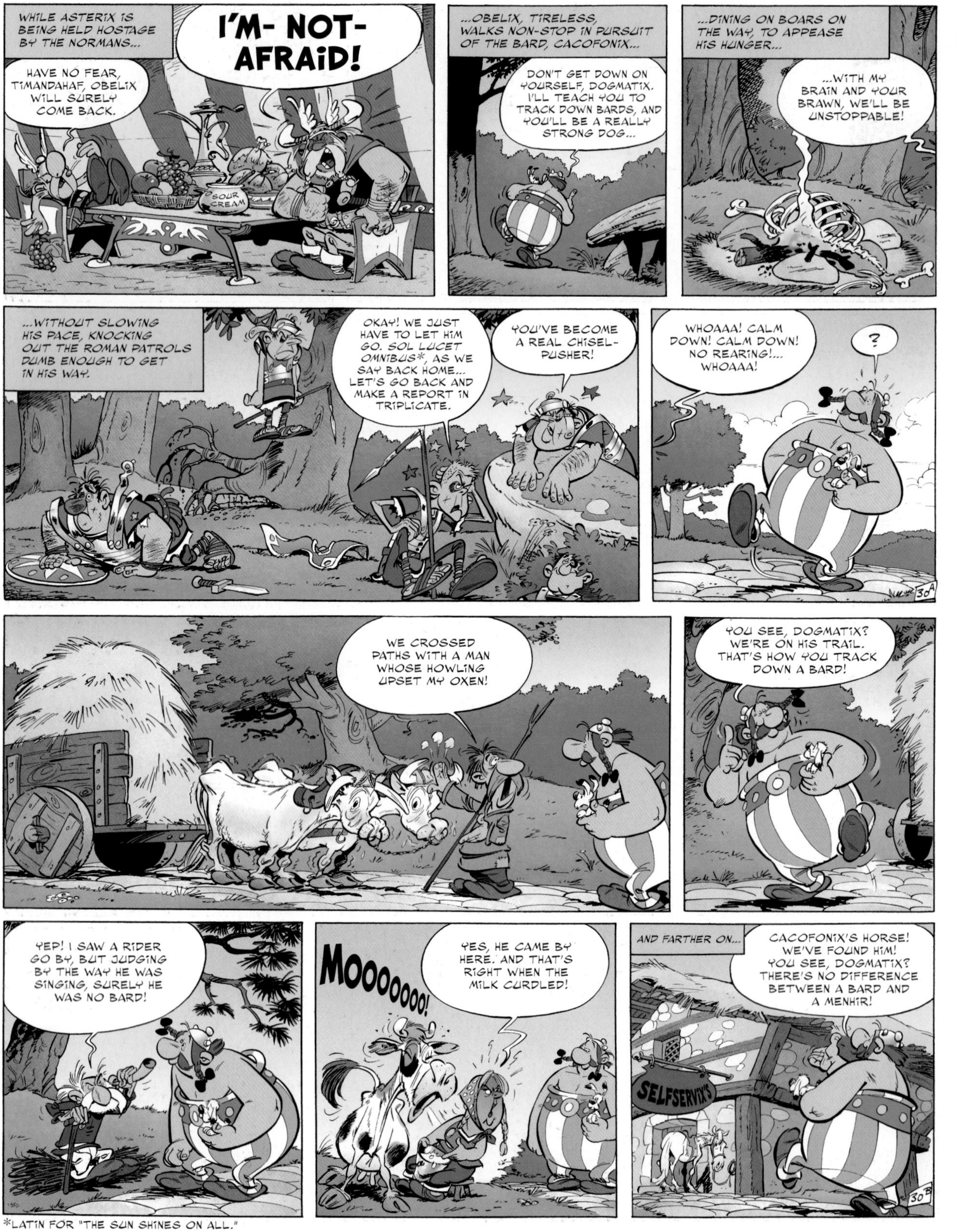

WHILE ASTERIX IS BEING HELD HOSTAGE BY THE NORMANS...
HAVE NO FEAR, TIMANDAHAF, OBELIX WILL SURELY COME BACK.
I'M- NOT- AFRAID!
SOUR CREAM
...OBELIX, TIRELESS, WALKS NON-STOP IN PURSUIT OF THE BARD, CACOFONIX...
DON'T GET DOWN ON YOURSELF, DOGMATIX. I'LL TEACH YOU TO TRACK DOWN BARDS, AND YOU'LL BE A REALLY STRONG DOG...
...DINING ON BOARS ON THE WAY, TO APPEASE HIS HUNGER...
...WITH MY BRAIN AND YOUR BRAWN, WE'LL BE UNSTOPPABLE!
...WITHOUT SLOWING HIS PACE, KNOCKING OUT THE ROMAN PATROLS DUMB ENOUGH TO GET IN HIS WAY.
OKAY! WE JUST HAVE TO LET HIM GO. SOL LUCET OMNIBUS*, AS WE SAY BACK HOME... LET'S GO BACK AND MAKE A REPORT IN TRIPLICATE.
YOU'VE BECOME A REAL CHISEL-PUSHER!
WHOAAA! CALM DOWN! CALM DOWN! NO REARING!... WHOAAA!
?
30A
WE CROSSED PATHS WITH A MAN WHOSE HOWLING UPSET MY OXEN!
YOU SEE, DOGMATIX? WE'RE ON HIS TRAIL. THAT'S HOW YOU TRACK DOWN A BARD!
YEP! I SAW A RIDER GO BY, BUT JUDGING BY THE WAY HE WAS SINGING, SURELY HE WAS NO BARD!
MOOOOOOO!
YES, HE CAME BY HERE. AND THAT'S RIGHT WHEN THE MILK CURDLED!
AND FARTHER ON...
CACOFONIX'S HORSE! WE'VE FOUND HIM! YOU SEE, DOGMATIX? THERE'S NO DIFFERENCE BETWEEN A BARD AND A MENHIR!
SELFSERVIX'S
30B

*LATIN FOR "THE SUN SHINES ON ALL."

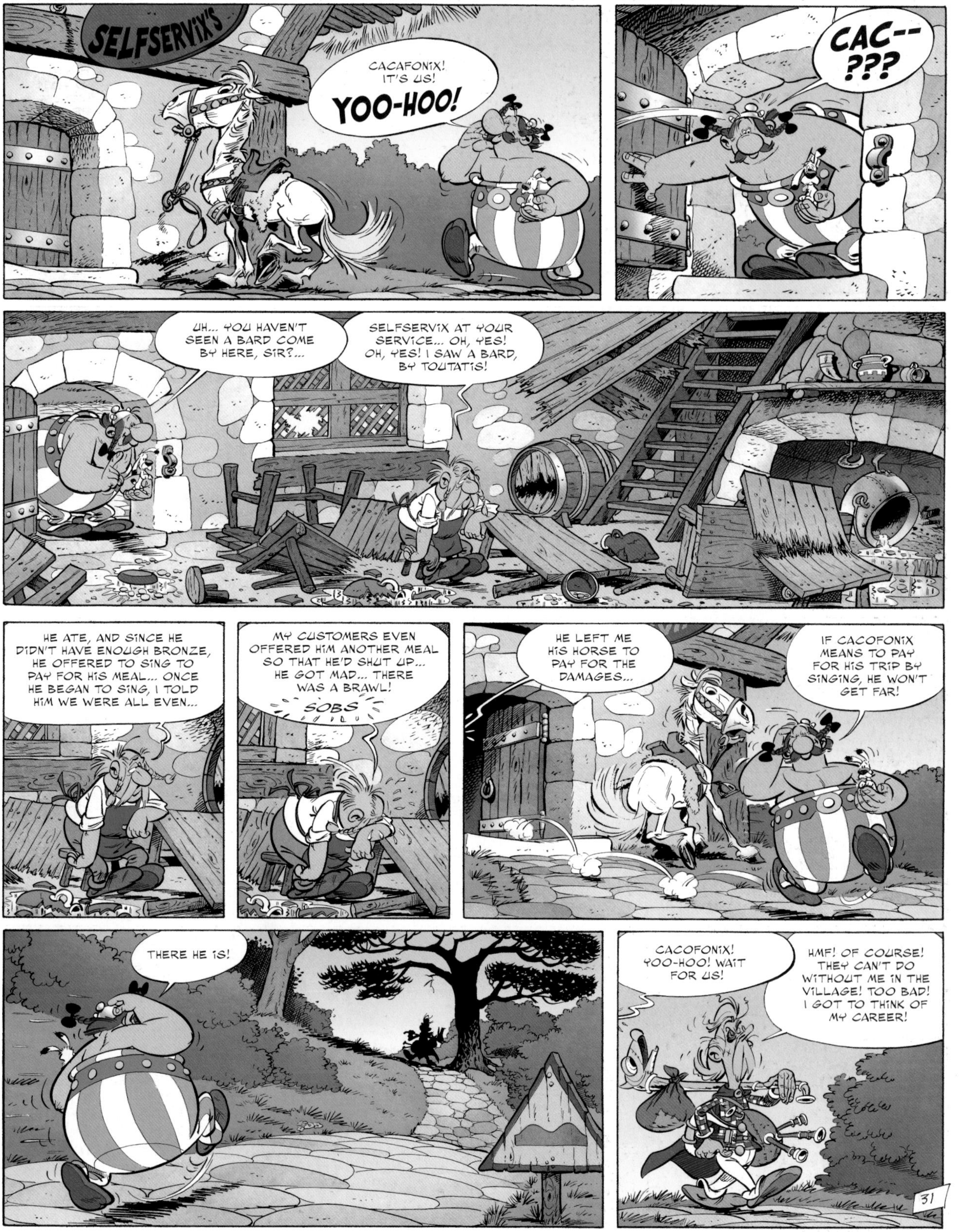
SELFSERVIX'S
CACAFONIX! IT'S US! YOO-HOO!
CAC-- ???
UH... YOU HAVEN'T SEEN A BARD COME BY HERE, SIR?...
SELFSERVIX AT YOUR SERVICE... OH, YES! OH, YES! I SAW A BARD, BY TOUTATIS!
HE ATE, AND SINCE HE DIDN'T HAVE ENOUGH BRONZE, HE OFFERED TO SING TO PAY FOR HIS MEAL... ONCE HE BEGAN TO SING, I TOLD HIM WE WERE ALL EVEN...
MY CUSTOMERS EVEN OFFERED HIM ANOTHER MEAL SO THAT HE'D SHUT UP... HE GOT MAD... THERE WAS A BRAWL!
SOBS
HE LEFT ME HIS HORSE TO PAY FOR THE DAMAGES...
IF CACOFONIX MEANS TO PAY FOR HIS TRIP BY SINGING, HE WON'T GET FAR!
THERE HE IS!
CACOFONIX! YOO-HOO! WAIT FOR US!
HMF! OF COURSE! THEY CAN'T DO WITHOUT ME IN THE VILLAGE! TOO BAD! I GOT TO THINK OF MY CAREER!
31

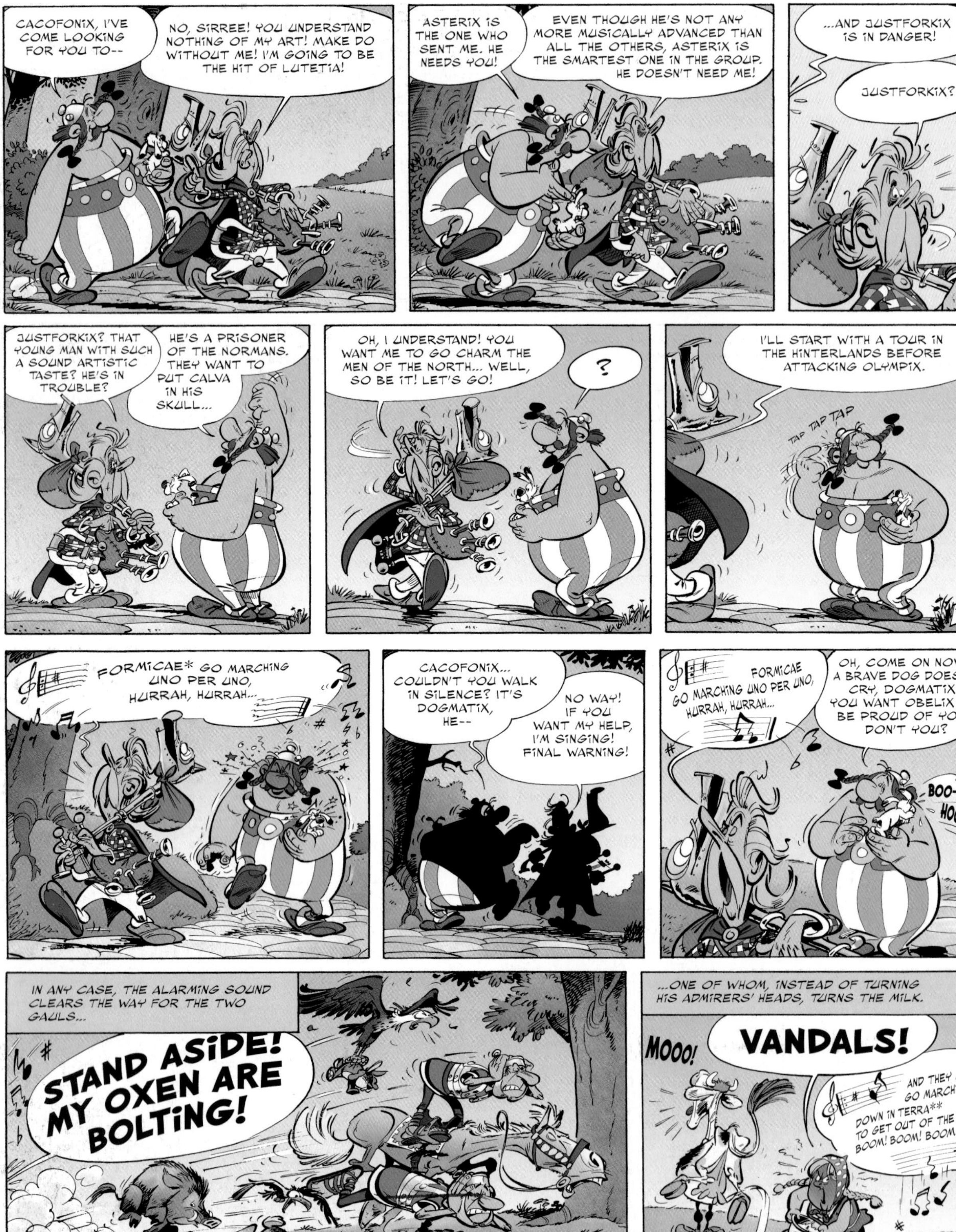

CACOFONIX, I'VE COME LOOKING FOR YOU TO--
NO, SIRREE! YOU UNDERSTAND NOTHING OF MY ART! MAKE DO WITHOUT ME! I'M GOING TO BE THE HIT OF LUTETIA!
ASTERIX IS THE ONE WHO SENT ME. HE NEEDS YOU!
EVEN THOUGH HE'S NOT ANY MORE MUSICALLY ADVANCED THAN ALL THE OTHERS, ASTERIX IS THE SMARTEST ONE IN THE GROUP. HE DOESN'T NEED ME!
...AND JUSTFORKIX IS IN DANGER!
JUSTFORKIX?
JUSTFORKIX? THAT YOUNG MAN WITH SUCH A SOUND ARTISTIC TASTE? HE'S IN TROUBLE?
HE'S A PRISONER OF THE NORMANS. THEY WANT TO PUT CALVA IN HIS SKULL...
OH, I UNDERSTAND! YOU WANT ME TO GO CHARM THE MEN OF THE NORTH... WELL, SO BE IT! LET'S GO!
?
I'LL START WITH A TOUR IN THE HINTERLANDS BEFORE ATTACKING OLYMPIX.
TAP TAP TAP
32A
FORMICAE* GO MARCHING UNO PER UNO, HURRAH, HURRAH...
CACOFONIX... COULDN'T YOU WALK IN SILENCE? IT'S DOGMATIX, HE--
NO WAY! IF YOU WANT MY HELP, I'M SINGING! FINAL WARNING!
FORMICAE GO MARCHING UNO PER UNO, HURRAH, HURRAH...
OH, COME ON NOW! A BRAVE DOG DOESN'T CRY, DOGMATIX! YOU WANT OBELIX TO BE PROUD OF YOU, DON'T YOU?
BOO-HOO HOO-HOO!
IN ANY CASE, THE ALARMING SOUND CLEARS THE WAY FOR THE TWO GAULS...
STAND ASIDE! MY OXEN ARE BOLTING!
...ONE OF WHOM, INSTEAD OF TURNING HIS ADMIRERS' HEADS, TURNS THE MILK.
MOOO!
VANDALS!
AND THEY ALL GO MARCHING DOWN IN TERRA** TO GET OUT OF THE RAIN, BOOM! BOOM! BOOM!
32B

*LATIN FOR "ANTS." **LATIN FOR THE "GROUND."

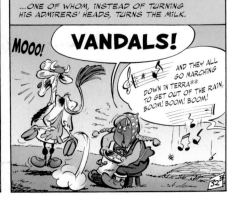

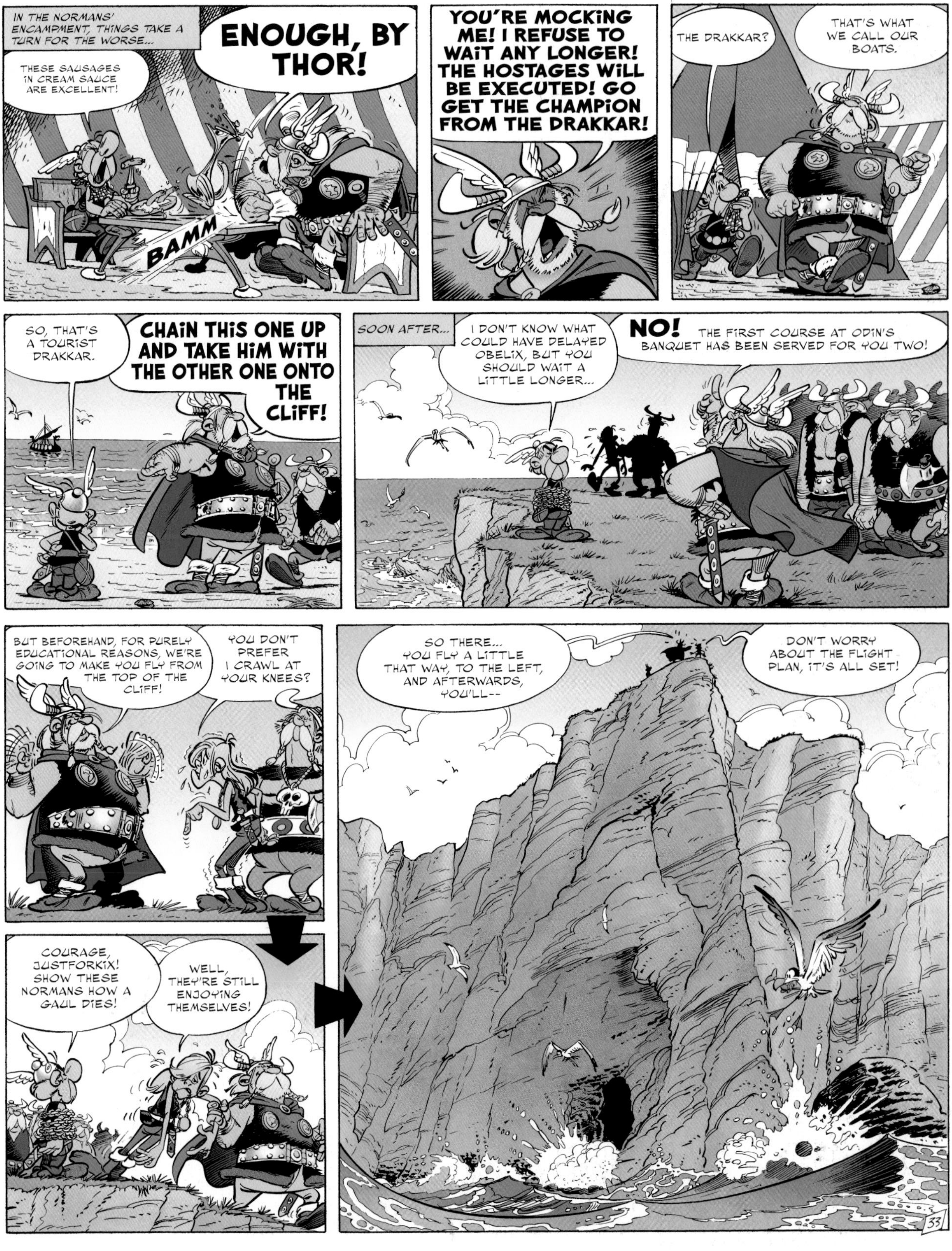

IN THE NORMANS' ENCAMPMENT, THINGS TAKE A TURN FOR THE WORSE...
THESE SAUSAGES IN CREAM SAUCE ARE EXCELLENT!
ENOUGH, BY THOR!
BAMM
YOU'RE MOCKING ME! I REFUSE TO WAIT ANY LONGER! THE HOSTAGES WILL BE EXECUTED! GO GET THE CHAMPION FROM THE DRAKKAR!
THE DRAKKAR?
THAT'S WHAT WE CALL OUR BOATS.
SO, THAT'S A TOURIST DRAKKAR.
CHAIN THIS ONE UP AND TAKE HIM WITH THE OTHER ONE ONTO THE CLIFF!
SOON AFTER...
I DON'T KNOW WHAT COULD HAVE DELAYED OBELIX, BUT YOU SHOULD WAIT A LITTLE LONGER...
NO! THE FIRST COURSE AT ODIN'S BANQUET HAS BEEN SERVED FOR YOU TWO!
BUT BEFOREHAND, FOR PURELY EDUCATIONAL REASONS, WE'RE GOING TO MAKE YOU FLY FROM THE TOP OF THE CLIFF!
YOU DON'T PREFER I CRAWL AT YOUR KNEES?
COURAGE, JUSTFORKIX! SHOW THESE NORMANS HOW A GAUL DIES!
WELL, THEY'RE STILL ENJOYING THEMSELVES!
SO THERE... YOU FLY A LITTLE THAT WAY, TO THE LEFT, AND AFTERWARDS, YOU'LL--
DON'T WORRY ABOUT THE FLIGHT PLAN, IT'S ALL SET!
33

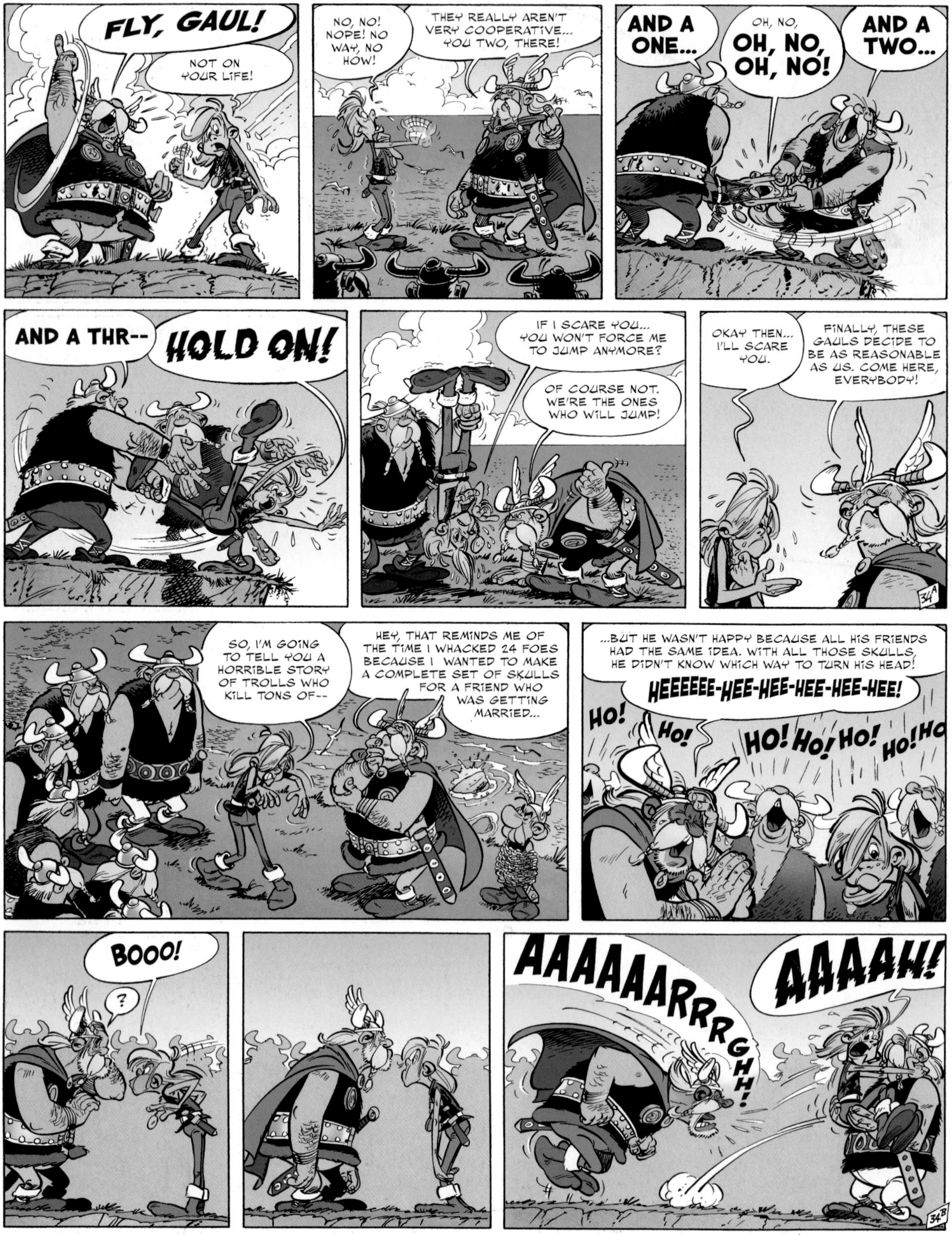
FLY, GAUL!
NOT ON YOUR LIFE!
NO, NO! NOPE! NO WAY, NO HOW!
THEY REALLY AREN'T VERY COOPERATIVE... YOU TWO, THERE!
AND A ONE...
OH, NO, OH, NO, OH, NO!
AND A TWO...
AND A THR--
HOLD ON!
IF I SCARE YOU... YOU WON'T FORCE ME TO JUMP ANYMORE?
OF COURSE NOT. WE'RE THE ONES WHO WILL JUMP!
OKAY THEN... I'LL SCARE YOU.
FINALLY, THESE GAULS DECIDE TO BE AS REASONABLE AS US. COME HERE, EVERYBODY!
34A
SO, I'M GOING TO TELL YOU A HORRIBLE STORY OF TROLLS WHO KILL TONS OF--
HEY, THAT REMINDS ME OF THE TIME I WHACKED 24 FOES BECAUSE I WANTED TO MAKE A COMPLETE SET OF SKULLS FOR A FRIEND WHO WAS GETTING MARRIED...
...BUT HE WASN'T HAPPY BECAUSE ALL HIS FRIENDS HAD THE SAME IDEA. WITH ALL THOSE SKULLS, HE DIDN'T KNOW WHICH WAY TO TURN HIS HEAD!
HEEEEEE-HEE-HEE-HEE-HEE-HEE!
HO! HO! HO! HO! HO! HO! HO
BOOO!
?
AAAAAARRRRGHH!
AAAAH!
34B

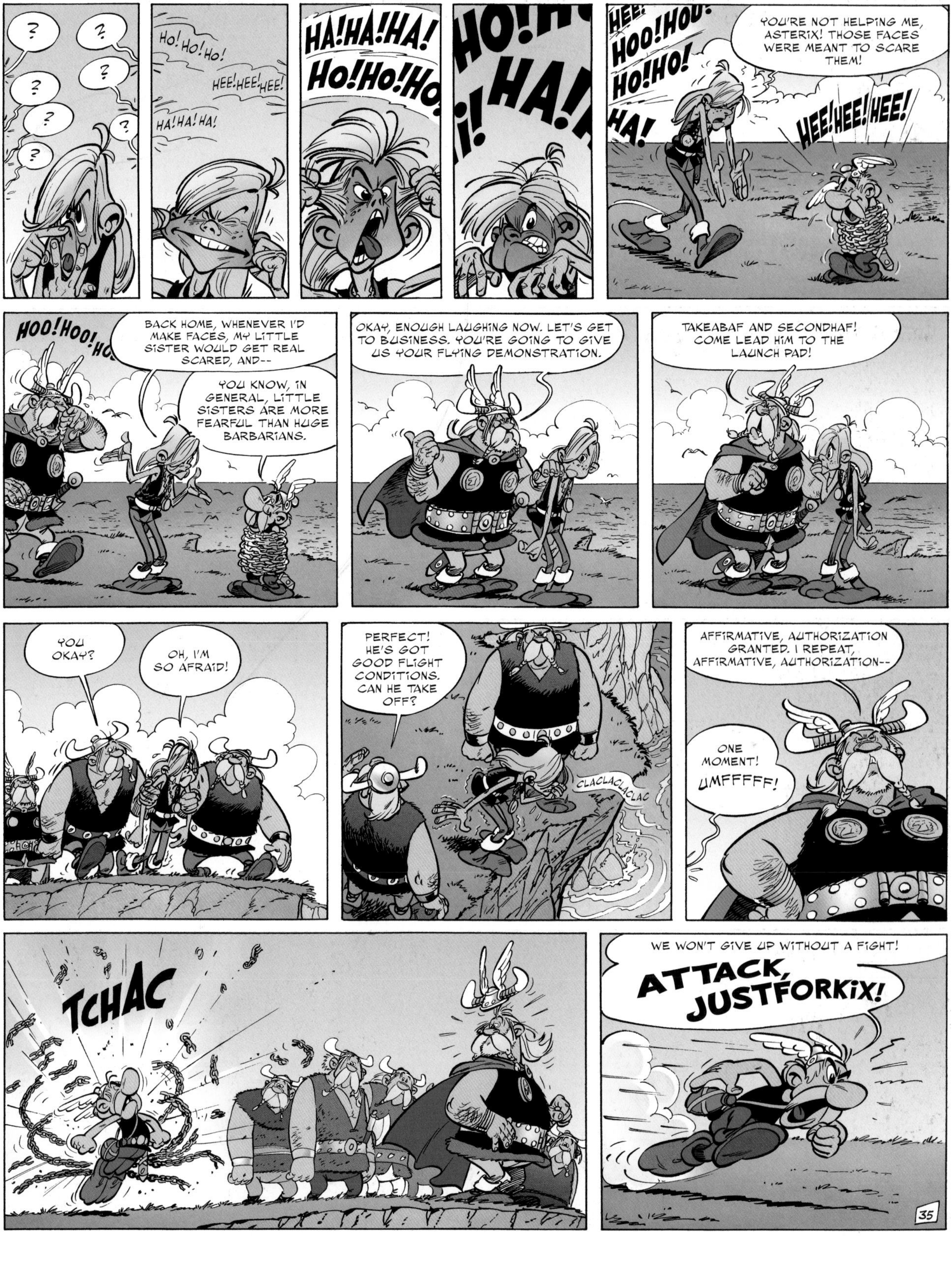
?
?
?
?
?
?
?
HO! HO! HO!
HEE! HEE! HEE!
HA! HA! HA!
HA!HA!HA!
HO!HO!HO!
HO!HO!
HA!HA!
HEE!
HOO!HOO!
HO!HO!
HA!
YOU'RE NOT HELPING ME, ASTERIX! THOSE FACES WERE MEANT TO SCARE THEM!
HEE!HEE!HEE!
HOO!HOO!HO!
BACK HOME, WHENEVER I'D MAKE FACES, MY LITTLE SISTER WOULD GET REAL SCARED, AND--
YOU KNOW, IN GENERAL, LITTLE SISTERS ARE MORE FEARFUL THAN HUGE BARBARIANS.
OKAY, ENOUGH LAUGHING NOW. LET'S GET TO BUSINESS. YOU'RE GOING TO GIVE US YOUR FLYING DEMONSTRATION.
TAKEABAF AND SECONDHAF! COME LEAD HIM TO THE LAUNCH PAD!
YOU OKAY?
OH, I'M SO AFRAID!
PERFECT! HE'S GOT GOOD FLIGHT CONDITIONS. CAN HE TAKE OFF?
CLACLACLACLAC
AFFIRMATIVE, AUTHORIZATION GRANTED. I REPEAT, AFFIRMATIVE, AUTHORIZATION--
ONE MOMENT!
UMFFFFF!
TCHAC
WE WON'T GIVE UP WITHOUT A FIGHT!
ATTACK, JUSTFORKIX!
35

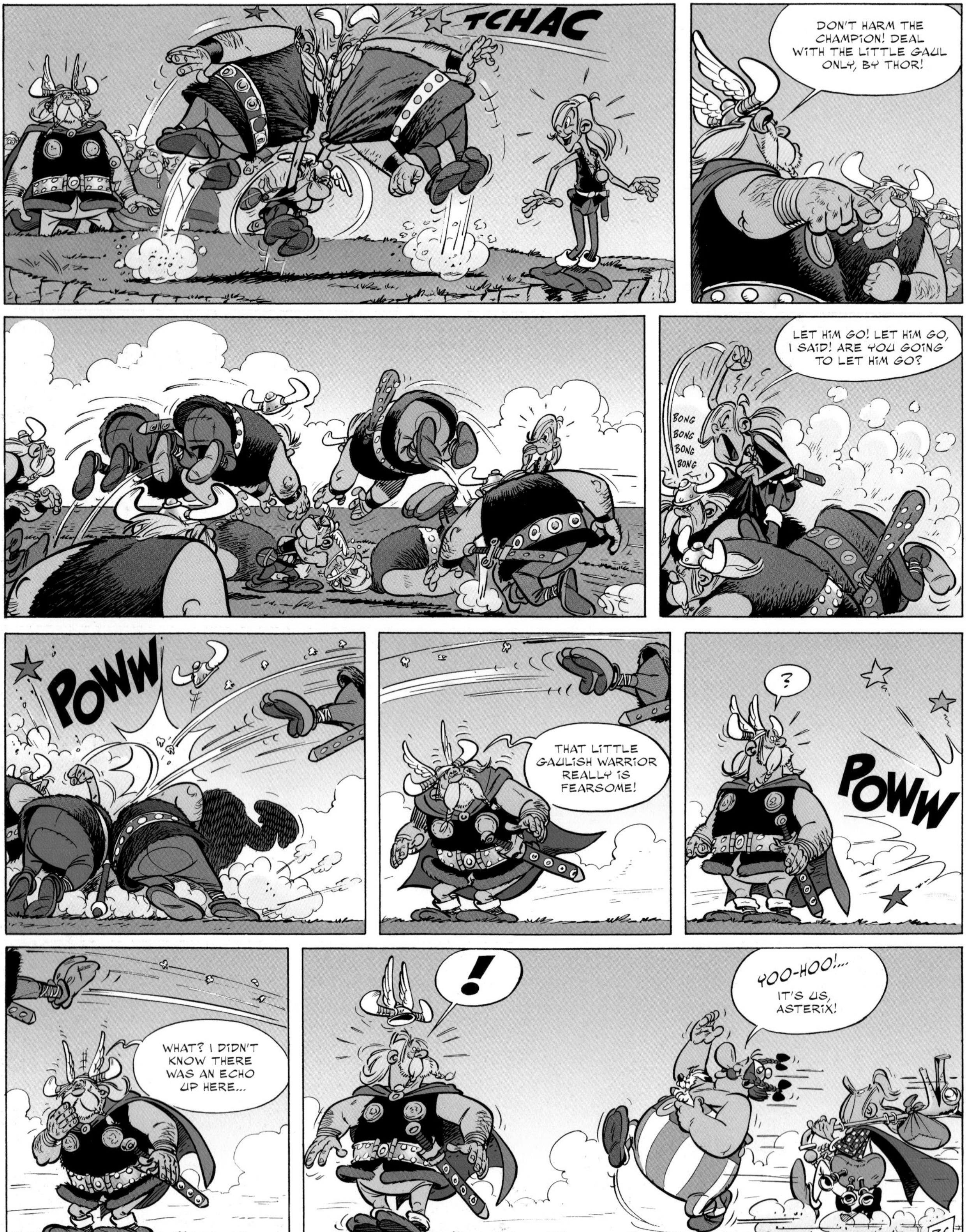

TCHAC
DON'T HARM THE CHAMPION! DEAL WITH THE LITTLE GAUL ONLY, BY THOR!
LET HIM GO! LET HIM GO, I SAID! ARE YOU GOING TO LET HIM GO?
BONG
BONG
BONG
BONG
POWW
THAT LITTLE GAULISH WARRIOR REALLY IS FEARSOME!
?
POWW
WHAT? I DIDN'T KNOW THERE WAS AN ECHO UP HERE...
!
YOO-HOO!... IT'S US, ASTERIX!
36

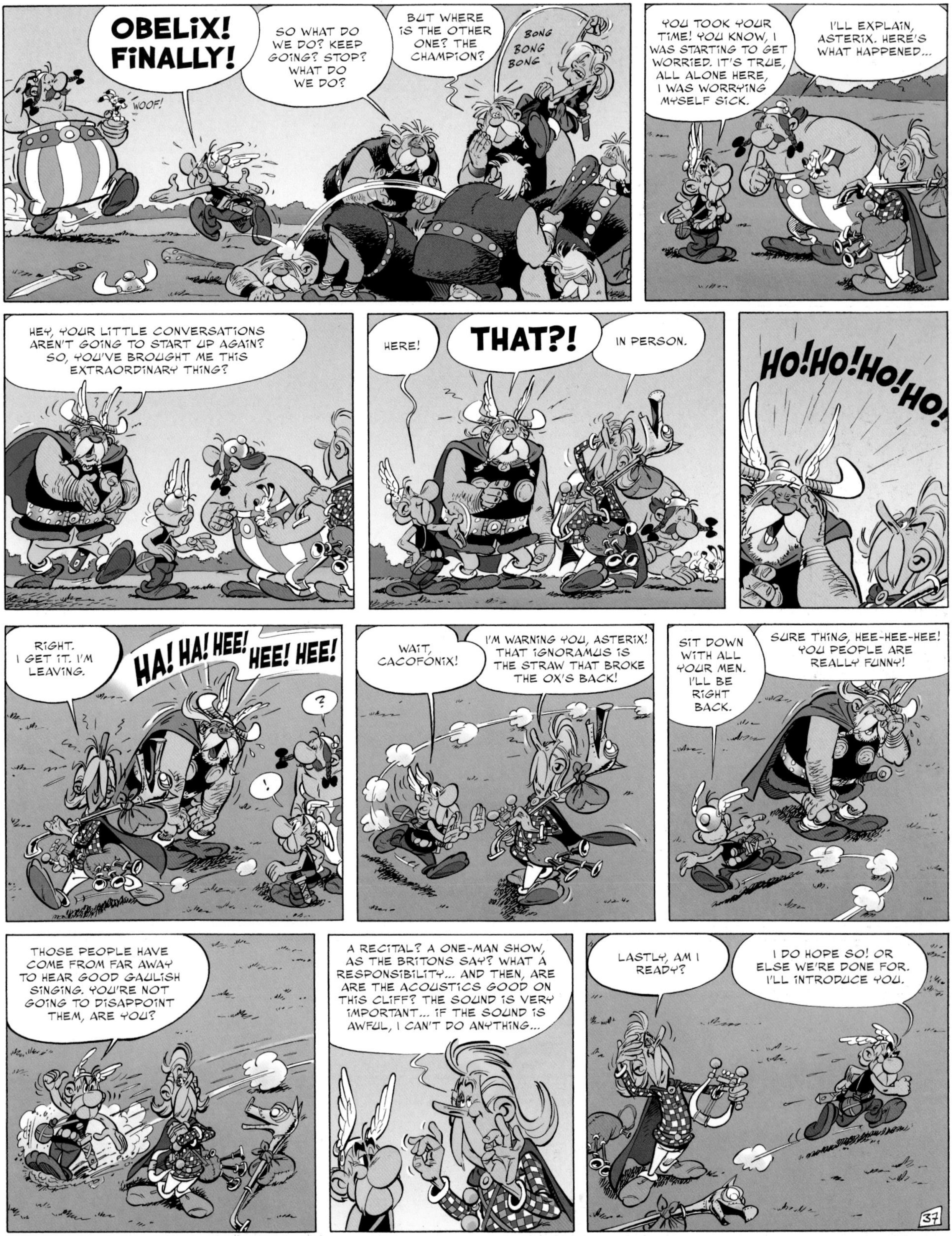

OBELIX! FINALLY!
WOOF!
SO WHAT DO WE DO? KEEP GOING? STOP? WHAT DO WE DO?
BUT WHERE IS THE OTHER ONE? THE CHAMPION?
BONG BONG BONG
YOU TOOK YOUR TIME! YOU KNOW, I WAS STARTING TO GET WORRIED. IT'S TRUE, ALL ALONE HERE, I WAS WORRYING MYSELF SICK.
I'LL EXPLAIN, ASTERIX. HERE'S WHAT HAPPENED...
HEY, YOUR LITTLE CONVERSATIONS AREN'T GOING TO START UP AGAIN? SO, YOU'VE BROUGHT ME THIS EXTRAORDINARY THING?
HERE!
THAT?!
IN PERSON.
HO!HO!HO!HO!
RIGHT. I GET IT. I'M LEAVING.
HA! HA! HEE! HEE! HEE!
?
!
WAIT, CACOFONIX!
I'M WARNING YOU, ASTERIX! THAT IGNORAMUS IS THE STRAW THAT BROKE THE OX'S BACK!
SIT DOWN WITH ALL YOUR MEN. I'LL BE RIGHT BACK.
SURE THING, HEE-HEE-HEE! YOU PEOPLE ARE REALLY FUNNY!
THOSE PEOPLE HAVE COME FROM FAR AWAY TO HEAR GOOD GAULISH SINGING. YOU'RE NOT GOING TO DISAPPOINT THEM, ARE YOU?
A RECITAL? A ONE-MAN SHOW, AS THE BRITONS SAY? WHAT A RESPONSIBILITY... AND THEN, ARE ARE THE ACOUSTICS GOOD ON THIS CLIFF? THE SOUND IS VERY IMPORTANT... IF THE SOUND IS AWFUL, I CAN'T DO ANYTHING...
LASTLY, AM I READY?
I DO HOPE SO! OR ELSE WE'RE DONE FOR. I'LL INTRODUCE YOU.
37

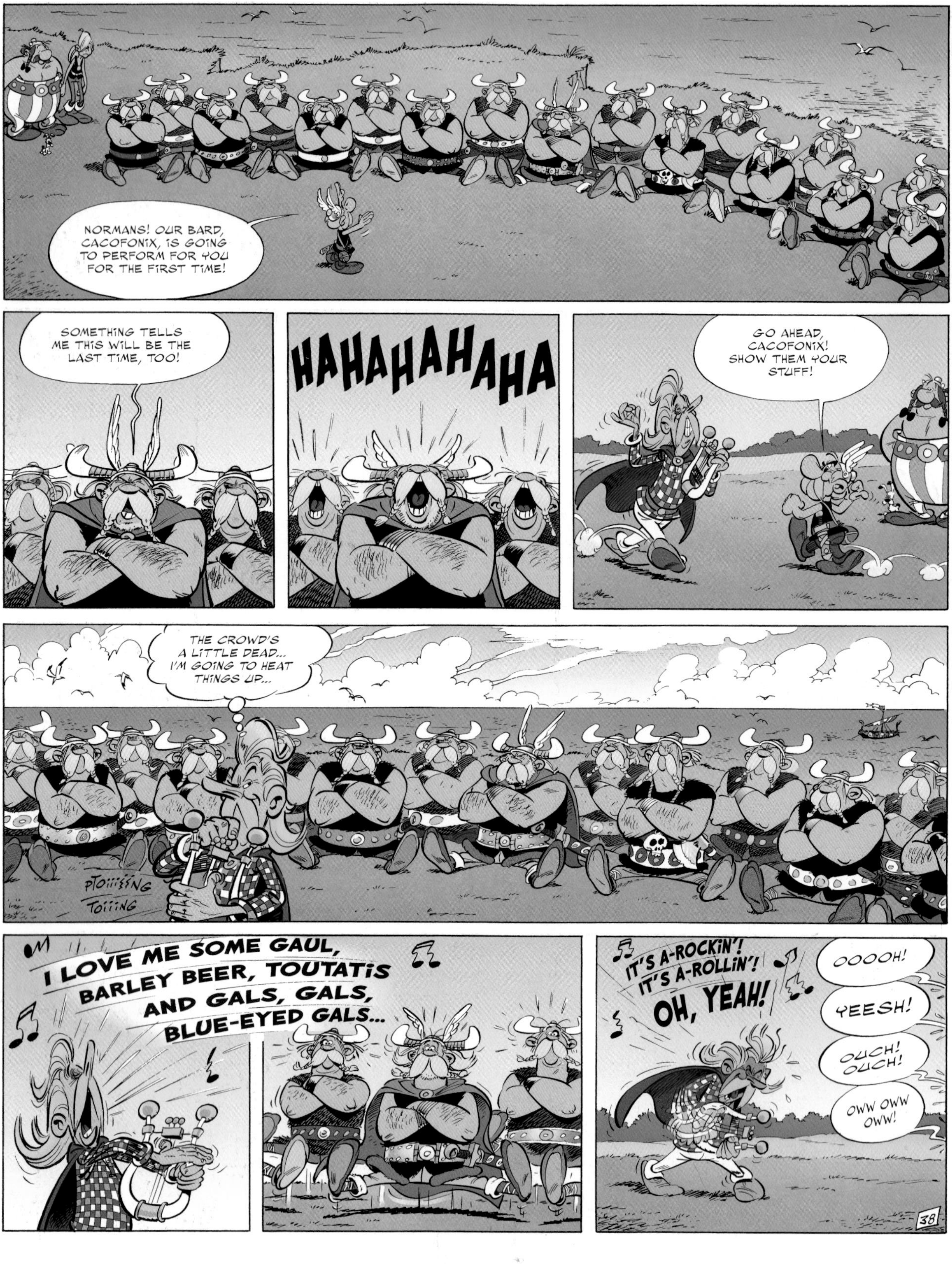
NORMANS! OUR BARD, CACOFONIX, IS GOING TO PERFORM FOR YOU FOR THE FIRST TIME!
SOMETHING TELLS ME THIS WILL BE THE LAST TIME, TOO!
HAHAHAHAHA
GO AHEAD, CACOFONIX! SHOW THEM YOUR STUFF!
THE CROWD'S A LITTLE DEAD... I'M GOING TO HEAT THINGS UP...
PTOiiiiiNG
TOiiiNG
I LOVE ME SOME GAUL, BARLEY BEER, TOUTATIS AND GALS, GALS, BLUE-EYED GALS...
IT'S A-ROCKiN'! IT'S A-ROLLiN'!
OH, YEAH!
OOOOH!
YEESH!
OUCH! OUCH!
OWW OWW OWW!
38

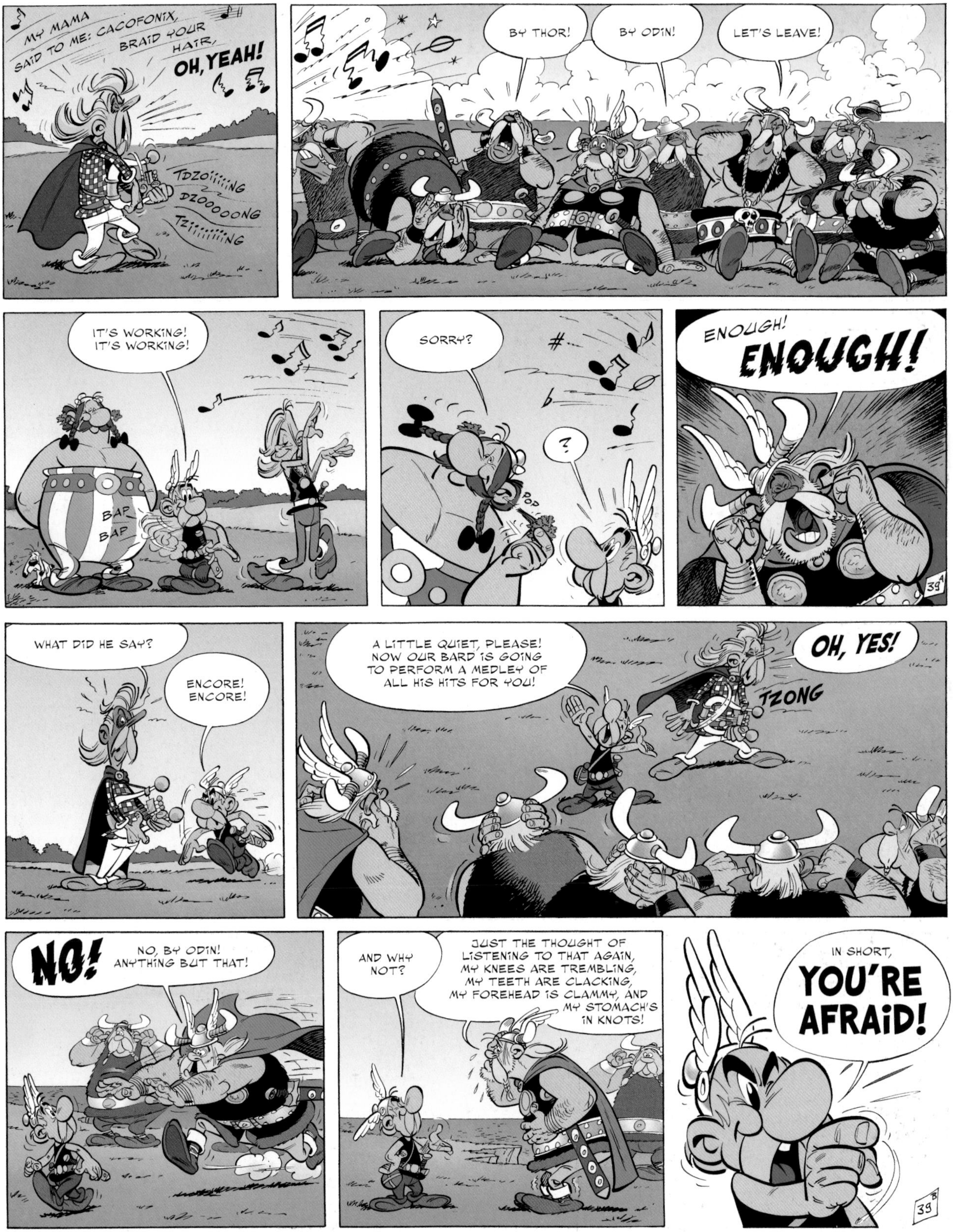
MY MAMA SAID TO ME: CACOFONIX, BRAID YOUR HAIR,
OH, YEAH!
TDZOiiiiiNG
DZOOOOOONG
TZiiiiiiiNG
BY THOR!
BY ODIN!
LET'S LEAVE!
IT'S WORKING! IT'S WORKING!
BAP
BAP
SORRY?
?
POP
ENOUGH!
ENOUGH!
WHAT DID HE SAY?
ENCORE! ENCORE!
A LITTLE QUIET, PLEASE! NOW OUR BARD IS GOING TO PERFORM A MEDLEY OF ALL HIS HITS FOR YOU!
OH, YES!
TZONG
NO!
NO, BY ODIN! ANYTHING BUT THAT!
AND WHY NOT?
JUST THE THOUGHT OF LISTENING TO THAT AGAIN, MY KNEES ARE TREMBLING, MY TEETH ARE CLACKING, MY FOREHEAD IS CLAMMY, AND MY STOMACH'S IN KNOTS!
IN SHORT, YOU'RE AFRAID!

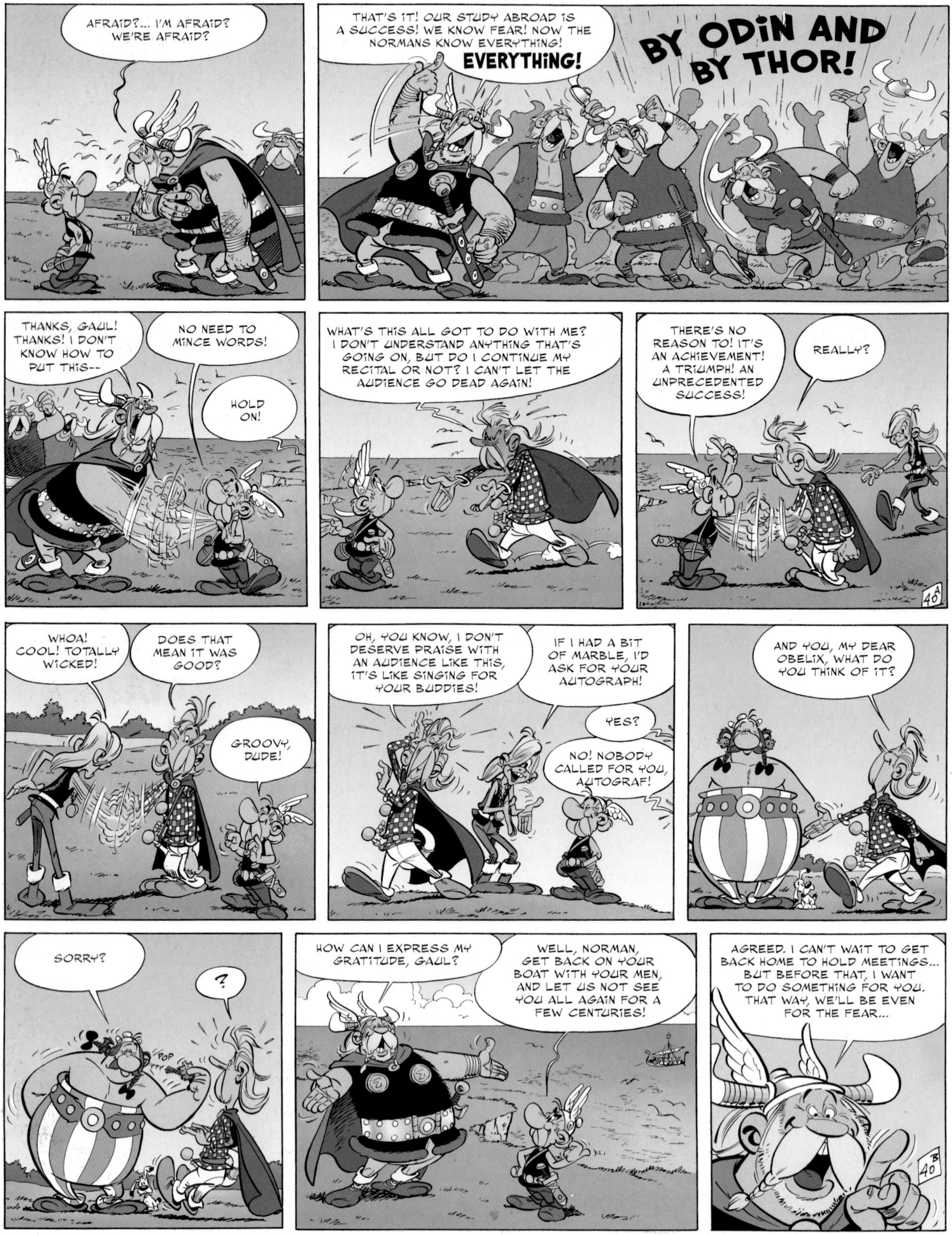
AFRAID?... I'M AFRAID? WE'RE AFRAID?
THAT'S IT! OUR STUDY ABROAD IS A SUCCESS! WE KNOW FEAR! NOW THE NORMANS KNOW EVERYTHING! EVERYTHING!
BY ODIN AND BY THOR!
THANKS, GAUL! THANKS! I DON'T KNOW HOW TO PUT THIS--
NO NEED TO MINCE WORDS!
HOLD ON!
WHAT'S THIS ALL GOT TO DO WITH ME? I DON'T UNDERSTAND ANYTHING THAT'S GOING ON, BUT DO I CONTINUE MY RECITAL OR NOT? I CAN'T LET THE AUDIENCE GO DEAD AGAIN!
THERE'S NO REASON TO! IT'S AN ACHIEVEMENT! A TRIUMPH! AN UNPRECEDENTED SUCCESS!
REALLY?
WHOA! COOL! TOTALLY WICKED!
DOES THAT MEAN IT WAS GOOD?
GROOVY, DUDE!
OH, YOU KNOW, I DON'T DESERVE PRAISE WITH AN AUDIENCE LIKE THIS, IT'S LIKE SINGING FOR YOUR BUDDIES!
IF I HAD A BIT OF MARBLE, I'D ASK FOR YOUR AUTOGRAPH!
YES?
NO! NOBODY CALLED FOR YOU, AUTOGRAF!
AND YOU, MY DEAR OBELIX, WHAT DO YOU THINK OF IT?
SORRY?
?
POP
HOW CAN I EXPRESS MY GRATITUDE, GAUL?
WELL, NORMAN, GET BACK ON YOUR BOAT WITH YOUR MEN, AND LET US NOT SEE YOU ALL AGAIN FOR A FEW CENTURIES!
AGREED. I CAN'T WAIT TO GET BACK HOME TO HOLD MEETINGS... BUT BEFORE THAT, I WANT TO DO SOMETHING FOR YOU. THAT WAY, WE'LL BE EVEN FOR THE FEAR...

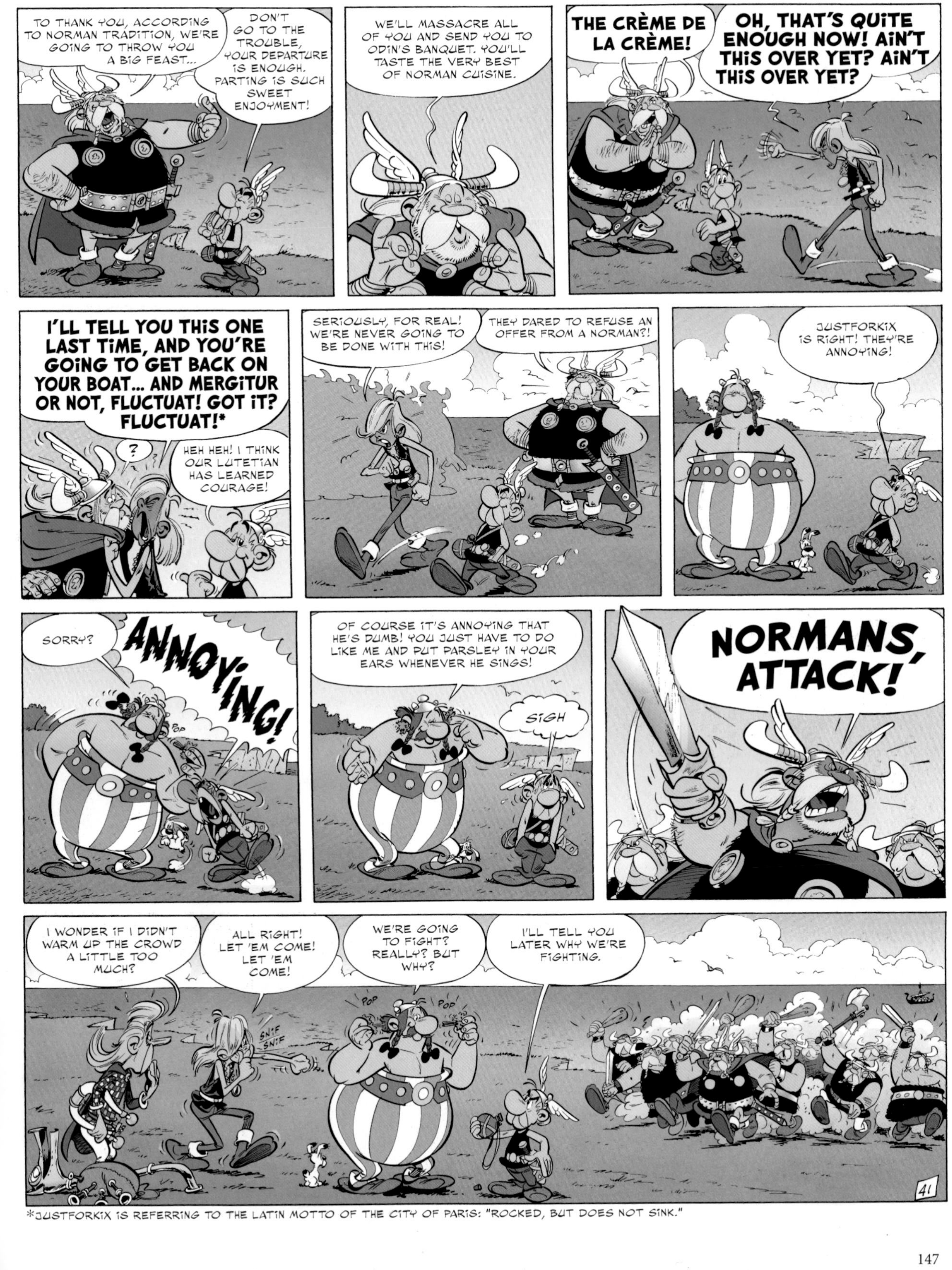
TO THANK YOU, ACCORDING TO NORMAN TRADITION, WE'RE GOING TO THROW YOU A BIG FEAST...
DON'T GO TO THE TROUBLE, YOUR DEPARTURE IS ENOUGH. PARTING IS SUCH SWEET ENJOYMENT!
WE'LL MASSACRE ALL OF YOU AND SEND YOU TO ODIN'S BANQUET. YOU'LL TASTE THE VERY BEST OF NORMAN CUISINE.
THE CRÈME DE LA CRÈME!
OH, THAT'S QUITE ENOUGH NOW! AIN'T THIS OVER YET? AIN'T THIS OVER YET?
I'LL TELL YOU THIS ONE LAST TIME, AND YOU'RE GOING TO GET BACK ON YOUR BOAT... AND MERGITUR OR NOT, FLUCTUAT! GOT IT? FLUCTUAT!*
?
HEH HEH! I THINK OUR LUTETIAN HAS LEARNED COURAGE!
SERIOUSLY, FOR REAL! WE'RE NEVER GOING TO BE DONE WITH THIS!
THEY DARED TO REFUSE AN OFFER FROM A NORMAN?!
JUSTFORKIX IS RIGHT! THEY'RE ANNOYING!
SORRY?
ANNOYING!
POP
OF COURSE IT'S ANNOYING THAT HE'S DUMB! YOU JUST HAVE TO DO LIKE ME AND PUT PARSLEY IN YOUR EARS WHENEVER HE SINGS!
SIGH
NORMANS, ATTACK!
I WONDER IF I DIDN'T WARM UP THE CROWD A LITTLE TOO MUCH?
ALL RIGHT! LET 'EM COME! LET 'EM COME!
WE'RE GOING TO FIGHT? REALLY? BUT WHY?
I'LL TELL YOU LATER WHY WE'RE FIGHTING.
POP
POP
SNIF SNIF
41

*JUSTFORKIX IS REFERRING TO THE LATIN MOTTO OF THE CITY OF PARIS: "ROCKED, BUT DOES NOT SINK."

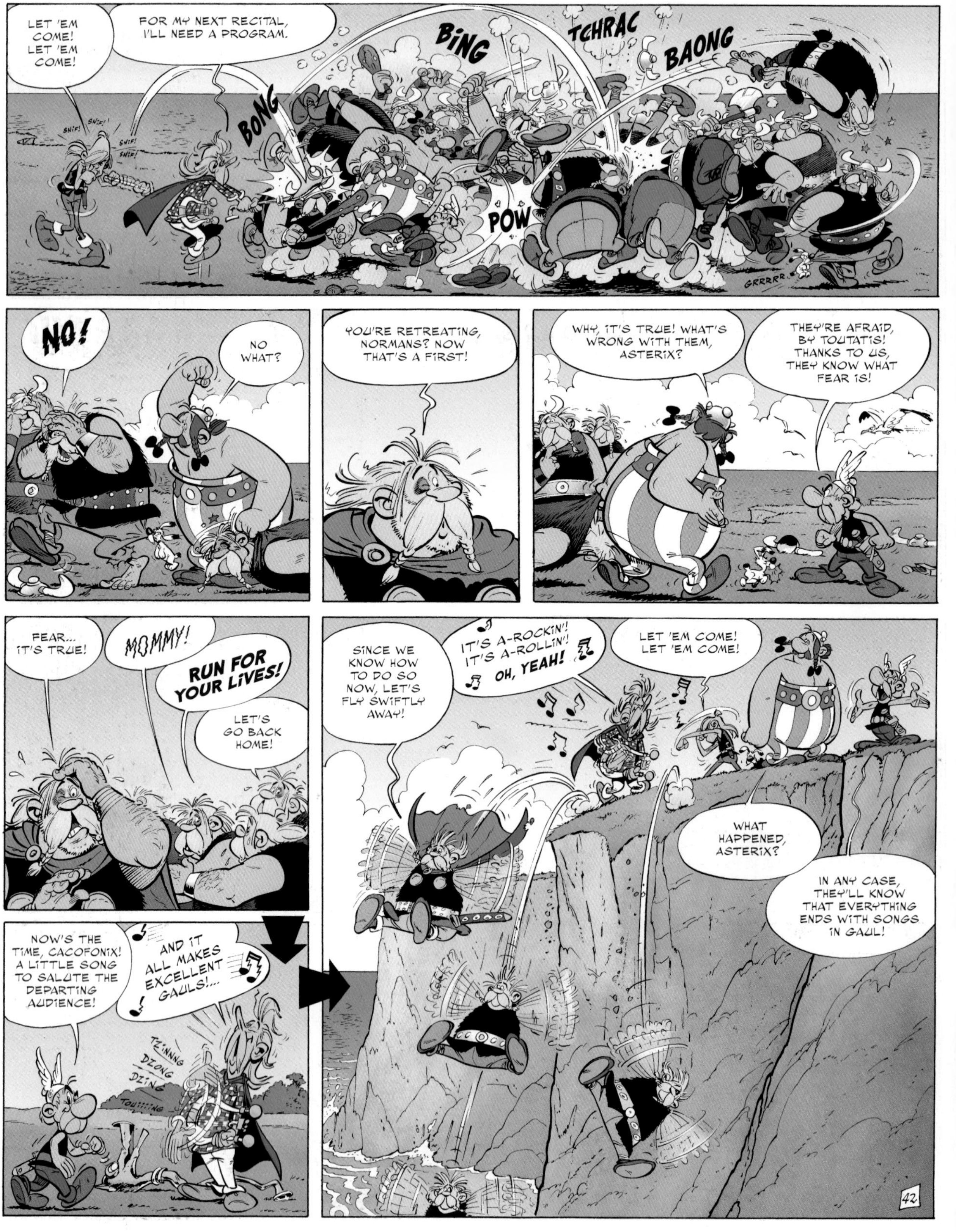

LET 'EM COME! LET 'EM COME!
FOR MY NEXT RECITAL, I'LL NEED A PROGRAM.
SNIF! SNIF! SNIF! SNIF!
BONG
BING
TCHRAC
BAONG
POW
GRRRRR
NO!
NO WHAT?
YOU'RE RETREATING, NORMANS? NOW THAT'S A FIRST!
WHY, IT'S TRUE! WHAT'S WRONG WITH THEM, ASTERIX?
THEY'RE AFRAID, BY TOUTATIS! THANKS TO US, THEY KNOW WHAT FEAR IS!
FEAR... IT'S TRUE!
MOMMY!
RUN FOR YOUR LIVES!
LET'S GO BACK HOME!
NOW'S THE TIME, CACOFONIX! A LITTLE SONG TO SALUTE THE DEPARTING AUDIENCE!
AND IT ALL MAKES EXCELLENT GAULS!...
TZINNNG
DZONG
DZING
SINCE WE KNOW HOW TO DO SO NOW, LET'S FLY SWIFTLY AWAY!
IT'S A-ROCKIN'! IT'S A-ROLLIN'! OH, YEAH!
LET 'EM COME! LET 'EM COME!
WHAT HAPPENED, ASTERIX?
IN ANY CASE, THEY'LL KNOW THAT EVERYTHING ENDS WITH SONGS IN GAUL!
42

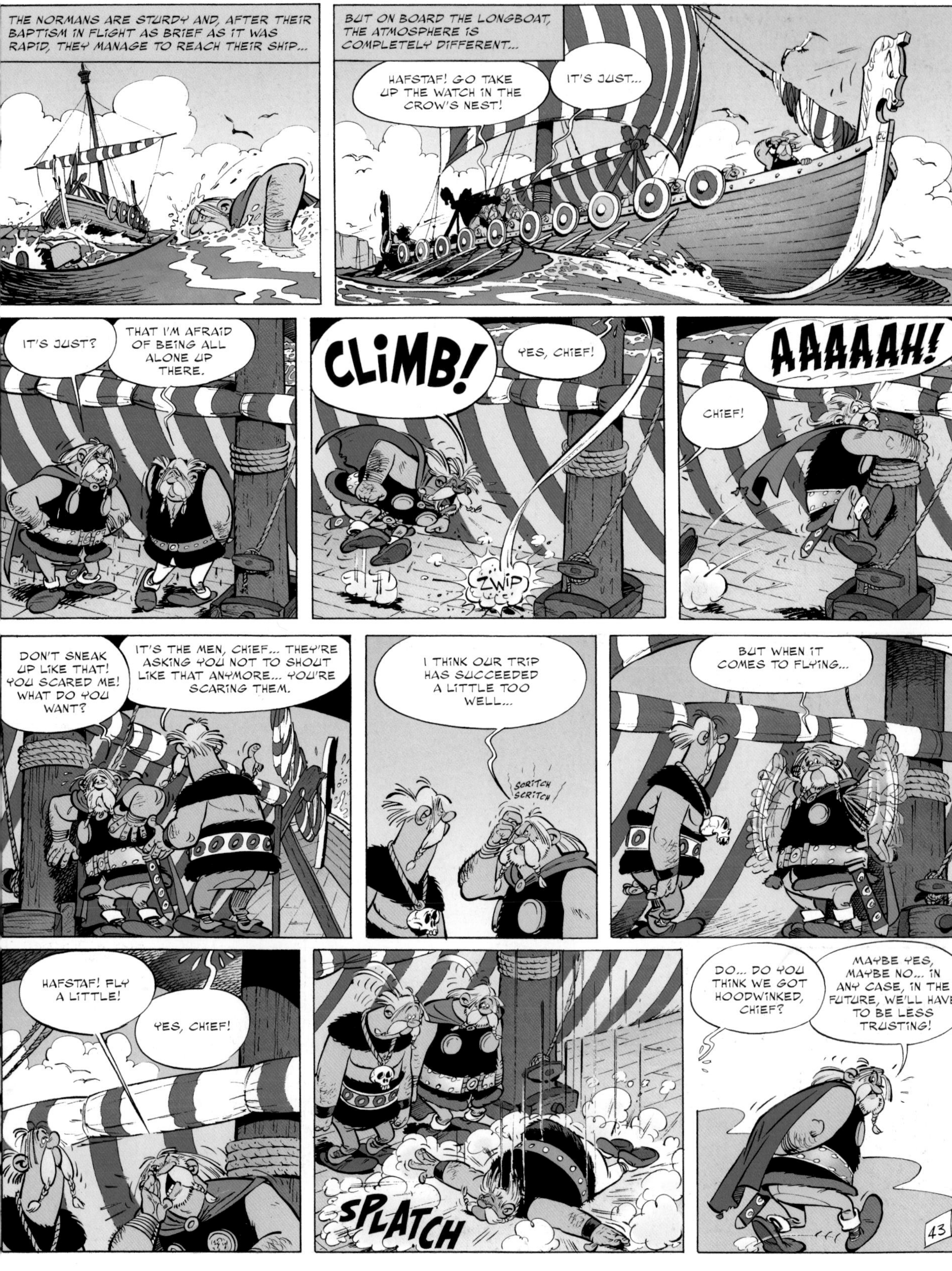
THE NORMANS ARE STURDY AND, AFTER THEIR BAPTISM IN FLIGHT AS BRIEF AS IT WAS RAPID, THEY MANAGE TO REACH THEIR SHIP...
BUT ON BOARD THE LONGBOAT, THE ATMOSPHERE IS COMPLETELY DIFFERENT...
HAFSTAF! GO TAKE UP THE WATCH IN THE CROW'S NEST!
IT'S JUST...
IT'S JUST?
THAT I'M AFRAID OF BEING ALL ALONE UP THERE.
CLIMB!
YES, CHIEF!
ZWIP
AAAAAH!
CHIEF!
DON'T SNEAK UP LIKE THAT! YOU SCARED ME! WHAT DO YOU WANT?
IT'S THE MEN, CHIEF... THEY'RE ASKING YOU NOT TO SHOUT LIKE THAT ANYMORE... YOU'RE SCARING THEM.
I THINK OUR TRIP HAS SUCCEEDED A LITTLE TOO WELL...
SCRITCH SCRITCH
BUT WHEN IT COMES TO FLYING...
HAFSTAF! FLY A LITTLE!
YES, CHIEF!
SPLATCH
DO... DO YOU THINK WE GOT HOODWINKED, CHIEF?
MAYBE YES, MAYBE NO... IN ANY CASE, IN THE FUTURE, WE'LL HAVE TO BE LESS TRUSTING!
43

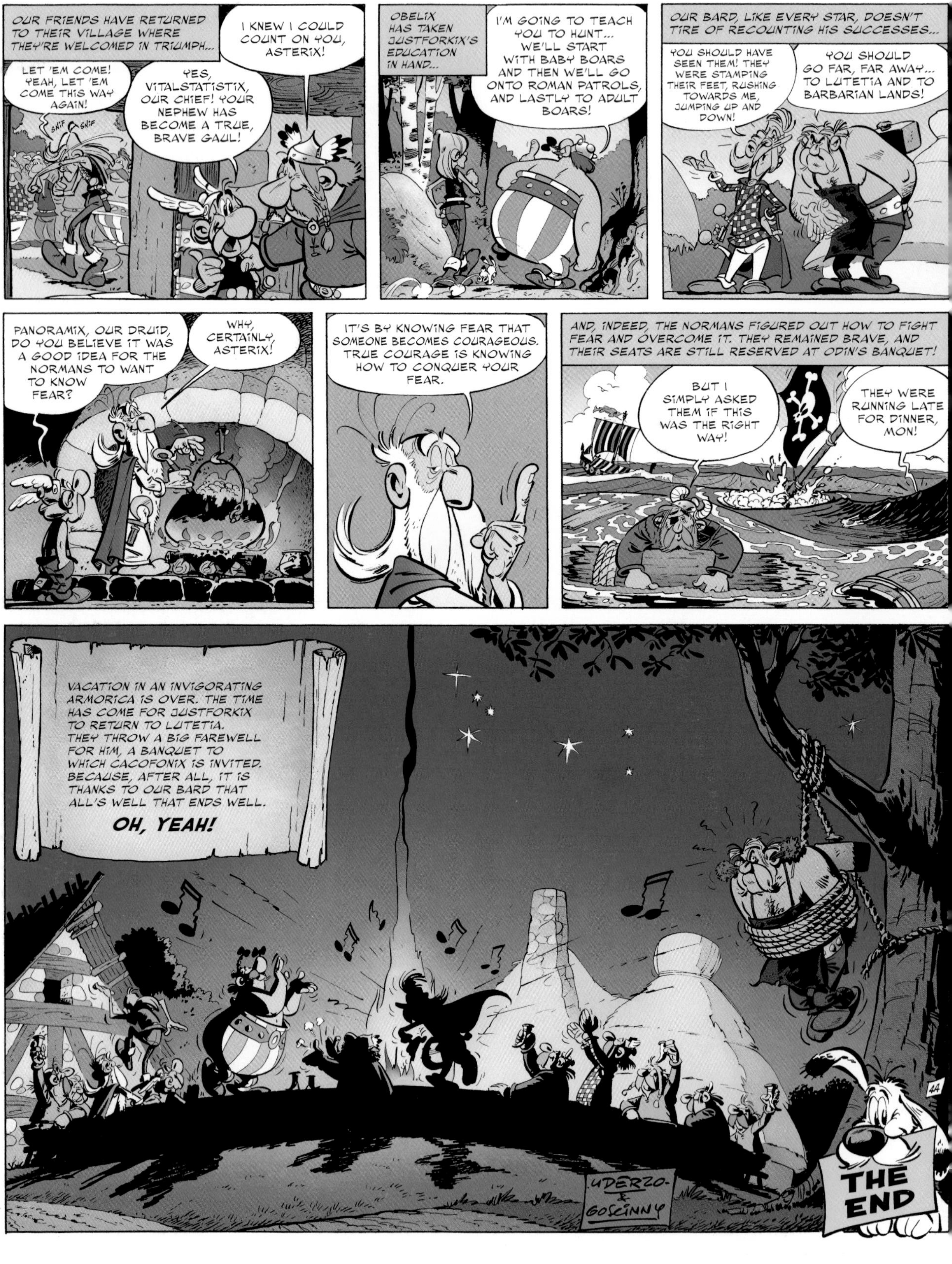
OUR FRIENDS HAVE RETURNED TO THEIR VILLAGE WHERE THEY'RE WELCOMED IN TRIUMPH...
I KNEW I COULD COUNT ON YOU, ASTERIX!
LET 'EM COME! YEAH, LET 'EM COME THIS WAY AGAIN!
SNIF SNIF
YES, VITALSTATISTIX, OUR CHIEF! YOUR NEPHEW HAS BECOME A TRUE, BRAVE GAUL!
OBELIX HAS TAKEN JUSTFORKIX'S EDUCATION IN HAND...
I'M GOING TO TEACH YOU TO HUNT... WE'LL START WITH BABY BOARS AND THEN WE'LL GO ONTO ROMAN PATROLS, AND LASTLY TO ADULT BOARS!
OUR BARD, LIKE EVERY STAR, DOESN'T TIRE OF RECOUNTING HIS SUCCESSES...
YOU SHOULD HAVE SEEN THEM! THEY WERE STAMPING THEIR FEET, RUSHING TOWARDS ME, JUMPING UP AND DOWN!
YOU SHOULD GO FAR, FAR AWAY... TO LUTETIA AND TO BARBARIAN LANDS!
PANORAMIX, OUR DRUID, DO YOU BELIEVE IT WAS A GOOD IDEA FOR THE NORMANS TO WANT TO KNOW FEAR?
WHY, CERTAINLY, ASTERIX!
IT'S BY KNOWING FEAR THAT SOMEONE BECOMES COURAGEOUS. TRUE COURAGE IS KNOWING HOW TO CONQUER YOUR FEAR.
AND, INDEED, THE NORMANS FIGURED OUT HOW TO FIGHT FEAR AND OVERCOME IT. THEY REMAINED BRAVE, AND THEIR SEATS ARE STILL RESERVED AT ODIN'S BANQUET!
BUT I SIMPLY ASKED THEM IF THIS WAS THE RIGHT WAY!
THEY WERE RUNNING LATE FOR DINNER, MON!
VACATION IN AN INVIGORATING ARMORICA IS OVER. THE TIME HAS COME FOR JUSTFORKIX TO RETURN TO LUTETIA. THEY THROW A BIG FAREWELL FOR HIM, A BANQUET TO WHICH CACOFONIX IS INVITED. BECAUSE, AFTER ALL, IT IS THANKS TO OUR BARD THAT ALL'S WELL THAT ENDS WELL.
OH, YEAH!
44
UDERZO & GOSCINNY
THE END

WATCH OUT FOR PAPERCUTZ

Welcome to ASTERIX Volume Three, collecting the seventh, eighth, and ninth ASTERIX graphic novels, "Asterix and the Big Fight," "Asterix in Britain," and "Asterix and the Normans," by René Goscinny and Albert Uderzo. Papercutz is dedicated to publishing great graphic novels for all ages, and ASTERIX is certainly a perfect example of just that. ASTERIX has been a best-selling series throughout most of the world for generations, and Papercutz is proud to offer a newly translated version of these classic comics to North America.

This is in no way a disparagement of the excellent British translations of ASTERIX previously done by Anthea Bell and Derek Hockridge. Those were done for a different audience at a different time, while we're focused on presenting ASTERIX to a modern American audience. In our translations, we've gone back to the original scripts by René Goscinny and have tried to be as faithful as possible, while being aware of what our audience will and won't be able to fully understand. For example, in Europe, many schoolchildren are required to take a course in Latin, while that's incredibly uncommon in North America. The British editions, therefore, include many Latin phrases… in Latin, assuming their audience will understand. While some of those Latin phrases are generally known over here, not all of them are. The solution was to simply add footnotes where and when these Latin phrases pop up, saving our audience the trouble of Googling.

Another surprising aspect of ASTERIX, at least to North American audiences, is how few actual ASTERIX adventures exist. Certainly, if a character was as popular as ASTERIX in the United States, he'd be appearing in all-new comicbooks every week. Just look at how many new Batman and Spider-Man comics are on sale at comic book stores every Wednesday (known as New Comics Day to comicbook fans). Unlike superheroes such as Wonder Woman or Wolverine, who have starred in literally hundreds of adventures in countless comics, Asterix and Obelix have starred in precisely 38 graphic novels in over sixty years. In other words, in just ten more volumes of this ASTERIX omnibus series from Papercutz, we'll have published every single Asterix adventure!

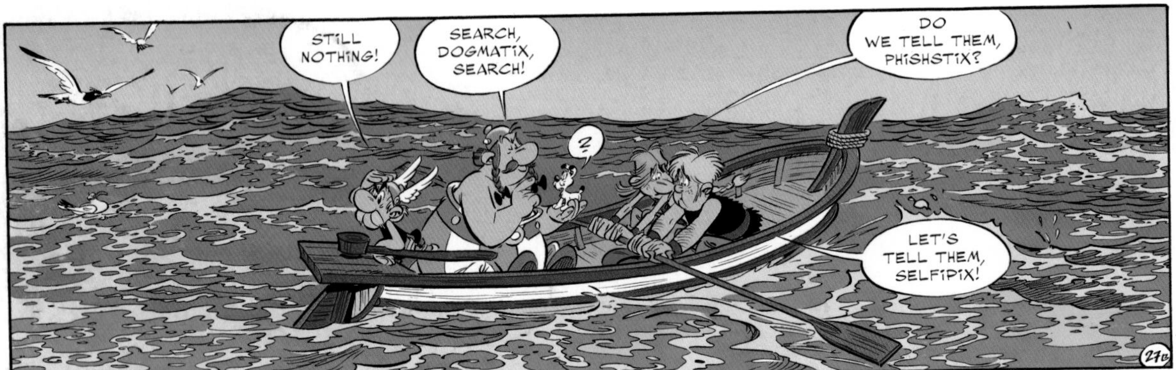
STILL NOTHING!
SEARCH, DOGMATIX, SEARCH!
DO WE TELL THEM, PHISHSTIX?
LET'S TELL THEM, SELFIPIX!

Coming up next is ASTERIX Volume Four, featuring "Asterix the Legionary," "Asterix and the Chieftain's Shield," and "Asterix at the Olympic Games." You don't want to miss it!

Thanx,

JIM

STAY IN TOUCH!

EMAIL:	salicrup@papercutz.com
WEB:	papercutz.com
TWITTER:	@papercutzgn
INSTAGRAM:	@papercutzgn
FACEBOOK:	PAPERCUTZGRAPHICNOVELS
REGULAR MAIL:	Papercutz, 160 Broadway, Suite 700, East Wing, New York, NY 10038